Honestly, We Meant Well

ALSO BY GRANT GINDER

The People We Hate at the Wedding
Driver's Education
This Is How It Starts

Honestly, We Meant Well

GRANT GINDER

FLATIRON
BOOKS
NEW YORK

HONESTLY, WE MEANT WELL. Copyright © 2019 by Grant Ginder. All rights reserved. Printed in the United States of America. For information, address Flatiron Books, 175 Fifth Avenue, New York, N.Y. 10010.

www.flatironbooks.com

Designed by Steven Seighman

The Library of Congress Cataloging-in-Publication Data is available upon request.

ISBN 978-1-250-14315-0 (hardcover)
ISBN 978-1-250-24424-6 (international, sold outside the U.S., subject to rights availability)
ISBN 978-1-250-14314-3 (ebook)

Our books may be purchased in bulk for promotional, educational, or business use. Please contact your local bookseller or the Macmillan Corporate and Premium Sales Department at 1-800-221-7945, extension 5442, or by email at MacmillanSpecialMarkets@macmillan.com.

First U.S. Edition: June 2019

First International Edition: June 2019

10 9 8 7 6 5 4 3 2 1

For my mother, Deborah Ginder

This is absurd,
that mortals blame the gods! They say we cause
their suffering, but they themselves increase it
by folly.
—HOMER, *THE ODYSSEY*, TRANSLATED BY EMILY WILSON

It's not the tragedies that kill us; it's the messes.
—DOROTHY PARKER

Honestly, We Meant Well

Sue Ellen

March 18
Berkeley, California

Ten minutes before the phone rings, Sue Ellen Wright—tenured professor of classical studies, beloved recipient of countless teaching awards, wavering wife, and mostly good mother—is wondering how, exactly, she got here.

"Teach? You okay?"

Blinking, she looks across her desk. There, one of her students slouches in a chair. His name's Connor McFarland, and he's a freshman, with a face still caught between the doughiness of adolescence and the resolution of everything else. Despite the weather (it's cold and raining), he's wearing a T-shirt, flip-flops, and a pair of mesh shorts. A San Francisco Giants hat is pulled low on his forehead, and from beneath its flat brim his eyes stare at her expectantly.

"I'm sorry." She tries to regain focus. "What were you saying?"

"I was saying that I think you made a mistake. I'm pretty sure I got this one right." Connor points to a picture on his midterm, which he's come here, to Sue Ellen's office, to dispute. It's an artifact that he was meant to identify and, in his defense, he has, albeit incorrectly: beneath the picture, in sloppy, blue ink, he's written: *BONG*.

"That's not a bong, Connor. That's a Corinthian urn from the fifth century B.C.E."

He spins the paper around so he can look at it again.

"But can't you see how it *could* have been a bong?"

"No," Sue Ellen says. "Actually, I can't."

He's been arguing about his grade for the better part of an hour. Twice now she's been tempted to kick him out. She wants to tell him that the 35 percent she gave him should have been a 25. That his answers were so dismal, so laughably bad, that halfway through grading the exam she actually began to feel sorry for him, and in turn padded his failing score with an extra ten points. (He spelled *Argos* correctly, she thought, as she added things up. That had to count for something.) Instead, though, she's let him talk, hoping that he'll hear himself when he tells her that the Agora was a movie theater. Hoping that, in that pivotal moment, he'll realize just how ridiculous he sounds.

"You'd put the weed here," he says, pointing to the vessel's base. "And then you'd drill a little hole and—"

"It's an urn, Connor. It can only be an urn."

He looks at her and twists his mouth to one side.

"I could have gotten that if you'd given us a word bank."

"Well, I didn't."

"Why not?"

"Because this is college."

He's in her biggest class—a fifty-student survey in classical archaeology. She's volunteered to teach it for the past decade—a fact that earns her ribbing from both her colleagues and her husband, Dean. *One of the most distinguished classicists on the West Coast,* they say to her, *and you spend your afternoons pointing to Sparta on a map.* She laughs along with them; she says that she's bad at geography, and she needs a reminder of where Sparta is each spring. The truth, though, is that she enjoys it—the wide-eyed energy that freshmen bring to the classroom, the way their optimism fools her into forgetting her own mistakes.

Or, mostly she does; she kind of does. While she'd never admit this to her colleagues (she finds it tedious and cliché when they complain about undergrads' laziness), privately she worries they might be right. She worries that kids like Connor are becoming less an anomaly than the norm.

He sits in the front row every day. He comes to class in varying combinations of sweatpants and hoodies, and fills one seat with his six-foot frame and another with his backpack, a green JanSport whose label has been covered with a Giants patch. He is, she suspects, good-looking—not to her, but to the young women who always elect to sit behind him, a pair of blondes and a redhead named Kristen, Kristin, and Kristyn. Watching them watch Connor, she wants to tell them not to worry—that, in a few years, once they've learned to appreciate men who care about proper hygiene and wear proper pants, they'll look back on this infatuation with a sort of hilarious disgust. Until then, though, they hang on Connor's every word. And, as it turns out, they're not alone. The whole class quiets when Connor speaks—never with a hand raised, always in a booming voice. More often than not, his questions aren't questions so much as critiques or challenges: last week, he told her he was skeptical of her recounting of the Battle of Thermopylae, citing the movie *300* as evidence. She still remembers how he took off his hat and ran a hand through a mop of oily hair.

"In *300*, it's just the Spartans who beat the Persians," he said, disappointed that he was the one teaching her.

Two rows behind him, she heard someone whisper: *He's right.*

"Three hundred?"

"It's a movie, teach. Check it out."

Later that evening, she recalled the incident for her colleague Charlene. Over a glass of wine she explained, with a bewildered excitement, how she had been forced to ditch her notes and spend the next hour teaching her students how to distinguish between Hollywood and fact.

Charlene listened and shook her head.

"There's always one of them," she said. "Usually there's more, but there's always one."

"One of what?"

"Some entitled eighteen-year-old man suspicious of female knowledge. They want to know everything, but they're not willing to work for it. And they're angry that you did."

"I don't want to turn this into some gender issue."

"Then you're an idiot." Charlene finished her wine. "You should see *300*, though. Those guys have great abs."

Now, Connor slouches down further and folds his hands across his stomach. "Maybe you're the one who's wrong," he says. "Maybe it actually *was* a bong, and you've been wrong this whole time. I mean, it's so old, who knows for sure? It's not like you were there."

He smiles, satisfied.

Sue Ellen says, "I don't think that's likely."

"And why not?"

Why not, Connor? Because there's something called context—the necessity of interpreting an object's meaning as part of a greater picture. Because as it turns out, pieces of old pottery aren't so different from middle-aged professors or failing college freshmen: it's only when we consider the sum of their stories that we can begin, maybe, to understand them.

She says none of this. She waits for the Teaching Moment to pass before she flips back to the first page of the midterm, which she slides across the desk to him.

"Connor," she says, "it wasn't a bong."

He folds the papers in half, then in quarters, before shoving them into the pocket of his hoodie.

Standing, he sighs. "I guess we'll just have to agree to disagree then."

"Yes," Sue Ellen says. "Yes, I guess we will."

Shaking his head, he leaves, and Sue Ellen locks the door behind him. Then she walks to her office's small window. Somehow, spring has crept up on me, she thinks. Back east, in places like Philadelphia and New York, the season arrives violently, in a single day. One moment sidewalks are slick, coated with gray, filthy ice; the next, they're sprouting tables and chairs, the seasonal appendages of a thousand eager cafés. With these changes also comes an unspoken but certain urgency, a tacit realization that Everything Must Be Done Because This Cannot Last. Berkeley lacks such drama—it doesn't muscle its way through the seasons so much as it slips into them, filling in empty corners over weeks and months. Gradually, the hills of Claremont Canyon become spotted with wildflowers; jackets are worn in the morning, then eventually left at home. When Sue Ellen first moved to the Bay Area, people warned her of this. She had just spent four years outside Boston, and her friends there told her that she would come to miss the way the seasons served to divide the year. They told her that without them her life would slip by—that, decades later, her memories, no matter what they contained, would all bear the same brassy hue. Twelve months ago, she would have told them they were right. The thirty years she's spent in California have been a pleasant blur—a sun-drenched montage of teaching, researching, marriage, and motherhood. But then this year happened. Now she'd tell those same friends their reliance on the seasons is simplistic and naïve. You don't need falling leaves or melting snow to mark time passing—mistresses and couples therapy get the job done, too.

Sitting down at her desk, she looks at a stack of ungraded papers and then beyond it, to a small framed picture of her family. In it, her son, Will, is holding up a wonky, overly frosted cake, while she and Dean smile behind him, barely containing their hysterics. It's an oldish picture; Will had baked that cake more than three years ago now, for Sue Ellen's fifty-second birthday. He had just started his freshman year at Berkeley, and he had ridden his bike home from the dorms to surprise her; Dean kept her out of the kitchen while he spelled out HAPPY BIRTHDAY, YOU'RE OLD in red sugar letters. It's an awful picture—Will, who's now nearly graduated, has puffy, hungover eyes, and she and Dean are smiling like maniacs. She wouldn't think of replacing it, though. It helps her remember how they were before.

When the phone rings, it startles her. She can't think of the last time someone called her on a landline, especially not the one in her office, and as she listens to the handset ring with what she imagines to be increasing urgency, she starts to worry that someone's died.

"Hello?"

She saves the call right before it flips over to voice mail.

"Yes, yes. Sue Ellen Wright, please." The voice belongs to a woman, and it's tinged with a heavy accent that Sue Ellen immediately pegs as Greek—Athenian, to be specific: quick, constant, pure.

"This is she," Sue Ellen says.

"Yes, wonderful. Dr. Wright, this is Gianna Galanis. We had the pleasure of meeting at the Society for Classical Studies event last year in San Francisco."

Leaning back in her chair, Sue Ellen works through the roster of events she attended in the past twelve months. A series of talks and conferences and symposiums that form a trail of memories, all of which invariably end with an image of Sue Ellen standing alone next to a catering table, contemplating the calories in a cube of cheese. Closing her eyes and thinking harder, she finally finds it: a Friday evening at the Hilton near Union Square. An opening-night reception in a carpeted hall called the Continental Ballroom. Gianna worked in development at the National Archaeological Museum, in Athens. She was small—Sue Ellen remembers that, too—no taller than five feet. The way she carried herself, though, like she was poised on a chariot, coupled with her explosion of raven curls, created a formidable impression.

"Yes. Yes, of course. How are you, Gianna?"

"I'm well, thank you. The world is falling apart and my country is in ruins, but I am well."

"That's lovely to hear." Sue Ellen clicks her web browser and opens the history tab: she had spent the morning before Connor arrived looking at shoes. "Still at the National Archaeological Museum?"

"I left the museum in October."

"Oh?"

What she needs, she thinks, scrolling down the page, is a pair of nice red flats. Red, or maybe green.

"I deserved more money than they could pay me."

"Isn't that always the case."

Zeroing in on a pair of espadrilles, she wonders what Gianna wants and how fast she can get her to hang up.

"What can I help you with, Miss Galanis?"

"Yes, I am sure you are very busy."

Sue Ellen struggles for an excuse. "I've got a faculty meeting in five minutes."

"I will only need three," Gianna says. "I left the museum to become the director of programming at Golden Age Adventures." There's a pause. "You've heard of it, obviously."

Sue Ellen opens a new window and types the name into Google.

She says, "Obviously," and watches as pictures of a small cruise ship load, its deck populated by gray-haired tourists in sun hats and synthetic T-shirts: a Cialis commercial at sea. On top of it all, arching along the shallow curve of a Photoshopped sunset, appears a slogan, at once perfectly inviting and devastatingly unaware of its own cruel irony: *The Ancients Await.*

"It's an expedition enterprise," Gianna says. "We organize educational vacations, catering to an older, more distinguished clientele."

"It certainly looks like it."

"In the first week of August we will be launching a new cruise called The Grandest Voyage Ever Made."

Sue Ellen minimizes Google and returns to her shoes.

She says, "Sounds ambitious."

"I came up with the title." Gianna pauses. Somewhere down the hall, Sue Ellen hears a door open and close. "It's a tour of some of the islands' most important sites," she explains. "With lectures occurring at each stop. We're offering it to our most active clients."

"How . . . wonderful."

"I think so, yes." Another pause, this time filled with something else: fingernails, clicking against a keyboard. "Last year when we met, you mentioned that you had done research concerning historical and religious memory in the context of Aphaía's temple on Aegina."

"Years ago. It was the subject of my dissertation."

"Yes, I read it last night."

"Oh, God, it's still floating around?"

"Dr. Wright, the memory of the internet is older than the internet itself."

"What a terrifying aphorism," Sue Ellen says.

"Thank you." Then: "I—on behalf of Golden Age Adventures—would be very honored if you'd join us at a welcome reception at the Hilton in Athens on the second of August, and then again on the third, when the tour reaches Aegina, to discuss your studies. The talk will be no more than an hour and will take place at the Temple of Aphaía on the island itself. We've found, Dr. Wright, that our clients are most impressed by *location*. Your travel expenses will of course be covered by the company, and we are also pleased to offer you a one-thousand-euro honorarium."

"You want me to come to Aegina."

There's a beat of hesitation before she says the island's name, and this fact surprises her—it is, after all, only a place.

"Yes, that's right. Athens, too."

"I've actually never been on a cruise before."

"Oh, you won't be on the cruise itself. Unfortunately, we reserve our rooms for paying passengers—"

"As opposed to passengers you're paying." Sue Ellen picks up a pen and twirls it around her finger. "So, I'm not going on a cruise so much as I'm giving a lecture."

"Correct."

"Where would I stay?"

"We'll provide a stipend to cover your lodging, and I'm happy to make a reservation for you at the Hotel Cosse, conveniently located near the island's—"

"No," Sue Ellen says, cutting off Gianna. "No, thank you, but I . . . I actually know of a place."

"On Aegina?"

"Yes. Not in the harbor, but close to it."

Gianna sighs, relieved. "Thank goodness," she says. "The Hotel Cosse is above a fish market and their bedsheets smell like mackerel."

Sue Ellen sets down the pen and closes her eyes. She sees a red dirt road, cutting through the shadows of a late afternoon.

"I'm flattered you thought of me," she says.

"I'm relieved to hear so. Our first choice declined the offer."

"How kind of you to point that out."

"Oh, no." Gianna laughs. "Please don't misunderstand me, Dr. Wright. *You* were always my first choice—"

"Really, you don't have to say that."

"—it was *everyone else* who wanted Peter Bollinger."

"Peter Bollinger from Yale? He's brilliant."

"Brilliant, maybe, but ugly. You are much nicer to look at."

"Again," Sue Ellen says, "how kind of you to say."

"I hope you'll consider our offer."

Sue Ellen turns to the window, where an ash-gray cloud has eclipsed the sun. She thinks of ungraded papers and unwritten lectures; of dozing students and their chirping cell phones; of Connor and his flip-flops and his millennia-old bongs. She thinks beyond that: to a year spent flailing. A year spent plugging leaks and patching holes as she has tried to keep her family's sinking ship afloat. And then deeper, to decades ago, when she was a younger woman, a student in her own right, boarding a crowded, sea-bound ferry. Closing her eyes again, she smells the island's pine needles and cypress trees. She hears the sound, as constant as lapping waves, of Christos's voice.

"I already have," Sue Ellen says. "I'll do it. I'll go."

Eleni

July 7
Aegina, Greece

"I'm trying it again!" Eleni shouts.

She turns the knob and stares up at the showerhead. Holding her breath, she listens as the promise of water moans beneath her. Somewhere downstairs, Stavros—a weathered Corinthian who her father, Christos, hired once as a handyman thirty years ago and who has since refused to leave—tinkers with a maze of rusty pipes. The window's open and there's a breeze, but it's too weak to drive away the bugs. A mosquito lands on the nape of Eleni's neck, and before she has time to slap it away she feels the faint pique of a new bite.

She closes her eyes and imagines herself somewhere else. A parallel world where lights turn on and ovens work and showers run; where existence extends beyond the four walls of this inn and the ragged coast of this island. A place where Eleni Papadakis lives the life she wants, instead of the one to which she's been sentenced.

"Anything?" she hears Stavros yell.

Opening her eyes, she squints at the showerhead. Dust gathers along its curves.

"Still nothing," she shouts back, and steps out of the tub. "Stay there. I'm coming down."

She finds him in the kitchen, smoking next to a tin of coffee beans. She considers asking if she can bum a cigarette, but instead says, "I thought I asked you not to smoke in here."

"Plumbing makes me anxious," he says.

"Haven't you been doing this for, like, thirty years?"

"What's that got to do with anything?"

He pinches the cigarette between his fingers and brings it to his lips. Leaning against the counter, he inhales and she watches as smoke seeps out from the corners of his mouth. His face, Eleni thinks, looks as if it's been roughly molded from wet, red clay; thick wrinkles crease his cheeks, and when he frowns his forehead collapses in half. She wonders if this is how her father would look, if he had been given the chance to age.

"This happened once before," Stavros says, ashing his cigarette in the sink behind him.

"What, all of the upstairs showers stopped working at once? You're kidding."

He shakes his head. "I'm not."

"When?"

"Four years ago, maybe? Five? You were at school."

Eleni pulls her hair back and ties it up with one of the rubber bands she keeps around her wrist.

She asks, "What'd Dad do?"

"He had to call in a part from Athens. Took about a week and a half, if I'm remembering."

"Shit," she says. "We don't have a week and a half."

Rummaging through the refrigerator, she finds a beer and cracks it open.

"Who are these guests again?" Stavros asks.

"I don't know." She holds the bottle to her cheek and winces at the cold. "Just some family. The mother said she stayed here before. Like, forever ago. Or at least that's what she wrote in her email."

"What's her name?"

"Sue Ellen Wright. Claims she knew Dad."

Stavros shrugs.

He says, "And they get here tomorrow?"

"Today. They're coming in on the five o'clock ferry."

"There are worse things in the world than sharing a shower."

Try telling that to a bunch of Americans, Eleni thinks.

She swallows a sip of beer and runs her tongue along her teeth. "You're sure you're not able to fix it?"

His cigarette dangling from the corner of his mouth, Stavros turns on the sink and begins to wash his hands. "I told you," he says, "plumbing makes me anxious."

"Remind me why I pay you," Eleni says, rubbing her eyes.

"Because your father didn't have the guts to fire me."

Eleni shakes her head. "This—this is why our country can't pay its bills."

Clinking the beer bottle against her teeth, she wanders out of the kitchen and into the inn's small dining room. Four square tables arranged haphazardly. All the surfaces, from walls to ceiling, painted in the same, noncommittal beige. Hanging above the bar, a chandelier that her grandfather appropriated from a condemned ship—a lamp made up of three smaller lamps, one of which lost its shade before Eleni was conceived. Three French doors that open to a row of tangled and overgrown hedges, beyond which lies a pool. On the west wall, the room's sole piece of art: a framed poster of Santorini, even though Santorini's more than two hundred kilometers away.

She pushes open one of the French doors and steps over a tangle of weeds and a broken tile as she makes her way out onto the patio. Finding a spot of shade, she stares out past the pool to Aegina Harbor, where a mess of boats dodge one another, their bows nearly kissing as they pull in and out of port. To the south, there's a spit of beach where, as a little girl, she would sit for hours on end, letting her shoulders and arms and spine darken to the color of ripe olives as she built sand castles. Her mother, Agatha, would call her from the rocks, tell her to come inside, eat something, keep cool in the relentless summer heat, and Eleni would ignore her. Would lie on her back and flex her feet as the tide sloshed around her ankles. Then, when Eleni was ten, Agatha died. Melanoma, of all things. She figures it was around then that she decided to hate the sun.

She hears the click of a lighter as Stavros starts in on a second cigarette, and she watches as cars crawl up the red hills leading up and out of town. Forty-five kilometers north, Athens smolders behind a scrim of smog, its buildings blending together into borderless gray huddles.

Her last morning in the city was over two and a half years ago. She sees herself waking up in her flat, a few blocks away from the physics laboratory in Zografou. To the left of her cot is her suitcase—her only one—and to the left of that are three boxes, packed heavy with her books. She remembers picking her way to the small refrigerator and reaching into it for the only thing that remained—a small peach. She cut it open and waited for the juices to run down her fingers, and when they didn't—the peach was three days away from ripe—she bit into it anyway, puckering at its sour toughness. And then what? She must have showered, and brushed her teeth, and taken the metro down to the port, but all of that seems to have been wiped clean from her memory. It's like the sea dragged it out of her, away from her; like the small channel between the mainland and the island ripped her clear of the life she had spent three and a half years building.

It was two weeks before that when her father called her and told her to come home. She was sitting in the park near the Olof Palme playground, sort of reading a back issue of *The Economist,* but mostly watching a pair of girls fight over a swing, when her phone rang.

Looking at the screen, she saw that it was him. Still, all she said was, "*Naí?*"

"It's time for you to come back." His voice sounded gravelly, gruff. She checked the connection on her phone. She had full service.

"Here we go again."

"The university's closed. I read it today in the paper."

Actually, it had been closed for a while—a week, to be exact. Another round of austerity measures, along with the closing of the banks, had led to massive layoffs and walkouts. Two of Eleni's professors had taken to holding class meetings in their apartments, which she had been attending with some regularity, and she was still engaged with the research on applied microeconomics she was doing for Maragos, her adviser. Ostensibly, though, the National and Kapodistrian University of Athens was nonfunctional. The bathrooms at the University Club hadn't been cleaned in three weeks, and most of her friends had started selling their textbooks on eBay. She conveyed none of these developments to her father.

All she said was, "Look at that, you're reading the paper."

"There's a ferry at eight o'clock tomorrow morning. That gives you time to pack up."

"Dad, c'mon. The university has closed before. It'll reopen."

"That's not what they're saying this time."

One of the little girls pushed her friend from the swing, and when she hit the ground her knees began bleeding. Eleni tucked her hair behind her ear and turned away.

Her father added, "Besides, I need help around here. Alec quit yesterday. I've only got Stavros left."

"Whose problem is that? I didn't get a degree in economics so I could sit around the front desk and wait for the phone to ring."

"What degree? Last time I checked you were still half a year away."

"Well, then I need to be here for when the university reopens."

"And what will you do in the meantime?" She imagined him sitting at his desk next to the kitchen, punching numbers into an old calculator, his gray hair curling around his ears.

"I have a job," she said. "I'm doing research for Maragos."

"Oh-ho, research. That's what we're calling it now." The girl with the skinned knee began to cry, and her friend sat on the swing. Eleni turned back to watch as she pumped her legs, forcing herself higher and higher into the air. "The only reason old men pay young girls to hang around them is so they can look down their shirts."

She hated him sometimes, most of the time. She said, "You're speaking from experience, I presume."

He didn't react. He never did, which killed her. All he said was, "You're coming home. Eight o'clock tomorrow morning, from Piraeus. Take a cab and I'll pay you back."

He hung up before she could say no.

She didn't go. If anything, she went out of the way to give her life in Athens a new sense of permanence. She shopped for nonperishable groceries—cans of beans and legumes that could sit in the cupboard, untouched, for a year. When she made dinner, she left the dirty dishes in the sink. At the florist three blocks from her flat she bought a potted plant, a fragile African violet that required great care and wouldn't bloom for another six months. On Tuesday of that week, she walked to the Economics Department at 10 A.M. and, just as she'd done for the past two years, poked her head into Professor Maragos's office to tell him that she was there and to update him on her progress compiling the data from the research he'd given her the previous month. He thanked her, and before he dismissed her he let his eyes fall from her face to the contours of her breasts. Recalling her father's words, Eleni felt a new, burning chagrin. She was torn between wanting to either stuff her body in a sleeping bag or rip off everything she was wearing; between either slapping Maragos to thank her father or sleeping with the old pervert to spite him.

She did neither. She completed her work for the afternoon, then went home to order takeout and stare at the new cans of chickpeas lining her kitchen shelves. The following day consisted more or less of the same, as did the day after that, and the day after that. Christos phoned her regularly—four times a day, give or take—and each time she guiltlessly let the call roll over to voice mail, feeling a certain glorious thrill as she watched his number vanish from the screen. When the weekend came, she recounted these small victories to her friends Sophie and Mina. They were drinking wine in a café in Thissio, doing their best to ignore the heat that weighed down the Athenian air.

"He's a fuck-head," Eleni said.

"A fuck-head who's insisting you come back to Aegina," Sophie corrected.

Eleni swallowed her last bit of wine. "Well, then that fuck-head will have to come to Athens and drag me home himself."

A week later, while she was getting ready to leave for campus, her landlady knocked on the door and told her that her rent check for that week had bounced.

"That's impossible," Eleni had said. "I . . ." She didn't finish the sentence. She loathed admitting that her father still transferred funds to her checking account each month. It robbed her of the right to be ungrateful.

"Well, it did. It bounced." The woman blinked her black eyes. "So, either pay or leave."

"Give me a week. Five days. I'll figure something out."

The woman scoffed. "I'm not running a charity."

Eleni thought of her father. Of the smug look he must have made as he called the bank. "That son of a bitch."

Her landlady said: "You watch your language, miss."

And that had been that. The next morning, after having been more or less evicted, she boarded an Aegina-bound ferry at Piraeus; by two o'clock that afternoon she was back at the Alectrona, tripping over the same uneven tiles that had given her bloody toes as a child. Over the past three years at the university she had learned how to hustle; she'd developed a general air of nerve and certainty, because certainty seemed to be the only ethos to which the men in her department responded. Now, she had a new thing to be sure of: she deserved better than to be back on this island.

She avoided Christos for the first three days she was home. Each night when he called her down to dinner, she pretended not to hear him and waited until he had gone to bed before venturing to the kitchen to pick at whatever leftovers languished in the fridge. She felt, more than anything, betrayed: it had been Christos who had encouraged Eleni to apply to the university, Christos who had prodded her to move to Athens once she was accepted. She could have screamed at him for this. *You can't send me away to be someone else,* she imagined saying, *and then act surprised by the person I've become.*

On the fourth day, when he asked her if she wanted to walk with him in the *eleonas* just south of Pachia Rachi and pick olives, she told him she was busy; she wasn't interested in his false camaraderie, his forced attempts at friendship. The *eleonas,* she wanted to remind him, were where they used to go to lose each other after her mother died. Under the guise of father-daughter bonding, they would drive to the ancient groves and then scatter themselves among the trees, drifting far enough away from each other that, at least temporarily, they could forget the other one existed.

She would have acted differently if she could have known what was to come six months later. She remembers the doctors telling her there was nothing that could have been done; that it was the fastest-metastasizing pancreatic adenocarcinoma they'd seen in their cancer-pocked careers. Between sobs she told them to shut up; she didn't care. She asked them why they were so insistent on explaining away an arbitrary cause for an effect that was so certain. They looked at each other and bit their lips; they said that was the job of medicine. Perhaps, they offered, she should talk to the priest that the hospital employed as a grief counselor. Her cheeks still wet, she found him—a young man cloaked in a black robe, busying himself in a small chapel adjacent to the maternity ward. She was angry and devastated, she told him. Angry that her father hadn't had the courage to tell her that he was dying; devastated that she hadn't had the compassion to sense it. The priest pointed to an icon of St. John Cassian, nailed to the chapel's Sheetrock wall, and quoted something about forgiveness from *The Philokalia*. Outside, a nurse helped a young mother into a wheelchair. The newborn in her arms began to cry. "These feelings are normal," the priest told her. "They're normal, and they'll pass."

Eleni stood up and gathered her things. She didn't want her pain to be normal, she said. She wanted it to be extraordinary. It was the last time she ever went to church.

It was winter, the slow season; the first guests wouldn't arrive for another six months. Without the structure of a schedule—the preparing of breakfast, the cleaning of rooms—the days of the next week merged together. Each afternoon, she took slow walks down the road that led to the Alectrona, a stretch of dirt forking off from the larger road that snaked east out of Aegina's central port. Overgrown pine trees sliced up the January sun and cast cool shadows over her. At night, she crawled into bed and folded her grown body into the dent her childhood form had made in her mattress. When she awoke, she spent the better part of her mornings staring at the same Sokratis Malamas poster hanging next to her door—the only thing that distinguished her own room from the four others in the inn. When that became too much—when she had grown tired of studying the room's wood floors, its rough, whitish walls—she'd pull herself to the window and watch birds land on the branches of the gnarled mastic tree that grew outside her father's old office, counting its leaves as they fell to the ground.

Then, on the fourth day, Stavros came to her. In his left hand, he held a black hat. Sweat matted his gray hair against his forehead.

He said, "You have to leave this room, *koritsi mou*."

She was sitting at her desk, staring at an open book. She hadn't bathed in four days, and she had taken on an increasingly yeasty scent, a mix of salt and filth and unbrushed teeth that made her think of regrettable mornings in Athens.

She turned to him. "I don't have to do anything," she said. "And I'm not your *little girl*."

Stavros cleared his throat. "Actually, legally you do: they're reading your father's will today."

"So let them read it," she said, fingering the pages of her book.

"You have to be there." He sat on the edge of her bed.

She protested again, but eventually she gave in. She showered, put on a fresh pair of jeans, and went to the courthouse in town. There, she learned that Christos had bequeathed to her everything he had owned, including the Alectrona. There was, though, one notable provision: if she wanted to sell the inn and pocket the proceeds, she could be legally allowed to do so only after two years. In the interim, the property's deed—and its operation—would fall under her name.

"I can't believe it," she said to Stavros on the way back to the inn. They were riding in his old VW Golf, and as the car jostled over potholes Eleni felt her throat pulse; at any given moment, she worried she might break down in sobs. She said, "Even from the grave, my father manages to fucking ground me."

"Maybe he was trying to do you a favor," Stavros said, shifting into third. "Maybe he thought that in two years you would come to love it."

"Just because you refuse to leave, that doesn't mean the rest of us want to stick around," she said.

They turned a corner and came face-to-face with the sun. Stavros squinted.

"And what, exactly, are you proposing you would do with it, if given the opportunity, *koritsi mou?*"

"I'd sell it."

"Ha."

"I would," she said. "I'd sell it like *that.*"

And now, finally, she has. Those two years are up, and she's found a buyer—*a developer.* In one month's time, Eleni Papadakis's four-year hiatus from life will, God willing, come to a close.

Still, Stavros had been half right: unloading the Alectrona wasn't as easy as she had initially assumed it would be. The market for broken-down inns on smoggy Saronic islands wasn't exactly booming—but then, the market for anything, anywhere, wasn't exactly booming. The economy had shrunk by something like a quarter in the past six years. Over half of the people her age were unemployed. The paper was saying that there was a new rule limiting cash withdrawals from the ATM to sixty-six euros, and people were still waiting in hour-long lines just to get that. A month before she put the property on the market, she heard about a friend of hers who had a car break down on the E75, just outside Kifissia. The girl couldn't afford to get the thing towed or repaired, so she hitchhiked the rest of the way into town. Five hours later, when she and her brother returned to see if they could get the car started again, they found the vehicle stripped of its tires and stereo, and the gas siphoned from its tank. Instead of filing a police report, they took a selfie of the two of them smiling next to the shell of the car and posted it to Facebook. As a caption, they used a line from Simonides: *Not even the gods fight against necessity.*

Eleni, though, had defied the odds, had toppled fate. Six months out from the two-year mark, she contacted a former classmate from her time at the university, a Macedonian grad student named Mehmet whose singular, defining characteristic was how many people he knew. She didn't explain what she was doing—just that she was looking to speak to someone interested in real estate acquisition. Within five minutes of emailing him, she had a response: *email my cousin's sister-in-law, Marija,* he wrote. *She might be able to help.*

Mehmet was right: Marija could. Not directly, exactly—she was a Swedish masseuse—but certainly indirectly. The company she worked for, Lugn Escapes, had for nearly a decade owned and operated a handful of high-end spas in Stockholm and its environs. Now, however, it was looking to expand its wellness empire southward, specifically into regions where its faithful clientele tended to travel during the Scandinavian winter, that long stretch of months when the days are replaced with a cold, reluctant twilight.

They sent a scout first. A real estate appraiser who was in charge of the company's foreign acquisitions. Before he arrived, Eleni lit a few candles and cleared away the Alectrona's older pieces of furniture: an ottoman she had been meaning to get reupholstered; an étagère where she kept, among other things, an antique teapot and her grandfather's wooden pipe, artifacts from her family's past whose value was purely contextual. She was worried that the appraiser wouldn't be able to see the Alectrona as anything other than what it was. Instead of imagining its future, he'd get bogged down in its past.

"Those things smell like bug spray."

Stavros said this to her, his nose buried in one of the unlit candles.

"They're lemongrass. I paid a lot of money for them."

"Well, they smell like bug spray."

"Stavros, if you're going to be an ass about this, then leave."

He didn't. He set the candle down, lit the wick, and passed his finger through its flame.

"Who are these people again?"

"They're investors. They're Swedish."

"They're turning us into an Ikea."

"They're turning us into a spa."

"A *spa*."

"Yes, where people can relax, or whatever."

"Where housewives can take a break from doing nothing."

"You're going to burn this place down." She took the candle from him and set it on the front desk. "And don't be sexist."

The scout's name was Oskar. He was tall and lithe, and had shoulder-length blond hair that he kept swept up and tied in a bun. Beneath the cuffs of his white shirt she could see ink on his wrists, the stark borders of tattoos.

"Great views," he told her, when he stepped out on the back terrace. His English was smooth, shaded with only the slightest accent. Beyond the standard pleasantries Eleni used with guests—*hello; can I call you a taxi; the Wi-Fi is down*—she hadn't spoken the language in months. She worried she sounded like a child.

"Yes," she said. "You can see all the way to the harbor."

"And the structure itself. You can feel the history."

"My family has owned it for four generations."

He smiled at her and, despite herself, Eleni blushed.

"Sublime. What . . . energy." He smiled again. "I'll be in touch."

He called two days later, named a price, and, after a few rounds of negotiations, Eleni agreed. Hanging up the phone, she floated through the next hour in a daze: just like that, she had managed to create a future. In six weeks, after playing hostess for one last family, she would be back in Athens. Before going to sleep that evening, she spent two hours in bed hunting for apartments online, her laptop propped on her knees. She did this often. Looking at real estate calmed her and let her imagine other mornings—ones spent with conveniences like ice makers and lamps that weren't pillaged from condemned ships. Now, though, instead of surfing wistfully, she searched for real, coming back again and again to a place in Kolonaki. A one-bedroom on Leventi, a side street off of Irodotou. Quiet, but loud enough that she wouldn't feel like she was back on the island, where the silence still keeps her up at night. It wasn't cheap (even with the economy hobbled, real estate wasn't exactly a steal), but it wouldn't break the bank, either. There would still be cash leftover to keep her afloat while she regained her footing in her old life. She would go back to school and finish her degree—that would happen first. Then she would get a job. Something that required her to wear suits, instead of jeans and a T-shirt. An analyst at Eurobank Ergasias, maybe, or a position in the Ministry of Finance. She would bring her country back from the brink of economic collapse, accomplish the thing at which the men who have come before her have failed so miserably; she would win the fucking Nobel Prize. Or, she wouldn't; she didn't care either way. She would be just as happy to come home from a run on Filopappou Hill and take a long shower in her new apartment. A shower that was built this century. A shower that actually worked.

Now, she finishes her beer and heads back into the kitchen, where Stavros is lighting his third cigarette.

"I wish you wouldn't look at me like that," she says to him, shutting the door.

"Like how?"

"You know how, Stavros. Like I kicked your dog or something."

"I don't have a dog."

"Fine, then like I spit on my father's grave."

Stavros doesn't respond. Instead, he offers her both of his palms.

"Oh, for God's sake," she says. "I couldn't keep the place, even if I wanted to. It's not exactly cheap to operate. And, in case you haven't noticed, it's not like people are banging down the door to stay here."

"We have three guests coming today."

"Yes, and they're the first three guests we've had in a month."

Stavros scratches behind his ear, where his hair has grown thick and wiry.

He says, "We still could have found a way to make it work."

"That's easy for you to say—you're not the one going into debt."

"But your father—"

"Please don't *but your father* me." A fly hovers an inch in front of her nose. She tries to snatch it and misses. "If he really wanted to chain me to this place, he would have made me hold on to it for longer than two years."

"Christos, he was not that kind of man."

"Not to you he wasn't."

A half inch of ash threatens to tumble from the cigarette's end. Rushing over, Eleni catches it with her empty beer bottle before it has a chance to spill to the floor. Stavros doesn't flinch; he just stands there, his eyes downcast, the creases along his cheeks quivering. He is, she realizes, about to cry.

"Hey." With her free hand, she gently takes hold of his chin. "Remember what I said: you're going to be totally fine."

This is true: she's promised him 20 percent of the Alectrona's sale price—if he's smart with it, he'll never have to work again. He'll live the rest of his life playing dominos, drinking *metaxa*, yelling at ERT1 as it warbles from the radio in his kitchen, and doing whatever else it is he does during those few, precious hours when he's not here, trailing her like some chain-smoking basset hound. She likes to think of it as a commission, of sorts. Not for helping her sell the place, but for allowing her to do so without too much of a hassle. For allowing her to reclaim her own life, burdened with only a reasonable amount of guilt.

"But what about you?" he asks her. Eleni releases his chin and steals one of his cigarettes from the pack he's set on the bar.

"What about me?"

"When will I see you?"

"Whenever you want. The ferry takes an hour. You can come over for Easter. You can come over for Sunday dinners. I'm going to Athens, Stavros, not Los Angeles."

"You know I don't like the ferry."

"Well, take a helicopter, then. You'll have the money."

Stavros fits his hat over his head and pulls the brim down low on his face.

"It's not about the money," he says. "It's about having somewhere to go."

Eleni lights the cigarette with a match from an Alectrona-branded matchbook. She had ordered two hundred of them last year, the result of a sudden and inexplicable burst of optimism during which she'd convinced herself that all the inn needed was a little bit of marketing. A siren's call—in the irresistible form of swag—to lure future guests. She's still got 195 of them left. The other five she gave to friends.

"I'm sorry, Stavros," she says. "You'll just have to find somewhere else."

Will

Trapped on a plane somewhere over southwest Europe, Will Wright punishes himself the only way he can: by banging his head against the window.

Stupid, he thinks, in time with the collisions. Stupid, stupid, *stupid*.

The person sitting next to him—a bald man in a black sweater and gray slacks—snores, and Will looks at him with envy. He's been asleep for ten hours. They took off from SFO, and then somewhere over Denver he reached into his pocket for an eye mask and a small white pill, which he took with a nip of vodka. "Wish I had one of those bad boys," Will had said. He grinned at the man, and the man glared back. At first Will worried that something had been lost in translation—they were flying to Greece—but then he remembered that before the man had drugged himself he'd been reading the last Dan Brown novel, in paperback, in *English*. So, no, he thinks now. Nothing was lost. The guy's just a dick.

He reaches up and pushes the call button to summon a flight attendant. He wants to know how much longer he's going to be stuck here before they land. Turning back toward the window, he presses his nose against the Plexiglas and looks down. Thirty-five thousand feet below them the sea spirals in blue, and green, and gray. They cleared Italy ten minutes ago, leaving behind the hills of Puglia and Molise for the tie-dyed Mediterranean.

"Sir?"

Will looks up and sees a blond flight attendant—the same one he argued with back in San Francisco. She's smiling down at him, her cheeks strained and her eyes puffy and reddened from the overnight flight.

"Is there anything I can get for you?"

She reaches forward and presses the call button, extinguishing a small orange light. The man next to him snores again, gulping for air.

Her smile widens; her eyes sadden. Even flight attendants get the blues.

"Do you know how much longer it'll be until we land?"

"Another hour and a half or so."

Will sinks further into his seat. He says, "We have been on this plane literally forever."

"*Literally* forever, sir?"

Will considers this for a moment.

"Any other questions?" she asks.

"A bottle of wine."

"Excuse me?"

"I'd like one of those little bottles of white wine."

She checks her watch. "You realize it's nine o'clock in the morning in Athens."

"Is it?"

"It is."

"Well then, I guess you'd better make it two."

Will watches the flight attendant as she makes her way back down the aisle, and then sinks further into his seat. He knows he should be embarrassed (chardonnay for breakfast is, objectively, embarrassing), but given the present circumstances, he decides to give himself a pass. When did things take such a precipitous turn? Spring break, probably. Or, if not spring break, then a week after, when his boyfriend, Rajiv, dumped him.

It was a Thursday, and he had invited Will to the Polar X-Press, a café that specialized in sno-cones that had just opened a few blocks from campus. Rajiv asked for a grape-cherry-mango concoction, and then before Will had a chance to order, he turned to him and said, "I think we should break up."

"Uh."

"I'm sorry, Will. It's just time."

Will looked down. He was still holding the menu—a thick, laminated placard that advertised cones with names like the Berkeley Blizzard and the B-Town Blast.

"Couldn't you wait until I ordered first?"

"Right—I'm sorry. Of course."

Will got a bottle of kombucha, which he hated, but Rajiv had offered to pay, and it was the most expensive thing on the menu. Then they sat down.

"I read somewhere that breakups should happen in neutral locations," Rajiv said. "And neither of us had been here before. So."

"Of course neither of us have been here. We don't eat sno-cones. We're twenty-two years old."

Rajiv licked cherry syrup from the edge of his lips.

"I wish you wouldn't yell," he said.

"You're joking, right? Christ, Rajiv—fourteen days ago we were camping in Baja. We were talking about moving in together." He looked at the bottle of kombucha, with its orange label and smug little top. "I think I deserve an explanation."

So Rajiv gave him one. In less than two months, they would be graduating, he said. And while the time they had spent together meant the world to him, the fact remained that he—Rajiv—was moving into a new phase of life, and he worried that Will was stagnant.

"I mean, you don't have a job yet, Will."

"What, and you do?"

"Yes. I do."

"Well, that's news to me."

It had happened two days before, on Tuesday. Fama, a brand-strategy firm with offices in San Francisco, had made an offer, and Rajiv had accepted it.

"Fama," Will said, repeating the name. "You mean the company where I was interviewing."

"You spoke so highly of it. I guess, well—look at it this way: you inspired me to apply." He reached across the table for Will's hand when he said this, but Will recoiled. He white-knuckled the kombucha bottle instead.

"And what, exactly, will you be doing at Fama?"

"I'll be a namer. I'll be naming things."

"You'll be naming things."

"Yeah. Brands, products. That sort of thing. Snack foods, mostly. Potato chips."

"Potato chips."

"They told me it was one of their more prestigious teams. I guess I did really well in the interview."

"Rajiv, that was the position I was interviewing for."

"It's weird, right? We could have been colleagues."

"No, actually, we couldn't have."

"Why not?"

"Because you stole my job."

Rajiv looked down into the melted mess of his sno-cone. He poked at the sludge with his straw and furrowed his brow.

He said, "You're upset."

Will nearly responded but stopped himself just before speaking. This had been a theme of their (now-dead) relationship: Rajiv would do something upsetting and, in turn, Will would feel upset. Before he had a chance to articulate these feelings, though, Rajiv would preempt them—he would say, as he just said now, *you're upset*. It was a declaration as much as it was a diffuser; in hearing Rajiv tell him what he felt, he no longer felt the right to feel it. Instead, he would spend the next ten minutes backtracking, explaining how his reaction had been wrong, and how Rajiv, blessed with a sense of eternal calmness—a stoicism that bordered, occasionally, on the catatonic—had been right.

Except this time. This time, Will said: "I am, in fact, upset."

Rajiv nodded slowly, his chin rising and falling half an inch.

"In all fairness, Will, you mentioned after your last interview that you didn't think you'd get it."

This was true. After his last trip to the Fama offices, he had met Rajiv in Union Square and told him that he thought his chances of getting the job were next to nil. Rajiv listened and then looked at him, stunned.

"But you were so sure before. You said that this was just to rubber-stamp it," he said. "What changed?"

Will had looked down and torn away a piece of the croissant they were sharing. He knew he couldn't tell Rajiv the truth—that it wasn't because of his talent, his ability to think up synonyms for such chip-specific terms as *ridged* and *twice-fried,* but rather something decidedly more complicated—and so he half lied. He said, "It's just a feeling I got."

Now, he tried to change the subject. He loosened the kombucha cap, then tightened it again. He said, "You told me you wanted to use your Spanish minor and start a literary nonprofit. You wanted to teach kids in the Tijuana slums to read."

Rajiv finished his sno-cone. His lips were now a mash-up of blue, purple, and a sickly sort of orange—the color, Will imagined, of a slug's innards just as they touched the air.

He said, "As it turns out, you were right: naming chips is more lucrative than helping orphans."

A week later, Will rode his bike home to his parents' house on Forest

Avenue. His senior thesis—twenty-five pages of quality fiction—was due to the university's English Department in less than a week, and since the breakup he had been unable to write a single word. He needed a change of scenery, he figured. He needed to work.

"'Perhaps some day I'll crawl back home, beaten, defeated,'" his father, Dean, said when he greeted him at the front door. "'But not as long as I can make stories out of my heartbreak.'"

"Hi, Dad."

"Sylvia Plath said that."

"Good for her."

Shaking water from his curls, Will slipped out of his coat. Dean took it from him and gave him a light check on his shoulder.

"Your mom told me what happened. Sorry to hear about the breakup, kiddo."

"The timing is not exactly ideal." He felt his throat tighten and an unbearable pressure build behind his eyes. Looking away, he kicked his shoes into a pile of slippers next to the front door. He said, "I haven't even started writing this thing."

"Do what Miss Plath did. Turn that pain into genius."

"With all due respect to Miss Plath, she also put her head in an oven."

Dean feigned a scowl, then smiled. "Don't sweat it. All the greats wait till the last minute. Did I ever tell you about the time I turned in a novel a year late?"

"You did," Will said.

"Did I?"

"Just last night, actually."

"Oh." He ran a hand over his bald spot. "So, I guess you know how the story ends?"

"You wrote an international bestseller that was translated into fifteen different languages."

"Sixteen, actually." Dean shrugged and opened his palms. "The Czechs finally came through."

"Really?" Will asked, mustering a smile. "That's awesome, Dad. Congrats."

Dean tousled his hair. "My point is there's always a silver lining."

"If that's true, I wish it would hurry up and show itself already."

"Hey, I already told you that I'd be happy to talk to Chip about getting you an extension." It was the third time Dean had made the offer. He still taught one fiction workshop a semester at the university and was close with the English Department's chair, Chip Fieldworth. It wouldn't be hard for him to make a phone call and wrangle a few extra weeks for Will to work.

"The offer still stands," he added now, leaning against the front door. "Just give it some thought."

"I appreciate the help," Will said, "but I think I can handle it."

He knew what people said about him: that while he had a lot of friends and was generally an upstanding guy, when it came to writing, he just wasn't very good. Yes, he was his father's son in some ways (blue eyes, too many freckles, acid reflux linked exclusively to white wine and kimchi), but he had nonetheless failed to inherit Dean's talent for prose. He was made aware of this during his first fiction workshop, a 100-level seminar taught by a graduate student who described things as either *jarring* or *problematic*. During that painful semester, when his classmates weren't calling his work solipsistic or reductive, they were criticizing him for lifting the easiest, most recognizable elements of Dean's aesthetic.

"It's time to kill your gods. Or, in this case, your father," he remembered the graduate student saying to him, after handing him back a draft of a story on which she hadn't bothered to make a single mark. "He sired you, now slay him dead."

Since that first class things had improved, though only marginally. With practice, he began to recognize a style that was vaguely his own and a voice that sounded, at least sometimes, like him. Still, he worried that whatever crumbs of encouragement he did receive were somehow offered as a sort of sacrifice to the department's worship of his father. His professors just wanted a blurb from Dean Wright for their next books, he figured, or they wanted him to put in a good word with his agent. Any way he cut it, there was no praise that Will could receive that seemed wholly his own.

It was for this reason that the job at Fama had been so attractive to him: finally, here was something he was *good* at, a success based on nothing but his merit. He hadn't told his parents about it—a decision for which now, after not being hired, he was profoundly thankful. While he was confident that his mother would have been proud of him, Dean, he knew, would have scoffed. Earlier, when Will had floated the idea of applying for a job at an ad agency in the city, his father had dismissed him. He told him that advertising copy was what real writers wrote when they were too bored to jerk off—and now, here Will was, about to shill for something as inconsequential as potato chips. Still, though, it was his—or, it *would have been* his, if things hadn't turned out like they had. He tried not to get too discouraged and poured his energy into looking for other jobs. With graduation approaching, he made appointments at the university's career center; he sent out cover letters and résumés blindly, feverishly. He scored interviews to answer phones at a nonprofit, to be a development assistant at the Pacific Pinball Museum, and, most recently, to read the newspaper to a rich blind woman in Pacific Heights. None of them, so far, had panned out. The nonprofit decided to hire an intern, and the pinball museum said—perhaps unsurprisingly—that it didn't have the funding to take on anyone new. When he left the blind woman's house, she told him she was sorry, but he just didn't have a reader's voice.

"It's a little too, well, homosexual," she said, grasping for the door handle. "I'm looking for the Marlboro Man, not Truman Capote."

He waited for her to say she was joking, and when she didn't, he bit his tongue. He told her that he understood and wondered if she could sense his scowl.

"Don't worry—you'll find something." She winked one of her sightless eyes. "People like you always do."

But that was only half the problem. The other half was Rajiv. A week after he dumped Will, Will's friend Cassie reported that Rajiv had started dating a sophomore named Logan from Laguna Beach. Will didn't believe it—he called Cassie a liar—but forty-eight hours later, an alarming number of pictures of Logan and Rajiv began appearing on Instagram. Now, every time Will glanced down at his phone he was assaulted by filtered and glossy shots of Rajiv and Logan kissing on Baker Beach, and along the Embarcadero, and outside SFMOMA, all of which were paired with horrific captions like #loveislove and #globalcitizens. They were, Will noted, the sort of flagrant displays of narcissism Rajiv had openly mocked while he was dating Will—displays in which he now (evidently) felt liberated enough to partake.

He successfully unfollowed Rajiv's feed a few days later. At the urging of one of his housemates, he managed to wipe his ex from his virtual life and focused ostensibly on more important things, like his senior thesis. The next day, though, after drinking too many beers and losing at Pub Quiz at the Albatross, he found himself huddled in the bar's bathroom, re-adding Rajiv on Instagram and Facebook. Twelve hours later, hungover and embarrassed, he discovered that any momentum he had developed toward his thesis had stopped dead; now, anything he wrote seemed trivial, or too small for his feelings. The only thing he could focus on was how Rajiv, in so many ways and in so many pixels, had broken his heart.

At his parents' house, he went to the kitchen and brewed a pot of coffee. Waiting for the percolator to warm up, he stared out the room's three bay windows where, a half mile ahead of him, San Francisco abutted the Pacific. The house itself was an old Craftsman—three stories of creaky floorboards and exposed wooden beams that Dean had bought in 1978. Will had been born and raised here, and while he knew both his parents had led lives before moving in, he had a difficult time imagining what form they took, so integrated and essential the place seemed to their beings. In each room were strewn bits of them—books they had written, research they had amassed, potted succulents they had abandoned, their once-pulpy stalks now mottled, decayed. Last year, when his mother forced Dean to move out for six weeks—when Will's parents' divorce seemed inevitable and imminent—he often found himself wondering what would happen to the house. Whether they would decide to sell it, or if one of them would stay, freeing the other from their messy domesticity.

Will lugged his backpack over his shoulder and made his way down the hall to his father's study, where he had taken to working whenever he came home. Once inside, he shut the door and collapsed into the chair behind Dean's desk. In front of him were stacked eight copies of *The Light of Our Shadows,* his father's latest opus, which, since its publication last fall, had sold over half a million copies, and which, according to Dean, would soon be available in Prague. It had been rereleased with a fresh cover design for its eighth printing—though Will was having a tough time distinguishing between this, the new book, and the other iterations of it he had already seen. He picked up one of the copies and inspected it more closely: same bloodred background, same pair of broken reading glasses. The only difference he could detect was that the title was now in a font two sizes smaller than his father's name.

He hadn't read it yet—he still hasn't read it. When Will was younger, his father's ability to write was a source of fascination for him. Sitting on the floor of his office, he would listen as Dean pounded away on the keyboard of his old iMac, pausing every ten minutes or so to crack his knuckles. None of those early works experienced as much success as *The Light of Our Shadows;* their sales were middling, and boxes of unsold copies were pulped. None of this mattered to Will. He tore through Dean's books; he reread them. He wanted to know what other stories lay bubbling inside his father—and, by extension, himself. Lately, though, as he confronted the limits of his own talent, that fascination had shifted to something else—fear, maybe, the crippling realization that he had no stories to tell, or that if he did, he'd never be good enough to tell them. And now he can't bring himself to read Dean's latest novel. He worries that doing so would be akin to staring into a fun-house mirror—one where instead of tiny arms or oversize legs, he's made up of a collection of stretched, bloated inadequacies.

Slumped in his father's chair, he let the book fall to the ground. Reaching into his shirt pocket, he fished around for the joint he'd brought with him but stopped himself just short of lighting it. No, he thought. Not until you've got a thousand words.

And then—well, and then.

It happened like this: In need of inspiration, he turned to his father's computer. Maybe Dean had a list of starters or something, Will thought. Some exercise that he used in class to jolt his students' imaginations. Or, at least that's what he told himself. Whatever the truth of his motivations were, the fact remains that he stumbled on the folder—the one marked (clearly! mockingly!) *unpublished stories*—by chance, hardly with an eye toward plagiarism. In fact, even as he started retyping the first five lines of the story he had selected onto a new page, he convinced himself that he would eventually change them and just use his father's prose to get the ball rolling.

But that's not what happened. Will kept going: word followed measly word and sentence followed measly sentence until, after an hour, he had transcribed the entire thing.

He didn't know if it was any good. From what he could tell, the plot concerned itself with a teenage boy lusting after the owner of a Laundromat, a forty-something woman called Mo. The style was a little different than the other stuff of his father's that Will had read: there were longer sentences, a freer use of punctuation and figurative language. Honestly, there were a few passages that he found a little clunky, or at least not to the level of writing that made Dean's other work such a hit. But this—all this—was a good thing. While there was zero probability that Dean would read the submission (only tenured faculty reviewed theses), Will still considered it more ethical to turn in something that was more in line with his own mediocre abilities, rather than something his father could have conceivably produced.

Before he could think—before he could let his conscience get the better of him—he opened a new email to his adviser and sent the file. Then he cracked the window behind the desk. He balanced the joint between his lips and, upon lighting it, took a deep, not entirely cleansing breath.

The flight attendant clears her throat and hands Will two small bottles of chardonnay.

She says, "Your wine, sir," in a voice of utter and absolute death.

Unscrewing one of them, he chugs half the bottle. They're starting to descend—he can feel his ears battling the pressure, the faint sinking as the plane dips beneath the clouds.

He thinks back to yesterday, once he was seated and waiting for the plane to take off. Using his iPhone, he had logged on to CalCentral, Berkeley's student portal—he wanted to check his grades before the flight attendant told him he had to shut off his phone. He didn't consider himself an obsessive person, though this—stalking the registrar—had become a compulsion ever since he submitted his thesis two weeks ago. There were countless 3 A.M. moments where he had woken with a jolt and reached for his phone. Countless nights out at a bar where the only way to stop himself from confessing his crime was to squint one eye and drunkenly pull up his transcript. Each time, he was looking for the same thing: if his grade for his senior thesis was still marked as *pending,* or whether it had been changed to *you're fucked*. He knew it was a worthless exercise—he had about as much power over when the grade was posted as he did over whether this plane plunged into the Mediterranean—but the act of checking provided him the illusion of control. Yes, he was strapped into the electric chair, but at least he got to decide when to throw the switch.

Now, though, as passengers hauled their bags into overhead compartments before takeoff, he saw that something on CalCentral had changed—notably, a number of his classes were graded. Holding his breath, he enlarged the screen and scrolled down. Then, sandwiched between *Buddhist Economics* and *Special Topics in Folklore,* he saw it: a line that read *senior thesis,* next to which was a clear-as-day A minus. Will stared at the letter, then refreshed the screen a few times. He wanted to see if the mark would vanish or change. It didn't, though; instead, it just stared back at him. Will Wright had, it seemed, *actually gotten away with it.*

The first thing he wanted to do was laugh, which was, admittedly, his go-to response in any morally dubious situation. Seeing someone skid on his ass down a flight of stairs, watching a friend step in dog shit—he couldn't help it, his body always convulsed in nervous giggles. It wasn't a lack of conscience that caused it so much as a recognition of conscience: he knew he should feel rotten, but mostly he was relieved. He suspected that in the future this might change, and remorse would catch up to him. For the time being, though, he was twenty-two. And, as a twenty-two-year-old, he was smart enough to know that feeling a little bit of guilt was better than dealing with actual consequences. He was smart enough to know that the important thing was not getting caught.

He took a deep breath to calm his giggles. Then he buckled his safety belt and sank his head against the back of the seat: he decided he could finally relax. In fourteen hours—in the time it would take him to watch seven movies—he would be in Greece. And while he had promised himself he would continue his search for a future during his time abroad (he had brought his laptop and a stack of semihelpful pamphlets from Career Services), he was also ready for a vacation. A break from the Bay Area's ceaseless summer fog and its job-nabbing boyfriends. A chance to trade in worries about what he was going to do with the rest of his life for a few weeks of feta, pita, and guys with good tans.

The flight crew announced that it was shutting the cabin door, and as they did so, his phone buzzed once against his lap—he had forgotten to switch it off after checking his grades. Picking it up, he glanced at the screen and saw that he had a new email. It was, he learned upon clicking it, a note from Ginny Polonsky, a rising senior at Berkeley and the new editor in chief of *The Berkeley Review,* the university's undergraduate literary journal. Reading further, his heart sank and then ricocheted to his throat: his story—his thesis—had been selected to be the featured piece of fiction in the *Review*'s fall issue. His adviser, Claudia Min, had been so taken with his work, Ginny wrote, that she had passed it along to the journal's fiction editors, who, in turn, passed it along to her. In addition to offering Will her *sincerest congratulations,* Ginny had a few questions ("as a new fan!"). *Like, for starters,* she wrote, *what inspired you? Have you ever even been to a Laundromat? Because you seriously describe it exactly as I've always imagined one. Also, on a more personal level, what convinced you to finally take a stance against your father with a story that's messier in its aesthetic, but also so clearly paying tribute to Dean's legacy? What's it feel like to come into your own? Oh, and finally, and this is sort of just for my own interest: how did you manage to capture the thoughts of a young member of the hetero-patriarchy when you're, well, just so gay?*

His palms sweating, Will tapped open a new email and began typing a response. *Look, Ginny,* he began again. *I'm flattered, but I'd like to talk to you about the story. I'm not sure if it's—*

"Sir, you need to shut your phone off and stow it for takeoff."

He looked up and saw a blond flight attendant staring down at him.

"Give me one second," Will said, returning to his screen.

"Sir, we've closed the cabin doors. If you don't shut your phone off, I'm going to have to ask the captain to come back here."

Will turned to her again. He said, "I don't think I can impress upon you how important this email is."

"And I don't think I can impress upon you how quickly I can get you thrown off this flight."

Somewhere in the rows of passengers ahead of him, his parents sit, oblivious. Originally, his father had booked three seats together. Upon arriving at the airport and printing their tickets, though, Dean realized that he had mistakenly selected a middle seat for himself. When he asked the gate agent—a mousy boy about Will's age with floppy hair and a soft voice—if there were any more aisle seats available, the agent immediately upgraded Dean and Sue Ellen to the last two first-class spots. Blushing, he murmured that *The Light of Our Shadows* had changed his life.

Will finishes the first bottle and reaches for the second. Where, he wonders, is his email presently? Floating. Idling in digital purgatory. He knows Ginny—knows her well, in fact. It's basically impossible not to: she's a ubiquitous presence in Berkeley's creative writing program. He can hardly remember a time when her voice wasn't the first one he heard during a workshop, or when her laugh wasn't the loudest at a party.

"She's always just, like, *there*," his friend Cassie said to him once. They were smoking cigarettes on the steps of the gym, and as Will listened he let ash fall on the tops of his shoes. "It's like she's an amoeba or something. Like she can split and multiply at superhuman speeds so she can be a billion places at once."

"There are multiple Ginny Polonskys," Will said. "That's the only viable explanation."

"Oh, Jesus," Cassie said, leaning a bit to the left so a pair of tan legs and running shoes could pass between them. "Can you even imagine?"

"It would be a lot of hair."

He knows what Cassie was getting at: Ginny Polonsky is, categorically, annoying as fuck. She is also a wholesale devotee of Will's father. And she's not alone: this past year there was a group of them, ten or so students who had been deemed, by Dean, to be talented enough to enroll in the one workshop he teaches. These Deaniacs, as Cassie called them, were of a certain type: sensitive gay men, primarily, and the headstrong women who love them. There was one straight male who was admitted. A ukulele-playing bro named Garrett, who considered himself enlightened, woke. He didn't last long, Will was relatively certain. Or, if he did, he ended up fading into the background; he quickly became aware that, really, he was just part of the problem.

Will works his jaw to pop his ears and rolls an empty bottle between his palms. Ginny Polonsky, he thinks. Of course she would want to publish the story; she probably just about wet herself when she read Will's name on top of it. But then, that was the point: at the end of the day, the quality of the story itself had very little to do with her decision; he wouldn't be surprised if Ginny hadn't even read the whole thing. Rather, she's probably publishing the piece to curry Dean's favor. *Look at me, publishing your son. Look at me, making you proud.*

For God's sake, Will thinks. I can't even plagiarize right.

The plane banks to the left, spiraling downward. They're meant to spend a few hours in Athens before catching the ferry to Aegina. His father explained this to him before they boarded the flight in San Francisco. They'll see the sights, wander through some ruins, eat a gyro or two. It was important to Sue Ellen—she wanted Will to experience the city. The last time she brought him here he was five years old, and the only memory he has of the place is tripping and skinning his knee at the Temple of Hephaestus. While he cried, his mother led him into the bathroom of a nearby McDonald's, where she washed dirt and gravel away from the wound. Now, pressing his nose against the window again, Will thinks he catches sight of the Parthenon, perched uneasily among the rubble of the Acropolis. At the mound's base, past the Odeon of Herodes Atticus and the shaded streets of the Plaka, Athens radiates outward—a mess of new and ancient.

"Jesus," Will says aloud, and the man next to him stirs. "I'm so fucked."

Dean

He's awful at red-eye flights.

He shouldn't be; after spending the last ten months crisscrossing the country to promote his book, by now he should have developed a system to ward off the gauziness of spending an abridged night on a plane. Drink two gins and eight glasses of water. Watch a rerun of *The Big Bang Theory,* listen to Elgar's "Mot d'Amour," do a Zen breathing exercise, and then pass out for six blissful hours. That sort of thing. He hasn't, though. Instead, he's just exhausted. While Sue Ellen had slept for nearly the entire flight, he spent the whole time trying to get comfortable, caught somewhere between an Ambien dream and the present. A few times he tried reading a book—a W. H. Auden biography that for the last five years he's been ignoring—but each time he gave up, preferring instead to listen to the flight attendants heat coffee and gossip in the galley.

They arrived here, at the Acropolis, twenty minutes ago. After clearing customs at eight o'clock this morning, they took a cab from the airport to a restaurant Sue Ellen knew of in Dexameni, near the city's center. At a table beneath a broken ceiling fan, they ate *bougatsas,* then took turns using the bathroom so they could brush their teeth. If it were up to Dean, they would have stayed there, drinking thick cups of coffee until he felt like he was running on something other than fumes. His wife, though, had other plans. A quick walking tour of the National Garden and a visit to Hadrian's Arch. To Dean's credit, he didn't protest, no matter how much he wanted to. Rather, he was well behaved, listening to Sue Ellen as she slipped into her lectures, not interrupting his son when he asked questions with obvious answers. He grumbled only minimally when Sue Ellen suggested they walk up Dionysiou Areopagitou, the pedestrian street that leads to the Acropolis, and was duly thankful when she negotiated for them to store their bags in the site's ticket office. He is, he thinks, being *a very good sport.*

Reaching into the back pocket of his jeans, Dean pulls out a worn white handkerchief, which he uses to wipe sweat away from his bald spot. He's worried that it's started to burn; he'd forgotten to rub sunscreen on it earlier this afternoon, and already he can feel the white patch of flesh darkening to a crisp pink. He wonders if Sir Arthur Evans had the same problem—if, when he was digging up Knossos, he was forced to take frequent breaks, ducking into the shade of an ancient temple to give his scalp a rest. Probably not, Dean thinks. Men were made from heartier stock back then. Sir Arthur probably baked out there without blinking an eye. He probably let his whole head get good and fried before the thought of a hat even crossed his mind.

A few minutes ago, Will, unprompted, brought Dean a bottle of water ("You don't look so good, Dad") before wandering off toward the Temple of Nike. Now, drinking it, he looks down and checks his watch: it's one forty-five, which means they've got another three hours before catching their ferry to Aegina, where he plans on downing a few poolside gin and tonics and signing off until tomorrow. Surveying the ground around him, he looks for a place to sit, some three-thousand-year-old piece of marble on which he might unload. He shields his eyes from the sun and looks toward the Erechtheion, where Sue Ellen is looking down, taking pictures of the ground with her phone. How many times has he heard her story about coming here as a teenage girl? How many times has she told him that, during her first visit to the Acropolis, she had sat on the steps of the Parthenon and cried? For this, he has persevered, he has sacrificed; he has ruined a perfectly good shirt with sweat and subjected himself to a sunburnt scalp in order to ensure his wife's happiness.

This is, after all, for her.

The sin for which Dean Wright is repenting was named Jasmine, and his agent, Sal, had been the person who introduced them. Two months before *The Light of Our Shadows* was released, he phoned Dean to tell him that, given the novel's growing buzz, he had reached out to a few Hollywood types who might be interested in optioning the book for film. Three of them—big studio guys whose tastes veered toward the superheroic, the high concept—had passed. The fourth, though, was interested. She was a fan not only of this current novel, but also of Dean's earlier work, and she wanted him to come in for a meeting.

"So, what, now I've got to fly down to L.A.?" he remembers asking Sal. He was sitting in front of his laptop, rereading a few prepublication reviews. In the kitchen, Sue Ellen was roasting acorn squash, and the smell—rich, nutty, thick with butter—wafted down the hall to his office. He cradled the phone against his shoulder.

"I'll pay for the ticket," Sal said.

"You mean you'll deduct it from my next check."

"Hombre, that check's going to be so big you won't know the difference."

"Why does she want to meet, anyway? Can't we just set up a call or something?"

He was doing his best to sound nonchalant, annoyed; he didn't want to let on that he had been practicing his red-carpet interviews for eighteen months.

"She wants to meet because she's a fucking fan, and she wants to turn your book into a fucking movie, and I already told her you'd fly down," Sal said. "Stop acting like I'm asking you to trek across the goddamned Andes or something."

"Okay, okay." Dean shut his computer. "I'll go."

"Good. Do your best to be charming."

"I'll try."

"And for the love of God, remember to tuck in your shirt."

"Fuck off."

She worked for a company called Tilt Pictures. It was a production house whose work, at least according to Sal, was often lauded at places like Sundance and Toronto, and whose offices were in the glassed-in upper floors of a skyscraper on Wilshire. Dean arrived in the afternoon and was greeted at the elevator by Jasmine's assistant, an enthusiastic young man named Danny with a wide smile and bracingly white sneakers. He shook Dean's hand, and by the time he had released it, he had already offered him a slew of beverages: water, coffee, Perrier, *matcha*. Dean declined them all, and Danny—smile still wide, shoes still blinding—led him into a glass conference room at the end of the floor. A fishbowl of sorts that looked out upon Tilt's office on one side and the grimy headache of Hollywood on the other.

She made him wait ten minutes. He remembers that now. Ten minutes of checking his breath, swiveling in his chair, and untucking and retucking his shirt. When she did finally enter, she did so carrying a copy of his first novel and a wineglass filled with sparkling water.

"Oh, God," he said, nodding toward the book. "Where'd you find that?"

"Just a little memorabilia to start things off." She sat across from him and offered him her hand. "Jasmine Ramos, by the way."

"Dean Wright." Her grip was firm; he felt her rings digging into his fingers. "I thought I asked my publisher to burn all the copies of that thing."

"Looks like I got the last one, then." She smiled. "And I don't know what you're talking about. *My Baby Takes Taxis at Dawn* changed my life. In fact"—she pulled the cap off a pen with her teeth—"I was hoping I could get you to sign it."

"You're just buttering me up."

"Guilty." Jasmine winked. "I had Danny order it on Amazon yesterday."

They continued like this—sparring, testing, flirting. She told him her vision for the book's adaptation. They would find a writer with studio chops, but someone who would still honor the integrity of the story. Keep it quiet and thoughtful, but with a mainstream sensibility. "*Dead Poets Society* meets *Scent of a Woman*," she told him, "but with a *Bird Cage* twist." Dean worked hard to impress her, dropping references to the Tilt films that he had researched, while he complimented her tastes. He hadn't expected to be attracted to her; when he walked into the meeting, he was mostly concerned with how wrinkled his shirt was and with the extra ten pounds he'd put on that year. And yet, here he was, laughing too hard at Jasmine's jokes, letting his eyes linger too long as she sipped seltzer from her wineglass. She was taller than Dean by a good two inches and wore a blazer better than he could ever hope to. Her dark hair was cut to the chin, in the sort of severe bob that he typically associated with Finnish secretaries, not Hollywood development execs. And when she yelled at Danny to bring her more water, it was in a clipped, staccato voice—a tone that was laced with a sort of annoyed authority that terrified Dean and turned him on.

After an hour and a half, she unbuttoned her blazer and leaned her elbows on the table.

"You want to take this somewhere else?" she said. "That kid's annoying me, and there's an awesome, depressing hotel bar two blocks away."

It was called the Dirty Duck, and when they got there they both ordered whiskey sours. Jasmine said the bar was famous for them, but after the third one she admitted that might have been a fib; really, she just liked the taste of lemon.

Later, he would swear he had no intention of sleeping with Jasmine— though this, of course, would be a lie. He knew within an hour or two of meeting her that, soon, they would end up in bed. He knew it in the way that a person knows certain things—that you're paying too much for a burger, or that a buxom blonde will be the first to die in a slasher film. There are signals. Little signposts that point to the inevitably of an ending. The thing that did shock him, at least at first, was his capacity for it. While he suspected he was handsome (twice he'd been told he looked like Gary Cooper), he still never considered himself a person who was suave enough for an affair. In grad school, long before he met Sue Ellen, his friends used to call him Turtle, for his propensity to shrink and disappear in front of women. And yet, here he was, setting up secret weekend getaways on Catalina. Here he was, closing the door to his office whenever Danny called to say he had Jasmine on the line.

Another thing that startled him: his remorse was surprisingly, almost addictively easy to ignore. Sure, he felt it, nipping at his heels whenever they checked into a hotel. It was, though, a minor emotion, an itch that, if ignored long enough, he didn't need to scratch. More than anything, he felt empowered, as if he had been reborn into a new, invigorating shape. With Jasmine, he wasn't the slob who left dishes in the sink or the taskmaster who scolded subpar grades; he wasn't confined to *husband* or *father*—roles in which, despite his best efforts, he sensed he had grown limp. Rather, Jasmine treated Dean like the writer he dreamt of one day becoming. She hadn't actually read *The Light of Our Shadows* (Danny, as it turned out, had a knack for giving great coverage), but still, when he talked about it, he felt like she was genuinely interested in what he was saying. She nodded at the right moments and asked him to clarify his more cumbersome thoughts. Instead of feeling like a burden or a hack, for the first time in a while he felt powerful—a man who held urgent opinions about topics like art, literature, and the future of Nordic cuisine.

He got caught on the most beautiful day of the year—that is, at least, what all the weathermen were saying. It was October. The fog had cleared from the bay, revealing the infinite promise of the Pacific. For once, San Francisco didn't look like the end of the world, but rather the beginning of it. In fact, it was so nice that Dean decided to go for a run. Lately, Jasmine's taut body had made him aware of the inadequacies of his own: the way a pillow of flesh sat just above his waistband, how his chest had grown soft and mutable. His new fitness regime wasn't some precursor for divorce; he wasn't dropping two pant sizes just to leave Sue Ellen, nor, he figured, did Jasmine expect him to. To date, the subject of his wife had never been discussed. There was a tacit understanding between them that the very thing that made them work was the implausibility of a future. A joint realization that as soon as whatever they shared became real—as soon as it became fleshed out with all the scars and warts of domesticity— that would be the instant they would both stop wanting it.

He entered the kitchen to find his wife sitting at the breakfast table. He was sweaty and parched from his run, so he poured himself a glass of water before coming over to give her a kiss. She didn't let him, though. As soon as he leaned down, she stood up and walked away.

"I know," he said. "I'm pretty gross right now."

"Who the hell is Jasmine Ramos?"

Her colleague Greta Weinstein had seen them—that's what Sue Ellen told him. Two days prior, Dean had gone to see Jasmine in Los Angeles (he had told Sue Ellen he had a reading in Orange County). On Wednesday night, they had gone to eat at a Tex-Mex restaurant in Venice—the same restaurant where Greta, who was in town for a conference at UCLA, had decided to have a quiet dinner of enchiladas. Instead, she had seen them kissing. She learned Jasmine's name when the hostess called them to be seated. Then she had phoned Sue Ellen. Dean was humiliated—for his wife, but also for himself. He had been an idiot and had gotten caught. Seconds earlier, his affair had struck him as exciting and original; now, he felt like just another schmuck.

He begged Sue Ellen to give him another chance, first in the kitchen and then in the living room, where she retreated after ten minutes. His shirt, a ratty gray thing with a hole in the left shoulder, dried as he spoke. In the beginning, it was heavy with sweat; half an hour later, it was stiff and crunchy—ducking his nose beneath his collar, he realized he hated his own smell. He told her he had made the biggest mistake of his life, and he meant it. She cried only once, when she asked Dean what had attracted him to Jasmine and he answered that she wasn't his wife. Aside from that, she listened, her hands folded resolutely in her lap, her eyes clear and trained on him. Then, around lunchtime, she stood up and made a sandwich. When she returned to the living room, she told him to pack a bag and leave.

He found a furnished short-term rental in San Ramon. An alcove studio with wall-to-wall beige carpet and vertical blinds that never fully shut and that he never fully opened. He never cooked anything—never, in fact, checked if the stove even worked. His meals, rather, were of the deliverable or microwavable variety: pizzas and Lean Cuisines and cups of dehydrated ramen. Eating these things, he was reminded of how he had lived in his early twenties, though this time his choices felt disrespectable and uncouth: he wasn't just being lazy, he was being a child. He called Sue Ellen twice—once on the first night he was alone, and then again four days later. Both times, he was redirected to her voice mail. Listening to her recorded voice, he would imagine her sitting somewhere in their house as she held the phone in her hand, staring at his number. Space, he intuited, was what she needed, though space was also the thing he was least inclined to give. He worried that in those stretches of silence, she would become more resolved in her disappointment, more certain of his sins. Still, he resisted his instincts and stopped calling. Forgiveness, he knew, could be a prickly thing.

Two weeks later she came to see him. He was lying on the couch, read-ing *The Day of the Locust,* when he heard her knock on his door. He was embarrassed to let her in, though he did, promptly. The apartment's fur-niture looked like it had been stolen from a Hilton Garden Inn, and there were half-empty takeout cartons in the sink. He hadn't managed to buy a laundry hamper yet, so his dirty clothes—socks, underwear, a pair of old khakis—formed a pile in the corner of the bedroom. He offered her some water, and when she accepted he considered it a promising sign. Leaning against the kitchen wall, she held the glass against her cheek. He watched her as she considered the apartment: the old television, the Formica counters, the splashes of marinara sauce on the floor.

Then she turned to him.

"I'd like for us to go to therapy," she said.

It was not so much a request as a demand; in the same breath, she told him that if he wanted to stay married, seeing a marriage counselor was nonnegotiable. And so they went, on Monday and Wednesday afternoons. Before long, these sessions fell into a predictable pattern: Sue Ellen would find refuge at the opposite end of the couch as Dean held his breath, ter-rified that, at any moment, she would announce that she was through with him. The counselor, Connie, had been recommended by a woman Sue Ellen knew in the Latin Studies Department. She was good, and not at all what Dean had expected. Connie wore no shawls, and her office boasted no collection of plants. Instead of sitting in some hideous recliner, she po-sitioned herself on an ergonomic kneeling chair—a squat pedestal with a sleek, Scandinavian aesthetic that kept her spine long and erect. Mostly, though, she was easy to talk to. Her voice hovered near a deep contralto, and—much to Dean's delight—she only rarely mentioned *feelings*.

And it worked: a month later the space between them on the couch had diminished. Sue Ellen was accepting Dean's apology, and Dean—his eyes filmy with tears—was reaching out to take her hand. The next day, they drove to San Ramon, where Dean canceled his lease and Sue Ellen brought boxes to help him pack his things. That night, he ate dinner with his family at the same Vietnamese restaurant he and Sue Ellen had gone to the evening she discovered she was pregnant with Will.

A tour group gathers along the eastern face of the Parthenon, a horde of twenty or so teenagers led by a stout woman holding a yellow umbrella. She points at something—one of the columns, Dean thinks, but from where he's sitting he can't be sure. Reaching down, he tugs a weed out from underneath the stone on which he's sitting and begins to tie its stem into knots. The Ottomans turned the temple into a mosque, he remembers having read, before deciding to store arms in it at some point during the 1600s. This turned out to be a bad idea: when the Venetians bombarded the city at the tail end of that century, they ignited the stored ammunition and blew off the roof.

He ties another knot in the weed's stem and, as a few drops of sweat work their way down his spine, he reminds himself that it had been his idea to come. And while his motivations may have been a hair less than pure, the fact remains: He was the one who, two months ago, first proposed to Sue Ellen that he and Will accompany her to Greece for the summer. He was the one who suggested that all the Wrights needed was a good family vacation.

It was midweek, a Wednesday afternoon, and he had surprised her at her office with lunch. The forecast, he remembers, had promised sun, but there was nonetheless a light drizzle, and by the time he reached the Classics Department, he looked shaggy and wet. After shaking himself off and removing his windbreaker, he began shuffling through the department's hallways, where there were stacks of flyers advertising study abroad opportunities in places like Naples and Alexandria and Rome. When he got to his wife's office, he didn't knock. Instead, he sat down, unloaded two turkey sandwiches on her desk, and said, "I think Will and I should come with you. To Greece, I mean."

"Uh, hi," she said, and set down the exam she had been grading. She took off her glasses and looked at the sandwiches, wrapped in white deli paper. "What are those? And why are you so wet?"

"Turkey. The one on the left doesn't have pickles." He pushed his hair out of his face. "And it's raining."

She spun in her chair and looked out the window, nodding. Spinning back, she said, "And to what do I owe the pleasure?"

"I just told you: I think Will and I should come to Greece with you this summer."

Sue Ellen unwrapped her sandwich and lifted up the top slice of bread, inspecting its contents. "You hate Greece."

"That's a lie. I love Greece."

"When we were there in '97 you flew back a week early."

"I had copyedits to work on," he said. "And besides, the Welsh weren't made for the Mediterranean."

She tore off a scrap of turkey and popped it in her mouth. "And you're suddenly no longer Welsh?"

"I've since learned about the magical properties of sunscreen." His phone buzzed in his pocket, and he reached down to silence it. "Come on," he said. "It'll be great. Our last chance to be together as a family before we release Will to the wolves."

"What if he gets a job by then?"

"I think the likelihood of that is less than convincing."

Sue Ellen tucked her hair behind her ears. "And you? What will you do?"

"I'll write."

"You'll write?"

"Yes, I'm a writer. I'll write." He took a bite of his sandwich and said, with his mouth still full, "Also, I've had a new book idea."

"Oh, *really*."

Dean said, "Yes, really," though this was far from the truth. He had experienced a few, precious bursts of energy since finishing *The Light of Our Shadows,* though he hadn't elected to invest in them with any reasonable degree of effort. Publicly, when his colleagues asked him when they might expect the next novel from Dean Wright, he complained about fear of failure, of not being able to write something that might live up to his past work. These anxieties, he would go on to explain, boxed him in creatively: his words had lost their rhythm. He appreciated the sympathy he got whenever he offered up this explanation—the pats on the shoulder, the assurances that *the juices would start flowing again.* The issue, though, wasn't writer's block; the issue was laziness. Putting together a novel was hard—impossibly so—and, despite how much he glorified the writing process for Jasmine, he often questioned whether he had the constitution for it. Sitting down at the computer, trudging through the awful monotony of prose—it was all such a tedious slog. The problem was that there was little else he was good at; he had endured the boredom of writing novels because it seemed like the only viable thing to do. It was for this reason that the most recent book's success brought such euphoric relief. Finally, there was an opportunity to rest on his royalty checks. Finally, there was an opportunity to stop.

Sue Ellen knew all this. Knew of his laziness, his keen desire to do nothing but watch reruns in his underwear. And that—all of that—was precisely why her smirk irritated him so much. If she really loved him, he thought, she would play along. If she really loved him, she would let him lie.

Sue Ellen peeled a piece of lettuce out of her sandwich, folded it in half, and ate it. She always deconstructed her sandwiches before eating them. She asked, "So what's it about?"

"A gorgeous classics professor giving a talk about a temple to a group of touring octogenarians."

"Oh, that's rich."

He wiped mustard from the corner of his mouth. "It's still in the early stages. I'm not really ready to talk about it yet."

Outside, the rain picked up, growing from a drizzle to a steady downpour. Sue Ellen said, "There's something you're not telling me."

"You're right. I was the second shooter on the grassy knoll." He waited for a beat, then smiled. He said, "Why is it so unbelievable that we want to come and support you in this?"

"It's not. It's just—"

"I know." He cut her off. He knew what she was going to say, and he couldn't stand to hear her say it again.

Instead, he set his sandwich on the desk and leaned over to kiss her cheek.

"We need this," he said. "I think this could be good for us. It'll be the final push to get us through this year."

She looked at him for a moment, then stood up. After pacing to the window and back, she shoved her hands into the pockets of her pants and said: "You promise not to complain about the sun?"

Dean raised both his hands. "Now I'm afraid you're just being unreasonable."

Sue Ellen sat down and tore some crust away from a slice of bread. Chewing it, she smiled.

She said, "Okay, let's go."

"Dad, I'm dying."

He glances up and sees Will standing over him. Trails of sweat dampen the front of his shirt.

"What?"

"I said I'm dying. Like, this place is cool and all, but the heat is killing me."

Dean looks at his watch. He says, "I don't know what to tell you. We've got another two hours until the ferry."

"What are we going to do until then?"

Dean stands and brushes off the front of his jeans.

"Jesus, Will, *I* don't know. Go find some shade. Buy another bottle of water. You're an adult—figure it out."

"Whoa." Will holds up his hands like he's under arrest. "What's gotten into you?"

"Nothing." Dean lowers his voice and rubs the bridge of his nose.

He wonders if it's possible to ever really escape his mistakes, or if he's just particularly good at repeating them.

He says, "Nothing's gotten into me."

Sue Ellen

July 7
The Acropolis and the Saronic Gulf

She rests her chin on her knees and looks south, where a cloud of smog chokes Athens. Squinting, she tries to make out the shapes of ships flooding in and out of the city's port, at Piraeus: the sharp angles of a sloop's mainsail as it catches the breeze; the broad, rusted girth of a tanker. She can't, though—the smog's too thick—so instead she lets her thoughts drift.

As the sun scalds the back of her neck, she lets her eyes cross and uncross, and the sea blurs in and out of focus. She thinks of its name, rolling its syllables over on her tongue, their impossible combination of vowels: *the Aegean.* Whenever she teaches her survey course on classical archaeology, she begins here, in the deep indigo, where Odysseus wandered homeless and homesick, where Poseidon sired Pelias and Neleus. She explains to her students how the etymology of its name is up for dispute; how some scholars say that *Aegean* is a derivation of *aiges,* the Greek word for waves, while others point to an ancient town, Aegae, where the name was supposedly born. She offers up other, more fantastical explanations, too: a fierce Amazon queen named Aegea, who perished sailing back from

Troy; an old Hecatoncheir called Aigaion—a giant of insurmountable strength who helped the Olympians oust the Titans. Finally: a king of Athens named Aegeus who, mistaking his son Theseus for dead, threw himself from a cliff into the churning surf.

"We can't be certain why we call it what we call it," she says, always, "which, actually, is half the fun."

Scratching a mosquito bite on her ankle, she shifts her gaze from the water to the city, its thousands of mismatched roofs and honking cars. Then she works her way back to the sight that has been fascinating her for the past ten minutes: not the Parthenon or the Temple of Athena Nike, but rather a woman. Italian, she's guessing, but she could be wrong; Sue Ellen's estimate is based solely on her raven hair, her perfect waist, her choice to wear a pair of kitten heels to a place whose name translates roughly to "The Rock." Whoever she is, she's taken about a hundred photos of herself with a selfie stick. It's an odd procedure to watch, one that's at once self-conscious and detached. The adjustments the girl makes in her arm are minuscule—not more than a single degree or two in terms of angle—and yet the results must be colossally different. Why else would she continue standing there, pouting her lips and making peace signs? Why else wouldn't she have just stopped?

Sitting on a bench facing the Acropolis's south slope, she wonders if the Greeks anticipated this. She wonders if, when Pericles instituted his marvelous plan for the reconstruction of the sanctuary, he had considered that, in two and a half millennia, a girl named Alessandra might trample through the Propylaea just to get a few shots for Instagram. She wouldn't be surprised if he did, Sue Ellen thinks. The Greeks were, after all, the people who gave us Narcissus. The only difference, she figures, is that while we have reality television stars, they had the gods; while we're stuck reading about Kim Kardashian, they had Aphrodite. But then, those two things aren't entirely separate, either: Greeks gossiped in the same way about Aphrodite's affairs as her students do about Kim's ass; both, as it turns out, are worshipped.

Glancing up once again, she notices the girl is looking at her—has, in fact, been watching Sue Ellen stalk her the whole time. Quickly, she looks down. She spreads her toes in her sandals and, a moment later, hears her name being called. Looking to her left she sees her husband, waving his pale arms above his head and pointing at his watch.

"Just a minute!" she calls out to him, and ventures another glance around. The selfie stick girl is gone, replaced by someone else: a man with a beard and a backpack, a comically big Canadian flag sewn onto it.

"We've got to go!" she hears Dean say. His arms still wave at her. "The boat leaves in an hour!"

For a final moment, she stares up at the Erechtheion. There, along the Porch of the Caryatids, six young maidens, carved from limestone, prop up the temple's roof. They've been there for two and a half thousand years. Ever since Phidias sculpted them to carry history on their shoulders.

An hour later, on the top deck of the ferry to Aegina, she grasps a bottle of Mythos between her thighs. Wedging the lighter against its neck, she flicks her wrist and pries off the cap.

"Where'd you learn how to do that?" Will asks her as she hands him the beer.

"I went to college, too, you know. Besides, we don't have a bottle opener, and needs must be met." The ferry lurches out of Piraeus, past the mouth of the harbor, and begins to pick up speed. Below her, deep in the boat's bowels, the engine rumbles and whines. In the row of seats to her rear, some French tourists show each other pictures they've taken on their phones.

She looks down at the lighter—blue, with a San Francisco Giants logo printed along its side.

"Is this yours?" she asks.

"Uh . . ." Will stutters. "I mean, I guess? I gave it to you."

"Yes, I know you gave it to me. I'm sorry. That was a stupid question. I should have said 'This *is* yours.'"

"Er . . ."

She turns the lighter over on her palm. Its paint is starting to chip.

She says, "Are you smoking again?"

"No." Will gulps from his beer. "Or, mostly no. Hardly ever."

Sue Ellen glances down at her son's backpack, where she sees a pack of Parliaments peeking out from the exterior pocket.

"Will, you know I hate it when—"

"I know." He cuts her off. "I've just— I've been stressed."

He leans his head against her shoulder and scratches his right ear. She does this, too, whenever she's got something on her mind. It's one of the countless tics, along with biting her fingernails and puffing her cheeks, that she seems to have passed on to him.

"Did you ever get a chance to look at that grad school stuff I sent you? I didn't realize there were so many M.F.A. programs in the Bay Area."

"I'd never get in," he says.

"What are you talking about? You got an A minus on your thesis."

He lifts his head and drinks from his Mythos.

"I don't want to be a writer," he says.

"Then don't be. There are a million other things you can do." She tries to pull him back toward her, but he resists. "Have you thought about the Peace Corps? Two of my colleagues have sons who did it and—"

"Mom."

She looks at him, but he doesn't look back. He keeps staring down.

"I'm not helping, am I?"

"No," he says. "I mean, I know you're trying to, and I appreciate it, but no. You're not." He leans forward and rests his elbows on the back of the bench in front of him. Reaching up, she runs her hand through his curls. He needs a shower—they both do.

Will says, "I'm going to end up, like, delivering pizzas for the rest of my life."

"There's nothing wrong with that," she says. "And besides, I think you'd be great at delivering pizzas."

"You have to say that. You're my mom."

"I suppose that does put me under certain obligations." She tugs lightly on his curls once, then lets them go. "But in this case, I'm speaking objectively. You've got a great smile and a flawless driving record. Domino's would snatch you up in an instant."

"Knock it off." He awards her a small laugh and stands. "I'm going to find Dad. Watch my backpack while I'm gone?"

"Sure, kiddo." She shields her eyes and looks up at him. "Where is he, anyway?"

"He went downstairs. He said the smell of the fumes was making him sick."

"It's worse down there." She can't help herself—instead of returning the lighter to Will, she slips it into her pocket. Once he's gone she'll go for the cigarettes. "There's no fresh air. No circulation."

"Yeah, well."

She looks at him for a moment longer. He purses his lips and blows lightly across the bottle's mouth, creating a low, sad whistle.

"I'm glad you came," she says.

"Yeah?" He stops blowing.

"Yeah."

He smiles. "I'll be downstairs."

She watches him disappear belowdecks and, after retrieving her own beer from beneath the bench, she turns her attention forward, to the ferry's bow as it cuts a broad wake through the water. She doesn't want to meddle. Her own parents were meddlers, and she knows how exhausting it can be, having that pressure looming, the weight of balancing a mother's interference with your own private anxieties. Still, it's hard work, biting her tongue, resisting the urge to fix a set of problems that aren't hers to fix. She wants to tell him not to worry, to accept that—at least for a while—things won't work out as he imagined. She wants to remind him of all the awful jobs she had before deciding to go back to school; of how, for ten abysmal months, she went door to door to dentists' offices, hawking bad art to display in their waiting rooms. More than anything, she wants to tell him how Purpose, that awful thing that greeting cards tell him he was born with and that he just has to *find,* is actually something he'll need to create; that it's not until he feels the monotony of life that he'll come to decide why he's living it.

She can't see Aegina yet, but she imagines it there, rising up from the waves. Holding the cool bottle against her cheek, she closes her eyes for a moment and lets the breeze whip through her hair. She thinks back to the first time she made this trip. She was twenty-five—she'd just completed her second year of graduate work at Berkeley—and she was like her son: terrified and clueless. She remembers queuing up at Piraeus to board this same ferry, her spine drenched with sweat beneath her backpack; she remembers looking out over the hundreds of heads in front of her, at the clouds of cigarette smoke as they mixed with the dank humidity of the port. She remembers thinking: What the hell am I doing?

The ostensible goal had been to get to Delos, in the Cyclades, where a former colleague of her adviser was studying the Stoibadeion alongside the French School of Archaeology. She was still struggling to find a direction for her dissertation, and her adviser had suggested that spending the summer doing fieldwork might jolt her creativity and give her a sense of focus.

"Dig around in the dirt for a while," she remembers him saying to her early that spring. She was sitting in his office, and in front of her on his desk stood a miniature statue of the Sounion kouros. The boy's left leg was rigidly fixed forward, as if he were caught in midstep, and his hands hung in half-fists at his sides. She remembers, very vividly, wanting to reach out and take hold of the thing. To grab the boy by his bare, flat ass and, without warning or motivation, shatter it on the office's cold tile floor.

Instead, she said, "Dig around in the dirt?"

"Why not?" Her adviser shrugged. "Dig around. See what comes up. I mean, that's all we really do anyway, isn't it?" He lit a cigarette. "Besides, from what I hear, they could use the help. The École Française isn't exactly what it used to be."

Sue Ellen looked at the kouros again. She thought of his leg split from his smooth pelvis. Of his head split from his stone neck.

She said, "Sure."

She never made it, though. To Delos, that is. Because in Aegina she met Christos, and what was meant to be a two-day layover turned into three months of something else entirely.

But now Christos is gone. And while she knows this, she nonetheless finds herself believing that she'll stumble upon him; that, upon entering the Alectrona's lobby, she'll discover that he's standing there, smoking a cigarette behind the inn's front desk. Thinking of him now, as she floats halfway between Athens and Aegina, she worries she might start to cry, might break down in sobs here, in front of these squabbling French tourists, with her husband and son nursing cheap Greek beer downstairs. She presses her sunglasses farther up the bridge of her nose and remembers when she first learned of his death. It was a month after discovering her husband's affair. As she worked to repair her marriage, she found herself googling Christos more and more often, scouring the internet for glimpses of a place where life might have turned out differently. It was an obituary she stumbled across—three sentences announcing he had died and was survived by his daughter, Eleni—sandwiched between bicycle ads on the *Aegina News* website.

At first, she refused to believe it. Instead, she chose to focus her attention on the fact that his daughter—the little girl she'd seen in the last picture he ever sent her—was now a grown woman. Although she had never met her, Sue Ellen always held Eleni in the same place she held Christos: a season of perpetual youth. Moments later, though, the reality seeped in, and her breath seemed to get caught in her throat. Dean was sitting across the table from her—she had brought her laptop into their kitchen in Berkeley—and he must have noticed her face turning ashen, because he set down his crossword puzzle and asked if she was feeling all right.

"The Classics Club was having a bake sale," she said. She had never told him about Christos, and she couldn't see the point of getting into it now. "I had too many cookies."

"Since when do you eat cookies?"

"I don't know." She stood. "Since today. Since I decided I wanted something sweet."

Dean looked at her for a moment, then rose to put an arm around her. He pulled her close and kissed her forehead.

She pressed her nose to his chest, breathing in a mix of laundry detergent and coffee fumes.

Pulling away, she said: "I'm going upstairs to lie down."

In her bathroom, she sat on the toilet and wept. She was there for at least an hour—maybe even two; she remembers watching the shadows shift across the awful beige carpet at her feet. She cried for Christos, but also for the thirty years that separated them, years during which they spoke occasionally, and then rarely and, finally, not at all. Once she was exhausted with being sad, she became angry. She hated Christos for dying and herself for being so affected by his death. She hated that she could be so devastated by someone who, in the terrible scheme of things, had occupied only a fragment of her life. Mostly, she hated that, in the years since she and Dean had bought the house, she had been too lazy to change the fucking carpet here, in the bathroom where she sat. She hated how the coarse tufts of nylon and polyester seemed to blink back at her, how they reminded her of how slowly and suddenly time passes.

Rubbing the bridge of her nose, she looks up. The French tourists are still fighting, and she tries her best to pick out a few words. It's useless, though. She hasn't spoken French since high school, and even then she hated the

language, all those swallowed *r*'s and tight, puckered *u*'s. Instead, she wonders if she should go downstairs. See if Will wants another beer and check
on Dean's nausea. She decides against it; she stays where she is, holding
the Mythos bottle with both hands, sinking into her annoyance of the
French.

It had been an impulsive decision to come. Gianna asked, and Sue Ellen
said yes; she booked her ticket before she checked her calendar. In the
weeks that followed, though, she worried that she'd made a mistake. Here
she was, fleeing from her family at the moment it needed her the most.
But then Dean had come to her. Had brought her a turkey sandwich and
begged her to tag along. At first she was skeptical—he really did hate the
heat—but after a few minutes of listening to him, she was convinced it
made sense. More than that: it was, perhaps, a perfect idea. Berkeley held
too many memories. Every building, every street bore some association
with the past year. Here's where she was drinking coffee when Greta
Weinstein called to say that she had seen Dean with another woman;
here's where she bought boxes to help him move back in. Greece would
allow them to escape, to find solid footing away from the scene of the
crime. Besides, what's that thing that Connie had told her? That in light
of her husband's affair she had two options: cut and run, or work toward
forgiveness. And for the latter to happen—for transgressions to be par-
doned and trust to be regained—there had to be equal effort and a will-
ingness to try.

There's also the matter of Will: chances are, she'll lose him come
fall. While she's always taken pride in being a mother *and something else*—
pride in being a woman who isn't rattled by clichés like a child no longer
needing her or the loneliness of an empty nest—Will's graduation has
shaken her more than she had ever anticipated. Since he had started at
Berkeley (she had been selfishly thrilled when his first choice, Northwest-
ern, turned him down), she had always had a sense of his schedule, of
where he was. She never imposed this on him, but she used it to free her
mind whenever teaching caused her to feel claustrophobic: *I'm at Classics,*

she would tell herself, imagining a campus map, *Will's at History, and Dean's at English*. Triangulating in this way calmed her; it reminded her of an existence beyond the walls of her department, the covers of her books. It reminded her of the life she lived in real time.

Half a mile in front of her, Aegina port begins to peek through the smog. Slowly, Sue Ellen starts to make out the Orthodox cross that sits atop the Ekklisia Isodia Theotokou, casting shadows along its red roof. Just to the church's north, small crowds gather in the waterfront cafés that line Leoforos Dimokratias. Watching as the scene gains focus, she wonders how much has changed since she was last here; she wonders if Elia still makes the best pistachio pesto, or if you can still get a shot of ouzo for a hundred drachma at O Kostas. She wonders if the best beaches—Marathonas and Kolona and Vagia—are still empty, still the domain of rock partridges and sea anemones, or if they've been discovered by the same northern Europeans who have conquered the rest of the Aegean.

Suddenly, the ferry groans to a stop, and deckhands scatter to tie the massive hull to one of the port's piers. There's a thud as the gangplank is lowered to the dock, and the French tourists jump, then start to laugh. Standing, Sue Ellen smooths out the wrinkles that line her khakis.

She says, to anyone who will listen, "We're here."

Eleni

July 7
Aegina

She hears the taxi before she sees it: wheels crunching on gravel, an engine coughing once and then shutting down. Standing behind the Alectrona's front desk, she tucks her hair behind her ears and applies a thin coat of lip gloss. Two hours ago, she went to town and bought some flowers—a bunch of white hyacinths and a single Roman orchid. She's arranged them in one of her grandmother's ceramic vases, which she's set just to the left of her laptop. Why not add a little pizzazz to the place, she thought, a little life—this was, after all, the last time she would be checking someone in. Inspecting the flowers now, though, she worries they look weird and sparse; there are too few stems to fill the vase she selected. Instead of admiring the hyacinths' blooms, all she can focus on is the empty space between them, the way the orchid droops beneath its weight. She should have bought more flowers, she thinks. Or she shouldn't have bought any flowers at all.

Outside, a car door opens and closes. Faint voices compete and form layers—prices being calculated and haggled over.

When she was alive, Eleni's mother was the one who checked people in to the Alectrona. She liked to tell her that welcoming guests—being hospitable—was an art. Getting people to feel comfortable in a place they had never been, anticipating their needs before they knew they had them: this all required a certain awareness, a domestic talent. As she grew older, Eleni thought of these lessons with a mix of sadness and regret. Before she got married, Agatha had wanted to be a journalist; a year before she died, she was lauding the aesthetics of throw pillows.

Now, as Eleni hears the taxi pull away, she runs through the list of dos and don'ts her mother left her: Memorize your guests' names before they arrive—you don't want to make them feel like another cog in the wheel, a way to pay the mortgage. When you show them around the inn, make sure to point out that the building was constructed over 150 years ago and once was the summer home of a wealthy Athenian family. If they ask who, make something up—a long, unpronounceable name, something with too many vowels to remember. Reframe flaws as personality and charm: those aren't cracks in the wall, that's just the original crown molding. In the morning, if you've run out of eggs and can't escape to the market, put out a bowl of muesli and some yogurt—call it a Greek breakfast.

The door creaks open, and she hears three sets of feet echo off the foyer's tile floor. Eleni looks up and smiles.

"*Yassas*," she says. And then, switching to English: "You must be the Wrights."

The next five minutes are a deliberate blur—all she can think of is how many times she's done this, and how she'll never have to do it again. She talks, asking them questions they don't have time to answer, filling the space with the steady hum of her voice. Once she's confirmed the details she already knows (*Where are you traveling from?* California. *It looks like we will have the pleasure of your company for four weeks?* That's correct), she produces a paper map of Aegina and unfolds it on the desk in front of her.

"Perhaps you would like to know a little bit about the island?" she says, uncapping a pen.

Sue Ellen thanks her and glances at her husband, then her son.

"That's very sweet of you," she says. "But they—we—have been up for almost thirty-six hours. Maybe we could—"

"You're exhausted, of course." Eleni nods.

She thinks of another one of her mother's maxims: *Ask them questions about their travel, even if it's small talk—there's nothing people love more than complaining about airlines.*

She says, "I hope your flight was pleasant?"

The husband looks haggard, tired. His clothes are wrinkled and his eyes are bloodshot. Sue Ellen, on the other hand, looks more or less put together. Her hair, a mix of blond and gray, is pulled cleanly away from her face, and her cheeks are fleshy, pink. She's wearing a blue T-shirt and khaki pants made from the sort of synthetic fabric that Eleni associates with hikers and rock climbers—no-fuss, fast-drying stuff that a person can wash by hand.

The husband arches an eyebrow. "It was awful," he says. "Torturous and interminable. Planes these days are criminal. We may as well have come over on the *Amistad*."

"Jesus, Dad," the son says, and looks to her apologetically.

Eleni doesn't catch the reference, but she smiles nonetheless.

"I am sorry to hear that," she says. "I will check you in and then show you to your rooms so you can get some rest. All I need, I believe, are your passports."

"Is that a pool?"

The son asks this. He's wandered a few feet down the hall that leads from reception to the hotel's dining room, which overlooks the rear patio. Looking at him, Eleni tries to get a sense of his age; she can't be much older than he is, surely, but still he looks so much softer, so entirely inexperienced. She remembers when she was a little girl, how she used to accompany her mother to the grocery store. Regardless of the hour, they'd run into someone—another woman, typically—with whom Agatha had grown up; this was a small island, and chance encounters were a sort of normalized plague. As her mother spoke, making small talk next to the tomatoes, Eleni would hang back and marvel at how much younger she looked than her peers; how while their hair had grown ashy and coarse, her mother's was still jet-black and smooth. What a wonder, she thought, that time could be both so sparing and so cruel.

"It is."

"Is it heated?"

"Of course," Eleni says. "By the sun."

Will looks at her for a moment, then smiles.

"Good one," he says.

They rummage through their bags for their passports, which Sue Ellen collects and hands to Eleni.

"I'll be right back." She begins to leave, ducking through the door that connects the foyer to the Alectrona's office, but she pauses for a moment. She takes a single breath and turns back around.

"Actually, there is just one more thing. We have . . . we have had a bit of a plumbing problem."

"What kind of a problem?" the father asks. He slings his bag over his shoulder, and the strap pulls at the collar of his shirt.

"We currently have one working shower. It's here"—she points—"in the downstairs bathroom."

"One shower."

"We're hoping to have the rest of the showers repaired within the week."

"Literally just *one shower.*"

Sue Ellen reaches down and takes hold of her husband's wrist.

"That hardly sounds like a problem."

Eleni smiles. "Please," she says, pointing to a small table next to the front door, where she's assembled a small spread of food. Fresh bread, cheese, two bowls of fruit. "Make yourself at home."

————

In her office, Eleni holds their passports in her right hand, fingering the documents' stiff corners as if she's cradling a deck of cards. Her phone vibrates against her hip and, setting the passports down, she reaches into the pocket of her jeans and sees that she has a new message from her friend Sophie, in Athens. A GIF of a pug falling off a couch, paired with a note: *Me after last night's fifth tequila shot.* Eleni watches the dog tumble to the ground a few times before typing: *Back among the living?*

Sophie replies in an instant: *Barely.*

Tequila always wins

Hard lesson to learn. When you back?

Soon—4 weeks

More like soon-ish

Whatever. Eleni chews on a strand of her hair. It tastes bitter, then floral: the faint traces of her shampoo. She types: *Last guests just got here.*

How many?

3. Mom, dad, son.

How olds the son?

Our age but gay I think

Why?

Because he's hot and polite

Fair. Find out for sure though

How?

Show him your tits and see if he blinks

Goodbye Sophie

Eleni sets her phone down and returns to the passports, opening them one by one, reading the names inside: *Dean, William, Sue Ellen.* The photos are of them, but also not: they show them as who they were, as opposed to as who they are. Fewer gray hairs. Fuller faces. A perm. She thinks of her own passport—she hasn't looked at it in years. Would she recognize herself, she wonders? Or would she look like an artifact—someone she used to be? The last time she left the country was four years ago, before Christos died. She had gone to London, as a member of her university's delegation to an undergraduate economic conference that was being hosted at King's College. There had been four of them—two men and two women—and the university had paid for them to stay in a hotel just across the river, on the other side of the Waterloo Bridge. She tries to remember what the United Kingdom's immigration stamp looks like, but she can't. Oh, well, she thinks. In less than a month she can go back and get another one. She can go on a world tour, if she feels like it, bopping around to different countries, collecting as many stamps as she wants.

She opens her laptop and begins recording the information she's required to collect. Names, birthdates, places of issuance. On the other side of the door, in the foyer, she hears the Wrights' voices echo against the tile. The sound startles her at first; the last guest to stay at the Alectrona left a month ago, and in the time since she's grown accustomed to silence, mixed with the churn of her own thoughts. Lifting her fingers from the keyboard, she stops typing and listens:

"Why do they always do that at European hotels?"

"Do what, sweetie?"

"Take your passports."

"It's an EU thing."

"You're making that up, Dad."

"How would you know if I was?"

"Did she mention what the Wi-Fi password is?"

"I swear to God, Will, you're going to die with that electric dildo clutched in your hand."

"Dean, please."

"Sue Ellen, did you hear what she said?"

"About what?"

"About the *showers*."

"Mom, what are these?"

"They're sour cherries."

"They're not bad."

"Sue Ellen."

"Yes, Dean, I heard what she said about the showers."

"Did you *know* that was the case?"

"Yes, and I thought I'd surprise you with it. No, of course I didn't know that was the case. Will, honey, go easy on those cherries."

"Well, are you even the least bit concerned?"

"About the showers? No. I am not concerned about the showers."

"I mean, that is *sort* of inconvenient, don't you think?"

"Mom, how warm do you think the pool gets?"

"It's July. It's had time to heat. I bet it's pretty warm. We can go swimming later on if—"

"Do you think she'll be sharing the shower with us?"

"She lives here."

"So—"

"So, yes, I'm assuming she'll be sharing the shower with us."

"What's Alectrona mean, anyway?"

"She was a daughter of the sun god, Helios. She died a virgin."

"Not a very promising name for a hotel, am I right?"

"Will."

"What, Dad?"

"Help me out here."

"With what?"

"The shower."

"I mean, is it really that big of a deal? Flint, Michigan, hasn't had clean water for, like, a thousand days or something."

"Yes, but that's *drinking* water. They still have water they can *shower* with. In *multiple showers,* no less."

"With all due respect, Dad, your priorities there strike me as a little bit off."

"Unbelievable."

"I'm serious about these cherries. Try them."

They stop, silent, when Eleni pushes the door open and steps back into the foyer. Will pops another cherry between his lips, and Dean looks at her with red cheeks, his eyes cast downward as if he's just been caught. She smiles and wonders if the Wrights know she could hear them. Despite all the weird things she's experienced during her stint as an innkeeper, this always surprises her the most: how quickly guests begin to ignore her. How willingly they go about their private lives forgetting that she's there, watching them.

She hands the Wrights back their passports.

For the last time, she says: "Welcome to the Alectrona."

Will

He's naked when the phone rings. He's just come up from the shower on the inn's first floor and for the past two minutes he's been standing in front of the mirror in his own room, trying to make sense of his curls.

"Hello?"

"Hi, Will?"

"Ginny. Yes. Hello." He sighs, relieved. "I've been trying to get ahold of you."

"Yeah, I can tell. I've got, like, twenty-seven missed calls."

He sits on the bed and feels the stiff quilt scratch at his bare thighs.

"In all fairness," he says, "those twenty-seven calls have come over the past five days."

He lies back and stares up. A deep crack begins in the left corner of the room's white ceiling and stretches to the middle of the square space, where it inexplicably vanishes.

Ginny says, "Well, I've been gone."

"Gone?"

"Yes. I've been gone. As in, not here."

"I know what *gone* means. Was your phone not allowed to *go* with you?"

She says, plainly, "I was at a silent retreat in Ojai."

He shuts his eyes. He had forgotten Ginny's ability to respond to rhetorical questions with legitimate—and wholly infuriating—answers.

"A silent retreat in Ojai," he repeats back to her.

"Yes. A *silent* retreat in Ojai. Phones weren't allowed." For good measure, she adds: "On the drive back I stopped in San Luis Obispo for a Paul McGregor reading. Goddamn *marvelous*."

A drop of water works its way from the underside of his groin to the back of his left knee. He wonders if he should put on some clothes.

His eyes still closed, he says, "My father says Paul McGregor's a hack."

"Well, some people say your father's a hack," Ginny bites back. "So."

"Do you think my father's a hack, Ginny?" Will says, laying his free hand on his stomach. "Would you like me to tell my father that you think he's a hack?"

There's a pause during which Will listens to Ginny's breathing meld with the cicadas buzzing in the mastic tree outside.

She says, "I'd appreciate it if you didn't."

"I won't," he answers, feeling—to his surprise—a little sad for her. "I was joking."

Sitting up, Will glances out the window. Dead pine needles blanket the Alectrona's small garden. Beyond it, Dean slumps, asleep, in a plastic blue patio chair next to the inn's bean-shaped pool. An old paperback sits open on his lap, and at his left is a wineglass filled with gin and tonic. Will looks at the clock hanging above the room's pine dresser: it's eleven eighteen in the morning.

Ginny asks, "Where are you, anyway?"

"What do you mean?"

"When I called you, your phone had one of those weird foreign rings. Why do they do that, I wonder? Like, why can't every country have the same ring?"

"I don't know. People like to be different." He runs a hand through his wet hair. "I'm in Greece with my parents."

"That sounds nice. Where in Greece?"

"Why does it matter?"

"Because I'm *curious*, Will. I'm a *curious* person."

He weighs the consequences of just hanging up.

He says, "Some island."

"You don't know the name of the island?"

"Aegina," he says, suddenly standing. "It's called Aegina, okay?" Reaching forward, he shuts the window's curtains. A midday twilight blankets the room. He cuts to the chase: "Look, Ginny, I need you to do me a favor."

She says, "Aegina's in the Saronic Gulf, right?"

"Maybe? I think so? But goddamn it, Ginny, *listen to me*."

She sighs. Will's certain that he can hear the sound of her eyes rolling. "A favor. *Oui. Dis-moi*."

"I need you not to publish my story."

"Um . . ."

He begins to pace, making half circles around the bed. "I just—frankly, I don't think it's ready yet, you know? Like, it still needs a lot of editing and I'm just . . . I'm not really comfortable with it being out there for people to read."

"Okay . . . I mean, you know that every thesis automatically gets submitted to the journal, right? Like, Claudia obviously told you that when you turned it in."

"No, I know, and she did. I'm just asking you to publish someone else's, instead of mine."

"That's weird."

"No, it's not. Or, fine, maybe it is, I don't care. Just don't publish it."

"Will."

"*Ginny*."

"You're selling yourself short, okay? For the past four years your stories have been . . ."

"My stories have been what, Ginny?"

"Not *unoriginal,* per se, but just not entirely inventive." Will hears a pop: a bubble bursting in Ginny's chewing gum. "No offense."

"Uh-huh."

"But then you turn in this! This masterpiece! And you say you won't let me publish it? You'll prove everyone wrong! They'll call you the second coming of Mailer, or Updike, or—"

"My father."

"That's your Freudian bullshit to work out—not mine. Me, I just need content."

"Ginny, I'm literally begging you."

"Oh, c'mon, Wright. Have a little chutzpah."

Will pulls at his curls until he feels them tug against his scalp. For a moment, he worries that he's lost her, that the line's gone dead.

"Ginny?"

"Yeah," she says, "yeah, I'm here. Sorry. Was just reading an email." His shoulders slump, and she continues, "Look, Will, we need the story, all right? We've already worked it into the layout. Besides, without it all we've got are a couple of shitty sonnets written by some lesbian from Roger's poetry workshop and a story about a pair of crickets. Literally—*a pair of crickets.* I get that you're nervous. Honestly, I do. I promise, though, it'll be great. Totally and awesomely great. In the meantime, I've got to jet. I was supposed to be at Fertile Grounds for this party, like, ten minutes ago. It's, like, one o'clock in the morning here. Anyway, *amuse-toi bien* in Greece."

"Ginny, no, wait. You don't understand. You—" Will starts, but the line goes dead.

"*Shit,*" he says, and tosses his phone on the bed. He stares at its darkened screen and considers calling her back. He could beg her, plead with her; he could feed her some contrived line about his *process* and try to appeal to her pseudoartistic sensibilities. But then, what would happen if she began to suspect something? What would happen if, in his own attempt to save himself, he actually revealed that he's become the thing he fears becoming most: a fraud? He imagines Ginny pointing at him and laughing, dropping her obnoxious little French bons mots as she explains what makes a real artist legitimate and Will not. No, he thinks. No, he can't call her back, at least not today.

Two nights ago, he almost told his mother. They were sitting on the Alectrona's back patio, drinking scotch and watching the sun dip behind the Peloponnese. This had become something of a tradition—at least, a tradition in the week that they've been in Greece. After dinner, the three of them gather here to have a drink and dissect the day and play dominos with the inn's old, chipped set. On this night, though, it was just Will and Sue Ellen. Twenty minutes earlier, after having lost his third consecutive game, Dean retreated to his room, taking the dominos with him.

"They're faulty," he had said to them, standing. "There are too many threes and not enough sixes."

Crickets had replaced the cicadas, and Will listened to them while he counted the stars. Earlier that afternoon, Sue Ellen had taken them to the monastery of Agios Nektarios in Kontos, a mile or two from the inn. She had been doing this since they arrived—filling their afternoons with excursions, acquainting them with the island's culture, its history. Two days from now, she had scheduled a more ambitious trip, this one to Delphi, on the mainland, to see the ruins of the oracle. He'll go along dutifully, just like he went along dutifully to the monastery. He listened as she told him that Agios Nektarios was a relatively recent saint—he died in 1920—and that the monastery was still run by a cadre of nuns. Hearing how excited she was, the way her voice lifted and increased its cadence, he encouraged her; he asked questions about what the nuns do all day (*I don't know—sweep, I guess?*), and if he could buy something from the gift shop (*I know we aren't candle people, but get a few anyway—they really are lovely*). She hadn't told him much about the time she'd spent on the island when she was his age, but watching the way the place transported his mother fascinated Will. For the past year he had watched her wrestle. Now, here she was, happy.

"Mom," he said now. Gnats were gathering over the Alectrona's pool. "I need to tell you something."

"Hit me," she said.

Will watched as she closed her eyes and leaned her head back against the wicker chair. She sighed and rested the glass of scotch on her stomach. He couldn't remember the last time he had seen her so relaxed.

"Nothing," he said. "This place is just really great."

Her eyes still shut, she reached out her right hand and wiggled two of her fingers, which Will took hold of and squeezed.

Now, glancing out the window again, he sees that his father has woken up, at least nominally, and is staring with a sort of half-drunk vacantness at his book. He normally isn't a heavy drinker, though, from the looks of it, he has committed himself to being a vacation alcoholic. Reaching down, he grasps blindly for his gin and tonic, his fingers shaking as they wiggle through the open air, searching for the glass. Finally, after a few frantic moments, he finds it and his chest heaves with relief. He's wearing a white linen shirt that he hasn't bothered to iron, and even though he's positioned himself in the shade, it's evident that he's started to sweat: damp spots pool around his armpits, the center of his chest, the dip of his belly button. Will continues to stare, right up until the moment when he senses his father can tell he's being watched. Just as Dean cranes his neck to look up, though, Will steps away from the window. He slips on a T-shirt, a pair of shorts, and his espadrilles. Then he grabs his backpack and his laptop, and he leaves.

In Aegina, he finds a place to lock up the old bike he's borrowed from the Alectrona and walks toward the harbor, where the cafés and restaurants are just beginning to seat tourists for lunch. He stops in front of a few of them and inspects the menus they've got on display, laminated photo cards displaying identical versions of grilled *xtapodi* and shrimp *saganaki,* the dishes' names written beneath them in seven different languages. He's not hungry—he realizes this while staring at a picture of souvlaki atop a plasticky mound of french fries—he forgot to eat breakfast this morning, but still, somehow, he's not hungry. Instead, he decides what he really wants is a beer, something to wash away the taste of Ginny, while he scours the internet for jobs. He finds a place with the fewest customers—a small bistro called Taverna Karalis—takes a seat outside, connects to its Wi-Fi, and waits for someone to realize he's there.

And finally, after ten minutes, someone does. He's just responded to another job posting—this one to write grant proposals for Friends of the Sea Otter—when he hears someone say, "Greek or English menu?"

Will looks up to see a waiter standing next to his table, holding two menus. The man's about his age—maybe a few years older—with dark hair that sweeps across his forehead.

"I'm American," Will says.

"Okay," the man says. "So, English."

"Actually, I'm not planning on eating anything." He pushes his sunglasses farther up his nose. "Just a beer, please. A Mythos."

"One Mythos." The waiter nods and tucks the menus under his arm. "You got it."

After he's gone, Will shuts down his computer and reaches for his phone. There, he finds a picture that Rajiv has posted to Instagram—a maddeningly attractive shot of him and Logan in Bernal Heights. Since the picture has been up, it's garnered forty-eight likes. There are also, Will notes, two comments, one from Rajiv's sister, Seema ("how cute are you 2?!"), and one from someone called @RichForYou ("lookin good studs"), whose profile picture features a backward baseball cap, a toothy grin, and a set of sexless abs. Will clicks the name and decides he doesn't know the guy. That doesn't stop him, though, from scrolling through his feed, a procession of sculpted pecs and dead eyes (here is @RichForYou surfing in a Speedo; here he is half naked in the snow) that at once infuriates and tantalizes Will: he'd happily hate-fuck him, he thinks, if he lived in a world where people like @RichForYou gave him the time of day. He knows he should stop here—after spending two minutes interrogating a picture of a baby koala perched on @RichForYou's left biceps ("makin new friend down unda"), Will knows he should put his phone down and focus on numbing himself with beer. And yet, he can't. Once he's done with @RichForYou, he returns to Rajiv's profile to see what other marsupial-bearing beefcakes he's opted to befriend.

There are sixty-four of them. He's not proud that he can spot this, but the fact remains: there are sixty-four of them. Most of them don't have handles as egregious as @RichForYou; rather, they err on the side of a subtler narcissism, adding tags like *official* and *thereal* to their given names, as if their identities were frequent targets of imposters. None of them is *actually* famous, nor have they, as far as Will can tell, *actually* accomplished anything. Still, that doesn't stop them or their followers from treating their posts with the sort of reverence most people reserve for a Vermeer portrait or the Sistine Chapel. Here, for example, is @TheCalebNation (this is an actual name—a real, actual name) standing shirtless against a wall. Behind him, painted onto the brick, are two Technicolor angel wings—which, given @TheCalebNation's position (hands behind back; left knee cocked just so), appear to be springing from his spine. Beneath the photo's 4,918 likes is a collection of a hundred fawning comments. @WesNWeho, for one, would like @TheCalebNation to *be his guardian angel.* Meanwhile, @Trevtastic wonders *who needs wings when you got those lats?* Reading them, Will starts to feel nauseated. Is this what Rajiv actually wanted all along? He tells himself no. He reminds himself of when they were first together—how, on cold mornings, Rajiv would hug Will from behind and slip his hands into the pockets of his hoodie. He decides that Rajiv doesn't know what he's doing. He's not thinking deeply— he just likes pretty things.

Clicking the camera option, Will holds his phone out in front of him and takes a quick selfie. It's awful: the lighting's all wrong, which has caused the upper half of his face—the good half, he'd like to think—to be darkened by shadows. He's also set himself at a bad angle; instead of the Aegean serving as the backdrop, he's managed to snap what appears to be the bar's exterior cleaning closet, a cubby stuffed with bleach, a bucket, and a red mop. He switches seats; he tries again, and then again. Each time there's something wrong. First, it's the lighting: the Aegean is there, but it's washed out and bland—it could be a lake in New Jersey. His appearance isn't helping things: in the past four pictures he's taken, he's had the charred appearance of a burn victim. There's also the matter of his chin, which has suddenly seemed to double.

Finally, after a few more attempts, he gets a good one—or, if not good, then passable. A shot where his nose isn't bright red, or where every freckle on his left cheek doesn't look like it's been excavated by a dentist's drill. Quickly, he posts it to Instagram, along with the caption *#Greece is the word*. Then he sits back. Across the street in front of him, a kid in an oversize tank top dribbles a soccer ball, occasionally flicking it up so he can juggle it off his knees. Watching him, Will wonders how long it's been. Thirty seconds, maybe? A minute? He isn't sure, though he wants to check. At first, this causes him to laugh—the absurdity of it all. He doesn't need to affirm his existence by incurring the favor of strangers; he doesn't need to stare at his reflection in some digitized puddle. But then, glancing at his phone, he feels something else—a nagging, or a tug. A nervous energy that starts at his elbows and ends at the tips of his fingernails. The need to look, to scroll, to assure himself that his efforts have been—at the very least—seen. And so, he picks up his phone. He opens Instagram and runs his thumb along the screen. Then, when he sees that there's nothing—no red hearts, no cartoonish speech bubbles—he immediately checks again.

"You want me to take one?"

It's the waiter, balancing a bottle of Mythos on a plastic tray.

"Uh, no, thanks," Will says, setting his phone down. He feels his face burn.

"You sure? You've been at it for a while."

"You mean, it's taken you awhile to bring me my beer."

The waiter lifts an eyebrow. He sets the beer down and says, "Touché."

"I'm sorry, that was rude." Will looks at the bottle, the beads of condensation working their way down its sides. "Your English is very good, by the way."

"I grew up in Astoria."

"Oregon?"

"Ha, no." He smiles. "Queens."

"Right."

The waiter nods, like he's expecting Will to say something else. When he doesn't, he places both hands on the small of his back and stretches it. His spine arches, and his shirt pulls against his chest.

He says, "Well, have fun with your photo shoot," and leaves.

Watching the waiter go, Will deletes the selfie. He takes down two swallows of beer, scrubs the moment clean, and returns to Rajiv's feed. The picture he had been looking at now has 120 likes, along with six additional comments, two of which are from people Will actually recognizes. This unsettles him. While the commenters aren't friends, they are sort of substantial acquaintances—or, at the very least, substantial enough that Will would have expected them to take his side, in the event they knew sides actually existed. So he scrolls down further, swiping past an image of Logan wearing a #PuraVida shirt and then one of him wearing no shirt at all. Finally, he stops on a shot of Rajiv wearing jeans, a button-down shirt, and a red tie. His left arm is draped over the shoulder of a man nearly twice his age, and in the background is a sign bearing Fama's logo—a yellow *F*, twisted to create the filaments of an Edison lightbulb.

Stoked to be joining the Fama Fam, the caption reads. *And big ups to this dapper gent for bringing me onboard. #FamaFam #Namer #Whatsmyname?*

Will doesn't have to stare at the image for long to recognize the man. He—François Tremblay—is the director of the firm's verbal department and Rajiv's new boss. He's also the person who conducted Will's last interview, the one he suspects stopped him from getting the job. Zooming in on François's crow's-feet, the streaks of gray in his hair, Will remembers the look François gave him when his assistant led Will into his office: a startled, unshielded jolt, like he had just seen the ghost of someone he'd forgotten once existed. For his part, Will pretended he didn't recognize him and did his best to stay calm. He thanked the assistant, shook François's hand, and sat in the open chair across from him—a red egg with a deep back and high arms in which he could never quite get comfortable.

"So," François said, looking at the résumé his assistant had handed him before leaving. "Will Wright."

"Yes, that's right. Ha. Get it? Wright, right." Will laughed and waited for François to join in. He didn't, though. He just kept staring at the résumé.

Here's what Will remembered, and François—at least at first—did not: they'd met seven years ago, when Will was sixteen.

It happened in Dolores Park, where Will had hung out nearly every nice weekend of that summer. The first time he went, he was a little drunk; his parents had invited some of his mother's colleagues over for brunch, and as Will helped clean up, he polished off the half-finished mimosas scattered around the living room. Then he packed a rucksack and announced that he was going hiking in Claremont Canyon. He wasn't out to his parents at this point—that would happen a year and a half later, over dim sum at Hong Kong Lounge 2 in Chinatown *(Will: Mom, Dad, I'm gay. Dean: Good for you, kiddo. Who wants some Fish Nugget Porridge?).* Still, he feared that if he told them the truth about his destination, they would somehow divine his intentions and start peppering him with questions. So—Claremont Canyon. A charade of compasses, maps, and hiking boots. A getup that he traded for flip-flops and a pair of knockoff Ray-Bans as he rode the train beneath the bay.

Once he emerged from the BART station, he went straight to the park. There, after surveying the crowded grass pitches, he spread a towel out next to the largest and most attractive group of men he could find and took off his shirt. He didn't know if he was worth being admired, but he didn't want to rush the moment, just in case he was.

François was the first person he met. After staring at each other for nearly an hour, he sauntered over. Will was lying on his stomach, flipping through his AP European History textbook, when he heard a deep, accented voice above him say *hey*.

Will looked up, shielding his eyes against the sun.

"Hey," he said.

"You mind if I sit down?"

"Uh." His palms had started to sweat. "Sure."

François lowered to Will's towel, propping himself up on a tanned arm. His dark hair was buzzed short, and he smelled like sweat and sandalwood.

"What's your name?" he said.

"Will."

"I'm François." He extended a hand, and Will took it. "Nice to meet you."

Will asked, "Are you French?" because he didn't know what else to say.

"Canadian," François said. "Quebecois."

"Like, from Montreal?"

"No," he laughed. "Quebec City."

Will looked down and picked at blades of grass. He felt suddenly stupid, like he should have known that François was from Quebec City, and that it had been ignorant to assume that any Canadian with a French accent was automatically from Montreal. He wanted to start over.

He said, only, "Oh."

François nodded, smiled, then laughed again. "How old are you?" he asked.

"Nineteen," Will lied. "How old are you?"

"Thirty-two." He glanced down at the textbook, which still lay open on the towel. "You're a student?"

Will shut the book and slipped it beneath his shirt, hiding its cover. "Yeah," he said. "I'm a student."

"Where do you study? USF?"

"No, no." Will shook his head. He thought for a moment, trying to think up something that would make his parents proud. "I study cultural anthropology. At Brown." He added, "I'm just home for a long weekend."

"Cool." François looked uninterested, and Will felt a pang of disappointment—he'd wanted him to be more impressed.

A cool breeze drifted up from the south, and Will felt goose bumps prickle his bare skin. To his left, a wiry gray dog chased a Frisbee down a small pitch.

"You want something to drink?" François asked after a brief silence. "I've got some stuff to make margaritas in my car."

They drove south, toward Bernal Heights Park, where François said he knew of a spot with an empty parking lot and a great view. For his part, Will focused on being unfailingly polite. He offered to make the first batch of margaritas, pouring too much tequila and not enough mixture into a giant orange thermos that François had stashed away in his backpack. Once they had arrived at the parking lot—which Will now remembers as being nothing more than a small shoulder off an abandoned access road— he waxed poetic about the vista, which was partially obscured by power lines and the ragged tops of trees. And during the unbearable silence that lingered when François killed the engine, Will found himself praising the car itself, noting everything from its cracked leather seats to the yellow Vanillaroma air freshener that dangled from the rearview mirror.

"I've always wanted a Jeep, particularly an old one," Will said, licking tequila from his lips. "But, you know, being at school in Providence it doesn't really make sense."

François nodded and slipped an arm around him, his hand dipping beneath the collar of Will's shirt.

He said: "Can I kiss you?"

"What?"

"I'd like to kiss you."

"Oh! Yes!" His voice sounded different, and he worried that he seemed too eager, like a waiter who'd just been asked for the wine menu. "Of course."

His tongue was thick. It filled Will's mouth with startling efficiency, pressing against his teeth as he coaxed his lips to open wider. He lingered here for a moment, pausing as he rearranged his body over the Jeep's center console into a position that allowed him to take more control of Will. Then, once he had found it—once he had one knee on the driver's seat and his own shirt was off—he began moving his mouth down Will's body, starting with the smooth pockets of his neck and ending, inevitably, at the zipper of his shorts.

Will finished quickly and immediately began to apologize. Then he offered—again a bit too excitedly—to return the favor, plunging his hand into François's pants.

"No, no," François said, wincing and then laughing. "It's okay."

Will's cheeks flushed.

He said, "You're sure?"

"I'm sure." François reached over and tousled his hair. He slipped the key into the Jeep's ignition, and the engine rumbled. "Where should I drop you off?"

Now, seven years later, Will thinks of how the memory seemed to creep up on François over the course of their interview; how it seemed first to stalk him, taunting him with a few spare details, before assaulting him with everything else at once. Neither of them acknowledged it. Rather, Will shifted and reshifted, working hard to sit up straight in a chair that would not allow it. François, meanwhile, read and reread his résumé. Occasionally he looked up and asked Will a question, but mostly he kept his gaze downward, his left palm resting atop a Slinky on his desk.

"So," he asked after a few minutes, "did you enjoy the case studies we asked you to do?"

"I loved them," Will answered. He leaned forward, and the egg rocked on its stand.

"Karen, who I believe you met with last week, seems to think you'd be particularly good on the Pringles account." He stretched a few coils off the Slinky, then let them descend. "She liked the name you came up with for their new chili flavor."

"Right. The Ridge-Cut Fire-Roasted Chipotle Potato Chip."

"Yes. That one."

"I thought 'ridge-cut' evoked the artisanal vibe that's so big right now, while 'fire-roasted' implied spicy without actually, you know, *announcing* it."

"Interesting."

"I'm fascinated by the narratives of foodstuffs," Will lied.

He smiled again, but not quickly enough; by the time his lips curled, François had already turned back to his résumé.

"And it says here you're graduating from Berkeley in a little over a month."

"Yes. In forty-eight days, actually. But who's counting, right?"

"Which makes you what, twenty-two?"

Here, François looked up, and in the slight narrowing of his eyes Will saw the workings of a certain arithmetic: the subtraction of years and ages, squared with memory and law. Watching it happen, he wanted to tell him to stop. He wanted to tell him that there had been other men, and other cars. That in the beginning, he'd kept his cruising to the confines of the park, but when that bored him—when the Castro clones started feeling monotonous and safe—he'd looked for other, more thrilling opportunities. The YMCA in Oakland. A Barnes & Noble bathroom frequented by straight husbands. Once, a town hall in San Mateo County. He wanted to tell him that he wasn't alone—without exception, his hookups were older, guys in their midthirties and early forties who looked at Will's youth just as François did, with equal parts suspicion and lust. To be with someone younger—someone who was more of a reflection of himself—struck him as impossible and dangerous. It would be admitting to something that was still a half-formed thought, like slicing open a co-coon while the caterpillar's still wiggling around inside. So, he kept it casual and transactional. The sort of behavior that was defined by its present, as opposed to its future. Still, it was thrilling. The first half of his adolescence he had spent in a numb fog; he had watched himself as if he were a stranger, half an inch removed as he fumbled with bra straps on friends' parents' couches. Now, he was suddenly aware of his own skin—how a man's hand felt as it reached beneath his shirt; how anticipation announced itself in goose bumps. Each time when he was finished, he'd take BART home, where, after a scalding hot shower, he'd sit at his computer and record his observations of what had just happened. He still had dreams of being a writer and was young enough to believe his life merited a story. As such, he took great pain in cobbling together these descriptions, recalling and committing to record the most minuscule of details: the pressure of a body on top of him, the bitter taste of cologne licked from a neck. Each file he tagged with the date and saved to a new folder he had created on his laptop—one that he called *Anatomy and Physiology*.

He told François none of this. As much as Will wanted to assure him that he was fine and undamaged—that what they had done had been as much his decision as it had been François's—he said nothing. He felt that to do otherwise would be rude or presumptuous; that it would force François to dig up bodies he had long since buried. Instead, he let him finish the interview, asking limp questions about an internship Will had last summer at a literary agency. When he was done, and when the only sound either of them could hear was the Slinky's coils rising and falling, Will did the only appropriate thing he could think of: he smiled and asked about next steps.

"I'm sorry?" François had set down his résumé and was now busying himself with an email.

"The next steps." Will said again. His voice felt small. He had the sense that he should be apologizing, though for what he wasn't entirely sure. "In terms of . . . the job. I just wanted to know what the next steps are."

"Oh." Francois turned back to his email. "I guess we'll be in touch."

"Another Mythos?"

Will squints up at the waiter. "I don't know. How many have I had?"

"Three, so far."

He thinks. He can't decide if he's hot, or drunk, or both.

"They're bigger than the beers where I'm from."

"You say that like it's a problem."

He says, "I probably shouldn't."

The waiter shrugs. "I guess that depends on what you've got to do today."

"Nothing," he says. "I have absolutely nothing to do today."

"And here I thought you had another photo shoot." The waiter smiles. "You should probably have a fourth. I'll bring you something to eat, too. You like olives?"

"Sure, olives, whatever." Will looks up at him again. He's handsome, in a way that Will suspects makes life easier for him—or, at the very least, gives him the confidence to offer olives to strangers.

The waiter lingers for a moment, and Will worries that he's been looking at him for a second too long and has been keeping him from his job. Glancing to each side of him, though, he sees that the rest of the outside tables are empty. The only other customer sits at the Taverna Karalis's small bar—a woman in a pink sun hat, picking meat from the bones of a grilled *barbounia*.

"From whence do you hail?"

"Huh?" Will asks.

"Where are you from?"

"Oh, sorry. San Francisco. Or, not really. More like Berkeley."

"I've never been."

Will watches as the woman gingerly pokes at the fish's head. When nothing happens, she sets the fork down, disappointed.

He says, "It's nice, mostly," and wonders how many more likes Rajiv's picture has won. A hundred, he bets. A hundred and fifty.

"How long will you be on Aegina?" the waiter asks.

"Like, three more weeks. My mother's doing some work here."

"You don't have a job back in Berkeley?"

"That," Will says, "is sort of a sore subject."

The waiter nods and bites his lower lip, as if to suppress a smile. Will wants him to leave—he wants him to bring him his fourth beer, then leave.

Instead, he asks, "And what are your plans for while you're here?"

"You're looking at them," Will says.

He turns away, looking toward the harbor. For a moment, neither of them says anything, and Will allows himself to get lost in the squawks of the gulls, the honks of motorists along the promenade.

"I'll go get you that beer—"

"That'd be great."

"—but also, I give sailing lessons, when I'm not working here." He sets a blue business card on the table. "If you don't have anything else to do, you should come by sometime."

Will picks up the card. The paper is flimsy, hardly thicker than an onion's skin. Across its top, large bold print reads THE SARONIC YACHTING SCHOOL, and then beneath that, in much smaller type, a name: DIONYSUS LOUKAS, INSTRUCTOR.

"Your name is Dionysus?" Will says.

"Dio for short. It's basically like being called John in the States."

"You're kidding."

He shrugs. "I don't know what to tell you."

There's a minor commotion from inside the restaurant, and they both turn to see that the woman in the pink sun hat has accidentally knocked her plate over; now, the *barbounia* lies twisted and broken on the floor, a heap of bones and skin and partially eaten flesh.

"I'm not much of a sailor," Will says.

"I figured." He smiles. "I wouldn't be inviting you to take lessons if you were."

Will scratches the back of his neck and thinks for a moment longer.

"I'm actually going to Delphi tomorrow," he says.

"For how long?"

"Oh, just the day, I think."

"Perfect—the school's closed on Saturdays, anyway."

Picking up the card, Will starts to hand it back. "Look," he says, "I appreciate the offer, but—"

"Just keep it." Dio reaches forward and collects the empty bottles sitting in front of Will. "In case you change your mind."

Sue Ellen

July 15
Aegina and Delphi

"Dean."

She shakes his shoulder once, then twice. Batting her hand away, he rolls over.

"Dean, it's time to wake up."

He grumbles something and moans.

His eyes still closed, he asks, "What time is it?"

"Five thirty," she says. "The ferry leaves in forty-five minutes. If we miss it, we'll miss the bus in Piraeus."

"Go wake up Will. I'll get up once he's up."

He buries his head beneath a pillow.

"He's up already." She snatches the pillow away and tosses it to the floor. "He's downstairs having coffee."

"We should get that boy a medal."

She flips on the room's lights, and he covers his eyes with the backs of his hands.

He says, "Christ, that's bright."

"You'll be okay."

A few minutes ago, she opened the curtains to the room's single window. Now, standing before it, she watches as the lower edges of the sky light with dawn. Higher up, the tops of trees disappear into the last traces of night, pockets of black and indigo and the faint silver of vanishing stars.

"Where are we going again?" Dean's sitting up now, wiping bits of sleep from the corners of his eyes.

"Delphi."

"How far away is it?"

"It's a two-and-a-half-hour drive from Athens." He tries to hide again, but she pulls the sheets off of him. "Knock it off," she says. "You can sleep on the bus."

"Remind me why we're traipsing all the way to Delphi?"

"Del-*phee*," she says. "Del-*phi* is the English corruption."

"I love it when you correct me before sunrise."

"Here, put these on." She throws him a pair of chinos and a gray polo shirt. "We're going because we're in the cradle of Western civilization for four weeks, and I'll be damned if we spend that entire time drinking gin and tonics by the pool."

"What if that's what they would have wanted?" He stands up, pulls on his pants. "What if Plato and Aristotle would have wanted us to drink gin and tonics by the pool?"

"They wouldn't have. You're thinking of the Cyrenaics." She kisses his cheek. "Be downstairs in ten minutes, or we're leaving without you."

He looks at her and arches his left eyebrow.

He says, "You promise?"

"Listen, it was your idea to come."

"I know," he says. "I was kidding."

———

They arrive at one o'clock in the afternoon. The trip takes two hours longer than Sue Ellen had promised, and they travel there by taxi, by ferry, by foot, by bus. She had tried to hire a private car in Athens—she explained this to them while they were trekking across the concrete docks at Piraeus, dodging puddles and benches and napping backpackers. There were two drivers whom she often used when she was in the city: one, a civil servant who had retired when he heard rumblings about more austerity measures; the other, a thirty-year-old Albanian named Behar. Neither was available—they had both escaped the city for the summer, with the temperatures it brought. So, Sue Ellen had booked her family three spots on a coach, a fifty-eight-seat behemoth that shuttled visitors to and from the oracle with promises of air-conditioning, snacks, and a guided, hour-long tour. Despite the pockets of rush-hour traffic that ensnared them, the drive itself had been tolerable, if not a little pleasant. While Will and Dean dozed, Sue Ellen leaned her head against the window and watched as Athens awoke, caked in its peculiar golden light.

She thought, intermittently, of Eleni. Of the way she greeted them when they arrived, like they were just another round of guests, a set of names to be remembered, then forgotten. How much, she wondered, did Eleni know? She hoped everything, but she suspected nothing, and this hurt her. Watching Eleni's eyes glaze over her, Sue Ellen felt a swell of rage toward Christos for not having at least spoken about her, for not integrating their story into some larger narrative. He had, essentially, reduced her to a memory and confined her to a single summer. This was, of course, unfair. She had done the same thing.

The bus departed the city on the E-75, heading north past Marousi and Kifissia and Agios Stefanos. After an hour, the Athenian sprawl became thinner; there was more space between suburbs, more stretches of highway framed by fields of dry brush, cypresses, and the distant promise of mountains. They pulled over only once, at a rest stop north of Thiva, before they headed west on 48, across the plains of Boeotia toward Mount

Parnassus. There, the driver smoked a cigarette, and Sue Ellen filed off with a few of the other passengers to get a cup of coffee. Will, bleary-eyed but awake, came to meet her, and she gave him a little cash to buy something to eat. Phyllo dough, wrapped in wax paper and stuffed with feta and spinach.

"It's still warm," he said, licking grease from his fingers.

She looked at it. A glob of cheese fell to the curb.

"That's because it's been sitting under a heat lamp," she said.

Once they arrived, they stuck with the bus's official tour for about half an hour. The guide, a woman named Dora, told them about the Castalia Spring, the Athenian Treasury, the polygonal wall. Then, as they approached the site's official museum, Sue Ellen managed to escape, blending into the stream of another group of tourists, urging Will and Dean and join her.

"We'll have more fun on our own," she whispered.

Dean clicked his tongue and adjusted his sunglasses.

"You're being smug," he said, grinning. "You think Dora's dumb."

Sue Ellen shepherded them up a few stone stairs.

She said, "I think no such thing."

Now, she stands with her son and husband in the orchestra of Delphi's theater, looking up at the crescents of stone seats that form the *theatron*. The Phaedriades, the two cliffs of Mount Parnassus, rise on either side of them. Their surfaces catch the early afternoon sun, reflecting it in bursts of white.

"They say they used to throw people off them," Sue Ellen says, "if they committed sacrilege against the sanctuary."

Will shields his eyes, squints.

He says, "That would . . . not be fun."

Standing behind her, Dean unzips her backpack and searches for the sunscreen. Once he finds it, he slathers some across the back of his neck.

"I bet Dora would have told us that, too," he says.

Sue Ellen reaches out her palm. Dean squirts a bit of sunscreen onto it, and she smears it across her face, feeling it sting the undersides of her eyes.

"Something tells me Dora's tour is a little more G-rated."

"Well, that would never do." He pokes her nose. "Everyone knows we're an R-rated sort of family."

Dean wanders away, exiting the old orchestra and making his way back toward the Temple of Apollo. Watching him go, she thinks of the last vacation they had all taken together. It was three years ago. Will had just finished his first year at Berkeley, and they decided to spend the month of August in Espelette, a town in France's Basque Country. Dean had planned everything. He leased a house and rented bikes, and, for one afternoon, enrolled the three of them in a semiprivate surfing lesson. Their instructor, she remembers, had been a Catalonian named Arnau. One at a time he would paddle out with them into the Bay of Biscay, shouting *Now!* and giving their foam boards a shove whenever a wave arrived. Will took to it easily—he had tried surfing a few times already, in Bolinas, and after half an hour of Arnau's instruction, he took off on his own, catching crumbling waves, finding steady footing. It took Sue Ellen a bit longer, but eventually she, too, got the hang of things. She managed to stand up on the board three separate times, the last for a minute-long ride that took her straight onto the pebbles of the beach. Dean, on the other hand, was not as lucky. No matter how much coaching Arnau gave him, he couldn't seem to lift himself to his feet. Time after time he tried and failed, getting rocked on each occasion by the foamy aftermath of a new wave. By the end of the session he had bruises, and his elbows were scraped and bloody from where they had collided with rocks. Still, he handled this humiliation with grace and humor. On the drive home to the house in Espelette, he even floated the idea of booking another session with Arnau, seeing how much fun they all had. From the backseat, Will gently cautioned against it. He suggested that instead they might go for a bike ride or a hike. An activity where there was less of a risk that one of them might drown.

But there had been bad bits to that trip, too. Will got so sick, for example, that they had considered driving him to the hospital, and in retrospect, they should have. One morning they had taken a bus across the Spanish border, to San Sebastián, where they had spent the day eating *pinxtos*. When they returned to Espelette, he was complaining about an upset stomach; by dinnertime, he was confined to the bathroom, vomiting. It was food poisoning—salmonella, they feared, from a bit of undercooked chicken that he had insisted on eating, even when she and Dean warned him against it. Throughout the night, they took turns checking on him, making him drink sips of water, and wiping spittle from the corners of his mouth. At around four o'clock in the morning, after finding him curled around the base of the toilet, Sue Ellen dug through her toiletry bag and gave him some antibiotics—a year-old Cipro prescription she'd gotten before a dig in Pylos.

She's amazed by how easily she's forgotten all that and has instead constructed her recollections of Espelette with halcyon snapshots: here they are surfing with Arnau; here they are laughing about how terribly they all speak French. Whenever she's supervised a field excavation, she has warned her students against this sort of retelling: when you're analyzing a shard of pottery, she tells them, the important thing is to look at it for what it is, not what you want it to be. When it comes to this trip, she wonders if she'll be able to ignore that advice and let the heavier realities—the betrayals and suspicions; the puzzle of rebuilding her family—dissipate. She hopes she will. She hopes that, over the coming years, her memories will rearrange themselves. That they will find a pattern that favors forgiveness instead of truth.

Will taps her shoulder and says, "So where did they get high and predict the future?"

He's rolled up the sleeves of his T-shirt. The skin on his shoulders has turned pink and dotted with freckles.

"Down there." She points to the ruins of the Temple of Apollo, where

Dean is standing, looking at his phone. "In the *adyton,* which was basically just a chamber beneath the main temple. And they didn't *get high.*"

"I thought you said they did." One of Will's shirtsleeves unrolls itself, and he reaches up to fix it, securing it again high on his shoulder. "I thought you said that whatever woman was the oracle basically just huffed until she was gone enough to ramble off a bunch of shit, and then a priest put that shit into a tidy verse, and *wham*—that was the future."

Dean slips his phone into his pocket. He crouches down and inspects something at his feet.

"It was a ritual, Will. They considered this place the center of the world. On the seventh day of each month, the Pythia was bathed in the Castalian spring, then led into the *adyton,* where she sat on a tripod chair and inhaled, possibly, either methane or ethylene fumes that seeped out of a fissure between two faults in the limestone directly beneath the temple. In small doses ethylene produces a disembodied, euphoric state, which can lead to incredible insight."

"So, basically, she got high."

Sue Ellen looks at her son. Sweat forms beads at his temples, and his curls hang loose and damp. High above them, a bird—an eagle, a hawk, a vulture—circles, its wings spread wide, motionless.

"Yes," she says. "Basically, she got high."

"How accurate was she?"

"*She* was actually a lot of people. When one Pythia died, another was selected to take her place. This happened for centuries."

Will looks down toward the temple, with its ancient stone foundations and its six remaining columns, their sides creased and cracked like knuckles.

"Thanks, professor."

Reaching over, Sue Ellen flicks his ear.

"Ow." He rubs the spot red. "That actually really hurt."

She says, "Yeah? Well, next time respect your mother."

Dean

He watches from a distance as Will laughs and pals around with Sue Ellen. He wonders what they're talking about, if they're conspiring against him. It's a fear that started when he was living in that horrid apartment in San Ramon and has never entirely stopped. Before, he was never aware of how delicate a balance existed between the three of them; with a single mistake, one of them could suddenly be on the outs. In exile, though, he often found himself concerned about what narratives were being created in his absence, the ways in which his family was evolving without him and because of him. Once Sue Ellen invited him back, this fear guided his parenting philosophy more often than he would like to admit; his decisions now are often prioritized by how much influence they might allow him to exert over his son. The goal is never to edge Sue Ellen out, more to make himself indispensable.

He told Will about the affair—this had been another requirement of Sue Ellen's, along with marriage counseling, and it terrified him. He sensed how his son had regarded him before, with an air of awe and reverence, and he worried that the news of Jasmine might change that. Instead of being worshipped, now he'd be despised, or, perhaps worse, pitied. His only hope, Dean felt, was that Will would look at his philandering as a sort of artistic inevitability: he loved Norman Mailer, and look how many times that son of a bitch cheated.

They met at a pub near campus on a Thursday afternoon. Will found them a spot to sit in the corner, next to an ATM, and Dean went to the bar to order them two beers. His hands shook as he carried the pints back to the table; foam kept slopping over the rims of the glasses and trickling down his fingers. For a few minutes, neither of them said anything. Or, if they did, it was filler about the Talking Heads album the pub was playing and a desire for the barman to turn the volume up.

Once he had finished half of his pint, Dean finally looked up.

He said, while trying to think of the perfect words to say, "So."

"You're having an affair."

"That is . . . very perceptive of you."

"Not really." Will folded his coaster in half. "Why else would you have moved out?"

"There are a lot of reasons marriages have problems."

"I guess I opted for the most obvious one."

"Can you forgive me?" Dean asked.

"Is it my job to?"

A woman approached the ATM, and Dean scooted his chair aside, making room for her.

"We're working it out. We will work it out." He drummed his fingers against the pint glass. "You know this doesn't have anything to do with you, right? I fucked up—this doesn't have anything to do with you."

"I'm an adult, Dad. I know people make mistakes."

Dean nodded.

"Can I offer you some, uh, advice, though? From son to father?"

"Of course."

"Don't do it again."

———

Now, he circles around the west side of the temple's foundations and looks out over the ruins, then beyond them. It's gorgeous, he thinks. Jagged gray cliffs dotted with cypresses and olive trees. A valley blanketed in a wild, primordial green. His phone buzzing in his pocket distracts him, and he reaches down to check it again: another email from Ginny Polonsky, bringing the new total to forty-one. Scanning the screen, he catches a few of the phrases the messages contain—*I need you; You're a dickless swamp walker; YOU CAN'T HIDE FOREVER. I'LL COME FOR YOU.* He closes his eyes and puts his phone away.

He had tried to stop. Two weeks before he proposed the idea of a family vacation to Sue Ellen, he had tried to end it with Ginny, an endeavor that resulted with both of them pressed up against the grubby bathroom wall of a diner in Walnut Creek. Again, though, that had not been his intention. In fact, he had invited Ginny to the diner in Walnut Creek (Diane's, he thinks it was called) to do precisely the opposite—to tell her that, despite the fun times they'd had, they would not be having fun any longer. Closing his eyes, he tries to remember how, exactly, he had explained himself. All he can think of, though, is the way her breasts squeezed together as she slathered thick pads of butter across her pancakes. The way she licked her fingers clean of syrup after taking her first, messy bites.

"Look, Ginny" is how he probably started.

"Yes, *Dean?*" (She always did this, Dean noted. She always stressed the pronunciation of his first name, ever since he'd told her to stop calling him Professor Wright, save for during moments of copulation, when he, in fact, preferred it.)

"I . . . I just think . . ."

He watched her pick up a strip of bacon, which she brushed against her lips a few times before finally taking a bite. Sunlight, tempered by a scrim of clouds, streamed through the windows, turning Ginny's hair the color of weak embers. Beneath the table, he felt her sandaled foot creep up his left leg, a single toe momentarily getting caught in the elastic band of his sock. Chewing her bacon, Ginny worked her foot higher. She had nearly reached his knee when their blue-haired waitress scuttled by, asking if they would like refills on coffee. Shaken, Dean had brushed Ginny's foot away. He crossed his legs, suppressing the bulge in his khakis.

The waitress left and he tried again: "I think we should stop this."

"Stop what?"

"This," Dean said. He picked up a fork and pierced the yolk on one of the two fried eggs he had ordered. Yellow muck bled across his plate. "All of this."

Ginny grinned. "I've heard that before."

Dean looked out the window. A Honda Civic pulled into the empty space next to his station wagon. He held his breath until he could see the driver and confirm that it was no one he knew. He said, "I'm serious this time. It's got to stop."

"Yeah? And why's that?"

"Because I'm married."

"Oh, please, Dean."

He dipped a spoon into his coffee and started stirring. He knew he shouldn't have told Ginny about Jasmine. He had done so because he thought it would make her like him more. He thought that if he gave her some indication that this wasn't just sex—that he was capable of carrying on an affair—she was more liable to keep sleeping with him. That, he realized now, had been a miscalculation.

And so, he accepted her edit and thought twice; he revised: "Because it's getting out of control," he said. "Because we're one red hair in the shower drain away from someone finding out."

"You mean from your wife finding out."

"Incidentally, that is who I'm most concerned about, yes," Dean said, adding, "but there's also Will."

"*Will?*" Ginny reached back and gathered her hair into a ponytail, straining her neck from side to side. Dean glanced at the white flesh and the smattering of freckles that darkened the left side of her chin. He re-crossed his legs, and she went on: "You said it yourself, Will's hopeless. He'd literally have to be naked in bed with us before he even suspected something was going on."

"I never said that."

"Yes, you did."

"I *didn't*." He thought for a moment. "When did I?"

"Two weeks ago. Tuesday afternoon in the laundry room. Right after I put my finger up your—"

"Okay, okay, maybe I did," he hissed, leaning forward. "I'm allowed to, though. He's my kid."

"Oh-ho, so that's how this works?" She slapped the table. "Now you've suddenly got a monopoly on who gets to be called an idiot?"

Dean scooped up a bite of egg, but it slipped, limp and wet, between the tines of his fork.

He looked at her and said firmly, "Do not talk about my son."

Ginny stared at him for a moment, as if she was searching his face for signs of a tell. When he didn't blink she finally turned away and let her hair fall back around her shoulders. "I'm sorry," she said. "It's just—is that why you brought me out here? Is that why you drove me all the way to Walnut Creek? So you could tell me that it's got to stop?"

"I knew you liked pancakes." He wondered how fast he could get the check. He wondered if Ginny would mind taking the bus home. "I heard this place had good pancakes."

"Yeah, well, they suck." She pushed her plate away. "They're dry as shit, and they suck."

"Would you like to order something else?"

"No, I would not like to *order something else*." She folded her arms across her chest and heaved a massive sigh. "In fact, if I'm being honest with you, I think I've lost my appetite."

"Ginny . . ."

"Yes?"

But he said nothing; instead, he just looked at her. Her green eyes had darkened to a stormy hazel. In front of her sat a box of yellow Splenda packets, and he watched as she arranged them and rearranged them, occasionally glancing up with an expression that was as desperate as it was vindictive. He knew that whatever he said next had the potential for gorgeously disastrous consequences. With a few simple words he could ruin Ginny's week—nay, Ginny's year. Conversely, if he pitied her and capitulated, he would have her groveling at his feet, thanking him for his magnanimity. He considered what those two outcomes might look like: on the one hand, here's Ginny, whispering sweet words of gratitude as she unzipped his pants; on the other hand, here's Ginny, throwing lukewarm coffee in his face as she stormed out into the rain. Both options, he admitted, carried with them the same, familiar effect: a wonderful tingling at the end of his dick.

But then, something strange happened: without warning, Ginny stood up. She took her napkin off her lap, dabbed the corners of her mouth with it, and just . . . stood up. It was as if she had suddenly become aware of just how seductive her own pliability was; of how Dean's own obsession with control had paradoxically given her the upper hand.

"I'm going to the restroom to dry my eyes," she said, folding the napkin into thirds and setting it back down on the table.

Leaning over, she added, "I'll leave the door unlocked."

Thirty minutes later the Wrights abandon the ruins for a restaurant a few miles down the road, a place called Epikouros with cloth napkins and, at least from some of its tables, a sweeping view of the surrounding mountains. Once they're seated, he orders a half liter of white wine, which the waiter delivers with a small basket of bread. The bread isn't good, or fresh; it's crusty and freckled with sesame seeds that keep getting caught in his teeth. He finds none of these facts particularly offensive. Rather, he's grateful for how he can eat the little slices without thinking, without appreciating. How he can slop them in olive oil and consume them purely as matter, which he does, over and over again, as he waits for his lunch to arrive. When it does, though, he's disappointed by what he sees: a lukewarm lamb chop, accompanied by rice and two wrinkled roasted tomatoes. He inspects them for a moment, poking them with his fork, letting their juices stain the plate red.

His tryst with Ginny in the diner had been the very last time. He made the decision to follow his wife to Greece right after he had finished. His pants were still around his ankles when he thought, with perfect clarity, Jesus Christ, we've got to get out of here. For starters, there was the issue of his faulty self-control—the diner had proven that much. More problematic than that, though, was the fact that Ginny had started to become, well, a little nuts. Typically, he would find this sort of behavior equally as seductive as it was troubling—he had no problem admitting a certain infatuation with crazy women—but with Ginny he found himself worrying that, sooner or later, he would get caught.

He had, to some degree, always suspected it would turn out like this. There were signs, even during their first encounter, when she was just another creative writing student vying for a place in his class. He remembers the first time she stopped by his office. It was November, two months into the fall term, and applications to Dean's upcoming spring workshop weren't due for another week. Still, the first thing Ginny did when she sat down across from him was slap a ten-page story on his desk, along with a letter of recommendation from Chip Fieldworth, the powdery old Victorianist who chaired the English Department.

"I want to study with you," she said, letting her shoulder bag fall to the floor. "I've read *The Light of Our Shadows* four times, and I want to learn everything you have to teach me."

Dean looked up from the book he had been reading, an old Forster hardcover, behind which he hid the stuff he actually liked: Lee Child thrillers. The occasional Jodi Picoult.

"We're not accepting applications until next week," he said, and waited for Ginny to reach down and pick up her bag. She didn't.

"I realize that. I thought, though, that it might behoove me to submit mine now."

"You mean that you thought it might give you a leg up on the others." He dog-eared his page and set the book down.

"Whatever. I guess that's one way of looking at it, sure."

She was wearing a light denim jacket, which she presently began working her way out of, letting the sleeves slip from her shoulders to reveal bare arms and a cream-colored top. The shirt, which she had cut to expose her pale midriff, had been stenciled with the word #BLACKTIVIST, even though (at least from what Dean could tell) Ginny was nothing if not very, very white.

"And why do you think you deserve to study with me?" he asked her.

She shifted in her seat, and her flesh doubled over in tiny folds against the waistband of her jeans.

"Because I can quote multiple paragraphs from everything you've ever written," she said, blinking. "And because I'm devastatingly talented."

"You don't think you've got classmates who've memorized my books? Or classmates who are devastatingly talented?"

She tucked her hair behind her ears. "I'm sure I do," she said. "But they're not here, are they?"

Dean smirked: he liked her swagger. Picking up his book, he said, "Get out of here, but leave your story."

He ignored her smile and focused on his book while she stood and gathered her things. Once he had heard the sound of her footsteps fade from the department's halls, he pushed himself away from his desk, picked up the stack of papers that she had left him, and poked his head into the office next door, where Chip Fieldworth was watering a trio of half-dead orchids.

"Who's this?" Dean said, waving the story in the air.

Chip peered over the rims of his glasses. "That's a piece of paper."

"Knock it off. You wrote her a recommendation for my class. Who is it?"

Chip set down his watering can and sighed. He was, per Dean's imagination, the sort of man who women in the early twentieth century might call a confirmed bachelor, someone who was so dandified, so entirely pastel, that his sexuality transcended any conventional categorization. He was, of course, gay, though he wore his homosexuality with a sort of chicness and savoir faire that Dean sensed had been lost on his son's generation. Chip, for example, knew how to wear an ascot. He knew how to quote Wilde and Burroughs, and how to talk about Verdi, and early American furniture, and chinoiserie. He had an ability that Dean admired to raise the aesthetic above the political and to treat artifice as truth. On three separate Sundays he had seen him in the city—on the borders of the Castro, more specifically—and each time Chip had been accompanied by a coterie of young men. They tittered around him, Dean later thought, like children in a Renoir painting, dappled in pale light.

Now, he squinted at the papers that Dean held.

"Ginny Polonsky," he said. "I had her in a seminar last spring. A positively exhausting young woman."

"Then God damn it, Chip, why'd you recommend her for my workshop?"

Chip turned and began sprinkling water over the orchid in the middle, a meager little plant boasting a single white bloom.

"Because she wouldn't leave my office until I agreed to write her a letter," he said, shrugging. "And I had places to be."

Dean looked down at the story. "Is she any good?"

"How do you suppose I would know?"

"Didn't you say she was in your class?"

Chip laughed. "You're assuming that means I read her work?" He stopped watering and turned back to face Dean. "I haven't the slightest idea if the girl's talented or not."

She was, Dean thinks now. Just—for the record, Ginny was talented. (*Is* talented—he needs to stop thinking about her like she's dead.) The rest

of the writers in her class all adhered to the same limp aesthetic, a simpering style of prose that seemed primarily concerned with things like
the undersides of someone's wrists, or the way the sun reflected off a collar-
bone. It was the sort of spineless stuff that at once assured them admission to any number of prestigious M.F.A. programs and made Dean fear
for the future of American fiction. Ginny, on the other hand—there was a
girl with actual promise. Granted, her stories weren't in the genre of stuff
he typically saw in an undergraduate workshop, though he suspected that's
also what made them so refreshing. While her classmates concerned themselves with the same soggy preoccupations (sad young women retracing
their families' pasts, for example, or lonely boys named Sasha picking their
way through Brooklyn), Ginny created wild, bizarre worlds. Her first
submission, he remembers, had been set on a planet called Druida—a
place where women ruled and kept men in giant hamster cages. Sci-fi,
you could call it, with a dose of slasher-feminism. When it came time for
the piece to be critiqued, her classmates didn't say much. Instead, they
looked at Ginny like she was nuts, a fact which further convinced Dean
that she was actually some sort of genius. Stephen King meets Philip K.
Dick, he breathlessly told Chip, but only if Ursula K. Le Guin had their
nuts in a vice.

He remembers the first time they had sex, in the kitchen of the group
house she lived in on Arch Street. After they finished the first time, she
slipped his finger into her mouth and bit down on it, stopping just before
her teeth pierced the skin. Then she slid the same finger inside of her,
demanding that he make her cum a second time as he recited lines from
his novel. Watching her sweat and chew her lip, he felt enlivened; he remembered what Jasmine had given him—a sense of prestige and domi-
nance. Immediately after they had finished, however, the guilt began to
creep back: there it was again, the familiar hollowing of his stomach, the
sudden rise in his throat. In Ginny's bathroom, he splashed some cool
water on his face and looked around for some soap to wash his hands. He
couldn't find any, though, so he used her strawberry bodywash instead.

They slept together four days later, and then the day after that; they continued sleeping together until the act became a habit, as opposed to a fluke. Between these occasions, he worried that something was wrong with him, mentally; he worried that his inability to be faithful signaled something larger, a sort of disease. The concern weighed on him so heavily that, after an encounter with Ginny that left him with bruises on his hips, he attended a meeting of Sex Addicts Anonymous—a wholly depressing affair held in the basement of a Presbyterian church in San Leandro, replete with foam cups, weak coffee, and sugar cookies that (at least in Dean's estimation) were shaped a little too much like vaginas. He didn't stay for the whole thing. The closest he ever got to returning was writing a story about one of the women who had shared—a twenty-two-year-old from Oakland whose fiancé left her when he discovered she had a thing for truck stops and the truckers who frequented them. His most recent novel aside, it's one of the better things he's written. In a month, it's going to be published in *The Paris Review*.

After lunch they begin the trek back to the bus, which is the first, negligible leg of a much longer trek back to the Alectrona. He stays put for a minute or so outside the restaurant while his wife and son go on ahead. Looking down, Dean sees a trail of ants threading between his feet. Above him, up the craggy slope of Mount Parnassus, are the specks of Delphi, the foundations of the ancient temple, beneath which used to sit the Pythia. How did the old consultants used to ask for advice? Did they take a knee? Whisper something in her ear? He knows Sue Ellen has told him, but he can't piece it together. All he remembers is that there was a sacrifice that took place, something involving a slaughtered goat.

He crouches down and drags a stick through the ants, scattering them in a frenzied, patternless mess. Quickly, they realign themselves and set about passing something—a bit of a leaf, it looks like—down their ranks.

Still crouching, Dean watches them for a moment, admiring their industry and their blind single-mindedness. Then he looks back up toward the mountain. He thinks of the Pythia, the world's most celebrated two-bit psychic, doling out fortunes to men of circumstance. Closing his eyes, he tries to see her: her purple veil, her frenzied eyes, her wild hair.

"Tell me what I should do," he whispers, and only hears the wind.

Eleni

July 19 and 20
Aegina

She rinses the old coffee from the *briki,* clearing away smears of brown from the small copper pot. Then she refills it with cold water and a heaping spoonful of grounds before setting it over the stove's blue flame. Slowly stirring the grounds, she watches as they dissolve, melding together to turn the liquid to a thick syrup. She takes her coffee like her father took his: thick, black, and silty, with the last few swallows requiring a healthy bit of chewing. *Jet fuel* is what Christos used to call it. *Ambrosia for the new millennium.* A thick foam starts to form along the water's surface, and she thinks back to how she used to watch him drink his coffee, back when she was a little girl. She would sit at the far end of the table here, in the kitchen, and stare as he lifted his demitasse to his mouth, taking monk-like sips while he slowly leafed through the paper. It would often take him an hour to finish a single serving—an hour during which the coffee surely grew cold, congealing to a bitter gel. Yet Christos never seemed to mind; he would still bring the tiny cup to his lips and blow on it with the same careful cadence that he used when the drink was piping hot. Lift, blow, sip; lift, blow, sip. Watching him was like staring at a metronome that was set to a single, lulling speed. This, though, was her father; he had a keen ability to ritualize the most mundane tasks. Grocery shopping, sweeping the Alectrona's floors, even filling the Volkswagen with a fresh tank of gas—the prosaicism of life became a sort of ecclesiastical procession, one that Christos performed with a deliberate exactitude.

She swallows her coffee in a single swig: she doesn't have her father's patience—she never has. She tried to develop it, once. She went to yoga and read books on mindfulness. But then, in the middle of a particularly insufferable ride on the metro, that illusion faded. Wedged between two sweaty armpits, she realized—with a sort of explosive relief—that she needed her agitation. Her body craved it with the same insatiability that it craved water, or nicotine, or air. She didn't want to *breathe through* her impatience as the sweltering train idled just outside the Agios Dimitrios station; she didn't want to *watch her thoughts* as the men around her pinched her ass. When the doors opened at the next stop—Dafni—she shoved her way off the train and immediately lit a cigarette.

So, no, there won't be patience for Eleni. Instead, there will be movement and chaos—the constant clamor upon which she's built her life. Brewing and drinking her second cup of coffee, she thinks of Christos. She misses him, and along with that she feels a pang of guilt. She imagines her father looking down at her and shaking his head. The poor son of a bitch disappointed, even in death.

"Okay," Stavros says. "Where do we start?" He's holding a four-pronged valve. Sweat glistens across his forehead.

"Don't do anything before I tell you to."

Eleni picks up the piece of paper she's set on the bathroom sink, a torn-out page from one of her old notebooks where she's written down some instructions for herself. Early yesterday morning she determined, after a series of blind and haphazard tests, that the problem with the showers wasn't a leaky pipe at all (she had assumed, wrongly, that all plumbing problems were caused by leaky pipes), but rather three faulty pressure-balancing valves. For the next two hours, while the rest of the Alectrona slept, she sorted through as many do-it-yourself repair guides as she could find on Google, cross-referencing their steps and looking up the jargon she didn't know. Then she called Stavros. She told him to be at the inn at ten o'clock the next morning and to swing by the hardware store in town on the way.

"Remember what I told you," he says now.

"Remind me." She's had too much coffee this morning. Her focus keeps jumping, landing one step ahead of where she wants it to be.

"Plumbing makes me nervous."

"It's not rocket science, Stavros."

"No—it's worse." He's got a cigarette tucked behind his left ear, which he reaches up to adjust. "All that *water*."

"Get a grip, you live on an island. I want to have these fixed before we close with Lugn." She looks through the square hole that she cut away in the shower's tile as she waited for him to arrive, a window that reveals a maze of pipes and, beyond them, a stained concrete wall. Turning back to the page, she says, "It looks pretty easy. There are only fifteen steps—"

"Fifteen steps."

"—the first of which is turning off the water." She glances up at him. "You turned off the water, right?"

"Yes, I turned off the water."

"Did you turn the right main, though? There are two of them in the maintenance—"

"I turned the one you told me to turn."

She arches an eyebrow, and Stavros arches one back.

"Here," she says, nodding to a toolbox next to the toilet. "Hand me that wrench."

He picks up the tool with his free hand but doesn't give it to her.

"Maybe I should do it," he says.

"Why?"

"Because it might be tight, and I'm stronger."

His shirt hangs from his shoulders. Beneath its open collar, his collarbones jut at sharp, fragile angles.

Eleni says, "I actually don't think that's true."

"You said the head and arm first?"

She sighs. "Yes—that's right."

He sets the valve in the sink and steps into the tub. Reaching up, he removes the showerhead and the pipe attaching it to its internal mechanisms. At first, things go smoothly; Stavros's hands are surprisingly steady, and he maneuvers the wrench with a confidence that causes Eleni to think that his distaste for plumbing might have been some grand charade. This confidence, however, is short-lived. Once he reaches into the wall to unscrew the valve from the water supply pipes, he's met with resistance—the wrench stops working, and he turns to look at Eleni.

"Let me take over," she says. "Or else give it a little more muscle, if you're able."

She's goading him, which is a mistake. It makes him more determined, less cautious; his eyebrows pulled together, he readjusts his stance and bears down.

The water begins as a trickle—a tiny rivulet that Eleni figures is buildup, a bit of excess moisture that's been caught in the dry pipes. With each quarter turn of the wrench, though, it grows; soon, water is spraying across Stavros's forearms. She tries to stop him—she says, "Uh, I don't think this is right"—but he's too single-minded in his efforts. With a final *clank,* the old valve falls to the floor, and a geyser erupts. Stavros stumbles back and falls to his ass in the tub. A pool gathers at his ankles.

"You turned off the wrong main!" she shouts.

"I turned the one you told me to turn!"

Water shoots at him and drenches his shirt. His hair—a wet mess of brown, black, and gray—hangs in front of his eyes.

"I'm drowning," he says. "My God, I think I'm drowning."

She helps him up and throws a towel at him.

"Stay here and try to keep the place from flooding. I'll go shut off the main."

Downstairs, she flips on the overhead lamp in the utility closet and cranks a rusted valve. There's a groan, the sound of pipes clanking and emptying, and then—finally—silence. She holds her breath for a moment and closes her eyes, leaning back against the concrete wall. It's dark in the closet, and cool. She wonders how long she can stay here, hiding from the mess upstairs, the flooded bathroom and Stavros's drenched, angry face. She wonders how long it takes for a problem to dry up on its own.

The next morning, she sits at the breakfast table in the kitchen, smearing Nutella on toast and drinking apricot juice. An hour earlier, Oskar emailed her a bundle of documents that Lugn Escape's attorneys had prepared for the deal's closing, which is scheduled to take place in Athens in a week. She understands the broad strokes of them—this is amortization; that is an encumbrance. When it comes to the details, though, she's lost, and that's unfortunate; she can't afford a lawyer, and she highly doubts Stavros understands the finer points of real estate finance. Still, she does her best to play ball—she's never been a pushover, and she doesn't want Lugn's lawyers to take her for a patsy. Opening a new email, she begins bullet-pointing the items she plans to push back on—namely, a provision that says she'll cover the cost of any needed repairs. She thinks, If they've got the cash to turn her bedroom into a sauna, then they've got the cash to patch the hole she made in the shower.

She fires off the points to Oskar, then angles her chair so she can look out the kitchen's single window and onto the back patio. It's ten thirty, but already the morning has lost its amber glow; everything, from the tile to the bark of the pines, is baked in hot white. She takes a bite of toast, and the Nutella instantly coats the roof of her mouth. It's the first time she's had it in years—when she got to school, she wrote it off as something kids eat—and she forgot how delicious, how perfect it is. When she gets back to Athens, she decides, she'll have it every morning—that's how she'll celebrate. She'll toss away the muesli, the bran flakes, and all the other healthy shit that tastes like soggy cardboard, and just eat spoonful after spoonful of Nutella instead.

There's a knock on the door and she says, "It's open." It will be Stavros, she suspects, apologizing for being thirty minutes late (again).

Instead, she looks up to see Sue Ellen Wright, standing with her hands in her pockets.

Eleni brushes crumbs from her lap and rises from her seat.

"Oh," she says. "Hello."

"*Kaliméra,*" Sue Ellen looks at the contracts strewn across the desk. "You're busy?"

"No, it's no problem. You need some fresh towels again?"

This is not the first instance of Sue Ellen coming to linger, and often this is the excuse that she uses: her husband has stolen both of their towels, and now she needs another. Each time, Eleni complies; she goes to the linen closet in the hallway that connects the kitchen to the dining room and gives her a fresh towel, along with a small washcloth. Now, she prepares to do the same thing, even though she suspects Sue Ellen's request is a lie: five days ago, when the family was in Delphi, Eleni went to clean the couple's room and found a stack of towels in the corner, dry and entirely unused. She doesn't pretend to understand the wants and wills of her guests—she just tells herself this is the last time she'll ever have to worry about them again.

But now, Sue Ellen stops her.

She says, "Oh, no, no. We're actually fine on towels. I . . . my husband's still sleeping, and my son's off doing God knows what. I just thought that I'd . . ." She takes a step deeper into the room and looks around. "You switched out the doors," she says.

"Pardon?"

"The doors—" She nods to the one behind Eleni, which leads out to the back patio. "They're glass now. Same with the ones in the dining room."

She adds, "They look lovely, honestly."

Honestly—they say this often, Eleni's noticed. All Americans do. *Honestly, I don't mind. Honestly, it doesn't matter. Honestly, the food was delicious.* She wonders if it's just some weird lingual tick, like how her father called all of his friends *maláka*, or if there's something more profound lurking behind it. She wonders if without the addition of *honestly*, the sentence being said would be rendered a lie; if English would suddenly become a language of half-truths.

"Oh," Eleni says. "Ha, yes, I guess I did. Thank you."

"And this—" Sue Ellen runs a hand along the table where Eleni's been working. "This is new, too."

"I got it two years ago in Pandrossou."

This, Eleni notes, is another thing that Sue Ellen has been doing: tracing her steps through the inn, identifying what's new and what isn't. She's hardly alone in this; the Alectrona's few repeat guests all seem to make a game of pointing out what has changed. Once, she got so annoyed with a Swiss man fetishizing a new lampshade that she took it off and replaced it with the old one in the middle of the night. The next morning, when he asked her where it had gone, she told him nothing had changed and that he must have been imagining things.

Now, Sue Ellen glances down at the contracts. "I hope I'm not interrupting your work," she says.

"You're not. I was just wrapping up." A spot of Nutella stains the end of Eleni's finger, and she discreetly licks it away. "Actually, you don't happen to know anything about real estate law, do you?" She laughs, though it's only a half-joke. "The only help I've got is Stavros, and he can hardly tie his own shoes."

Sue Ellen smiles. "No lawyers in this family, I'm afraid. Why do you ask?"

Eleni pulls her hair back and ties it off. "I've got an offer from a company that wants to buy the Alectrona. Lugn Escapes, it's called."

"I don't think I can say *Lugn*."

"You've heard of them? They're Swedish."

"I haven't." Something flickers across Sue Ellen's face—a mix of clouded emotions that Eleni can't read. "I didn't realize you were selling the place."

"We're actually set to close in a week and a half, two days before you leave. Don't worry, though—they've promised they won't kick you out."

Eleni laughs, but it comes out guttural and harsh. Sue Ellen doesn't seem to hear her. Instead, she's looking at the kitchen counter, drawing circles around a small, euro-size stain that's been there since before Eleni was born. For a moment, Eleni says nothing. She watches as Sue Ellen moves on from the stain to the stovetop to the old door swinging open behind her. She remembers the Swiss man, and she feels a sudden surge of sadness. She thinks, Our ghosts don't haunt us as phantoms, but as lampshades and doors. All the bits of life we refuse to forget.

Stepping forward, she sets her fingers on Sue Ellen's forearm.

She says, "Look, I know I just ate breakfast, but would you be interested in grabbing some lunch?"

There's a place she used to go with her mother, back when she was a little girl. A bakery in Perdika, on the southwest side of the island. They would drive there on Saturdays, when her father was busy paying the Alectrona's bills, and when Agatha, with her witchy maternal intuition, sensed that Eleni needed to get out of the house. It didn't have a proper name—it was called, simply, Perdika Bakery—and they probably never would have frequented it had Agatha's cousin Maria not owned the dress shop next door. Typically, they arrived in the late morning, once Maria had finally gotten around to opening her store—a small, overcrowded operation that specialized in baptism gowns. For a few minutes the women would chat, the conversation darting between topics that, to Eleni, seemed foreign, and adult, and exciting: so-and-so's sister leaving her husband for a man she met in Glyfada; the new Proton supermarket near the harbor, which charged too much for produce and bread. As they spoke, she would hang back listening near the front door, shifting her weight in her sandals and running her fingers along the gowns' stiff lace. There was a picture of her wearing one of these in her father's office, a glossy portrait of her dressed like an infant bride, her soft head covered with a white bonnet. It terrified Eleni whenever she saw it. Even though, at eight, she was hardly tall enough to see over the Alectrona's bar, she didn't like to imagine there was a time when she was so breakable.

Before long, her mother would come to her and rest her hand gently on top of her head.

"Let's go," she'd say, "before you stain one of these things and Maria makes me pay a fortune to have it cleaned."

They would go next door, then, and on most occasions, Maria would join them; the shop rarely had visitors—there were only so many baptisms happening on the island at any one time, and besides, the year before a larger store had opened closer to the port, a two-level place that sold not only tiny dresses, but larger ones, too, along with other apparel, like T-shirts, tie-dyed wraps, and beach towels. At the bakery, Agatha would commandeer one of the two small tables outside, and as she and Maria got settled, she would hand Eleni a thousand drachmas—enough to buy a small bottle of orange juice and a *bougatsa*. They were, by Eleni's estimation, the best pastries on the island: the phyllo dough crisp and flaky; the semolina custard warm and oozing from its edges. She always ate them slowly, trying to distinguish the individual flavors as they marched across her tongue.

Now the bakery is gone. So is Maria's store: a decade ago, she sold it to a company that rents motor scooters before moving to Tripoli with her girlfriend. There had been a going-away party for her, Eleni remembers, but she hadn't been able to attend. Christos said she had too much homework. The end of the school term was approaching, and her grades had started to slip.

"Huh," Eleni says, "I guess it closed."

"What about Giovita?" Sue Ellen asks, in Greek. "Is it still open?"

"You know Giovita?"

"That's the place next to Saint Sosti, right?"

"Right, the one with the blue-and-white tablecloths. Great French fries. It's been there forever."

"Well, good thing I was here forever ago."

They find a free table and, flagging down a waiter, Eleni orders for both of them. A bottle of moscofilero to drink. To eat, Cretan salad, fried calamari, and a grilled mullet, which arrives to the table whole, the two tips of its tail crispy and charred. Picking up a knife, Sue Ellen begins to remove the fish's meat from its bones, peeling the flesh away to reveal an opaque and milky spine.

"So when you were here forever ago—that's when you met my dad?" Eleni says.

It's the only thing that comes to mind. Since they sat down, their conversation has circled around things like the color of the water and how much the island has changed, and she doesn't know how much more of it she can take. For someone whose profession requires so much of it—or maybe, actually, because of it—she finds small talk particularly torturous.

"Yes, that's right," Sue Ellen says. "I came here as a graduate student. I was supposed to spend the summer in Delos, but . . . for a number of reasons, I think, I ended up staying here. I studied Aphaía's temple and wrote about it quite a bit in my dissertation. That's the subject of my lecture, actually." She wipes a bit of olive oil from the back of her hand. "I think I mentioned the lecture when you and I were emailing about my reservation, didn't I? Yes, I thought so. It's for Golden Age Adventures, which is one of those cruise companies for old people. God, wait, can I say that? I mean, *I'm also old*." She feigns horror. "In any event, I stayed at the Alectrona. This is when your grandfather was still alive, and Christos was helping to run it."

Sue Ellen finishes dissecting the mullet and scoops a filet onto both of their plates.

"Why'd you decide to study Greece?" Eleni asks.

"Honestly? Because I knew it was sunny here." She takes a sip of her wine, and Eleni laughs. "No, I'm serious. I grew up in Port Angeles—do you know it? It's fine, not a lot of people do. It's this tiny town on the Olympic peninsula, in Washington, just across the water from Canada. The weather there—God, it's awful. It rains pretty much all the time. People like to say that it's worse in Seattle, but they're lying; in Port Angeles, you're always a little bit cold and a little bit wet.

"Anyway, from there I went to college at Amherst, in Massachusetts. It didn't rain as much, but it was still cold. *Freezing.* I remember my first winter, there was this stretch of about three months where the high didn't get above seventeen degrees, which is—what—something like negative eight degrees Celsius? I'm terrible at math. Whatever it is, I think it was actually the next semester when I took an introductory course in classical studies. I was so tired of being cold that I wanted to read about somewhere warm."

She refills both their wineglasses and empties some of the Cretan salad onto her plate.

"And from there . . . I don't know." She smiles. "I guess I just fell in love with the whole idea of this place, you know? All those stories of goddesses and heroes. Homer, Thucydides, the Peloponnesian War. There's a romanticism to it, obviously, but it's more than that. I like uncovering things, I think. I like how you can look at something as distant as the past to explain a mystery like the present."

Eleni can't help but grin—it's a lovely thought, even if it is a little delusional. She suspects it must be easy to be nostalgic for the way things were, once you've managed to escape them. When history is the chains that bind your ankles, though—well, she would like to see what Sue Ellen says then.

A fly lands on the table, and Eleni brushes it away. On the street next to them two boys chase a girl. Behind them their *giagiá* trails, yelling at them to slow down.

"Listen," Sue Ellen says. "Tomorrow I'm hiking up to the temple, just to get myself reacquainted with the space. How'd you like to come with me?"

"That's so sweet of you to ask," Eleni says, and she means it. "Unfortunately, I think my whole day is going to be spent looking over contracts."

"Ah, yes. That's right."

Sue Ellen picks at the fish, which is now a heap of scales and bones. She digs beneath them, as if she's trying to uncover something.

"I'm sorry," Eleni says. "I may be totally misreading things here, but are you upset?"

Sue Ellen looks up and shakes her head, like she's suddenly woken up from a dream. She smiles.

"Me? Oh, God. No, I'm fine." She reaches back and gathers her hair with both hands. "If I'm being honest, I guess there was this part of me that thought maybe one day I'd end up here."

She lets her hair go, and she laughs.

"But that was crazy," she says, finishing her wine. "That was another life."

Sue Ellen

Aegina and Berkeley
Then and Now

Then

"I'm going to miss my ferry," Sue Ellen said, glancing down at her watch for the fifth time that minute. "And the next one to Delos isn't until tomorrow night. If I don't get to the Stoibadeion by Wednesday, it's not going to be pretty."

"You'll get to the Stoibadeion by Wednesday." Christos didn't turn around when he spoke. He was a few yards ahead of her, and she watched his calves flex as they trudged up the hill. "We're very close."

For a moment, she considered if she could escape. Lie about an injury, maybe. A pulled muscle that prevented her from hiking up old Greek roads to see old Greek temples dedicated to old Greek goddesses who no one really knows. *It's a rare thing,* she imagined saying, *but my doctor says Aphaía aggravates it.* She grinned and looked down, stepping over a branch that had fallen onto the road. She would do no such thing, she knew; she would stay, and follow him up to the site, past the pistachio trees, the tiny parked cars, and the gift shop selling obscure ice-cream bars and not much else. And she would do it primarily because she was afraid. Ever since arriving in Greece thirty-six hours ago, she had felt more like an intruder than she had ever felt before—a feeling that only grew in intensity when she reached Aegina last night. On the plane to Athens, she had counted on her dread dispersing once she landed; she figured that once she successfully ordered her first meal in Greek, had her first glass of dry assyrtiko, any anxieties she felt about her future, about what she was doing with her life, would vanish. That, though, had been naïve thinking. She had slept a grand total of one hour the night prior, and those sixty minutes came in fits and starts, during pockets when her mind became too fatigued from worrying and slipped, however briefly, into twilight. Now, fighting exhaustion, she worried that if she were to bolt she would betray her own self-doubt. Suddenly, Greece would see her for the fraud she was.

There was also, she knew, the matter of Christos. Lugging her suitcase through the inn's front door, she'd found him standing next to a small ficus tree, pouring a glass of water into its deep pot. She hadn't expected this: the sight of a handsome man her own age, watering a strange little plant. But then, what had she expected, exactly? She knew nothing about the Alectrona, only that she was to stay there for one night before continuing on to Delos. She had booked the hotel because it was cheap, and because the travel agent with whom she spoke said that it was a ways outside town; after twenty-four hours of traveling, Sue Ellen was keen to avoid the raucousness of the harbor.

"*Me léne* Sue Ellen. *Ékho kanéi krátisi.*" She smiled, then said, "*Póso eseís?*"

He glanced up at her.

He said, in English, "More than you can afford."

Sue Ellen's cheeks flushed, and he shrugged. "You ask me how much I cost," he said, tilting the last few drops of water out of the can and smiling. "Though I think my name is what you want to know? It is Christos."

Handing him her suitcase, she wanted to tell him she knew that. She had been studying modern Greek, along with its ancient counterpart, for the past six years. She was fluent—she knew how to ask someone's name. Instead, she followed him as he showed her to her room, wondering if she had made a mistake. Maybe she would have had better luck dealing with the cries of drunk tourists in town, the stench of their cigarettes. She had never been very good with desire.

She was loath to admit any of this—she still considered herself to be above infatuation, above a schoolgirl crush. And yet, no matter how hard she steeled herself, his voice softened her; no matter how resolved she was to write him off, his eyes—old, knowing, set deep in too young a face— drew her back in. So much so that when he proposed he show her the temple the next morning—an offer made casually, dutifully, over breakfast—she had immediately said yes.

"Okay," he said now, stopping just short of the road's end. "We're here."

She circled to his left side and adjusted her sunglasses. A hundred yards ahead of them, the temple stood in a clearing of trees, and then beyond it, a panorama of the Aegean. She immediately recognized the structure as Doric; it lacked the ramlike volutes of the Ionic order or the baroque embellishments of the Corinthian. Its columns—their shafts striated with flutes; their tops crowned with simple, circular capitals—were arranged in a peripteral hexastyle fashion: a single row of twelve peripheral columns flanked each side of the naos, while a row of six lined the temple's front and back. The entirety of the structure rested on a crepis, a plateau that lifted the temple a good six feet off the ground, where a group of teenagers—three boys and one girl in a yellow halter top—lounged, smoking cigarettes.

"Late Archaic," Sue Ellen said. "Reminds me of the Athenian Treasury at Delphi. A similar sort of distyle."

"I have never been," Christos said.

"You should go. It's spectacular."

"It's difficult." He slipped his hands into the back pockets of his jeans. "My father needs my help."

She nodded, trying not to focus on how much she loved the sound of his Greek. How it smoothed over the harsh angles she associated with the language, the sharp consonants she heard being tossed around the streets of Athens.

A fly landed on her shoulder, and she brushed it away before approaching the temple. Christos stayed where he was for a few moments, then followed her.

"If you were to draw a straight line between here, the Parthenon in Athens, and the Temple of Poseidon in Sounion, you'd have an isosceles triangle," he said.

"Actually, that's not true," Sue Ellen said, studying the flutes on the column nearest to her. A few yards away the girl in the yellow halter top slapped one of the boys, and the others laughed. "A lot of people say that, but Schwandner maintains the distances are different."

"Schwandner?"

"Ernst-Ludwig Schwandner. *Ludovikos*, in Greek, I think," she said. "German archaeologist."

Christos scratched his arm. He said, "Oh," and she now felt terrible for correcting him. She wanted to reach out and touch his shoulder, apologize, ask him to continue with his theories, his invisible triangles. She didn't, though. Instead, she stepped up onto the crepis and wandered between a set of columns, toward the naos. Picking through the rubble, she thought of what little she had read about the site: how the architects devised a double colonnade to support the temple's massive flat roof; how here, where she was standing, there used to be an ivory statue of Athena; how the archaeologists originally thought the site was dedicated to her until they found an inscription, tiny and history making, carved into the stone: APHAÍA.

A moment later, she felt warm skin brush her right arm: Christos, standing closer to her than he had ever stood before.

"They say she was fleeing from King Minos, on Crete, who was enamored with her," he said. "And that to escape him, she threw herself into a fisherman's net. Artemis made her a goddess, and she came here."

Sue Ellen bit her lip for a moment. Then she couldn't help herself. She said, "Incidentally, that's only one version of the myth. Another one says that she was once a nymph, and that there was a god who was trying to rape her." *What was wrong with her?* "She came here, to this thicket, to get away from him. The name she was originally worshipped by—Britomartis—even means 'Sweet Virgin.'"

"You . . . are very knowledgeable."

"I guess," she said. "But it's also the only thing I know."

A breeze moved through the pines and whipped a strand of hair across Sue Ellen's lips. Turning to face her, Christos reached forward to remove it before leaning in to give her a gentle kiss.

"Then I am sure you know what her name, Aphaía, means," he said, placing his fingers on her sunburnt cheeks.

Sue Ellen closed her eyes.

She said: "To disappear."

Now

She doesn't need to be here—at the temple, that is—and yesterday Dean was keen enough to point that out.

"Why do you keep going back there?" he asked her. It was seven o'clock in the morning, and he buried his head in a pillow as she leaned over to tie her boots. "You've done all your research, and it's not like these geriatrics from the cruise will be able to hear whatever you've got to tell them anyway."

Sue Ellen tightened her last knot and stood up. "Be kind to your elders."

"May I remind you that *we*, technically, are elders."

"Now you're just being defeatist."

She walked to the mirror, where she buttoned her shirt and pulled her hair back.

"It helps me think," she said, finally.

"Huh?"

"You ask me why I keep going back there, so I'm telling you. It helps me think."

"Thinking," he said, rolling over, "is something with which you've rarely had a problem."

She hadn't been lying. Or, mostly she hadn't been. There's more to it than simply thinking, though. There's the sound the wind makes as it rattles the pines; the way the morning light softens the brutality of the temple's slow ruin. There's the tug of the past, when she's able to close her eyes and believe—at least for a second—that she's twenty-five years old again, here for the very first time. In those moments she allows herself to imagine different realities, competing histories of what her life would look like if she had made *this decision* or forgone *that choice*; what her life would look like if, against all odds, she had stayed. Maybe therein lies the silver lining behind Christos's death, she tells herself: for all the heartbreak that it's caused, she can now, at last, move past it. She can stop thinking of what could have been, because what could have been is finally gone.

Then

She missed the ferry that afternoon, along with the one the following day, and the day after that. She would track the boat's departure on her watch, a cheap black Timex with a broken second hand and a cracked face. The minutes would tick by—each one impossibly slower than the last—and she would imagine the lurching of the ferry's hull as passengers crowded its deck, the belching of its exhaust as it coughed its way out into the gulf. She would close her eyes and picture herself there, among the suitcases and tourists and cigarettes, fighting that familiar mix of nausea and irritation as they inched toward Athens. But then that moment would pass; she would shake herself awake and smile.

A week later, he took her north of town, to see the Tower of Markellos. That night, once they had returned to the inn, Sue Ellen found herself straddling him, pressing his shoulders into the new chaise longue his father had just set out by the Alectrona's pool. His breath was sweet—a mix of honey, watermelon, and the lukewarm athiri they had been drinking all day: kissing him was like sucking on drugstore candy. To her surprise, he was also timid. The removing of clothes, the arranging and rearranging of limbs, the new ways of balancing on the chair's taut plastic straps: all of this was left almost entirely to Sue Ellen. When they were finished, she laid her head against Christos's bare chest and listened to the cicadas swarming in the branches above them, their hum rising and falling like a set of shallow hills. Running her tongue along her teeth, she licked away traces of wine, of sugar.

"I should be on Delos," she said.

Christos was quiet and still for a moment. Then he began threading his fingers through her hair.

"What's that thing that Plutarch is famous for saying?" he said, his voice buzzing against her cheek. "'Fate leads him who follows it, and drags he who resists.'"

"Since when do you quote Plutarch?" she asked.

"Since I read him as a teenager." He kissed the top of her head. "America's not the only place they have books."

Another week passed, and it had become excruciatingly clear to her, to everyone, that she no longer had plans to leave. On that Tuesday, she snuck into the Alectrona's office and phoned her adviser. Told him that her interests had changed, and that she would be staying here, on Aegina, to do her research instead.

"But they were expecting you at the Stoibadeion almost two weeks ago," he said, his voice delayed and detached over the long-distance line. "I spoke to Lambert yesterday. A group of Canadian volunteers just showed up, and he's been fighting to keep your cot free. The poor old Frog is going to be heartbroken."

"I highly doubt that."

"Researching with the École Française. Spending the summer under one of the best classical archeologists in the business. You're really missing an opportunity here, Sue Ellen."

She cradled the phone against her ear and pressed herself against the office's wall.

"I think I've found something better here," she said.

"Well, I highly doubt *that*."

"That sounds more like your problem than mine."

"Maybe, but that will change when it comes time to present your dissertation. I hope you're prepared to defend whatever mess of pages this decision results in."

"I am." She wrapped the phone's cord around her finger. "And I can't begin to tell you how much your confidence in me means."

"Well, Christ, Sue Ellen. What am I supposed to tell Lambert?"

"Tell him whatever you want. My ferry sank. I'm lost at sea. I got kidnapped by Apollo and I'm living in Thebes." She said, again: "Tell him whatever you want."

"Sue Ellen . . ."

In the kitchen, a light flickered on. Leaning away from the wall, she saw a leg, then an arm, then a face: Christos, grinning at her as he rummaged through the icebox for a piece of fruit.

"I've got to go," she said, and hung up.

He was busy on weekdays. His father relied on him to help keep the

Alectrona afloat, and Sue Ellen felt guilty whenever she willed him away. Still, sometimes she did. She'd be reviewing some new research at a table in the corner of the dining room, and she'd look up to catch his eye as he poured coffee for another guest. He would wink and say something pleasant, and an hour later they would be on two of the inn's bikes, stifling their laughter as they pedaled away. They went to Kipseli, and Pachia Rachi; they spent long afternoons at Souvala, where they read and drank lukewarm cans of Pils Hellas and sunned themselves on the rocks. Weekly, Sue Ellen would hand Christos an envelope containing twenty thousand drachmas, which was less than what she owed for the room but was all she could afford. She had never been a freeloader, she told him, and she wasn't about to become one now. Christos protested at first, but eventually relented, with a single condition: he would take her money, but he would only use it to buy the retsina they drank each Saturday, when they hiked up to watch the sun set behind Aphaía's temple.

"Won't your father catch on?" she asked him. They were sitting on the pool's edge, their legs floating.

Christos drew slow circles on the water's surface.

"I do the books," he said. "Besides, the old man's terrible at math."

A month more slipped by: soon it was August, the heat growing infernal before surrendering to autumn. On one of those thick evenings, Sue Ellen lay in bed, a copy of Pausanias's *Hellados Periegesis* propped open on her chest. Beside her, collected in a loose stack, were a few drawings she had done of the temple. Three weeks ago, her camera had stopped working. She couldn't afford to buy another one, so she committed herself to producing a series of sketches—diagrams, really—that she hoped would somehow inform her dissertation. For the past hour she had been flipping between them and Pausanias, unable to focus; every time she had a halfway decent idea, her thoughts drifted to a week from now, when she would be leaving Aegina and returning home. Twice she had brought the subject up with Christos, but both times he'd batted it away. For this, she was thankful. Leaving him wasn't inevitable, so long as it was just another joke. She started to doze, the book still splayed across her, when there was a light knock on her door. Rubbing her eyes, she said, "Come in." She didn't need to ask who it was; she knew it could only be him. His parents only spoke to her when they were required to; for the most part, they left her alone. They regarded her with a mix of deference and suspicion that struck Sue Ellen as both sweet and uncomfortable, and with which she dealt by acting overly, if not performatively, gracious.

"What's the book?" Christos asked, quietly closing the door behind him.

"Pausanias," she answered, showing the cover to him.

He crawled onto the bed and slipped a foot beneath the thin sheet. She was wearing an old pair of plaid boxer shorts, and his toes felt warm as they brushed against her calf.

Taking the book, he dog-eared her spot and flipped through a few pages.

"Looks like a lot of work," he said. Reaching over her, he picked up the sketches. "You draw these?"

"My camera's busted." She stole the book back from him and set it on a bedside table. Linking her leg around his knee, she pulled him closer to her. "If I don't draw what I see, I won't remember what I saw."

"They aren't finished," he said.

"What are you talking about?" Sue Ellen took one of them back. "In this one you're looking east from the opisthodomos, into the naos."

Christos retrieved a pen from the bedside table and removed the cap with his teeth. Using Sue Ellen's thigh as a surface, he drew two stick figures into her drawing, leaning against a column.

"I wish you wouldn't do that," she said, and didn't stop him.

"You want them to be accurate, don't you?"

She took the drawing from him.

"You made my hair look like Doris Day's." Reaching beneath the sheets, she found the button of his shorts and unfastened it. "If accuracy is the goal, I'll guess I'll have to draw one of me leaving."

Christos wiggled out of his shorts and kicked them to the foot of the bed.

"What, you can tell the future now?" he said. "It's not like that's happened yet."

Sue Ellen propped herself up on her elbow. He was smiling, the corners of his eyes creased with shallow crow's-feet.

"Christos," she said, "I love you, but I'm leaving."

"That," he said, "would be a very complicated picture to draw."

"Seems like it would be a pretty necessary one, though."

Christos brushed hair away from her eyes.

He said, "How about we start with something easier? Like a kiss, maybe. I could draw a kiss."

Sue Ellen collapsed backward, her head falling on the pillow.

"Stick figures don't have lips," she said.

He pressed his mouth against her cheek, then her chin. He continued working his way downward, stopping for a moment at a spot on her neck. She wondered if he could feel her pulse, how it quickened.

"No," he said, before he dipped his head beneath the sheets. "No, I guess they don't."

It rained the morning she left. Not a downpour—that would be unthinkable in August—but a spritz. Enough to dampen the docks in the harbor and send waiters scrambling to move their tables inside. She remembers standing on the quay with soggy hair, watching puddles evaporate and smelling old, wet wood. Beside her, Christos fidgeted, rocking back and forth on his heels as he twirled a set of keys around his finger.

"I can call someone to pick you up at Piraeus," he said. "It is . . . it can be such a madhouse there, it might be nice to have someone to meet you."

"I'll be fine."

With her right hand, she reached up and twirled a cheap gold necklace looped around her neck. He had bought it for her yesterday, after he drove her around the island on the back of a scooter that wasn't his. At the end of it hung a small pendant with a picture of Hermes. The patron protector of travelers, he reminded her.

She felt something brush the fingertips of her other hand: Christos, taking hold of her.

Two hundred yards offshore, the bow of the ferry emerged from a curtain of fog. It blew its horn once, then twice, sending bellowing vibrations from Sue Ellen's toes to her kneecaps. Reaching down, she grabbed her backpack and slung it over her shoulder.

"It's twenty minutes late," Christos said.

"In this country that's right on time."

He twirled his keys faster.

He asked, "You'll call?"

"I told you I would," she said, and allowed herself to grip his fingers tighter.

"Promise me."

"I promise you I'll call."

And she had. She'd called him from a pay phone in Piraeus, where a line of other people yelled at her, telling her to hurry up, and then again from New York, where she waited for her connecting flight back to San Francisco. She called him the second after she dropped her bags in her apartment in Berkeley, and another time the next afternoon, once she had met with her adviser to get a dressing-down for her summer antics. She had called him, in fact, every day for the next week, until the moment she remembered she was a grad student—or, more specifically, a grad student without a budget for countless long-distance phone calls—at which point she suggested that, maybe, they should write letters instead.

At first she regretted this decision; she had become so accustomed to the sound of his voice, and she feared how much she would miss him in its absence. This fear, though, turned out to be ill founded. His letters carried a fullness that she hadn't realized their phone conversations, addled with the crackles and delays of long distance, lacked. Pressing her nose to the paper, she imagined smelling him; in the curves of his letters—his alphas, and omicrons, and omegas—she saw the soft contours of his ears, the subtle fullness of his lips. They were also, she soon realized, able to take their time. Free from a ticking clock, from the counting of so many dimes and nickels, they were able to return to the languid, rambling discussions with which they had filled their days on the beaches of Aegina. They could debate, again, the role of myth and regret—the sort of questions that seemed too distant, too unanswerable, when Sue Ellen was imagining her phone bill.

Another thing: the weeks between letters also allowed her to escape. Whether she wanted this or not is now a moot point, because the fact is that it happened: without hearing from him every day, without the constant pull of his presence, she was able—however regretfully—to return to her life in Berkeley. Slowly, her thesis began to take shape—began, in fact, to impress her adviser, who, up until spring, had still been treating her as something of a bête noire. And suddenly, there were also other men, lovers who slipped in during the increasingly long pauses between Christos's letters. At first, she dated as a form of retaliation; Christos told her that he had met someone, a woman named Teresa, and Sue Ellen felt a sudden need to prove that while she ached for the past, she, too, had a future. For two months, she saw a stockbroker who lived in Pacific Heights—a man named Gary with sharp suits and slick hair, who she dumped when she found out he'd voted for Reagan. There were also Reggie and Malik and Steve. A horticulturalist named Charles who taught her how not to kill her plants. She didn't love any of them—she knows that now, and she knew that then—but she hardly considered that a problem. She wasn't interested in love—she was interested in distraction.

She assumed Dean would fit the same bill. When she met him at one of the university's graduate-student mixers, she singled him out as someone she could have a little fun with, another body who would fill the hole in her life left by Christos—a space that changed daily, depending on what shape her memories took. But then a strange thing happened: she fell for him. It was a product of his curiosity, his earnestness, his uncertainty. For the previous three years, she had been dating men who were nothing but sure—about their work, about their lives, about their sex. It didn't matter if their thing was botany, or the Soviet Union, or cunnilingus; when they talked to her, she felt like she was sitting in the back row of a lecture. Dean, on the other hand, listened. He didn't interrupt when she talked about California politics, nor did he try to correct her understanding of trickle-down economics. And when they slept together, he was genuinely interested in what pleased her; when he asked her if she liked something, it wasn't a statement, but an honest question. Other men had called her difficult—actually, she just needed to be heard.

A year later, when they got engaged, she sent Christos an invitation to the wedding. It was a rash move; after polishing off a bottle of wine one night, she wrote his address on an envelope, fixed it with a few extra stamps, and slipped it into the mailbox outside her apartment building. For a moment she stood there, her hand on the rusted handle, the streetlamps flickering above her. She told herself she was being friendly, mature; they had both moved on, and she wanted him to know what was happening in her life. Beneath that, though, was something else: the giddy terror of self-sabotage. A message, written between lines of calligraphy on cheap, white stationery: *Here's your last chance, maláka. Come and get me.* When she awoke, hungover, the next morning, she held a hand over her eyes to block out the light. She calmed her nerves by telling herself the invitation wouldn't make it to Aegina in time. And even if, by some miracle of the Greek postal system, it did, it would be too last minute; Christos would never be able to afford a flight.

But then he showed up. Not to the wedding itself, but to her apartment two days before it. He knocked on her door with the same rhythm that he used to knock on her door at the Alectrona—one short rap, two long ones—and when she opened it, he was there, holding his hat in both of his hands. For a moment, they stood there, staring at each other. Christos offered a timid smile, and Sue Ellen threw her arms around him. She held him an unnaturally long time; twice he gently tried to pull away, but she clutched him harder. She didn't want him to see her face. She worried that if he did, he would immediately see what she was feeling—the sudden regret of getting what she thought she wanted.

Finally, once she had gathered herself, she said, "Jesus Christ."

"Actually, it's Christos."

She laughed and wiped her eyes.

"That's not funny," she said.

In the apartment, she cleared a spot on her futon for him to sit. Then she brewed a pot of coffee and filled two mugs. His she kept black—after four years, she still remembered how he liked it; hers she topped off with two fingers of whiskey.

"I just—" she started. "I just can't believe you're here."

"I got your invitation," he said. "I called the airline and reserved a seat an hour later," he said.

"What were you thinking? That must have cost a fucking fortune."

"I don't know." He shook his head. He looked foggy, tired. "I just—I just did it. I was somewhere over the ocean when I realized that you might not want to see me, and that, maybe, it was a bad idea."

"Don't be ridiculous, of course I want to see you."

"But you think it was a bad idea."

"No," she said, too quickly. "Or, if it is, it's not your fault. I—it wasn't fair of me to invite you."

He nodded. "I hadn't been on a plane in so long. I kind of forgot that you couldn't tell the captain to turn around if you changed your mind."

They were both quiet. A siren passed outside, and Christos blew a cloud of steam from his mug.

He said, "I was hoping that you might reconsider getting married."

Standing, she sipped from her coffee, swishing it around until she felt the whiskey burn her gums. She ran her hand through her hair, then over her face. She kept it there for what she knew was too long, blinking her lashes against her knuckles, listening to the clock as it counted the seconds on the wall.

"I have an idea," she said to him, finally.

"What?"

"Let's go to the city."

They ended up in Golden Gate Park. There was a pair of windmills there that, for all the years she had been living in the Bay Area, she had never been motivated enough to visit. Then, two years before, she'd read a story about them in the *Chronicle* and was reminded that they existed. Apparently, they had been built in the early 1900s as a cheaper way to pump groundwater to the park. A few years later, though, electricity replaced the need for air, and the windmills were left to crumble. Now, an effort was under way to restore at least one of them—the so-called Dutch windmill, in the northwest corner of the park. She explained all this to Christos, in the same way that she might explain the excavation of Pylos or Troy. She hadn't mentioned his proposition since they had left Berkeley, and now she hoped that, in cordoning it off with some other history, she might escape it altogether.

"The sails are one hundred and two feet long," she said.

Christos wasn't looking. His head was turned west, where the park ended and the ocean began.

He said, "Fascinating."

It was a breezeless July day. Clouds hung idle in the sky, and the windmill loomed, frozen. Ten yards away, down a small slope of grass, a group of twentysomethings sprawled out on a bedsheet, drinking bottled beer and toggling with the knobs on a portable radio. After a minute or so they landed on a station, and Soft Cell's "Tainted Love" began drifting through the park. Leaning back on her elbows, Sue Ellen worked her feet out of her Keds and focused on the music—she had heard that song everywhere this summer, and now she wanted to see if she could forget the words. Next to her, Christos sat with his legs crossed and plucked blades of grass. He had on the same shirt that he'd worn when Sue Ellen first checked in to the Alectrona four years earlier, a blue oxford with a pea-size grease stain on its bottom hem. She wondered if he remembered, and then decided that he did. It was easier that way, to paint him as a person capable of such petty manipulations, even when she knew that he wasn't. Even when she knew that he owned a total of six shirts, three of which he actually wore.

"Where are you staying?" she asked him.

"At a hotel."

"Which one?"

"The Roadway Inn, in Oaktown."

"Oak*land*. How is it?"

"The soap is wrapped in plastic," he said. "But at least I don't have to iron the sheets."

"You can't win them all, I guess."

"Tainted Love" ended and was replaced with a DJ's voice. *You're listening to KFRC. Nonstop hits for a nonstop city.*

Christos asked, "Do you want to marry this man?"

"That's a shitty question." She pressed her heels into the soil. It was hot, and the earth beneath the grass felt cool. "How's Teresa?"

"She's gone. There's— I'm seeing someone else. Agatha is her name."

"Does she know where you are?"

"I said I had business up north. In Thessaloniki."

"That's convenient."

Sue Ellen dug through her purse for her cigarettes before remembering that, a week ago, after promising Dean that she would quit before the wedding, she had thrown the pack away. Now all she could find was an old stick of gum. She broke it in two and handed one half to Christos.

"What would you do if I told you I didn't want to marry him?" she said.

"I would tell you to come back with me." He chewed, the gum cracking between his molars.

She listened for another song but heard nothing. The twentysomethings were gone; they had packed up their radio and their blanket and left.

"Well, I can't do that," Sue Ellen said.

"Why not?"

"Because."

There was more to say, a flood of explanations that churned against her teeth. *Why not?* Because, Christos, we are too late. Because I have fallen in love with someone else; because I have made a choice. Because despite what our poets tell us, we contain no multitudes, no alternate endings. We are like Homer's Dawn, who was not marigold, or violet, but was rose, and only rose. We are epithets. Dean the Lost, Christos Who Regrets, Clear-Eyed Sue Ellen. Singular reductions that strip us of all the people we wish we were but can never truly be. And to forget this is to truck in fantasy. A life of second chances that call to us, luring our ships closer and closer to the gun-gray rocks.

She told him none of this. Instead, she repeated herself. She said, again, "Because."

Collapsing back onto the grass, she stared up at the windmill. There was still no breeze, but she told herself that if she focused hard enough she could will the wings to move. They didn't, though, and it wasn't until Christos leaned over to brush some hair from her face that she realized that she had started to cry.

"*Agape mou,*" he said. "What's wrong?"

"Nothing."

"I don't believe you." He was still leaning over her, and she could smell the gum—stale peppermint—on his breath. When he kissed her, she let him, if only for a second—she wanted to see if she remembered how he felt—and then she turned her head away.

"I'm sorry. I shouldn't have done that."

"No," she said, "you shouldn't have."

He looked up at the windmill and pulled his knees up to his chest.

"Well," he said. "You can't win them all, I guess."

The next morning, she woke early and drove to his hotel, the Roadside Inn in Oakland. In four hours, her parents would be arriving from Washington; in twenty-four hours, she would be married. She didn't know what she wanted to happen in the meantime—to be convinced, maybe. To hear Christos make his case, then make it again. To be reminded that, in spite of her recent decisions, there were choices she could still make. It was a rash, stupid decision, and as she merged onto the exit from the highway, she turned up the radio and cursed herself. She didn't know what she was thinking: a day wasn't long enough to change a life.

She rang the bell on the front desk, and ten seconds later, when no one had appeared, she rang it again. A half-empty rack of tourism brochures stood in the lobby's corner, along with a percolating Mr. Coffee machine. From where she stood she could smell it—weak grinds, mixed with whatever industrial bleach the cleaning staff used the night before. Next to it was a fake plant—a silk Kentia palm, its leaves a startling and perfect shade of green. She was hungry and a little hungover. Yesterday, after leaving Christos in the park, she had gone to have an early dinner alone and ended up drinking a bottle of wine. When Dean called in the evening to check in, she told him that she was expecting a call from her mother, and she needed to keep the line free. She was worried about talking to him for too long. She didn't want him to know she was drunk.

Turning, she prepared to ring the bell again. This time, though, a woman stopped her.

"Twice is enough," she said. "In fact, I heard you the first time."

"I'm sorry"—Sue Ellen read the woman's name tag—"Barbara. I'm just . . . I'm sort of in a rush."

"Check-in isn't until two."

"I'm not checking in. I'm looking for someone."

"We don't give out room numbers without guests' permission."

Barbara wore a denim shirt and a pair of burgundy corduroys. She smelled like cigarette smoke and rose perfume, and in her left hand she held a half-eaten bran muffin.

"Maybe you can phone him for me, then."

"Maybe you can tell me his name." Barbara picked up the phone and sneered. Sue Ellen saw a gash of red lipstick on her front tooth. She considered telling her, and then didn't.

"Christos," she said. "Christos Papadakis."

Barbara set the phone down and took a bite from the muffin.

"Mexican guy?"

"He's Greek."

Barbara wiped something from the corner of her lip—a crumb—and flicked it to the floor.

She said, "Whatever he is, he's not here. He left last night."

Eleni

At first, Sue Ellen's stories come unpredictably and in trickles. Her past, it seems to Eleni, is like a fistful of sand: occasionally a few grains escape, slipping through cracks between her knuckles. There's little rhyme or reason to it. A chair reminds her of a hike, while a hike calls to mind a day at the beach. Eleni does her best to indulge her, listening with an uneasy charity. She watches as Sue Ellen disappears into herself, her eyes glazing over and her lips curling into a smile. Stopping her there, at the edge of nostalgia, would be worse than impolite, she figures. It would be cruel.

Two days after their lunch in Perdika, they stand shoulder to shoulder in the Alectrona's kitchen preparing dinner. Eleni's never considered herself much of a cook—tonight will be the seventh time in eighteen days that she's made the Wrights moussaka—and so she was relieved when, earlier today, Sue Ellen asked if she might help. Now, she watches as she finishes slicing half an onion, which she stirs into a saucepan, along with cinnamon, ginger, and ground lamb. Her eyes water at the scent, and so it's through a film of tears that she watches Sue Ellen wipe her hands on a dishtowel and reach up to unclasp her necklace.

"It's too long," she says, setting it on the counter. "It gets in the way when I cook."

Eleni picks it up. From its chain hangs a pendant the size of a small thimble.

"It's pretty," she says.

Sue Ellen throws a pinch of allspice into the saucepan.

"Your dad bought it for me," she says.

Lifting the necklace to the light, Eleni inspects the pendant more closely. There's something on its surface, she sees—the cryptic remains of a half-erased face.

She says, "You're joking."

Sue Ellen reaches past her for a wooden spoon.

"That surprises you?"

"The only time my dad bought me jewelry, it was a mood ring. He let me wear it for one day before he told me to take it off because he was worried that when it turned green it was too suggestive."

Sue Ellen shrugs and stirs the lamb. "The gods used mortals to act out their follies," she says. "I suspect that parents do the same with their children."

Eleni sets the necklace back on the counter, pooling its chain in a loose circle. Then she reaches for an eggplant, which she begins to cut into thick, meaty slices.

"When did he give it to you?" she asks.

Sue Ellen smiles. "The day before I left," she says. "I was in my room packing when I heard this terrible honking coming from outside the inn. The two other guests who'd been staying there had left that morning. They were this British couple who were always complaining about not having enough ice in their drinks. God, I can still remember their faces. Anyway, I thought they might have forgotten something—they came with enough luggage to last them the whole summer, even though they were only there a week. Your grandparents weren't there, which means it must have been Sunday; the only time they both left the inn together was when they went to church. So, the honking continues, and I start to get worried that something might actually be wrong, so I go downstairs to see what it's all about.

"It was your father. He was sitting on the back of this beat-up red scooter, yelling at me to get on. He hadn't even turned off the engine. I asked him where he got it, and he told me not to worry about it. I pressed him again, and he said he borrowed it, and he'd return it before whoever owned it knew it was gone." Here, she shakes her head. "God, we went everywhere. Souvala, Cape Tourlos, Portes. Honestly, I think we probably drove down every road on the island. When we were done we drank negronis down near the harbor, and he bought me that."

She sets the spoon down and picks up the necklace, wrapping the chain around her finger.

"It's cheap, obviously. He bought it at one of those souvenir shops that has racks and racks of worry beads. The pendant used to have a little engraving of Hermes. It's been rubbed away, mostly, but if you look closely and sort of squint, you can still see one of his winged sandals. Either that, or it's just a scratch." She hands the necklace to Eleni. "Hermes was the patron and protector of travelers. Thieves and orators, too, but for your father, travelers were most important. He said he wanted me to have a safe trip."

"A safe trip where?"

"Home, I suppose. Or wherever I was going."

The lamb sizzles, and Sue Ellen uses the spoon to scrape it away from the pan's edge.

"You can have it, if you want," she says.

"The necklace?"

"Sure. Would you like to keep it?"

Eleni looks down at it, the chain running along the lines of her palm.

"Yes," she says. "I actually think I would."

There are more memories. Sweeping pine needles from the Alectrona's front stoop, she hears of how, on those rare afternoons when she and Christos were the only two people in the inn, they used to clear the tables from the dining room, put on records, and dance.

Setting down the dustpan, she says, "He loved Joe Dassin."

Eleni angles a pile of pine needles with her broom.

"I don't think I know him," she says.

"French guy. Big in the seventies." Sue Ellen stands and empties the pan. "Great hair, but he sang some really god-awful stuff."

Later, when Eleni's heating the *briki* to make her afternoon coffee, Sue Ellen tells her how, on a weekend in June, she and Christos had taken a trip north, to the island of Skopelos.

"Your grandparents shut the inn for the last two days of the Apostles' Fast, so they let us skip town. To get there we had to take two buses and what had to have been the slowest ferry in Greece, but it was worth it. I dragged him to Agios Ioannis, this little chapel on top of a huge rock along the coast. The only way to get up or down from it is this *terrifying* set of steep stone stairs. On one side you've got the cliff's face, and on the other side, nothing, at least back then. No rope, no guardrail—just a hundred-meter drop to the rocks. Going up, Christos was fine, but on the way back, he froze. Only way he could do it was to sit on his ass and scoot himself down, one step at a time." Sue Ellen laughs. "He was so pissed. I don't think he spoke to me again until dinner."

Eleni smiles.

"That's hilarious."

She fills two demitasses, handing one of them to Sue Ellen, then taking a scalding sip from her own. She doesn't say what she's really thinking: that she never knew her father was afraid of heights.

That night, she sits at the desk in her bedroom, passing the necklace back and forth between her hands as she waits for her laptop to power up. In a week she's scheduled to be in Athens to sign the closing documents with Lugn's attorneys, and she needs to reserve a spot on an early ferry.

Earlier today, she had invited Sue Ellen to come with her. When she mentioned that she needed to be in the city the following evening for a reception at the Hilton, Eleni promptly suggested they ride over together. Ultimately, though, Sue Ellen declined the invitation; there was some writing she intended to do that morning, so whatever ferry she took would need to be in the afternoon. Eleni smiled and, surprised by her disappointment, said she understood.

"It's probably for the best." She laughed. "I always end up passing out and drooling on ferries, anyway."

Now she books a spot on a ten o'clock hydrofoil, which will put her in Piraeus around eleven. Once she's finished, she brushes her teeth and crawls into bed. For the next hour, she stares at the ceiling, unable to sleep; she keeps replaying the stories she's heard of her father. They play on loop—a supercut of Christos scooting downstairs, stealing a moped, and doing the twist in the dining room. They haunt her until they start to disappear, at which point she goes searching for them again.

Still awake around midnight, she hauls herself back to her desk and her laptop. Tapping her fingers on each side of the screen, she thinks for a moment, letting her eyes adjust to the blue light. Then she searches for images of Agios Ioannis, the church Sue Ellen and her father visited on Skopelos. The Wi-Fi is weak; it takes awhile for the results to load, though when they finally do she clicks on the most detailed photograph she can find, a panoramic shot of the site, the Aegean pressed up against the sky. She's never been to Skopelos. Work has certainly never called her there, and when she was at the university, she preferred to take her holidays on the mainland—what's the point of going to an island, she figured, when you've spent most of your life trying to get off one? Now, zooming in, she stares at the little chapel, perched atop its giant rock. She wonders if you can hear the surf when you're that high—if the sound of the waves travels, or if it vanishes halfway up the cliff. It's one of those questions Christos could have answered for her, she realizes, if she'd ever thought hard enough to ask. Looking closer, she's surprised to see that there are people in the photo. She can't tell much about them, other than that they're there— tiny, faceless smudges on the stairs and at the chapel's door. She picks one of them—a red dot near the cliff's edge—and decides that it's her father. Smoking a cigarette as he surveys a new patch of sea.

After saving the image to her desktop, she returns to Google, this time typing in Joe Dassin, the singer Sue Ellen had mentioned. For a few minutes, she reads snippets of his biography: born in America; grew up in Europe; married twice; died during a vacation in Tahiti. Then she scrolls down further. There, toward the middle of the page, she finds a link to a video of him singing. The footage is black-and-white, and grainy; lines cut across his face as he leans into the microphone. She can't tell what he's saying, but even still, she's inclined to agree with Sue Ellen: it's soupy, maudlin music. The sort of stuff that she imagines makes French grandmothers weak in the knees. When it's over, she says, aloud, "Jesus, Dad, this is really bad," before reaching down and playing it again.

And then, two days later, she learns the rest. Sue Ellen's fist springs open, and the memories that are left within it come pouring out.

Early in the afternoon they ride bikes down to Aegina Marina, on the east side of the island. Sue Ellen swears there's a market there that sells Aegina's best sour cherries, and she wants to pick up a few jars for her son before they fly home. "They're too sweet for me, but he's addicted to them," she says once they've left the store. "Then again, I guess cherries are better than heroin." Afterward, they get lunch and drink two beers along the quay before beginning the ride back to the Alectrona. Ten minutes in, though, there's a pop, followed by a fierce hiss. Sue Ellen has run over a broken bottle, and now her back tire sags, flat.

"I'll call Stavros," Eleni offers, digging in her pocket for her mobile.

Sue Ellen leans down and plucks a shard of glass from the rubber.

"Actually," she says, "how about we walk."

It's then, in the hour that follows, that she unspools the rest of her history with Christos: a kiss and missed ferries; a wedding invitation and a botched, last-minute trip to California. Eleni is silent as she speaks, focused only on the sound of Sue Ellen's voice and the uneven slap of the tire as it rolls over rocks and dirt. Every so often a car will pass, its driver beeping the horn and waving, and in those moments Sue Ellen stops and waves back. Then she waits, keeping quiet until the car has disappeared behind a bend or a cloud of red dust—nervous, it seems, that someone else might hear what she has to say.

Now, as she finishes, Eleni stops walking and turns around, her left hand steadying her bike.

"So, you were in love with him," she says.

Sue Ellen adjusts her backpack.

"We were very young," she says. "It was before he met Agatha."

"You don't have to apologize. You can say you were in love with him."

Overhead, a warbler alights on a branch, beating its wings a few times before settling. Sue Ellen watches it, then turns to Eleni.

"Okay," she says. "Yes. I was in love with him. Very much so, as it turns out."

"And do you regret not staying with him? Or not going back with him, when he asked you to in San Francisco?"

"That's a very personal question."

"I'm sorry." Eleni rests the bike against her hip. "We can talk about something else."

Sue Ellen lifts her sunglasses and sets them on top of her head.

"No, it's fine. It's just something that I've thought a lot about."

"And?"

"And no. I don't regret it."

Cicadas buzz in the brush on each side of the road. The sun, well into its descent, ducks behind a pine tree.

"Why not?"

Sue Ellen scratches a mosquito bite on her right ankle with her left foot. Her shoes, once white, are now caked in red soil.

She says, "Because I couldn't keep running away to what was behind me."

"But if you loved him . . ."

Sue Ellen looks at her.

"Have you ever been in love?" she asks.

"Of course," Eleni says, though this is a lie. She suspects she's gotten close, one time with a classmate she used to tutor in calculus, another with a bartender who worked at an Irish pub near the university. Both affairs ended quickly—her classmate left school to work for his uncle up north; the bartender met a rich girl from Ekali and stopped calling back. A flame snuffed out as soon as the match was lit.

"So, you know what I'm talking about, then," Sue Ellen says. "You fall in love, but you make other plans. Life, unfortunately, is longer than a summer."

It's dusk by the time they finally arrive at the Alectrona. Above them, the night's first stars pierce a scrim of purple and blue. Sue Ellen offers to help change the bike's flat tire, but Eleni tells her not to worry, they can take care of it tomorrow. They're both exhausted, anyway, and she wouldn't mind cleaning up a bit before dinner. Alone in the bathroom, she wets a washcloth and scrubs her face, watching in the mirror as her cheeks grow red and clean. Letting the faucet run, she finds herself thinking of what would have happened if Sue Ellen had stayed. It is, admittedly, a curious thing to picture—a version of the past where Christos never met Agatha and Eleni was never born. But it's also one that's vital and unburdened by regret. Where Christos danced, and bought cheap jewelry; where he was willing to fly halfway around the world because he had fallen madly and improbably in love.

Will

They are, if nothing else, a family of books: books they read, books they study, books they collect. Books they dream of someday writing; books they stress over and abandon; books that win fortune and fame. He remembers when his mother kicked his father out. Dean had brought with him his suitcase, some boxes, and a trash bag full of books. It was unclear which ones he'd selected until, days later, Sue Ellen asked Will if he'd seen her copy of *The Complete Works of Sappho*.

"I haven't," he told her. It was Saturday afternoon, and Will had come home to check on his mother. They were both in the living room, where he had draped himself over an easy chair. Now he hauled himself up to join Sue Ellen in front of the bookcase. For the most part, it was full—overflowing, really. Dog-eared and decaying editions of Anne Carson and Aristophanes, of Steinbeck and Szymborska and Calvino, grew in piles on the floor. On the shelves, though, there were a few conspicuous holes: empty slots where titles had been removed.

"I guess Dad took it," he said.

For a moment, his mother said nothing. Down the hall, halfway to the kitchen, an old grandfather clock—the same one that Will had broken as a teenager and had to pay a thousand dollars to have repaired—chimed four times.

"He hates Sappho," she said.

"Maybe he decided to give her another try."

"No, I don't think that's it," Sue Ellen said.

She tucked her hair behind her ears and reached for a copy of *Elektra* instead.

So, yes: a family of books. Books as secrets; books as betrayals; books as a means of cryptic but unmistakable revenge. Books that—in Will's case—are forgotten, not at home, but in the seat-back pockets of Athens-bound planes. It was a copy of *The Brothers Karamazov* that his father had given him three years ago, after his first tumultuous year at Berkeley. He hadn't read it yet, he just couldn't get into it, though he suspected this was his own fault, not Dostoevsky's. Dean agreed with him and had taken to mocking him for it with a sort of relentlessness that Will suspected was only appropriate when discussing Russian literature. So, on the ferry to Aegina, when he demanded that Will sit down and read—when he told him that he was already seasick, and if there was one thing that would make him actually vomit, it would be having to endure another nanosecond of his son's pacing—Will panicked. He fumbled through excuses before admitting, sheepishly, that he had left the book on the plane.

"Well," his father said. His cheeks had taken on a pale green pallor. "That wasn't very smart."

"I'm sorry," Will said. "I promise I'll buy another copy when we get back."

"Don't bother." Dean wiped his forehead with a handkerchief. "Best to leave it for someone who will actually read it."

Now Will wades waist-deep into the Alectrona's pool while, on opposite ends of the stone deck, his parents flip through paperbacks. They're both splayed out on green chaise longues and are, for the first time this trip, wearing bathing suits: Dean has opted for a pair of red trunks, Sue

Ellen a black one-piece. Running his hand an inch above the water's surface, he looks at his father's legs, which are drooped on either side of the chair. They're white, but with a faint pinkish tinge; beneath the skin, veins sprout purple branches. There's hair, but it's mostly gathered around his ankles and calves; anywhere above the knee, the strands are sparse and patchy. It always sort of startles Will, seeing his parents in various states of undress. It's why he was happy they had to wear wet suits when they took surfing lessons in France. He knows they have bodies, of course, but checking in on them like this—seeing their naked and unshielded selves—reminds him that they're old and that, by extension, he is no longer young.

Planting his hands against the rough stone, he hauls himself up out of the pool and sits on the deck. From behind him, he hears his mother say, "Will, sweetie, what do you say about getting us some beers?"

He does. He wipes his feet down with the edge of his mother's towel and trots across the hot stone to the Alectrona's kitchen. He pops the tops off two bottles of Mythos before grabbing his phone from his room and returning to the backyard.

The hotel's Wi-Fi is spotty, particularly here, on the back terrace, but once he snags a strong enough connection, he opens Instagram and returns to Rajiv's feed. He's held off looking at it for three days—a feat that he pegs as something bordering on heroic—but now, with nothing else to do, he figures he'll allow himself to indulge. The new posts are, by and large, the same as the old ones: pictures of Rajiv and Logan with their shirts off, paired with quotes about being true to yourself, loving who you love, and not listening to the *haters,* even though, as far as Will can tell, there aren't any *haters* to be found. The only real difference he can spot is an increase in photos taken at Fama. Rajiv eating cupcakes with François in the office's dessert bar. Rajiv, with François standing next to him, holding a mock-up of a tube of potato chips. *Proud to announce Pringle's newest flavor, named by yours truly,* the caption says. *Thanks to big man F for all his <3 and support.* Zooming in on the picture, Will squints and reads the copy printed on the tube: THE RIDGE-CUT FIRE-ROASTED CHIPOTLE POTATO CHIP.

He whispers: "You fucking thief."

Then he deletes Instagram and downloads Grindr instead.

Or—no. Perhaps more specifically, he re-downloads Grindr, as Grindr has a curious tendency of disappearing and reappearing on his phone, depending on factors ranging from boredom to intoxication to loneliness. This is, however, the first time he's opened the app here, on the island. To that end, he doesn't know what he expects to find—though, for being in Greece, he is a little puzzled by how few, well, *Greeks* appear to be within his general vicinity. Rather, Aeginan Grindr seems to have been colonized almost exclusively by tourists. Still, he plays along; he engages in his standard ritual of scrolling and zooming and poking pictures of headless torsos. He reduces himself to a single photo and adopts the app's mindless vernacular *(hey, whats up, into?)*. Once he's exhausted his possibilities, he refreshes the screen, watching the images reload into a new (though actually the same) checkerboard of flesh. This lasts for about ten minutes, a period during which Sue Ellen leaves the pool deck to make a sandwich and Dean looks up from his book to ask, "What are you doing over there?"

Will clicks on a thumbnail—a zoomed-in shot of a biceps, a ghost arm that's not attached to a body or face.

"Nothing, really," he says. "Just playing around."

Dean picks up his book again.

He says, "I never knew *just playing around* required so much focus."

Will doesn't answer. He's just received a new message—a four-word missive from a blank black box.

It says: *Look who it is.*

He types back *who is this* and a moment later receives an answer in the form of a picture: the waiter, Dio, leaning against a redbrick wall.

Oh ha hey

You never came sailing

Sorry went to delphi w my family

oh right. how was that

great—found out what my future will be

and?

pretty bleak

A minute passes and Dio doesn't respond.

Then Will's phone buzzes.

Dio says: *wanna get a beer or something*

Will looks at his father. He's fallen asleep and has draped his book across his face like an eyeless mask.

He types *sure.*

He's worried that he's wearing the wrong thing.

This is what Will's thinking as he watches Dio disappear into the bar to order their third round of drinks. Had they not arranged to meet on a hookup app, it would have been easy; he would have traded in his wet trunks for a pair of shorts, thrown on a shirt, and biked into town. The context of the app added a layer of complication, though. While he was *relatively* sure they would not be having sex, he was also not *entirely* sure; the pressure of it, however obscure, was still there, haunting the periphery of their conversation. As such, while he was getting ready he had felt a certain obligation to appear, to some extent, sex-worthy. What sex-worthy meant in Greece, though, was still something of a mystery to him. So he ironed a blue oxford. Inspecting himself in the mirror, though, he decided that a button-down was too stuffy, too *Talented Mr. Ripley*; this wasn't a date, and he didn't want to show up looking like he thought it was. He traded it in for a tank top, a white one that Rajiv always used to say made him look tan, before Rajiv left him for Logan from Laguna Beach and a life of stealing Will's names for potato chips.

Now he's sure he made the wrong choice. While the shirt might make him look tan, it also makes his arms look skinny and his shoulders too thin. He feels like a hanger, the cotton draping off him, swallowing him up. Maybe he should have gone for the oxford, something that made him look a little older, a little more serious.

"Mythos is basically piss water," Dio says, setting two glasses filled with a clear liquid down on the table. "I thought this time we could try something a little bit stronger."

He's wearing a striped shirt and jean shorts that nearly reach his knees. A few days ago, when he had been his waiter, Will guessed Dio was a year or two older than him; he sees now, though, that he's probably approaching thirty. Crow's-feet crease the corners of his eyes, and there are gray patches in the stubble of his beard.

"What is this?" Will asks, picking up the glass.

"Ouzo."

Will sniffs it. His eyes water.

Dio reaches out with his own glass and knocks it against Will's.

"You can't come to Greece without drinking it at least once."

Will takes a sip, and it burns his throat, leaving his mouth feeling rancid. Running his tongue over his teeth, he stares at the glass and watches the liquor grow cloudy as a single ice cube melts. Then he goes for a second sip. It tastes like licorice, he decides—the black, tarry kind his grandparents used to eat.

He says, "It's delicious."

"It's not. No one thinks it is, except for old *pappouses* who've burned all their taste buds off, anyway. But you're a good man for lying."

"I actually don't know if I can finish it."

"Sure you can—it'll put some hair on your chest. Just give it a second. Forget how bad it tastes, and take it all down in one swallow."

The bar that he's brought them to is called Captain Ioannis'. It's on the harbor's main drag, though at the opposite end of it from Taverna Karalis, the restaurant where Dio works. Inside there's a lukewarm commitment to a nautical theme: two of the barstools are wrapped in rope; a lifesaver hangs above the bathroom door. Outside there are a handful of tables, and it's here where Will and Dio sit. For most of their conversation the focus has been on Will, and this makes him uncomfortable. He doesn't want to be perceived as someone who talks solely about himself. Each time he tries to ask a question, though, Dio immediately responds with another one, swerving around answers like they're traffic cones. The result has been a sort of extended interview in which Will has described, among other things, his mother *(lovely)*, his father *(brilliant)*, and his postgraduate plans *(uh, not yet defined?)*. He has offered up opinions on the Alectrona, and Eleni Papadakis, and the food on Aegina. Once in a while, Dio will respond with an insight (the Alectrona: *I can't believe it's still around;* Eleni Papadakis: *terrifying;* the island's food: *it's not as fresh as you think*). Mostly, though, he just sits, nodding. Rambling on, Will wonders if Dio's actually listening or if he's just happy not to talk.

But now he senses an opening: Dio downs the rest of his ouzo, and before he has time to ask something else, Will says:

"So, Queens?"

He swallows, grimacing. "Astoria. Born and sort of raised."

"When did you move here?"

"When I was fifteen, after my mom died." Dio looks into the empty glass, then sets it on the table. "Fuck, that stuff is rough."

"I'm sorry. About your mom, I mean."

"Oh, it's fine. I mean it's not, but it is."

"How'd she die?"

"Liver failure."

"Was she—"

"An alcoholic? No. As it turns out, she just had a really bad liver."

"Wow."

"That was a joke. She had a pint of gin every day for lunch." Dio looks behind him, back toward the bar. "After telling you that, do you think it'd be tacky for me to order another drink?"

"Uh, no? Or, I don't know? She was your mom—I think that's probably your call."

Dio doesn't go to the bar. Instead, he stays seated. He cracks his neck, angling it from side to side, before stretching his arms over his head. As he does so, the bottom hem of his shirt raises an inch, exposing a landscape of skin and hair, a single small mole.

Will looks down. He swirls around what's left of his ouzo and wonders how long he can delay finishing it.

"So why'd you move back to Aegina?" he asks.

"My dad grew up here. As soon as it was just the two of us, he started making plans to leave Astoria."

"He didn't like New York?"

"He hated it." Dio works his knuckles, pressing his thumb on top of each one until there's a quiet crack. "It was my mom's idea to move, I guess. They met here, when they were teenagers. The way he tells it, they had this storybook romance. Walks on the beach, moonlight swims, dancing. Really, the whole nine yards. It can't be true, though. I mean, my mother fucking hated dancing."

He reaches for Will's glass, and Will doesn't stop him. He just watches as Dio finishes the ouzo, the muscles in his throat contracting as he swallows.

"Anyway, I think what actually happened is that Mom saw Dad as a meal ticket and a way to get out of here. His family had a little bit of money, at least at the time, and I think she probably told him that she would agree to marry him if he agreed to move to New York."

"He never told you any of this?"

A stray cat curls itself around Dio's leg, and he kicks it away.

"No," he says. "Not directly, at least. She trained him pretty good to keep his mouth shut. After she died, though—I was thirteen—he started to let things slip."

"Like what?"

Two yards from their table, at the border of the patio and the sidewalk, the cat begins preening itself, licking its paws and cleaning its face.

"Oh, just that it had been her idea to come to New York, and that he had always hated it. I remember him having this total breakdown once after coming back from the store. The trains were all fucked up, and it was raining, and his grocery bags got wet and ripped, and when he showed up at our apartment his arms were filled with these soggy boxes of cereal and the pockets of his coat were stuffed with soup cans. He started scream-ing that hell would be better than the city, because at least in hell you know things are miserable, whereas the city promises you convenience but then secretly conspires to make even the smallest things hard."

He runs a hand over his head, working knots out from the dark waves of hair. "Anyway, he started making plans for us to leave that night. I know it sounds morbid, but I think he actually ended up being happy that Mom died. It meant that we could come back here."

"Were you happy to come back?"

"Me? Fuck, no. I was furious. I told him that as soon as I was old enough to be on my own, I'd be back in Queens. I was fifteen, though. And when you're fifteen your entire world consists of what's in front of your face."

"And now you're . . ."

"How old am I? I'm thirty-two." He tears at a fingernail with his teeth and spits it over his left shoulder. "I'm thirty-two, and I'm still here."

The sun clears the patio's awning, and for a moment Will is blinded. He reaches for his sunglasses, then blinks, letting his eyes adjust. Across the street, a long line of boats is tied up against the quay, a wall of hulls and masts that rocks gently with each new wake.

"Where's your dad now?"

"Here, on the island. He lives in town, about fifteen minutes from here."

"You live in town, too?"

"I live with him."

"Ah."

"Yes, I know. I'm thirty-two, and I live with my father."

"No, no." Will blushes. "It's not that. I'm sorry. It's just—that must be hard."

"It is. I want to kill him half the time." He drums his fingers on the table. "He's old, though. He needs my help."

"Does he . . . does he, like, know about you?"

"Does he know what about me?"

"Does he know that—I don't know, does he know that you're here, with me?"

"You mean does he know that I use the wonders of modern telecommunications to expand my social circle and meet people who are not from this fucking island? No. He does not."

Will thinks for a moment and says, "I always tell people that Grindr is the best guide for tourists."

"So do I." Dio smiles. "But I think we're saying two different things."

Will stretches his legs out and accidently brushes up against Dio's calf. Pulling them back, he apologizes.

"You apologize too much, you know that?"

Will nearly says he's sorry but stops himself. He asks, instead, "You got plans tomorrow?"

"I was thinking of taking one of the school's sabots out in the afternoon, depending on the wind."

"What school?"

"The Saronic Yachting Academy. The place where I teach, and where you never showed up."

"Very funny."

"Yeah, well, I'm a funny guy." Dio looks at their bill and throws a few euros on the table. "You want to come?"

"Okay." Will takes a deep breath. "O-*kay*."

He squints. Gripping both ends of the rope between his sunburnt fingers, he twists it and recites aloud: "You make a hole, then the rabbit comes out of it, and then goes around the tree, and then dives back through the hole, and . . ." He pulls the rope, but nothing happens. Or—nothing that's supposed to happen happens; instead of a clean bowline knot, all he's left with is a tangle of nylon.

"Shit," he says, and drops the rope to the floor of the boat, one of the Saronic Yachting Academy's tiny sabots. The collar of his T-shirt is caked with salt and sweat. Beneath him, water sloshes against the hull. He says, again: *"Shit."*

He woke early that morning and, in lieu of a shower (they're still broken), he dove into the Alectrona's pool. Then, over breakfast in the dining room, he tried to engage Eleni in something resembling a conversation. This didn't quite work—it never does. He always gets the feeling that she's a little too busy, or a little too bored, and so, per usual, he ended up finishing his coffee in his bedroom, taking down the last sips as he spent half an hour looking for jobs. This didn't quite work, either; after an hour of tweaking cover letters he got anxious, which invariably led to thoughts of Dio, and his hair, and that inch of skin above his waistband. He felt a surge of anticipation and nerves. A lightness in the knees that caused him to think that, maybe, Rajiv leaving him was a good thing—that, without that catastrophe, he might have forgotten how fun it was to have a crush.

Now Dio hands Will the rudder. "Don't get frustrated," he says. "That doesn't help."

He picks up the rope and Will watches as he begins to untangle it, his rough fingers prying at the knot. As he works he crouches down, resting his ass on his tan calves. His white shorts are stained with grease, and his neck strains as he fusses with Will's mess.

He says, "You've managed to create something pretty complicated here, Mr. Wright."

"I think the rabbit hates me."

"That's a lie," Dio says, finally managing to loosen the rope. "The rabbit loves everyone."

"I don't know if I love the rabbit."

"But you must!" He coils the untangled rope and slides it beneath the bench where Will sits. Then he tousles Will's hair. "The rabbit is what teaches us our knots."

Will says, "I think I hate the rabbit."

He's wearing a life jacket, which digs into the base of his neck, and he reaches up to pull it away as he looks out over the harbor. A hundred yards in front of him a gull bobs along the peaks of tiny swells, every so often leaning over to dip its pointed beak beneath the surface.

"Okay," Dio says, adjusting his sunglasses. A small wave slaps the side of the boat, spritzing Will's face with salt. "Okay, we're going to tack. Remember what I told you?"

"I think so."

"That's good enough."

Reaching down, Will picks up the mainsheet and begins to pull, tightening the sail as the boat gains speed. Quickly, the sabot heels over to the starboard side, the lips of its hull scraping the water's surface.

Dio crouches down and switches to the port side of the boat, where he huddles next to Will. He says, "*Naí*, good. Now steer us into and across the wind."

Will grasps the rudder's handle and swivels it to the right, pivoting the bow. The boat rights itself and Will holds his breath. Then, suddenly, the wind catches the sail again: the mast creaks, and the boom swings inches above their heads. Now heeling to port, they scramble over to the starboard side.

Dio laughs. "You're a natural!"

"A natural who can't tie bowlines."

He nods. "We'll work on that."

An hour later, Will angles the sabot's bow toward the dock as best he can and watches as Dio leans out to catch hold of it. His hips pass over the lip of the hull and the boat rocks precariously to the right; closing his eyes, Will half expects to hear a heavy splash—the sound of his body plunging into the water—but instead is greeted by a dull thud: the sabot, softly meeting its berth.

"Good," Dio says, swinging a leg up and out of the boat. "Now hand me the docking line."

Will does, and Dio holds it as he scrambles onto the dock. It's not easy work; the tide is low, revealing a crosshatch of barnacles and bird shit on the pier's pilings, and to follow Dio and exit the sabot Will has to do a half pull-up, gripping the dock's splintered wood before hauling his body out of it. Once he's standing on solid ground, he runs his teeth over his lower lip and a fleck of skin comes loose: he needs to buy some ChapStick.

"Here," Dio says. "Give me the dock line, and I'll tie us off."

Passing the rope beneath a rusted cleat, he makes a series of figure eights and pulls the loose end of the line, tightening the knot. Three feet below him, the sabot rocks gently, succumbing to the ebbs and flows of the tide.

Dio stands up. He slings both their life vests over his left shoulder, then takes his sunglasses off, letting them dangle from a set of blue, neoprene Croakies.

"I've got a proposition for you," he says. "I'm being paid to sail a boat to Hydra this coming Friday. It's this thing I do sometimes—sail rich people's boats to other islands so they're there when they arrive from wherever they're arriving from. Which, in this case, is Munich, I think. Anyway. It's a big boat. About fifteen meters. I can't handle it on my own. I was wondering if you'd come along to help me."

"You're kidding." Will laughs.

"Why would I be kidding?"

"I've been sailing for, like, three hours."

"These are boats, not spaceships."

Will pulls his left heel out of his espadrille, scratches it against his right leg, and then slips it back into the shoe.

"I don't know," he says. "What if I screw something up?"

"Impossible. You're a natural."

"I think the rabbit would disagree."

Dio cleans his sunglasses with the bottom hem of his shirt and slips them on again.

"Fuck the rabbit," he says. "You're coming."

Eleni

August 1
Aegina

Three hours before she's scheduled to be in Athens to sign the Alectrona's closing documents with Lugn, Eleni knocks on the door to Stavros's house and waits. Then, after a minute has passed and he still hasn't answered, she knocks again. She keeps knocking, her knuckles aching as she calls his name, until, finally, he's there, creaking the door open with a rueful hesitation.

Looking him over once, she says, "Oh, for God's sake, Stavros."

He's donned his best mourning garb: a pressed black suit, paired with a thin matching tie. On his head, he's set a wool cap—also black—which he presently pulls down, adjusting the brim so it nearly shields his eyes. It is, all in all, not a terrible look: the slacks have a flattering cut, and the jacket fills out his shoulders—he appears solid and sturdy, instead of just short. How curious, Eleni thinks: the man can't button his shirt when he comes to work, but cleans up nicely for imaginary funerals.

"A little dramatic, don't you think?" she says.

"It's a sad day."

"I'm going to Athens to sign a contract. That's all that's happening."

"That's one way to look at it."

"And what, pray tell, is the other way?"

He shrugs. "That we're experiencing a death."

She ducks beneath his arm and into his house. "Your ability to turn a piece of property into a person is truly remarkable."

She moves from the foyer to a cramped dining room. There, on a card table, sits a black demitasse, an ashtray, and a newspaper. To the left of the table is a small bookshelf, which holds, among other things, four framed pictures of Stavros and his long-dead wife, along with a small television, switched to Skai TV. When was the last time she was here, she wonders? Fifteen years ago, at least. Maybe even more. It had been for a holiday. Easter. They had just returned from midnight mass and Stavros hovered near the stove, where he prepared the *magiritsa*. He didn't know much about cooking—the best Eleni had known him to make was pasta with melted butter—and every so often she'd hear him yelp or curse. A knife grazing his finger, she thought, or boiling broth searing his skin. Christos, meanwhile, cleared a spot on the floor, a square in between the sofa and a coatrack, where he set down a few cushions and two of the eggs that he and Eleni had boiled and dyed red two nights earlier. Her father coaxed her to sit and, as she listened to Stavros chop dill and onions, he handed her one of the eggs. Then, with the one he had kept for himself, he gently tapped hers and said, *"Christos anesti."*

Eleni smiled. She loved playing *tsougrisma;* it was her favorite part of Easter. Looking down at the bloodred shell, she inspected it for cracks. When she couldn't find one, she tapped his and said, *"Alithos anesti."*

It was, she thinks now, the first time she had played the game with him. In the past, it was her mother who entertained her, knocking her egg against Eleni's as Christos busied himself roasting a lamb. But by that Easter her mother was gone—she had died a few months earlier, in February—and the burden of tradition fell on Christos. It was not a natural fit. He was never comfortable with the theatrical side of parenting. Still, at least early on—before Eleni grew to share his suspicion for sentimentality; before she learned that keeping him at arm's length was easier than admitting she needed him—he did his best to try.

Tightening his grip on his egg, he tapped hers again. *"Christos anesti."*

Again, nothing happened, so she took her turn. *"Alithos anesti."*

This time, there was the fragile sound of a shell cracking. Turning his egg over, Christos pointed to a thin, hairline fracture, along which he ran his finger.

"You beat me," he said. "Well done."

Eleni smiled. "Now I'll have good luck for the rest of my life."

Her father had reached out and set his palm against her cheek.

"Yes," he had told her. "You will."

Now, she tries to rid herself of the memory—the unsettling mix of nostalgia and contrition it stirs in her; the feeling of waking from a dream she can't seem to forget. She skirts past the card table and looks out onto the house's terrace, a walled-in square of tile that contains a hose, an unemptied ashtray, and a terra-cotta pot.

She says, "Growing dirt, are we?"

From somewhere behind her, he answers: "I was getting ready to plant a fig tree. A small one. A *fiddle leaf* fig tree."

"In those clothes?"

"No matter the tragedy, life must endure."

Her back still turned to him, she rolls her eyes.

Then she says, "I like fiddle leaf figs. I'll help."

"You'll help? That's a first. Where's the hidden camera?"

"Knock it off before I change my mind."

He taps her shoulder and hands her a trowel.

"Here," he says. "I'll go get the tree."

She steps out onto the terrace and listens while Stavros bangs around inside. After a few minutes, he emerges carrying a bag of soil in one hand and the tree in the other. It's as tall as she is but looks weak and breakable—a thin stalk topped with ten green, lyre-shaped leaves. The roots are contained in a burlap sack tied together with a piece of twine, and as Stavros teeters toward her, the whole trunk sways, threatening to topple over.

"Careful," Eleni says. "You're going to kill it before it's had a chance to live."

He ignores her and sets the tree down in the pot. Placing his right hand on the small of his back, he stretches.

"Okay," he says. "I'll hold it. You untie the bag."

Eleni nods and does as she is told, reaching down and pulling gently on the twine. The sack unfurls, releasing bits of fertilizer. Pushing them aside, she works the fabric down farther until, finally, she's holding the root cluster, a maze of knots and gnarls, encased in a cone of soil. Carefully, she removes the burlap and sets it down on the floor.

Stavros says, "Grab that bag of soil. The one right there, next to my foot."

"Why can't you be this sure of yourself when it comes to plumbing?"

With both hands she lifts the bag and begins to pour its contents into the pot, distributing the soil on all sides of the roots. Once the bag is empty she crouches down again, this time digging her hands into the dirt, forming it, giving it a sense of integrity and shape.

"You're giving me that look again," she says.

"How do you know how I'm looking at you? Your head's in a pot."

"I can feel it, Stavros. I can *feel* your looks."

For a moment he's silent; all Eleni hears is the sound of the fig leaves, lightly brushing each other in the breeze.

"I just think it's interesting, is all," he says, finally.

"You're going to have to be more specific than that."

"I think"—he clears his throat—"I think you're distracting yourself."

"From what?"

"From going to Athens. From signing something you don't want to sign and giving away something you're not ready to lose."

"How convenient." She straightens the tree's trunk, edging it to the right. "I'm helping you—that's all. You help me, and now I'm helping you."

Stavros ignores her. He says, "An hour ago you called me to say that you had to catch the ferry. You said that you didn't have time for me to drive your dry cleaning up to the Alectrona, and that you'd just pick it up here on the way to town because you were—and I quote—*in a huge rush.* And yet, now here you are, up to your elbows in fertilizer, helping me plant a fig tree."

Eleni looks down and lets her hair fall in her face. She keeps her fingers in the soil, burying them up to the second knuckle. The dirt's cool, and as she digs deeper, she can feel it working its way beneath her nails.

She leaps to her feet.

"You're right," she says. "This is a waste of time."

She looks for a cloth to wipe the filth from her hands, and when she can't find one, she uses the lapel of Stavros's jacket.

She says, "I've got five minutes. Tell me where you put my clothes."

She realizes immediately that there's a problem: the haul of laundry he gives her is too thin, too light; she's able to balance the three hangers on her little finger.

"Stavros," she says. "Where's my suit?"

"What do you mean?" He's poured himself a glass of orange juice, and a shred of pulp clings to his mustache.

"I mean *where's my suit?* I dropped off a skirt, a blouse, and a blazer. All that's here are three shirts."

"Oh." He licks his lips. "I think those are mine."

"Yes, I can see that." She takes a breath; she doesn't want to snap at him again. "But where did you put the rest of it?"

"That's all there was. I gave them the ticket, and that's what they handed me."

The color drains from her face, and Stavros sets down his glass.

"There must have been a mix-up," he says. "Here, I'll call them."

Eleni presses the heels of her palms against her eyes and shakes her head.

"I don't have time for that," she says. "My ferry leaves in half an hour." Then: "*Shit.*"

"What's wrong with what you're wearing? You're just going to sign a piece of paper."

"Says the man planting trees in a funerary suit." She uncovers her eyes and blinks away the stars. "And look at me. I can't wear jeans and a tank top to close a deal."

"Why not?"

"Because, Stavros! Because I'm an adult, not an animal! Because these people are *Swedish*!"

"What's that got to do with anything?"

"I just mean that they're all probably going to be wearing, like, J. Lindberg suits, or something, while I look like *this*."

"I don't know who J. Lindberg is."

"That's not the point," Eleni says. "The point is I can't show up wearing this, and I don't know what to do."

"What about one of my shirts?" He rips away the plastic from the hangers and thumbs through the options. "The blue one, I think. It'll bring out your eyes."

"My eyes are green."

"Close enough." He tosses her a threadbare oxford. "You can change in the bathroom."

She looks ridiculous. The shirt is too big in some places and too small in others; staring at herself in the mirror, she's reminded of her older classmates at the university as they traipsed out for their first job interviews. Girls and boys pretending to be grown-ups, playing dress-up in their hand-me-down suits. Now, standing in the muted light of Stavros's bathroom, she does her best to make the shirt work—rolling up the sleeves so they don't dangle at her knuckles, grabbing a handful of fabric and tucking it into the back of her jeans. Turning to the left, she looks at her profile. It's not bad, but it's not perfect, either; the shirt looks like it fits until it hits the waistband her jeans. There, it bunches and folds over itself;

she looks like she's pregnant with a stack of pancakes. Still, she figures it's better than the alternative. Reaching up, she gathers her hair with both hands and ties it back into a loose bun, collecting and adjusting the stray tendrils that fall across her eyes. Then she slips her hand into the pocket of her jeans. She fishes around until her fingers brush against a thin gold chain. Pulling gently, she retrieves the necklace—the one that her father gave Sue Ellen, and Sue Ellen gave to her—and clasps it around her neck.

Suddenly, Stavros thumps against the door.

"You're going to miss your ferry," he says.

She emerges from the bathroom and finds him standing in the living room. He's draped his jacket over the card table and loosened his tie. In his left hand, he holds a small paper bag.

"Keep the shirt," he tells her. "It looks better on you, anyway."

"You're lying." She makes a final adjustment to the sleeves, pushing them up so they cuff just above her elbows. "What's in the bag?"

"I made you a sandwich. Tomato and cheese and a little bit of ham."

"Stavros—"

"What? You might get hungry."

She knows she won't, but she takes it anyway.

"Thank you," she says.

"Come on, I'll give you a ride to the boat."

His car is parked on the street, and when she ducks into the passenger side the heat is assaulting; even through her jeans, the seat scorches the backs of her legs. She stuffs the paper bag into her purse, which she rests on her lap. Then she rolls down the window and drapes her arm outside.

"Put that up," Stavros says, starting the car. "I'll turn on the AC."

"I will in a second, once it stops blasting hot air."

He looks at her for a moment.

"That necklace," he says. "I've never seen you wear jewelry before."

"It's new," she says. She doesn't know why she lies. When she recalls this moment in ten years, and then again in twenty, she still won't know why she lied.

Stavros shifts into first and pulls away from the curb.

"It looks old."

"It's not old—it's just cheap."

The air from the vents begins to cool and, feeling it flush against her face, Eleni reaches down to crank up the window.

"Stavros," she says. "I'm sorry."

"For what?"

"I don't know. I'm sorry if I disappointed you. If I am disappointing you."

He banks the car around a corner and doesn't say anything. Then, releasing his grip on the gear stick, he takes her left hand and brings it to his lips.

He says, "You couldn't, *koritsi mou*. Not even if you tried."

In the corner of the conference room there's an essential oil diffuser, and every sixty seconds it burps up a cloud of eucalyptus-scented mist. She knows this because she times them—the burps, that is—watching a clock on the wall as it counts down to the next fragrant emission. Ten minutes ago, they left her alone, *they* being Oskar, a lawyer named Hugo, and a tall, striking blonde in a black pantsuit—a woman called Freja who, from the way she whispered directives to the two men, Eleni gathered is their boss. Someone had forgotten a signature page in the closing documents— this is what Freja explained to her with clipped English and a joyless smile—and now they had to go find it. Why it required three people to retrieve a single piece of paper baffled Eleni, but she didn't dare ask questions; instead, she begged Freja not to worry, going so far as to apologize for any inconvenience that she might be causing, as if the forgetfulness of Lugn Escapes' staff was somehow her fault. Freja didn't correct her. Instead, she played along: she waved away Eleni's apologies as if she were too gracious to accept them, then offered her something to drink.

"A little something to hold you over," she said. "While we fix this . . . mistake."

Eleni looked at Oskar, who winked.

"Uh, sure," she said. "That sounds nice."

She was presented with an octagonal plastic bottle filled with a silt-toned sludge. Before drinking it, she tried reading the label on the bottle's back (she was, at this point, alone), but to no avail—the ingredients, along with whatever else the label advertised, were written in Swedish. She tasted it, swishing the concoction around like a mouthful of pudding before promptly spitting it out, back into the bottle. She wanted to like it, but as she searched through her purse for some gum, she couldn't think of a time when she had tasted something so awful. Compost, mixed with gull shit and spoiled chocolate milk.

The diffuser hiccups, and Eleni stands. A few minutes ago, she thought the smell was relaxing—luxurious, even, in the way she imagines most day spas to be. Now, it strikes her as overpowering; tears gather in the corners of her eyes. Trying to escape it, she moves to the opposite corner of the room, where there's a large window overlooking the street and, beyond it, Syntagma Square. She's been here, in this building, before—she recognized it as soon as she stepped into the lobby. Alpha Bank has offices on the second floor, and when she worked as a research assistant for Maragos, he used to send her here to deposit checks. Now, though, she's higher up—on the twenty-seventh floor—and as she looks down she thinks of how she's never seen Athens from this vantage. Pressing her nose against the window, she thinks about what color she'll paint her new apartment once she moves in. She thinks about what life will be like when she doesn't have to worry about plumbing or lost dry cleaning. When she doesn't have to wear Stavros's old blue shirts.

"I'm sorry about the delay." She turns to see Oskar, standing at the entrance to the conference room. He's wearing the same white dress shirt that he wore when he came to the Alectrona—or, at the very least, a similar version of it—except now the sleeves are rolled up a bit higher;

instead of just the edges of his tattoo, Eleni can now see the final six inches. A bird, she thinks it is, its beak tangled in a thicket of thorns. In his left hand, he holds an iPad, encased in a black leather portfolio. Raising it, he says, "In the meantime, I thought you might like to see this."

"What is it?"

He smirks. "A present."

"Can you just tell me what it is?"

"How impatient we are today!" Oskar slides the iPad across the conference table. "They're mock-ups. I thought you'd get a kick out of seeing how we're going to renovate the property."

Eleni looks at the first image, and as she does she feels her heart clawing at her throat: the Alectrona is unrecognizable. Not just remodeled, but entirely gone. In the old structure's place now stands a collection of single-story bungalows, laced together by a fern-lined path. In the mock-ups that follow, she sees blond women in bathrobes, sipping tea as they dangle their ankles in warm baths; Pilates instructors, realigning sets of thin hips on a bamboo floor; moneyed couples laughing, enjoying the brown sludge she just spat out. And then, finally, at the end of the road where Christos taught her to ride a bike, a sign: LUGN ESCAPES: RETURN. RELAX. REDISCOVER.

"You said you were going to renovate it," she says, looking up, "not demolish it."

"I think *demolish* is a pretty strong word. We're just building something else."

"Yes, by destroying the thing that came before it."

He looks at her strangely, but not unkindly. "I'm sorry," he says. "I guess I'm having a difficult time understanding what you expected would happen. When we first met you seemed so eager to get rid of the place."

Eleni's cheeks flush—suddenly, she feels very foolish. She knows that he's right: she's finally doing the thing she's been waiting so long to do. She shouldn't be concerned about what happens in the Alectrona—nor, in a matter of minutes, will she have a right to be. Both of those facts should elicit within her a profound and palpable joy. And yet, all she can seem to focus on is the sound a wrecking ball makes as it collides against a wall. The pile of rubble and debris that follows, wrapped in the phantom smell of dust.

"This is where my room was," she says, pointing to a bungalow with a bright green roof. "And this is where my father's room was. That's where he and my mother slept, when they were alive."

Oskar cocks his head to get a better look at the image.

"Ah, yes," he says. "The *Gökotta*."

"The what?"

"The *Gökotta*. It's a Swedish practice of rising early to hear birdsong." He says this slowly, satisfied with the description. "We'll sell breakfast goods there. Seed bars and acai bowls. Smoothies, too, like the one you drank."

"I didn't drink it."

"You should—it's very good for you. Delicious, too."

"It tastes like a dirty puddle."

"That's just the raw parsnips. You learn to love them."

He smiles, the same smile he gave her when they first met and he was appraising the Alectrona. Looking at him now, though, she sees something different. Whereas earlier he had struck her as mildly charming, now he seems slick. The sort of person who could weaponize a wink and bend life to his will; who spent summers in places that were cool and winters in places that were warm; who referred to those seasons not just as set times of a given year, but also as verbs that he owned—actions existing in his past, his present, and his bright, unblemished future.

Eleni says, "I think I should go."

"But we haven't even—"

"I know, and we're not going to."

"*Eleni.*"

He reaches a hand out to her shoulder, but she ducks away.

Grabbing her purse off the conference room table, she says, "I'm leaving."

Dean

He finds her on the Alectrona's back patio, staring at her laptop at a table overlooking the pool. She's built a makeshift desk for herself: at her right are two open books, stacked on top of each other; at her left is a forgotten cup of coffee, along with the old Rubik's Cube she plays with whenever she's trying to think. From the door where he's standing he watches her for a moment, marveling at the way she manages to re-create herself wherever she goes: this desk, or some iteration of it, he's seen in at least four different cities on just as many continents. His wife is, above all else, a creature of habit. For all her exploring and search-ing, her summers spent among the dusty ruins of forgotten worlds, one of her most remarkable talents is this—an ability to create patterns and routines, to suss out order from any breed of chaos. Setting the Rubik's Cube down, she leans closer to the laptop's screen, an inch from the computer. Still watching her, Dean smiles: twice now he's told her to get a stronger prescription for her glasses, but on both occasions she shooed him away.

"One of these days you're going to fry your eyes," he remembers saying to her the last time.

"So, let me." Her nose was basically touching the screen. "At least when I'm blind I'll be able to say I saw life up close."

Above her is a trellis—a lattice of splintered wood and nails that supports, along with two empty pots, an enormous bougainvillea vine. Looking away from Sue Ellen, he studies it for a moment: the way its blossoms cluster in tight bouquets, how the midmorning light gets tangled in its knots. For the first time since they arrived, there's a breeze—finally, Dean doesn't feel as though he's being swallowed by the heat—and during one of its stronger moments it knocks away a few of the vine's petals, sending them spiraling toward the ground. One of them, the smallest, lands on Sue Ellen's left shoulder, at the exact spot where the neck of her T-shirt sags, revealing a patch of pink skin. She ignores it—she goes on staring at the laptop, scrutinizing whatever image has caught her attention—and after a minute more of watching her, Dean approaches and plucks it away.

"Hey," he says, and hands her the petal.

"Jesus, you scared me." She pinches the bloom between two fingers and turns it over once. "And hey yourself."

He takes a sip of her coffee, which has grown cold.

"What's doin'?"

"Working. Or, trying to, at least." She stretches her arms over her head. "You?"

"Same."

This is only partially true: a half hour ago he was, in fact, trying to work, though he suspects his efforts were noticeably less admirable than his wife's. Earlier that morning, he had set up his laptop in the Alectrona's dining room, whereupon he announced, to no one but himself, his intention to write. Before he acted on that intention, though, he had to check his email. In April, he had gotten word that a small liberal arts college in the Northeast had assigned *The Light of Our Shadows* to all of its incoming freshmen. This was a disappointment: Why was it always the teeniest of institutions that were putting his books on their syllabi? What did he have to do to be required reading at, say, Michigan State? His agent tried to convince him otherwise. Sales beget more sales, he had told Dean, and if his next royalty statement didn't prove that fact, then, by God, he would eat his hat. And so, after breakfast, Dean had fired up his laptop and signed into his email. Surely the statement would have been sent to him by now, he figured, along with whatever other news had managed to trickle in from the outside world. This had been a mistake. There was no royalty statement, no sign of how many dollars he had added to his name. Instead, there was a note from one Madison Assendorp—a character claiming to be the new bookkeeper at the agency. In it, Ms. Assendorp explained that she had just taken over the tracking of royalties last month, and that, given the volume of work before her, statements would be arriving two to three weeks later than usual. Irritated, Dean fired off a quick reply—*Lovely*—and then decided it was probably safer to just google himself instead. It had been a few weeks since he reread the reviews of his book, and he figured he could use a little pick-me-up.

Somewhere around the thirteenth page of results, though, after he'd reread raves from the *Argus Leader* ("Provocative, engaging, and—most importantly—humane") and the *Idaho Statesman* ("A thing of breathtaking beauty. This is Wright at the top of his craft") he began to feel anxious. What if he didn't have another book in him? What if he'd said all he had to say? His own experiences, after all, were hardly literary. He was a guy, a *dude*. Caucasian, and heterosexual, and from Abbottsville, Ohio—a town whose defining characteristic, at least while Dean was growing up, was its ability to breeze through national crises, be they economic, social, or cultural, unscathed. This changed in the eighties, when the food-processing factory outside of town closed, and half the men in Abbottsville lost their jobs, and bowling leagues were replaced by opioids and malt liquor. By then Dean had left, had trucked out west to Berkeley, where, instead of experiencing the dereliction of middle America, he was reading books— just books. Even his politics are uninteresting—he's liberal, with digestible socialist tendencies, and any conservative opinions he does have tend to be vague and innocuous. A suspicion of trigger warnings and a preference for purebred dogs—that sort of thing. He supposes he could write about being a teenager again, but that feels a little dicey. The goal is to be taken seriously, and he doesn't want people to think he's dipping his toe into YA.

Opening up a new search window, he typed in a few terms: *book ideas, ways to rewrite Ulysses,* and then, finally, *painkiller withdrawal.* Yes, he left Abbottsville without any plans to ever return, but did that mean he couldn't write about the place from the safety of the West Coast? Did that mean he couldn't infuse that particular brand of poor, American suffering with the insight and experience he's gained from, well, *living somewhere better*? One of his best friends from high school—an electrician's son named Bo Reynolds—died from an Oxycontin overdose. Dean had, in fact, attended the funeral. He didn't last long—twenty minutes into the reception, after struggling through conversations about things like duck hunting, Paul Ryan, and automotive repair, he'd slipped out the back door and drove to a Burger King. There, sitting in his rental car, he ate two Whoppers and cried—because of Bo, yes, but also because of the overwhelming mix of relief and guilt he felt for having escaped. Now he wonders: Is there a story there? Would he—could he—write about Bo, as Bo? From a market perspective, it wasn't a terrible idea: white poverty was chic now. Readers—the same ones who read Wallace, Franzen, and Knausgaard—were ravenous for accounts of the *forgotten middle class,* that marooned segment of the population which, despite its basic *whiteness,* they now regarded with the same exotic fascination that they had typically reserved for ethnographies of cannibalistic Guineans or fundamentalist Mormons. Still, when he set his fingers on the keyboard—when he was confronted with the despotic brightness of a new, blank page—he realized he couldn't. Instead, all he could think about was the life that he, Dean, had managed to avoid: Bo, and his pain, and his opioids. His nights wondering how the American Dream had eluded him and his mornings spent vomiting and shitting out his addiction—the one thing that, before it killed him, managed to provide him with momentary relief.

Sue Ellen's still reaching her arms up, and now he reaches down and sets his hands against her ribs. She flinches, and he does his best to ignore it.

"It's quiet here without Will asking us if he should work at Friends of the Sea Otters," he says.

"Our son the sailor. Who knew?"

"Should we have let him go?" Dean releases her and takes another sip from her coffee. "I mean, he went on a boat to some island with a total stranger."

"You don't think going on a boat to some island with a total stranger sounds a little romantic?"

"No, and I don't think you do, either."

Sue Ellen considers this for a moment.

She says, "No, you're right, it sounds like hell." She takes the coffee back from him. "But I think at his age a person's notions of romance are a little . . . I don't know, less tainted."

"Tainted by what—reality?"

"That, and the inevitability of being disappointed."

She swirls what's left in the cup and lets it settle before drinking it.

"This is cold," she says. And then: "I'm sorry, I shouldn't have—"

"It's fine." He scratches a mosquito bite on the back of his neck. Conversations have become like this, like minefields. They'll be skipping along at a clip that feels just close enough to normal when a word will suddenly carry a new and treacherous connotation. Then, in a blink, they'll find themselves retracing their steps, picking through scraps and collecting broken pieces.

He says, "I don't know how we could have stopped him, even if we wanted to. He's twenty-two years old."

She plays along: "You're right. It's not exactly like we can send him to his room."

"You were never a fan of doing that, anyway."

"Grounding a kid feels so unimaginative. There are more creative forms of torture."

"Remember when you made him research the history of child labor in Mesopotamia?"

Sue Ellen smiles. "Remember when you made him write a book report on that Bill O'Reilly screed? What was it called?"

"*Killing* . . . I don't know, *Killing* somebody. I sort of feel bad about that, actually: in punishing my kid, I earned Bill O'Reilly two dollars in royalties." He leans against the table. "Christ, Sue Ellen, when did we get so old?"

"I don't know." She runs a finger along the rim of the coffee cup. "I really, really don't know."

"I mean, this cruise you're lecturing to—are we going to do that? Are we going to go on an old person's cruise?"

"You're acting like it's a requirement or something. It doesn't look half bad, though." She adjusts her laptop so he can see the screen, where she's pulled up the Golden Age Adventures home page. "I mean, if you go on the Italy trip, you get unlimited gelato with every meal."

"Of course you do. It's the only thing you can eat without your dentures." He leans down so he can get a better look at the company's offerings. "Ooooh, Fun in the Fjords sounds promising—I've always wondered whether walkers work on ice."

"You're awful." Sue Ellen giggles and scrolls down a bit. "Personally, I'm partial to Enchanting España."

"Oh, so what, you're planning next year's vacation now?"

"You bet your ass I am. Get your Depends ready."

And then, suddenly, they're both silent; the future is another minefield. A place filled with plans they dare to only half make.

"I don't know what I'm going to say to these people," she says finally. "That's why I was looking at the site, I mean. I'm just—I'm trying to figure out what I'm going to say to them."

"When's the reception in Athens?"

"Tomorrow afternoon." She takes off her glasses and rubs the bridge of her nose. "I'm headed in tonight, though, on the six o'clock ferry."

"I'm still happy to go with you, you know."

"No—I mean, thank you, but don't worry about it. I'm going to be spending most of tomorrow morning at the museum, anyway. You'd just be bored."

He picks up the bougainvillea blossom and presses it against his palm.

"Hey," he says. "Let's go do something."

"Like what?"

"I don't know—something other than sit around and talk about being geriatrics on boats."

"Okay . . ." She leans back in her chair and laces her fingers behind her head. "There's a set of ruins over at Kolona that you've never seen. We could go there, and then maybe to—"

"No. I'm tired of looking at old, broken shit." He lifts her to her feet and kisses her cheek. "Let's check out something new instead."

They decide on Paralia Klima, a cove that forms a shallow dimple in the island's southern tip. A few days ago, Sue Ellen mentioned that she wanted to do some snorkeling—she hadn't seen a single live fish when she was here forty years ago—and after doing a little research Dean decided this was the place to go. A taxi drops them off between two cypress trees, and he surveys the beach, a mixture of coarse sand and pebbles lined with rows of umbrellas loaned out by the hour. For the middle of the week, he's surprised how crowded it is, even for the high season: nearly all the prime real estate has been claimed by a towel or a lounge chair, and the water, clear and placid, is dotted with bodies. To their left, a hut with a thatched roof sells Heineken and potato chips, and from its insides a speaker blares a tinny recording of an old British pop song. They look around for a few minutes before finding an open plot, and then, once staking it, they crouch down in the sand and unload two sets of rented snorkeling gear.

"I don't remember the last time we did this," Dean says. He hands Sue Ellen an orange mask and slips a green one over his head.

"Seven years ago," she says. "We were in Kauai. Will was a freshman in high school—we went for his spring break."

They begin to undress, both of them peeling away their shirts, their sandals, their shorts.

"How do you remember this shit?"

"Do this, it stops it from fogging up." She spits on the mask's lens and rubs it around with her finger. "And I remember because we let him bring that girl with him—the one he was dating."

"Yes." Dean nods. "Yes, you're right. Alana Rothstein. She decided she was vegan the night we went to that luau where they roasted the pig." He spits in his mask. "We let them stay in the same room and everything. Because, like—"

"Because what was possibly going to happen." Sue Ellen grins. "God, I don't know how parents with straight sons do it. I mean, with Will all we had to worry about was acting surprised when he finally told us."

Dean bites his lip for a moment. He spreads his saliva against the plastic, pushing it up into the mask's corners.

"Yes," he says, finally. "I guess we really lucked out."

They wade into the surf, and Dean lifts onto his toes, doing his best not to slip on the smooth stones underfoot. The water's lukewarm, but he shivers as it climbs his thighs and circles his waist. Once they're ten meters out, they lower their masks and glide onto their bellies; with slow, deliberate strokes, they make their way toward the rocks. He had forgotten, he realizes, how bewildering and alien the experience of snorkeling actually is. The tide swirls around his ears, creating, with its quiet roar, a sort of paradoxical silence, a whiteness punctuated only by his breath, which, at first, comes unsteadily, in anxious gasps. He finds himself clenching his jaw and grinding his teeth into the plastic mouthpiece.

Every so often a spoonful of water will splash down the snorkel's tube as he tries to breathe. He exhales against these intrusions, propelling them back into the air in sprays of mist and salt.

The strangest part is the mask itself. Looking through it he feels like he's not swimming but floating, somehow detached from the space around him. The scratches and grime on the inside of the lens remind him that, as much as he's here, in the water, he's somehow still outside of it. Every so often Sue Ellen will tap his arm and point to something—a mullet darting between two rocks, or a clump of urchins forming a bed of black spines. There aren't many colors; this isn't the Caribbean, and the fish they do see come in muted shades of silver, blue, and gray. Still, they chase them when they see them. They kick their feet faster and occasionally dive down beneath the surface, peeking into places they aren't meant to be.

He had been stupid with Ginny—worse than stupid, he had been careless. In terms of both his stumbling again so soon after his affair with Jasmine and also the brazenness with which he had conducted himself. Twice he'd thought that they had been caught: the first time when he ran into Ginny's roommate while leaving her apartment; the second when Chip caught them sitting an inch too close on a bench. At the end of the day, though, he managed to emerge unscathed. He'd ended things and escaped the girl; now he's floating in the Aegean alongside his wife.

Will he tell her? No, he decides, watching Sue Ellen as she propels herself with a lazy flutter kick. No, he won't. For as much as Connie extolled the virtue of radical transparency in a marriage, he's always believed that the most compassionate thing a lover can do is lie, particularly now, when they're finally getting back to stable ground. *Does this dress look good?* Yes. *How's the meat loaf?* Delicious. *Did you sleep with your student?* No. The only rationale for answering otherwise, he thinks, is a sort of selfishness—a need to unload your own guilt by telling your wife the thing she doesn't want to hear. Connie pushed him on this. Once, when he came to her alone, she'd asked him if he would ever consider admitting something to Sue Ellen even if he knew it would hurt her. It was two weeks after he had started sleeping with Ginny and, looking back now, he hardly considered the question a coincidence. Connie, he gathered, had a sense about these things.

"No," he said, crossing one leg over the other. "No, I wouldn't."

"And why not?" Her voice was cool, free of any music.

"Because I think I've probably hurt her enough."

They're in the water for nearly an hour before they remove the snorkels from their mouths and decide that maybe they've seen all there is to see. Back on the beach, Dean unfurls two towels and spreads them out next to each other on the sand. Reaching deeper into the backpack they've brought, Sue Ellen retrieves an apple and a bottle of water.

"Thirsty?" she asks.

"Actually, yeah," Dean says. "But how about I get us two beers instead?"

He does, and when he returns Sue Ellen has reclined back on one of the towels. Her bathing suit is already dry—now, faint tracks of salt form whirls on the Lycra. Dean lies down next to her, propping himself up on an elbow and opening the beers.

Handing her one, he says, "That was fun. Not a lot to see, but it was fun."

Sue Ellen takes a sip of beer and holds it in her mouth for a moment.

"Greece," she says, swallowing. "Good on ruins, bad on fish."

Dean laughs. Resting his beer in the sand, he reaches out and sets his free hand on top of Sue Ellen's. She doesn't brush it away, so he leaves it there, letting his fingers fall in the spaces between her own.

"I'm glad we're here," he says. "I'm glad we came."

Next to them, a woman haggles for a free half hour beneath an umbrella. He listens to the sharp clip of her voice alongside the other, smoother sounds of the beach: gulls squawking, swimmers splashing as they dive into the water.

Slowly, Sue Ellen rotates her hand and begins lacing her fingers around Dean's. She leans her head against his shoulder and tightens her grip.

Pebbles—bits of the beach caught between their palms—press into the creases of his skin.

She says, "Me, too."

She showers when they return to the Alectrona, and because the inn is empty and he feels the promise of connection, Dean waits an excruciating five minutes, then goes in to join her.

"I, uh, thought I might come in there with you," he says, opening the shower door. Sue Ellen turns her back, raising her arms to cover her breasts. Water streams from the back of her head and down her spine.

He stammers—he didn't realize fixing a marriage could make him as nervous as a first date. "I—er, it's the only shower that works."

She takes a bit of water in her mouth and spits it out.

"Uh, sure. If you want to."

Closing the bathroom door, Dean removes his trunks and squeezes inside the stall alongside her. It's a tight fit, and only one of them can be under the showerhead at once. Standing half-dry at her rear, he covers his hard-on with both hands and catches the splashes as they bounce off her shoulders. At their feet, water spirals around the drain, carrying shampoo suds and stray hairs with it. Inching his toes forward, he tickles the backs of her ankles.

"Oh, sorry," Sue Ellen says, turning to face him. "I didn't realize you weren't getting wet."

She moves to trade places with him, but he stops her and pulls her body into his. He wraps his arms around her and, immediately, she goes rigid; her arms return to shield her breasts, and she ducks her chin into her shoulder. He expects this, but that hardly helps. Of all the horrors of the past year—the second glances and mixed messages; the strained, existential silences—the way his wife recoils from him is, bar none, the worst.

And yet now something shifts. Her shoulders relax, and her hands, once balled into tight fists, open. Without guidance, she walks her fingers across Dean's waist and around to the small of his back; she buries her head against his chest. Reaching up, he adjusts the showerhead so water hits both of them, and as his wet hair mats against his forehead and eyes, he leans down to kiss a curve of flesh along her neck. She tastes like soap, and salt, and something else—a flavor that's specific to her skin, and that he's unable to describe as anything other than *Sue Ellen*. Now, her hands still against his back, she holds him with a bit more force, digging the tips of her blunted nails into his ass. This, though, causes him to slip; jutting out an arm, he braces himself and catches Sue Ellen before they both go tumbling through the glass door.

"Let's go upstairs," she says, switching off the water. "Before we break our necks."

They've had sex in the past year—this is not the first time. The night he moved home from the apartment in San Ramon they slept together, for instance, and again the night after Dean suggested that he and Will join her in Greece. Both of those occasions, however, had a feeling that was undeniably political: sex as a treaty, or a marker of some minor marital success. Neither of them carried the sort of passion that he's presently sensing as he watches his wife jog up the stairs and toss the pillows from the bed. And while yes, there is still some hesitancy—a look that lasts a second too long; a timid *so*—Dean will take whatever fire he can get. He will latch on to the tiny smiles and satisfied murmurs, the little signals that Sue Ellen has, finally, at least sort of, relaxed.

They will allow him, at the very least, to rediscover her body—a block of bones and flesh and neurons that, over the past year, has been less a person than a crisis to address. Feeling her weight upon him now, he is reminded of the subtle joys she possesses: a scar on the inside of her left thigh; the way her hair always manages to escape the hook of her ears. She's not as young as Ginny or Jasmine, and this fact is inescapable: her skin is tough, and she's hardly acrobatic in bed. Still, he finds himself at first relieved and then excited by her age. Ginny's softness was cloying, the pockets of flesh like unbaked meringue. Besides, while her youth made him feel powerful, it also made him feel old; when she walked her fingers across his stomach on the way to his groin, he always wanted to apologize for his paunch, for the hairs sprouting from his belly button. Sue Ellen, though, knows these things about him. She has seen him submit to time and is now familiar with him—in the way she touches him, and kisses him, and whispers the same, practiced words in his ear.

When they're finished, she turns on her side and he holds her from behind. They're still above the bedsheets, though beneath them are strange imprints—not their full bodies, but rather parts of them: an ass cheek here, a scapula there. Neither Dean nor Sue Ellen says anything. He suspects they're both worried that if they comment on the past thirty minutes, that if they acknowledge it happened, something will shift, and this tiny step forward will be erased. So instead, they lie there, trying—with some success—to match the rhythm of each other's breaths as they watch dust motes swirl in pillars of afternoon light.

After twenty minutes of silence, though, Sue Ellen breaks away. Wrapping her towel around herself, she stands up and leans over to kiss the top of Dean's head.

"Where are you going?" he asks her. He was dozing, and he blinks away sleep.

"It's five o'clock," she says, slipping on her pants. "If I don't leave now, I'll miss my boat."

Ginny Polonsky

She locks the stall door and turns to stare at the toilet: a hair floats in its water; a single square of paper clings to its base. From the center of the automatic flusher a red light blinks at her, taunting her, she thinks, with its detached all-knowingness. Doing her best to ignore it, she considers her next move: if she lays her suitcase flat, she'll have nowhere to put her feet, whereas if she leaves it standing up, balanced on its twin black wheels, she'll have nowhere to put her knees. Sighing, she gathers her hair into a loose fist and secures it with one of the hair bands she keeps looped around her wrist. This is the problem with airport bathrooms: they're always too small. They've hardly got enough room in them to fit a body, let alone a body *and* a suitcase *and,* when it comes to Ginny, a moderate size rucksack—which, at the moment, she's doing her best to wiggle out of without knocking down the stall's two walls. Thank God she doesn't have a coat, she thinks, looking around for a hook (there isn't one). If she had a coat, she'd be really fucked.

She stands for a moment longer, and then she unbuttons her shorts.

Stacking her things to the left, she folds her knees in the opposite direction and squats, hovering an inch above the toilet's seat. In the world outside the stall's scratched door, a faucet turns on, then off, then on. A cell phone rings and a woman sneezes. Inside, Ginny Polonsky closes her eyes. Then, just before she's set to pee, she spins around and vomits.

There isn't much there, she sees, once she opens her eyes. She supposes that makes sense; the last thing she ate was a salad in San Francisco, before she boarded the red-eye to Frankfurt. Wiping her mouth with the back of her hand, she checks her watch. It's ten thirty at night. That means she's been here, on her German layover, for ten hours, and she's got another seven to go; her connection doesn't take off until tomorrow. She should probably get something to eat in the meantime. Then again, maybe not: from what she's seen so far, all German airports have to offer are pretzels and bratwurst and beer.

The puking started a few weeks ago. And it happened so often, and with such vile force, that her roommate had finally asked her if she'd bit the bullet and turned bulimic. She—the roommate—was blond, and was called Scarlett, and was a junior in the university's Media Studies Department. They hadn't lived together for long. Only a semester, really, ever since Ginny's old roommate—a political science major named Karen Liu—left to study abroad in Ghana. They hadn't been friends, exactly (Karen liked live music, whereas concerts gave Ginny hives; Karen worshipped the 49ers, whereas Ginny was categorically opposed to football's brutality), but they nonetheless shared an interest in basic decency and responsibility. Karen knew not to leave the lights on when she left the apartment and to shop local instead of at the big chains in El Cerrito Plaza. She knew that banana peels should always go in the compost bin below the sink and that feminism wasn't feminism unless it was intersectional. Scarlett, though, knew none of these things—or, if she did, she certainly didn't care about them. At least one morning a week since Scarlett had moved in, Ginny found herself digging empty tubs of Greek yogurt out from the garbage and transferring them to the recycling bin. Twice, she had opened the apartment's front door to the television blaring to an empty house.

They rarely spoke—Scarlett had treated Ginny like a ghost ever since they got into a fight over foam coffee cups—but this hardly bothered Ginny. Whereas Scarlett celebrated her privilege, Ginny had the good sense to loathe her own. And frankly, she wouldn't have it any other way. Otherwise, what's to keep her in check—what's to keep her from throwing away recyclable yogurt tubs—if not the cultivation of her own, deliberate guilt? This, Ginny wagers, is the unbearable burden of being aware, of being conscious. It's a responsibility to which she's committed herself happily, dutifully: she will persist as recompense for the Scarletts of the world, those latte-loving hordes, content to brunch into oblivion. And if she's painted as earnest or sanctimonious, she'll shrug it off: sometimes, being friendless is the price for being Good.

Standing up, she buttons her shorts and zips up her fly. Behind her, the toilet wheezes and chokes before finally flushing. Then, slinging her rucksack over her left shoulder, Ginny leaves the restroom and goes to find a corner where she might nap. Her stomach churns and gurgles once, then quiets itself. She'll buy something to eat, she decides. A bag of almonds, or one of the weird yogurt drinks she always sees Europeans drinking. Kefir, she thinks it's called. God knows what they serve on Olympic Air, and she's got awhile yet before she reaches Athens.

"Bloody Mary mix," she tells the flight attendant, a man her father's age with graying hair and a pink ribbon pinned to his vest.

He offers a weak smile and begins rummaging through the steel drawers on his cart, pulling out tiny bottles one by one, searching for the makings of Ginny's drink.

"And hey," she says to him, once he's found the can. "Take it easy on the ice."

This time he doesn't smile; he sets the items down on her tray, along with a creased napkin and a pack of pretzels, and then lurches his cart onward, pushing it farther into the bowels of coach. Once he's gone she opens the can of Bloody Mary mix and empties it, watching as the red slop climbs the sides of the cup. Two ice cubes crackle and pop, and she sloshes them around a bit, giving them time to melt. Then, raising the glass to her nose, she sucks in a peppery, restorative breath. Finally, she takes a sip.

Reclining her seat, she lets her eyes wander up, past the heads in front of her, the mess of hair and scalp and dandruff, until her gaze settles on the plane's ceiling. She traces the outlines of the small air vents in the ceiling above her row, the reading lights wedged between them, the genderless flight-attendant call buttons. She doesn't mind flying, the taste of recycled air, the constant pop of pressurization. In fact, she might even like it.

There's something communal about cheating gravity in such close quarters. Part of it, she figures, also has to do with class. She can think of no other place where the distinction between the haves and have-nots is so strikingly clear as on an airplane. She imagines what must be happening in the patrician environs of first class: the champagne being served in crystal, alongside fresh cookies and warm nuts. She thinks of the decadence of real flatware, versus the plastic forks being rationed out in coach. The divide thrills her. Or, if not the divide itself, then the mutual bitterness it breeds. Looking around, she feels a swell of pride for her fellow seatmates in steerage. A bond that she attributes to the resentment they all must feel toward the indulgence unfurling at the front of the plane, behind that gilded curtain that shutters off first class from the rest of them.

She remembers how, a few years back, she flew on a Cubana Airlines flight from Mexico City to Havana. The plane was old; while she's since read that the newer jets in Cubana's fleet have designated classes, this one certainly did not. At first, this excited Ginny: Communism! she recalls having thought. How lovely. She had always considered herself more or less a Marxist, and seeing that ideology play out in the world of aviation tickled her. Quickly, though, that excitement faded; instead of angry or agitated, the other passengers just looked sad. Watching them trudge to their seats, she decided she would rebook her return flight on another airline—Air Canada, maybe, or AeroMexico. She hadn't wanted reality so much as something to resent.

But anyway, she makes her best decisions on planes. It's got something to do with being that much farther from earth and that much closer to death. A mix of rising and falling, of physics and ontology, that strikes a certain chord of clarity in her mind. Take last week, for example. She was on a Delta Shuttle back from visiting her sister in Los Angeles when she decided, with a lucidity she had lacked since summer's beginning, that she would fly to Greece and find Dean.

"You need to forget about him," her sister had said. They were at a restaurant in Silver Lake—a kitschy Mexican place called El Cóndor, where the napkins were folded to look like fans. Elsa had ordered for the both of them, and Ginny watched as she dunked a *papa brava* in aioli. "He sounds like a schmuck."

"Unfortunately, I don't think it's that simple."

"Don't be melodramatic. Anything's that simple if you want it to be."

"Maybe you're right."

Ginny took a gulp of water and chewed on bits of lime. She hated how her convictions evaporated in front of her sister—how, suddenly, she questioned her hard-won beliefs about politics, art, and sustainable agriculture. Or, that's not entirely true. Half of her hated it. The other half welcomed the respite, the opportunity to be indifferent and agnostic.

"Of course I'm right," Elsa said. She pushed the plate toward Ginny and added, "Are you going to have any of these or what?"

"I've stopped eating eggs."

"They're potatoes, Ginny."

"There're yolks in the aioli."

"Of course." Elsa looked down and poked the sauce with the tip of a *papa*. Bits of garlic jiggled on its surface. She said, "Berkeley's got to be crawling with guys."

"I don't know what you're talking about."

"I'm saying that if it's a guy you're after, you've got plenty around you."

Ginny stabbed the remnants of her drink with her straw. She said, "I'm not interested."

"Why?"

"Because they're mindless slobs."

Elsa leaned forward, planting both her elbows on the table.

"Ginny," she said.

"Yes?"

"Are you a lesbian?"

"How passively homophobic of you."

"Because if you *were*, I'd still love you, you know."

Ginny smiled—it was what her sister wanted—and then she threw an ice cube at her. It was easier than getting into an argument about what she knew Elsa was already thinking: that Ginny didn't have her long legs, or her lean hips, or her manageable hair; that her rejection of the boys at school was born from self-loathing, as opposed to the fact that she— actually, really—found 99 percent of them to be repulsive.

"Maybe it's an older-guy thing," Elsa said, once she'd brushed the ice from her lap. "If you hate all the dudes your age, maybe it's an older-guy thing."

"*Dudes,*" Ginny parroted. "You need to stop working in Hollywood. You need to leave L.A."

"Well, is it?"

She said, "No, it's not an older-guy thing."

Next to them, a mariachi band started playing "Happy Birthday" to a table of teenagers. Elsa rolled her eyes and looked back at Ginny.

She asked, "Why aren't you drinking?"

"I am drinking."

"You're drinking *water.*"

Ginny shrugged. "Since when is water not drinking?"

"Oh, my God." Elsa leaned over the basket of *bravas*. "You're pregnant."

Ginny fished out a second ice cube and threw it, this time knocking her sister right between the eyes.

"Knock it off," she said. "And no. I'm not."

Except yes. She was. Obviously, she was. It was an unfortunate discovery she'd made two weeks ago, the day before Scarlett accused her of being bulimic. In addition to feeling a new and unshakable queasiness (they were right, Ginny now realized: morning sickness didn't just happen before lunch), there was also the matter of her Mooncup, which, just when she thought her period had started, remained bloodless and empty. She had gone to the drugstore and bought a pregnancy test, even though she knew already what the result would be; she and Dean had hardly been careful when they had sex in the bathroom of that diner he had taken her to, so she knew what she was up against. Still, though, she marveled at the awful cliché of it all—the peeing on a stick, the watching of a timer, the squinting at two pink marks. Holding the completed test in her fist, she recalled, strangely, the time her father had taken her and Elsa to see the Grand Canyon, back when Ginny was in grade school. She remembered standing at the lip of the crevice, looking down, and being perfectly satisfied: the sight, while amazing, was exactly as she expected it would be. Discovering she was pregnant was very much the same. The collision of horror and pride, of helplessness and power—it all coincided perfectly with how she had imagined this situation would play out, should she ever find herself in it.

Her first thought was to take care of it—this, she'll proudly admit, also met her expectations. She would call her gynecologist and make an appointment. But then something happened: the world, or fate, or chance decided it had other plans for Ginny. For starters, it was Saturday, which meant the soonest she could call her doctor's office would be in two days' time. There was also the issue of the book—Dean's book—which she'd stumbled upon that evening, after googling the best foods to eat before an abortion. Picking up the book and cracking its spine, she thought back to the first time she happened upon it, just two days shy of her twentieth birthday. She had come into San Francisco with her mother to go fabric shopping; Cece, motivated by nothing but suburban ennui, had recently decided to reupholster a sofa, and there was a bolt of Japanese silk being held for her at Sal Beressi's shop in the Mission. At some point, Ginny broke away. She told her mother that she had some errands of her own to run and that she would meet her at two o'clock at Delarosa, in the Marina, where they had a reservation for lunch. After that, she wandered, eventually making her way to a bookstore on Valencia where, while browsing the new releases table, she happened upon the bloodred cover of Dean Wright's novel. She must have read a hundred pages in the hour that followed. She bought the book and read a hundred more. She sat on the curb outside the store, she remembers, her knees pulled to her chest as she gripped the cover in both hands. It was an eye-blue day, the sort that turned every street corner into a postcard, but Ginny didn't care; it could have been pouring rain and she still would have sat there, devouring his words. She felt herself floating, unmoored and unsettled, but also understood—finally, finally understood.

Now, as she sucks Bloody Mary mix away from ice cubes, she thinks back to the passage she flipped to on that Saturday night—the one that would redirect her fate. It was a scene she knew well. The protagonist's girlfriend—the troubled (but actually misunderstood), bisexual Belinda, awash in lust and longing, realizes the person she's meant to be, while trapped on a stalled BART train. As she drank in his words alongside her own annotations, Ginny's thoughts coalesced around a perfect singularity. In that moment, she forgot about Monday, and consuming a fiber-rich meal before having her procedure. She forgot about her own devastation and the scourge of a vanishing man. Now she had but one goal: she would find Dean, and she would go to him. She would confront him and demand an explanation.

Will

August 2
Hydra

The island of Hydra is some forty-seven miles away from the Port of Piraeus in Athens and a twenty-minute ferry ride from the eastern coast of the Peloponnese. When you approach it from the north, it's not much to look at: a craggy collection of rocky hillsides, cypresses, and olive trees, all washed out in the same muted sepia, the colors fading like those in a painting that's been exposed to too much sun. About halfway down the northern coast of the island, something shifts: a small cove appears, along with a harbor, the white masts of sailboats, and a crescent cobblestone quay. As Dio guides them to port, Will scrambles to the bow and takes in the view: houses—not just in the predicable white, but in varying shades of gray, red, and blue—climb the surrounding hills. He stares at them until his eyes cross. Until their tile roofs reflect in bursts off the water.

The sail here had been easy—or at least that's what Dio says as they tightrope down the gangplank onto the harbor's stone dock. Will did his best to keep up, hauling in sheets as they tacked, coming about when he was told. It came easy to him—he seemed to have an instinct for interpreting wind, for anticipating gusts by the way they lifted mist from the tops of waves. And the boat was spectacular—even with his anemic knowledge of sailing, he knew enough to notice that. A sixty-five-foot yacht called, regrettably, *Finja's Fantasy,* with teak decks and a cobalt-blue hull. A floating penthouse, Dio had called it. Not the kind of boat that you'd want to race, but not a bad place to spend a weekend.

"Let's get beers." Now, Dio drapes his arm around Will's shoulder and leads him off the dock. "Lugging that much boat around makes me thirsty."

The port is small and hugs the narrow crescent of the cove. Souvenir shops, jewelers, and restaurants dot the waterfront, their tables and patrons spilling out onto the stone quay. There are no cars on Hydra—the only way to get around is on foot or by pack animal—and outside a bar called the Pirate, Will nearly collides with a donkey with a white LG washing machine strapped to its back. On the west edge of the cove, atop a slope crowded with villas and steep stone stairs, are a pair of windmills with skeletal fans. Watching them turn, just barely, Will breathes in the familiar scent of salt and petrol, but also something else: fish, he thinks, and lemons. A pocket of alarmingly fresh air.

Outside a small market wedged between a bank and an alley, Dio stops them. Later that evening they're meant to attend a dinner that the owner of the boat, Klaus, is hosting, he explains, but they've got hours until then. In the meantime, he's hungry.

"I figure we can buy some food," he says. "Take it somewhere and go for a swim."

He hands Will a basket and fills it with two oranges, a loaf of bread, and a block of halloumi cheese. Then, making his way past a crate of cucumbers, he opens a case filled with cold drinks and grabs two tallboys of Alfa.

"You think this will be enough?" he asks.

"Uh . . ."

"You're right." He puts the cans in the basket and grabs two more. "We'll get some sour cherries, too."

They walk west along the quay, following the curve of the harbor past a clock tower, a statue of Andreas Miaoulis, and a harem of stray cats. At the lip of the port, the path leads them up a small incline to a point where, as they stand in the thin shadow of a windmill, the Aegean stretches out before them. The sun blazes—Will's shirt is sweaty; the cotton clings to his back—and as he stares at the water he shields his eyes with his hand, trying to gain a sense of their position. Directly north across the water, Dio says, is Metochi, a small village on the mainland that provides ferry service to Hydra, and where, at the age of seventeen, he drank too much cheap gin and vomited on his crush, a girl named Callie who he only saw twice more.

"Once when I gave her back her shirt, which I washed," he says. "And once when she dumped me."

"That hardly seems fair," Will says.

On the opposite side of the slope Dio guides them down a crumbling stone staircase. At the base of it is a small concrete platform the size of Will's bedroom in Berkeley—a smooth slab of rock that, aside from a few names graffitied on its surface, is empty.

"If we keep walking we can get to Vlychos Beach," Dio says. "To be honest, though, it's not that great. It's pretty, I guess, but it's just always so crowded." He pulls his lips to one side, thinking. "Besides, the restaurant that's there is always blasting the worst music. Like, old American pop from five years ago that you forgot about and didn't want to remember."

They set the grocery bags down and Dio points to a swim step to his left—a metal ladder that reminds Will of municipal pools.

"Just be careful of the top step," Dio says, peeling off his shirt and unbuttoning his pants. "Last year some kid busted it trying to do a backflip. Broke his nose and everything."

A trail of dark, coarse hair runs from his chest to his abdomen, following a topography of lean muscle. As he bends over to lay his shirt and jeans down on the rocks, Will notices more: a freckle on his left shoulder; a twin set of shadows formed by the sharp angles of his hips;

sweat gathering in the grooves of his lower back, dampening the waist-band of his briefs. Then, as Dio stands up again, Will—worried that he's staring—looks away.

He reaches into the bag of food, cracks open one of the Alfas, and takes a long swig. Setting the can down on the rocks, he reaches into the bag again, this time retrieving an orange. For a moment he holds it to his nose, trying to pick up the bitterness of the rind. Then he begins to peel it. He digs his fingers into its skin and winces as acid bathes the cuts on his hands.

There's a splash, and Will turns to see Dio disappear into the sea. He holds his breath and imagines the roar of water flooding his ears, the taste of salt on his lips. Juice from the orange drips from his wrists to his chest to the tops of his thighs. From the distant belly of the port he hears the peals of a church bell, the horn announcing a ferry's approach. Then Dio surfaces, brushing hair from his eyes.

Dinner is at a restaurant called Plato—a smallish place with white table-cloths on the port's main drag. Klaus has rented it out for the evening, and by the time Dio and Will arrive, at eight o'clock, it's already filled with Swiss, British, and Athenian weekenders—a mostly middle-aged crowd with faces turned leathery by the sun. Klaus himself is a big man, both in size and personality, and at first Will finds him fascinating: his preter-natural ability to conjure a room's attention, the hearty Teutonic slap he gives women's shoulders. He reminds Will, in many ways, of his father. Soon, though, the fascination fades. After Klaus sends Will his third shot of *tsipouro*, Will decides the posturing—the unapologetic loudness—is too much. Necking down the liquor, he now suspects Klaus is testing him, see-ing if Will could roll in whatever boys' club he's created on the island. He thinks back to his early years at Berkeley, of the uncomfortable anticipa-tion he'd felt whenever he walked into a fraternity party, the sudden sense of otherness. He thinks of how, like Klaus, those boys would always make sure he had a shot in his hand, or a beer, or both. Half their hospitality, he knew was well-intentioned: this was Berkeley, and they were liberals. The other half was fueled by something else, a subconscious skepticism. A wanting to see if Will could shed whatever notions he had of being gay and, at least for the night, belong.

Receding into one of the restaurant's corners, he finds an empty seat and watches Dio float between the guests. Dio's wearing a blue linen button-down with the first three buttons unfastened and the sleeves rolled up to his elbows. On the walk over he told Will that he hardly knew any of the people who'd be at the party, and yet here he is, doling out hugs and shaking hands. Soon, Klaus is kissing both his cheeks and introducing him to people—*Look at this guy,* Will imagines him crooning, *look at this guy who I let sail my yacht.* From his chair in the corner, Will tries to catch Dio's eye. He'll wink at him, he thinks, or give him a subtle nod. Something to suggest that they're compatriots, and that they're suffering through this charade together. Dio, though, ignores him; he keeps palling around with Klaus, and Will feels himself sinking deeper into the background. I'm an idiot, he thinks, as he picks a scab on his finger. I'm an idiot, and this was a terrible mistake.

Freeing the scab, his finger oozes a pinprick of blood.

"You're new."

A woman his mother's age sits at another table across from him. Her gray-blond hair has been cropped to a bob, and she wears a blue sleeveless dress, the neck of which sags slightly, revealing a thin gold chain. A glass of red wine's in front of her, and with the first two fingers of her left hand she grips its stem, swirling the base in tight circles. Will watches as a few drops escape the glass's lip and splatter across her stomach.

She says, "Oops."

Dipping a corner of the tablecloth in a cup of water, she daps it for a moment on the stain. Then, giving up, she lets the thing go. Says, instead, "Well, shit."

"What do you mean I'm new?" Will asks her.

"I mean I haven't seen you before." British, he realizes. A posh, tony accent. "I mean you're *new*."

He glances down and sees blood pooling in the creases of his knuckle. Quickly, he wipes it away with his other hand.

"I came with Dio," he says, pointing. "Dionysus."

The woman surveys the crowd and takes a sip of wine.

"Don't know him," she says. "But what a head of hair."

A half-moon of pink lipstick stains her glass.

"He works for Klaus. Sailed his boat over this afternoon. I helped." Will crosses his legs.

"Ah, you work on boats."

He doesn't say yes and he doesn't say no. Instead, he looks across the restaurant, where Dio is finally glancing at him and offering him a tiny nod. It's the sort of gesture that would be negligible, meaningless, but that given Will's present circumstances (alone, sunburnt, caught in the irrational throes of a crush) lifts his spirits and ropes him back in. He's fine being powerless, he figures, so long as he's not forgotten.

"Well, that explains why I don't know you," the woman says, filling the silence. "I hate boats. Get dreadfully seasick."

"That seems . . . inconvenient."

"It makes getting off the island a bit of a production, if that's what you mean."

"I'm betting there are worse islands to be stuck on."

"*Mmm.*" She looks at him for a moment and squints, like she's sizing him up. "You need a drink," she says.

She stands, disappears into the scrum, and returns a minute later, this time holding an uncorked bottle of red wine and a second glass.

"I couldn't find a waiter, so I took this from the back," she tells Will, reclaiming her seat across from him. "But I know the owner, Tony. He won't mind. And if he does, well. Then Tony will mind."

She fills the glass to its brim and hands it to him.

"So, what—you, like, know everyone on the island?"

"I've lived here on and off for thirty years, and there aren't that many people to know. Less when you consider that most of the locals wouldn't be caught dead talking to me."

"But aren't you a local?"

"You don't have a cigarette, do you?" Will checks his pockets; he shakes his head. "That's probably for the best—I don't actually smoke." She takes another sip of her wine, leaving a second arc of pink, this one only slightly fainter than the first. "I mean the Hydriots," she says. "The lot who were born here. They've got a thing about fraternizing with outsiders. And that includes other Greeks. My next-door neighbor's family has lived here for three generations, and she orders carry-away food from Tony twice a week. Each time she asks him to put it in an unmarked bag because she doesn't want her friends seeing her spending money at a restaurant that's owned by an Athenian." She reaches up and adjusts her necklace. "And if you're Albanian, forget about it."

"That's nuts."

"Even paradise can be a drag."

Careful not to spill it, he drinks some of his wine. It's warm, and the tannins leave his mouth dry.

He says, "I'm Will, by the way."

"Polly."

Will reaches out his hand, but realizes, in the next instant, that they're too far away from one another; that, even if she were to extend her own arm there would still be six inches of space between them.

He asks, "Want me to move to your table? We're sort of far apart."

"Don't trouble yourself. Distance lends a little enchantment." Polly takes another swig, then tucks her hair behind her ears. Leaning forward, she says, "Will. *Will.* Tell me where you're from. I detect a certain American accent—not of the neo-fascist variety, but something else. New York, maybe. Or Boston."

Will grins.

"Close," he says. "California."

"That'll do, too." Polly nods. "And you've come to the Aegean to work on boats."

"Well . . ." He shifts in his seat and rolls up the sleeves of his shirt—a white oxford that he had stuffed in his backpack, along with a toothbrush, when Dio told him to bring something other than T-shirts and swim trunks. "That's only, like, marginally true. I came here—or, actually, to Aegina—on vacation with my parents. I'm only on Hydra for a night."

"Aegina with your parents." Polly's eyebrows lift. Thin wrinkles divide her forehead. "How harrowing. Thank goodness you've escaped."

At the other end of the restaurant comes a loud crash, and they both turn in time to see Dio, along with a man twice his age, help Klaus up off the floor. Next to him, a chair lies toppled. Half standing, Will sees that it's missing one of its legs.

"Christ, he's such a brute," Polly says. "A nice guy in the end, but a brute regardless. Though I suppose you can't ask for much more than that when it comes to arms dealers from Cologne."

"He's an arms dealer?"

"*Mmmh.* Black market and everything. From what I understand, he really made a name for himself in Iraq during the two gulf wars."

Will tries to picture this buffoon, who just fell off a chair, negotiating deals with tyrants in smoke-filled rooms. He wonders if Dio knows.

Polly passes him the bottle of wine.

"I'm kidding," she says. "He worked in telecommunications. Bet early on Motorola and then got out before flip phones turned into smartphones. Arms dealing is more fun, though, don't you think? I know it's a nasty rumor to spread, but what else is a girl supposed to do? I mean, look around—I haven't got a lot of material to work with."

Will laughs and tops off his glass. "Stick with arms dealing."

"Smashing. It'll be our little secret. Klaus, the Iraqis, and a few AK-47s." She drains her glass and licks her lips. "Before when I asked for a cigarette I wanted to just look a bit affected. Now I'd actually kill for one.

In any event, tell me about these parents of yours on Aegina. Are they as dashing and well-mannered and fascinating as you are? I've got no children of my own, and I'm enthralled by people who do."

A man in a navy blazer—Tony, Will assumes—delivers a platter of four red mullets to a table in the center of the restaurant. The fish have been grilled whole and lie on a bed of lettuce and quartered lemons. Their eyes are a collection of black opals, catching bits of light.

He says, "Oh, they're much more dashing and fascinating than I am."

"With those dimples? I refuse to believe it."

Smiling again, Will lets his eyes fall to the tablecloth. A few crumbs of bread gather near the saltshaker. He brushes them away, collecting them into the palm of his left hand.

"My mom's a classics professor," he says. "That's why we're here. She's giving a talk on Aegina as part of some cruise. She's actually in Athens right now, I think. She has to go to a dinner, and she wanted to spend some time at the National Archaeological Museum."

"Have you been there?"

"To the museum? Once, when I was a kid." He lets the crumbs fall to the floor. "I don't really remember it."

"It's about as gorgeous as a bomb shelter."

"I read this article once about bomb shelters built by billionaires. Some of them are more gorgeous than you think."

Polly laughs.

"All the same—and I certainly don't mean to disrespect your mum; I'm sure she's lovely—but I don't see how studying a bunch of rocks and pottery shards is any more fascinating than sailing an arms dealer's yacht to Hydra. And with the god of wine, no less."

"Theater, too."

"Pardon?"

"Dionysus," Will says. "He was the god of theater, too."

"Well, whoever he is, he's a looker, don't you think?"

"I don't know. I hadn't really noticed."

"Oh, darling. Yes, you have. I've been watching you notice all night."
She winks, but it doesn't quite work; instead of looking charming, she just
looks drunk. "Don't worry, though. I've always said that if I'm to die I want
to come back as either a Spaniard or a homosexual. They seem to have
the most fun. You're good on wine, yes? Yes. Good. So, your mother digs
around for old things, and you fall in love with men named after Greek
gods. What's your father do?"

Will leans back and slips both his heels from his espadrilles.

"He's a writer. A novelist."

"Is he any good?"

"He's brilliant," he says. "His book was translated into sixteen languages."

"Well, that's something, isn't it?"

"It is."

At the table in the center of the restaurant, he watches as Klaus tears
into one of the mullets.

"Well, don't be coy," Polly says. "What's his name?"

"Dean Wright. The book is called *The Light of Our Shadows*."

"Don't know it—but then, I'm not much of a reader. All those words,
you know?" Polly thinks, twirling her necklace around her finger. "But
Jesus Christ, that title."

Will curls his toes and scratches his elbow. He thinks for a moment
and says, "You don't like it?"

"Who would?" she says. "Shadows don't have light."

Will and Dio leave the restaurant at midnight, and they're back on *Finja's
Fantasy* by twelve fifteen. Klaus has a house in town—a villa overlooking
the port with four spare bedrooms—but he would prefer it, Dio explains,
if they slept here, on the boat.

"I think he might be expecting guests," he says.

"It's after midnight." Will watches as he teeters up the gangplank, then he follows suit. Below him, the water's inky-black. "Who else could possibly be showing up?"

"I don't know." Dio reaches out his hand, and Will takes it, steadying himself. "I don't know."

They're quiet for a moment. Will listens as the sea, lapping against the hulls of boats, mixes with the other sounds from town. Voices chasing each other with echoes; music turned metallic and crisp in the night.

He says, "Forget about Klaus."

Dio doesn't answer. Instead, he chews on his lip. He unlocks the door leading belowdecks and pockets the key.

"I'll get us some ouzo," he says.

"Oh, I think I've had enough."

Will sits on a bench in the cockpit and slips his hands into the pockets of his khakis.

From down below, Dio calls: "There's no such thing as too much ouzo."

"That," Will says, "is categorically untrue."

Still, a moment later Dio remerges, a glass of clear liquor balanced in each hand.

"Saw you talking to Polly."

He hands Will a glass. The smell of the stuff's enough to make him sick, but he takes a sip anyway.

"You know her?"

"I know *of* her." He kicks his feet up onto the steering wheel. "She's nuts."

Will thinks of Polly's hair, the way she looped it behind her ears when she leaned forward. He thinks of how she laughed at his jokes.

He says, "I liked her."

"No one's saying you can't. Doesn't mean she's not a loon, though."

His ears burn; he's drunk, and he's getting defensive. He tells himself he doesn't know Dio, or Polly, for that matter. At the very least, he doesn't know them well enough to fight.

Instead, he asks, "Why do you think she's a loon?"

Dio shrugs and tosses back his ouzo like it's a glass of water. "Just what people say. She showed up five years ago and said she was an artist. Turns out she'd never painted anything in her life, though, and once she started, no one wanted any of her stuff. So, six months later she became a real estate agent. Sold Klaus his house."

"She told me she'd lived here on and off for thirty years."

Dio lights a cigarette.

He says, "She lied."

"But why?" Will watches smoke curl. "I mean, don't you think that's weird? I think that's weird."

"Who knows? Like I said, she's a loon." He balances the cigarette between his lips and refills his glass. "She had a kid and a husband back in England. Liverpool, I think? Liverpool or Manchester. People say she left them and ran off with her brother-in-law, and then when *he* left her she came here, to Hydra. Wanted to disappear, or restart. Same thing, really." Ash floats down to the water. "The kid was young. Five, I think."

"And you know this just from what, gossip?"

"Klaus," Dio says. "He knows what's going on, and he told me. I guess whenever she's drunk she tries to get in his pants."

Will finishes his ouzo. Dio's pack of Karelias sits on the bench between them, and he takes one, lighting it without asking if it's okay.

"I think Klaus is an asshole," Will says.

"Really? Because I think you're running your mouth."

Will doesn't respond. To his left, there's a faint splash—drunk teenagers, throwing rocks from the quay. On all sides of him lights bleed across the water.

He finishes his cigarette and announces, "I'm going to bed," then waits a moment, hoping Dio will stop him.

But Dio doesn't. Instead, he takes a long drag from his own cigarette and, before exhaling, says, "That's probably a good idea."

"I'll sleep on the couch in the galley."

Dio nods, and smoke escapes the corners of his lips. "There's a blanket underneath the bench down there if you get cold."

There's a new formality in his voice, and it causes Will to feel a sudden sting. How wrong he had been for coming here, he thinks. For believing that his affections would be returned by this improbably beautiful man, in this improbably beautiful place. For having faith that sun, and salt, and Hydra would iron out something so obviously one-sided into an equation that was balanced, reciprocal. Standing now, he stumbles, knocking his knee against the steering wheel. He's had too much ouzo, he realizes, and now he's drunker than he had hoped to get. As opposed to dulling his embarrassment, though, this amplifies it. He feels like a teenager again, mixing bad margaritas in the back of François's jeep. It's been over six years since then, and in that time he thought he had been doing the messy work of growing up. But then, there was the disaster with Rajiv, and now there's this humiliation with Dio—two instances in which he thought he knew someone, only to be proven wrong. Reaching down, he rubs the sore spot on his knee. Just when he thought he was on the verge of becoming an adult, it turns out he's only a kid.

From behind him, he hears Dio say something—a sentence in Greek that Will suspects is hardly complimentary.

"I don't know what that means," he says.

"You drank your horns. It means you're wasted. It's just an expression."

"Yeah, well, whose fault is that," Will tells him. "Anyway, I don't speak Greek even when I'm sober, and like I said, I'm going to bed. So."

"Oh, come on, don't be so sensitive." Dio's voice warms again, and now he grins. "Sit back down and let me teach you some."

"Forget it." Will shakes his head. He's tired of smiles and winks and tiny nods, he decides. Of all the insignificant ways that over the past twelve hours Dio has managed to keep him hoping, even when he suspects that all hope has been lost.

"Please?" Dio asks.

"I appreciate the offer, but it's a lost cause. My mother tried to teach

me but it was useless. To me, it just sounds like a bunch of people scream-
ing at each other."

Dio props himself up on his elbows. "Repeat after me: *kaliméra*."

"I know how to say *kaliméra*."

"So, you can speak Greek. Now, try this: *eímai amerikanós*."

Will folds his arms. "*Eímai amerikanós*."

"Close," Dio says. "Close, but the *k* is a bit softer. Try it again."

He does, but the syllables don't work; they get tangled up somewhere
between his lips and his tongue and emerge as a pile of mush.

"See? Pointless. Can I go to bed now?"

Dio laughs.

"Don't get frustrated. Here—" He reaches forward and touches Will's
face, placing a finger on each side of his mouth. "Do you mind?"

Will shakes his head.

"Okay, good—now try again."

He takes a breath, and Dio gently pushes on the corners of his cheeks.
Then he begins; as he speaks Dio presses harder, manipulating the shape
of his mouth, the movement of his tongue. It works—for the first time, Will
feels he's actually speaking Greek. Except, he's not able to finish the sentence. Before he reaches the end, Dio has his lips pressed against Will's,
coaxing his mouth open, catching the words as they tumble out.

He can't sleep. Each time he starts to drift he opens his eyes again to look
at Dio's body: the way the moon, glowing in the cabin's porthole, turns
his shoulder the same pale silver as the sea; the way his hair looks like it's
been carved from stone. At around three o'clock in the morning he slips
out of bed and into the yacht's main cabin. There, in the galley, he finds a
chart table stacked with maps and a GPS locator; two framed pictures of
Klaus holding just-caught fish; and, against the opposite wall, a set of
shelves lined with books. They're technical volumes, mostly, guides for

sailing in places like the Caribbean and the Côte d'Azur. Among them, though, are a few novels—a German translation of *The Alchemist*, a mass-market printing of some John Grisham thriller that Will's pretty sure he's already read. And then, between *The Magus* and *Travels with Charley*, he spots a familiar red spine, emblazoned with his own last name. He stares at it for a moment; he wants to make sure he isn't seeing things. Then he reaches for it. He tucks the book beneath his arm and takes it with him up to the deck.

It's cooler outside, and the air is fresh. It's not until he's sitting with his back against the mast that he realizes how stuffy it was down below. A few lights still shine along the quay, but otherwise the island sleeps. The houses that climb the hillside are now quiet; the moon casts their roofs as dark silhouettes. Will props his knees up and rests the book against them. The jacket is already worn—the upper right-hand corner of it is actually torn off—and on the title page there are stains from three drops of coffee. Still, the spine is curiously smooth and uncracked; it's like instead of reading the novel, Klaus has been using it as a coaster.

Now he reads the first bit, which is mostly exposition: here is a boy named Trip; here is his family, here are his friends, and here is his house. In the hands of a lesser writer, it'd be boring, prosaic stuff. Given the Dean Wright treatment, though, the chapters sing: his sentences surge with an undeniable electricity; his insights cut sudden and deep. Once again, Will succumbs to a mix of despair and wonder. He'll never achieve this degree of genius, but at least it's responsible for half his DNA. Somewhere around the fourth chapter, though, after a particularly graphic scene of Trip masturbating to thoughts of his fifty-year-old cello teacher, Will's eyelids become heavy. He's been reading for the better part of two hours, and now it's nearly morning. He'll head back belowdecks, he decides. He'll take the book with him and finish it back on Aegina. Tell his father he read it, and how proud he is to be his son.

Standing up, he stretches his arms above his head and feels a light breeze prick at his bare chest. He looks at the novel one last time, flipping through the pages, fanning himself. As he does so, though, he notices something. Two words, to be specific. Blinking at him like a pair of head-lights, parked in a dense fog of sentences: *Dolores Park*. He stops his flip-ping here and looks closer. He thinks, Huh.

Will opens the book again. He breaks its spine, and he reads:

James held his breath as the man approached. His limbs felt as if they were floating, hovering an inch above his towel and the park's grass. His heart beat as if it were not his own. He could see it, pounding and thrashing in his own caged chest. The man stood above him now, his broad shadow darken-ing the European history textbook that James had brought to read, and that he now endeavored to hide. James could smell him: sweat and patchouli, the musky scent of lust. The man cleared his throat and spoke. "I'm François," he announced, in an accent that James would soon learn was Quebecois.

He goes back and reads it again, and then again. It is, he soon realizes, all there: the clandestine trips to Dolores Park, the car rides to aban-doned gravel parking lots: all described in his words, the prose that he labored over as a sixteen-year-old. He looks at the pages with the same detached fascination that he imagines someone who's just had his arm ripped off looks at the stub where the limb used to be—a terrifying sense of wonder that hovers for a moment before the pain and horror set in. And then? And then. He becomes startlingly aware of how naked he is—both in the literal sense (he's only wearing his underwear) and—worse—the figu-rative one. He thinks of mannequins in department store windows be-fore the employees have gotten around to dressing them. He thinks of himself standing there, with the rest of the world gathered on the other side. He's got nothing to cover himself up, just a bunch of fumbled seduc-tions and stinging humiliations: instead of clothes, the horrible accuracy of his youth.

Now committed, he reads more, his fingers leaving wet prints as he flies through the pages. He is not the entire story—*The Light of Our Shad-ows* is always billed as an ensemble drama, and the book certainly con-tains other plots. Between all those moments, though, is Will. The Barnes

& Noble he used to cruise in Danville and the YMCA in Oakland. The parking lot outside the town hall in San Mateo, where a married council-man asked to kiss Will's neck and then started to cry. His secrets, pinned to the pages like butterflies, wings brittle and outstretched. He thinks of what reviewers kept saying about the novel after its release. They called it a chorus, and Dean a master of voices. Yes, Will thinks, that's right: *a master of voices.* The praise appeared so often—on the pages of *The New York Times* and *The Washington Post;* during an interview Dean did on NPR—that, as a joke, Chip Fieldworth went on eBay and bought Will's father a ventriloquist's dummy. A creepy wooden guy in a suit with a mouth that didn't stay closed. It sat in the corner of the Wrights' living room for two weeks, joining them for Sunday dinners and nights in front of the television. Finally, Sue Ellen said she couldn't stand looking at it anymore and threw the doll away. Leaning against the boat's mast, Will shakes his head. How stupid he had been for reading those reviews and not putting two and two together. For not realizing that one of the voices Dean had so adeptly mastered was his own.

It's nearing three o'clock in the morning, but still he forges onward, un-able to stop. Here are the protagonist Trip and his girlfriend, Belinda, hav-ing sex in the Lazy River of a water park in San Jose; here is his mother, Diane, demanding her husband watch as she chases a handful of off-market Quaaludes with a bottle of Sancerre. Then, after fifty more pages, he finds himself again—or, if not himself, then at least himself as James—riding BART. It's a moment he doesn't recognize; for the first time, he in-habits not one of his memories, but rather his father's fiction, and for this he feels a momentary sense of relief. It's an ordinary scene—James (or Will) is on the red line, his ears plugged with headphones as he rides from Embarcadero to Oakland. But then Dean pulls the rug out from under his readers: an earthquake hits, and the tunnel collapses. In total darkness, James listens as children scream and their mothers hold them close, whispering assurances. Pushing his nose to the pages, Will finishes the chapter by the faint glow of the anchor light rocking slowly above him:

"Everything will be okay," the mothers said, and "we'll be home soon."
These were empty promises—above them, cracks in the tunnel were widen-
ing, and soon the bay would swallow them whole. Closing his eyes, James lis-
tened, thankful for their capacity to lie in the face of certain death. This
would be his final thought: as the walls collapsed and crushed his fragile body,
he would wonder whether he had lived his life with the purity of these mothers.
Whether, despite the lies and the betrayals, the selfishness and the deceit, he
could say that he honestly meant well.

Then all was black.

Will slams the book closed and looks up.

He says, "That son of a bitch killed me off."

Sue Ellen

August 2
National Archaeological Museum, Athens

There's a group of teenagers huddled around a statue of Hermes, and they're using their phones to take pictures of his dick.

From where she's standing, near a case of Minoan pottery, Sue Ellen watches as they snicker, zooming their lenses in and out, comparing the results of their handiwork. Had she ever done that? Not that she can remember. Or, no—maybe once, during her freshman year at Amherst, when she enrolled in her first art history class, and every Tuesday and Thursday morning became a parade of tits, testicles, and plump Renaissance asses. Thinking a bit harder, she can recall the piece that had sent her into hysterics. A Neroccio de' Landi painting of the Madonna and Child, where the infant Christ bore a striking resemblance to her aunt Bethanne. She had pointed this out to her roommate, Elaine, and they'd spent the better part of two minutes biting their lower lips, trying to contain themselves. When the next slide held a more detailed image, though, they lost it, doubling over at the sight of Christ-cum-Bethanne's potbelly, chunky thighs, and olive-shaped prick. After class, she had received a scolding; the professor, a humorless medievalist named Calhoun, told her that he didn't tolerate giggling girls, and if he caught her acting so child-ishly again he would expel her from the lecture.

She shaped up after that. Not because she had any respect for Calhoun—she hated the man; he looked like an iguana—but because she was in-sulted by the implication that she was some tittering coed, another girl who had come to Amherst for a ring instead of a degree. She committed herself to being serious and stern. *Nakedness* became *nudity,* and encoun-ters with genitalia a sort of high-minded challenge. Once, during a trip to the Met in New York, she came across a carving of Perseus and, just to prove to herself—and to Calhoun—that she could, she stared at the hero's penis for nearly half an hour, willing the thing into namelessness. A slab of stone, swept slick and smooth by time.

"Falla finita!" A young woman—a teacher, Sue Ellen guesses—scolds the group and begins snatching up their phones, dropping them into a deep, black purse. *"Vi comportate come i bambini."*

Still laughing, they scatter into one of the museum's adjoining galler-ies, a room dedicated to early Cycladic funerary work. Sue Ellen watches them and, once they've disappeared, turns her attention back to the piece of pottery she's been pretending to inspect. It's drab and unimpressive: a squat terra-cotta pot flanked by two vases adorned with lilies and papy-rus. Listening to the shuffle of whispers around her, she pulls herself away. She links her hands loosely behind her back and glides over to the statue of Hermes. Once she's there, the god's belly button aligned with her nose, she digs through her pack for her reading glasses: she decides, finally, that she needs a better look.

It's a nice dick—she can't deny that. Around her, the room clears of people—for a moment, she's alone—and before she can overthink it, she reaches for her phone and snaps a picture. Maybe she'll send it to Cal-houn, she thinks, if the old lizard is still alive. She'll keep the email simple—no subject line or text. Just the photo, grainy and out of focus, of the messenger god's package, dressed in nothing but dust and Attic light.

Pinching her eyes shut, she rubs her temples: last night she accidentally got drunk, and now she can't seem to claw herself out of her hangover. This had not been part of the plan. Her ferry arrived at Piraeus at seven o'clock and in the middle of a cloudburst. Using her bag as an umbrella, she leapt over puddles and fought through a thick crowd gathered at the port's gate. She found a cab, which, after sitting in rush-hour traffic for nearly an hour, finally delivered her—damp, but not soaking—to the Athens Hilton. She had stayed at the hotel once before, for a conference she'd attended in '97, and her room was exactly as she had expected it to be: clean, boarding on sterile; impersonal, air-conditioned, and cold. Usually when she traveled she preferred to stay somewhere more authentic, or with a little character (*dirty* is what Dean would say. *Dirty and ill-managed*). Now, as she sat on the bed—as she felt the crunch of the stiff sheets beneath her—she decided she was glad she was here, as opposed to some B and B in Lycabettus. She liked the anonymity of the place, the way a person could stay at a hotel like this and completely forget herself. For two nights, she could pretend she was someone else. She could pretend she wasn't Sue Ellen Wright, Professor of Classical Studies, but rather a room, a number—724, specifically. A faceless customer that did things like watch pay-per-view and binge on room service and drink overpriced bottles of sauvignon blanc.

She opened the thick green curtains hiding the windows and stepped out onto the balcony. There, set in the middle of a plastic patio table, was an ashtray. Looking at it, she wanted a cigarette. She hadn't smoked in twenty years, but being here alone, she wanted nothing more than to suck one down. Looking out at the patchwork of roofs, avenues, and awnings, she remembered how, a few weeks ago, she had taken Will's Parliaments while they were on the ferry—had confiscated them, along with his lighter, and buried them beneath her wallet. Now she reached for her purse and dug through it for the pack. She smoked one and lit another with its butt.

She took a shower next. A long one, without fear of using too much water or hogging time in the bathroom. Then she threw on a fresh pair of khakis and a clean shirt and headed out for the evening. There was a long line of cabs waiting in front of the Hilton's lobby, their drivers leaning against the cars' hoods, arguing and smoking, so she opted to walk. First west, toward Syntagma Square, and then northeast, rounding the southern edge of Mount Lycabettus and into the quieter, posher streets of Kolonaki. It was a clear night—the clouds from the afternoon's storms had vanished—and as she walked the streetlamps above her began to buzz and flicker on. She ate at a restaurant she loved in the neighborhood—a French place; she needed a break from feta—and when she was done, when she had polished off a plate of passable coq au vin and a half liter of Bordeaux, she smoked two more of her son's cigarettes and set about walking again.

She thought, strangely, of Jasmine. She tried not to, but she did. Questions emerged from the place she had learned to bury them, a corner of her mind that she only allowed herself to access on nights like this one, when she was alone and a little drunk, wandering the streets of Athens. She remembered the phone call from her colleague and the fights that followed; she remembered Connie. The past year hadn't felt like life so much as a challenge. A test to see how capable she was of creating an equilibrium in which they all might survive.

Maybe, though, she had been unfair to Dean. She thought of how he nervously asked to join her in the shower, the boyish hesitation with which he took her hand on the beach. In dwelling for so long on how he had wronged her, she had turned him from a partner to an adversary—an enemy whose words she needed to parse and whose motives were inherently suspect. It was a thought that had first dawned on her during one of their last sessions with Connie. Watching him speak from the opposite end of the couch, she found herself recoiling from his apologies, rejecting them for the sake of rejection. She left that day more disgusted with herself than with him; in the name of self-preservation, she had turned her back on resolution. The next morning, she called him and invited him to move back in. "I'll buy the moving boxes," she even offered. "I'll help." Forgiveness, she decided, wasn't forgetting someone's sins. It was remembering who they were before they committed them.

Near the corner of Skoufa and Iraklitou she ducked into a bar without bothering to look at its name. She needed a nightcap, she decided, something to help her get a little rest. Inside, it was a typical dive: too dark in some corners and too light in others; so many lit cigarettes that the bitterness of burning nicotine drowned the stench of smoke. At the end of the bar she found an empty stool and, after flagging down one of the two bartenders, she ordered a whiskey. As the man prepared her drink, she glanced forward, where she caught her reflection in the scratched mirror that served as the bar's backsplash. She wasn't whole—all she could make out were bits of her cheeks and wisps of her hair; fragments obscured by half-empty bottles of vodka, gin, and rum.

The bartender set her drink down, and before she took her first sip, she knew she needed another.

"Swiss."

She turned to her left, where a boy and a girl were sitting, smiling at her. He was wearing torn black jeans and a leather jacket, even though it was ninety-two degrees. She was more appropriately dressed—jeans, still, but paired with a tank top and heels. They could have been Will's age, she thought, smiling back. Will's age or older—twenty, or maybe closer to thirty-five. She had always been terrible at telling how old people were.

She said, "Pardon?"

The girl turned to the boy, and then back to Sue Ellen.

"We . . . uh, we have a bet that you're Swiss."

"American."

The girl smiled and the boy handed her five euros.

Sue Ellen grinned, took too large of a sip of warm whiskey, and said: "I actually hate the Swiss."

"Yes," the boy said. "They're pussies." Then he pointed to his friend. "Her father's Swiss."

Sue Ellen leaned forward and began to apologize, but the girl stopped her.

She said, "You don't see me living in Zurich, do you?"

What happened next? They exchanged names. He was George; she was Lena. They asked Sue Ellen if she was alone, and when she said yes, they bought her a drink—a rum and Coke, which she hadn't had since she was twenty-two (incidentally, they were twenty-two); they wouldn't take no for an answer. And then, because she didn't want to seem ungrateful, she bought them both drinks in return. It went back and forth like this for an hour—Sue Ellen trading rounds with two people half her age. At first, she felt self-conscious: What must they think, looking at her? Here is a woman who lost her way. These insecurities soon passed, though. Around the third or fourth drink, she started feeling not so much anxious as just plain drunk. This was welcome; it distracted her. Whereas she had forgotten what it felt like to socialize with people in their twenties—the strangeness of their slang; the ways in which she could be intimidated by youth—she knew what it felt like to be wasted.

"Sue Ellen."

Here was George, leaning toward her, his breath warm with rum.

"*Ti kánis*, George. What's up."

He smiled and set a lit joint in the ashtray between them.

He said, "You like hash?"

She looked at it for a moment, watching its ragged tip burn. *Did she like hash.* Yes, George, of course she liked hash. She had never been a puritan, and the notion that age somehow erased the need for vices was—at least to her—one of the more hilarious myths about growing old. Now, did she *smoke* hash? Did she *partake in it with any frequency*? That was a different question; she was, after all, a mother, someone bound by the burden of example. But then, were these her children? Did she owe them the same guidance? Looking at George, she tried to imagine Will sitting in front of her. They were about the same height, she figured, and carried themselves with the same lose confidence—an easy mix of fey masculinity (George, she had come to suspect, was also gay). What would she do if he were, indeed, her son?

Picking up the joint, she decided not to think about it. She decided that here—free of her son and her husband—she would just get stoned instead.

It turned out to be the right choice: ten minutes later, Lena suggested they go to a dance club, and the hash—God bless it—softened Sue Ellen's judgment just enough for her to agree to tag along. First, though, she excused herself to the restroom. Locking the door, she ran her fingers through her hair, working out the knots, smoothing down the frizz. Reaching into her purse, she found some strawberry ChapStick, which she applied generously, until her lips took on a glossy, pinkish tinge. Then, leaning forward, she pouted and made a face—something, she thought, that approximated sexy. She winked at herself and laughed.

The club was called Cinderella, and while this made her laugh, too, she did her best to keep her giggles to herself, using the crook of her arm to shield her face as she burst into periodic hysterics. Lena ordered the three of them a bottle of Johnnie Walker and two liters of Coke (this was, she explained, how things were done), and as she set about mixing their drinks, Sue Ellen leaned against a black wall and watched George dance among a scrum of sweaty bodies. He moved nimbly, his body rolling and gyrating to the thick beat of a song she thought she knew but couldn't place—a remix or Abba, or some other Scandinavian artist whose music was particularly suited to a place like this. Above him, a hundred disco balls spun at varying speeds, their gilded surfaces tossing flashes of iridescence across his cheeks, nose, and thin, bare arms. The floor left her dizzy—a patchwork of different squares that lit up with the beats of the music; an endless barrage of green, blue, and red lights, against which George's body would temporarily disappear, his flesh becoming shadow. Every so often he looked over at her and beckoned her to join him, and while she initially declined, by the third invitation she relented; she refilled her drink and she danced.

It felt delicious. Even now, in the excruciating haze of the morning after, when each step she takes causes her head to feel like it's about to explode, she can admit that: dancing felt delicious. The sweat dripping down her back, the way the hash made her limbs weightless, buoyant—it was heaven.

Sue Ellen told George this. Swaying her hips toward him, she said, "George, this is heaven."

He looked at her and shrugged; the music was too loud, he couldn't hear.

So she tried again. She pressed her lips against his ear, and yelled, "THIS IS HEAVEN!"

He shook his head and tossed back a few whiskey-soaked ice cubes.

"No," he said. "Heaven is in London."

This confused her, but Sue Ellen didn't mind; she liked his nonchalance.

"I HAVE A SON! HE'S ABOUT YOUR AGE!" She was still yelling, her mouth an inch from his cheek. "HE'LL NEVER BELIEVE I CAME HERE WITH YOU!"

"Introduce me." George bobbed his head from side to side, like he was waiting for a better song.

"I SHOULD! I THINK YOU TWO WOULD GET ALONG!"

"Probably. I like Americans." Sue Ellen was smiling, and George reached out to tap her incisors. "They have nice teeth."

A woman passed behind Sue Ellen, jostling her and causing her to spill a few sizable drops of whiskey on her Keds.

"GEORGE, I'M SO STONED!"

"You can stop shouting now."

"George, I'm so stoned."

He leaned over and kissed her cheek.

"Tomorrow we'll go somewhere better," he said, and looked down at their feet. "We could have gone tonight, but we're not wearing the right shoes."

What did she say to that? She can't remember now. All she knows is that she kept dancing and drinking whiskey-Cokes until finally it was four o'clock in the morning and George and Lena were screaming at each other in one of the club's mirrored corners. She started to work her way over to them, scooting past couples making out with drunken ferocity, but she stopped once she was in earshot; the subject of their argument, it turned out, was her.

"You always do this," she heard Lena say. Her Greek was slurred and soggy, thick with a German accent. "You always fucking invite me out and then totally ignore me."

"You were the one who said we should come to Cinderella." George poked an ice cube with his straw. He sounded bored. "I hate this place."

"That's not what I mean." Lena's voice wavered, and she shook her head. Her eyes she had painted with dark, smoky mascara, and her lips were bloodred. Looking at the girl's reflection in the mirror, Sue Ellen felt her own heart break. Lena didn't know what she was doing; Lena was trying too hard.

She said: "What I *mean* is that you'd rather dance with some random American *in pants* than hang out with me."

George tossed the straw to the ground and ate another of the ice cubes.

He said, "I mean, you're not that good of a dancer."

It was at this point that Sue Ellen thought about interjecting; as Lena fumed, she considered throwing herself between them to explain that (1) she was not some *random American in pants,* and (2) there was no need to fight, especially here in Cinderella—a club that, in Sue Ellen's estima-tion, was the happiest place on earth. A moment later, she decided against it; watching them argue, she realized that this was a fight they'd had be-fore and a fight they would continue to have. The drama of Lena's needi-ness and George's ennui would play out until, finally, he decided he didn't actually like her and he stopped returning her calls. He would find new friends—other bored young men whose insecurities more closely resem-bled his own—and on the off chance that they ran into Lena, he would explain to them that they used to hang out, but that she had a crush on him and got clingy and weird, and she was never really that fun, anyway. They would nod and understand. Of course, neither George nor Lena could predict this, not now, in Cinderella's fantasia of lights, where their youth elongated the present into a mythic infinity, a place where friend-ships didn't crumble and sons didn't leave and marriages didn't falter.

And so, Sue Ellen left. She let them have their fight and call her an American in pants, while—smiling—she slipped out into the blistering night.

The welcome reception the next evening begins at five thirty and is held in the restaurant on the Hilton's roof. At Gianna's request, Sue Ellen dresses nicely, trading in her khakis for a white sundress and her Keds for a pair of heels. She rides the elevator to the top floor, where she checks in with a Golden Age Adventures employee manning a registration desk just outside the restaurant's entrance. She signs in and picks up her name tag, a sky-blue lanyard with a white badge that reads SUE ELLEN WRIGHT, PH.D.: SCHOLAR AND HOST.

The restaurant is called the Galaxy, and its interior is futuristic—at least she wagers that it was once futuristic, back when it was first designed and the future was imagined to be a place bathed exclusively in neon purple light. She wanders through it, past knee-high tables and sleek white chairs, wobbling on her heels, wondering where everyone is until, finally, she turns a corner and discovers a glass door to the terrace—a wide, open expanse of the roof with a bar, a band, and seventy-five sweating seniors. They're gathered in groups of four or five, and as she weaves through them, she picks up whiffs of their heavy perfume: patchouli, sandalwood, and cypress. There already seems to be a loose hierarchy, even in this early stage of the trip: the more seasoned cruisers are dressed in linen blazers and floral scarves, and talk exclusively about where they've sailed and the lines they like best ("Lindblad was a delight; Windstar, never again"). The first-timers, meanwhile, gather at the crowd's edge. They wear wrinkle-free shirts and collapsible hats, and their conversations meander and stall: how long their flight was *("endless"),* and the weather ("hot, but nothing like Palm Springs."). Pushing deeper, past a woman in a pink vest and Velcro Eccos, Sue Ellen tries to remember if she's ever seen this many old people in a single place. Both of Dean's parents had passed away by the time they met, and when it came to her folks, they had insisted on dying at home. She had tried to persuade them otherwise—there was a senior living facility called Sunset Village in Tacoma—but they had been adamant ("Who says our sun is setting, anyway?") and soon she stopped arguing. She acted disappointed; visiting them during trips back to Port Angeles, she would let Will run around the overgrown backyard as she pointed out to her father all the things that he and Sue Ellen's mother might trip on, all the things that might break a hip.

Now she wonders if she should have tried a little harder. At the very least, time spent wandering the halls of Sunset Village would have better prepared her for this—knobbed knees and swollen ankles and three wobbly walkers. Making her way over to the crowd's edge, she hails down a cater waiter and, surveying his tray, plucks off a canapé—a piece of brittle toast topped with a euro-size round of watermelon and a square of dry feta. As she chews, she leans against the Plexiglas railing and does her best to look youthful, fresh. Still, she can't seem to process the fact that she's closer in age to the blue-haired horde before her than she is to George and Lena. It's not as though she *feels* old. Which causes her to wonder: Do they? Are they shocked when they look in the mirror and are confronted with sagging skin and drooping ears? Do they feel betrayed by their sore feet, their heavy lungs, their uncooperative bowels? Or have they accepted that the war they're waging with their bodies is one of attrition—a prolonged battle that they will inevitably lose?

She's thirsty, she decides—the sun's been against her neck for the past ten minutes—so she makes her way over to a bar on the opposite end of the roof. She considers ordering a whiskey but quickly decides against it; last night's Johnnie Walker is still there, clinging to the insides of her cheeks. Instead, she picks up the cocktail menu. Printed on a small placard, it advertises drinks with names like Persephone's Party and Calypso's Chantey. The bartender asks her what she wants, and she feels herself starting to panic: she worries that whichever drink she chooses, she won't be able to say its name without doubling over in laughter.

Finally, after ten seconds of dallying, she steels herself.

She says, "Give me Hera's Heartache, extra tarragon."

It turns out to be the wrong choice—a Long Island iced tea, but with the salty aftertaste of beef bouillon. Still, she drinks it and smiles at the bartender; it took him five minutes to make it, after all. Then, just as she's about to retreat to her post by the railing, she hears a voice—deep, male— say her name.

"Sue Ellen Wright?"

Turning, she sees a man about her age, with a pair of aviator sunglasses and a shock of snow-white hair. He's wearing a tan dinner jacket, and beneath it his white button-up is streaked with beads of perspiration.

"Charles Winkler," he says, extending a hand. "From the University of Richmond."

The drink has been sweating against her hand, which she wipes dry before taking his.

"Charles," she says. "Of course."

"Oh, don't worry—we haven't met before. I just—" He cranes his neck and gazes around the terrace. "They told me one other lecturer would be here, and you're the only person who doesn't look like the crypt keeper, so I figured it must be you."

"Ha." She glances down at her name tag and shows it to him—proof of her existence. "Well, you were right. Here I am."

"Is this your first one of these things?"

"It is, as it happens," she says, nodding. "And you?"

He laughs.

"Me? No, I'm an old hand at this point."

"Oh?"

"*Mhhm.* Last summer it was In the Steps of Odysseus with Viking, and then Virgil and His Contemporaries with Norwegian the summer before that."

He smirks and raises an eyebrow.

"I'm becoming a veritable pro."

"Well . . ." She sucks down more of Hera's Heartache. "Well, that's really something."

Charles shrugs. "It's not a bad gig, if you think about it. A few grand to drink shitty drinks and give a Cliff's Notes version of the same lecture you've been giving for the past thirty years." He swats a fly away from his nose. "Of course, this time none of us will actually be *on* the boat, but honestly—and take it from me on this one—that's a blessing in disguise."

She shakes the ice in her glass. Fifty feet to her left, she sees Gianna, clothed in a black sheath dress and a pair of dauntingly high stilettos. She presses the tips of her fingers together as she bows, shallowly, to two guests—a couple in matching cargo pants, the pockets filled and sagging.

She says, "I don't know, floating around the Aegean on a yacht for a few weeks doesn't sound half bad."

"You'd think that." Charles laughs. "But you'd have a change of heart if you saw fifty geriatrics get norovirus in a span of two hours."

"That happened?"

"Last year, about ten miles off the coast of Crete. Totally apocalyptic. By the end of it, there wasn't a single working bathroom." He nudges her with his elbow. "So, believe me—you're better off on Spetses."

"Aegina," she says.

"Pardon?"

"I'm on Aegina."

"Ah, yes. Aphaía and all that. My apologies." There's a silence, an empty space where Sue Ellen watches a man adjust his fanny pack. She considers plotting her escape.

Charles sighs. "Well, this is what we are now, I suppose."

"Pardon?"

"Oh, come on, Sue Ellen. You know what I mean. This is what our job is now. Acting as script consultants on rip-offs of *Indiana Jones*. Writing op-eds for newspapers about the importance of studying the classics right before the fall semester starts, even though we know that the real money is in computer science. Giving ten-minute lectures to a bunch of seniors who overpaid for a themed cruise: three neat facts about the design of the Acrop-olis. Education, like everything else, has become a pop commodity."

"I tend to disagree."

"Yeah?" He looks at her glass. "What's that you're drinking?"

Sue Ellen swirls her straw. She doesn't want to tell him.

"A Long Island iced tea," she says.

"Really? Because mine's called Zeus's Zest."

Another waiter approaches them with a tray, this one topped with mini tortes stuffed with goat cheese. Charles takes two. Sue Ellen politely declines.

She asks, "So what, exactly, are you proposing?"

Charles makes a sucking sound, like he is slurping something off his teeth.

"I'm proposing you find another one of these things next year, and then the year after that," he says. "I'm proposing you drink all the allit-eratively named drinks you can."

Staring at him, she wonders if she's strong enough to toss him over the edge of the roof, and if she is, how long it would take him to reach the sidewalk.

But she also knows he might be right; the futility of her job digging up old things in order to explain a world that no longer exists has recently been weighing on her more heavily than she cares to admit. She doesn't have the bandwidth to consider the implications of that realization now, though—not tonight, when her brain trudges through a lingering hang-over. Instead, she glances around the party, trying to find someone else—a lone straggler, nervous and fidgeting—who she might befriend. But as she scans the crowd, something else catches Sue Ellen's eye: a girl walking in her direction, her wild hair pulled back into a loose bun, her hands work-ing to smooth the wrinkles from an oversize blue shirt.

"Sue Ellen," Eleni says, once she's standing before her. "I was wonder-ing if we could talk."

Eleni

She doesn't know where to look as they ride the elevator down from the Hilton's roof, so she fixes her eyes forward, at the car's twin mirrored doors. Above her, a small screen counts down from fourteen, chiming each time they pass another floor. It's a pleasant sound, a nice sound, one that fills the space between Eleni and Sue Ellen unobtrusively but fully; each time Eleni worries the silence is growing too dense, it's there—*bing*—saving them both from making the sort of stilted, stale conversation that elevators uniformly demand. As she stares forward, she tries to catch a glimpse of Sue Ellen in the door's reflection. As they descend past the seventh floor, she reaches up to fix her hair; somewhere between four and three, she picks a piece of lint from her dress.

The elevator reaches the ground floor and the doors slide open. Initially, Eleni thought they might go to a restaurant or a café—something a little more personal than a hotel. It's hot, though, mercilessly so, and the idea of asking Sue Ellen to abandon the Hilton's air-conditioning for the city's shadeless sidewalks feels like too much of an imposition, particularly now, when Eleni has already interrupted her at work. Instead, she leads her past a wide gold pillar to an empty leather sofa tucked away in a corner of the lobby. In front of them is a glass table, on top of which sits a vase containing a bushel of white hyacinths and a magazine called *Athens NOW!* Beneath the cover model, printed in a sleek, modern font, is a headline in English: NOT YOUR GRANDMOTHER'S ATHENS.

"What are you doing here?" Sue Ellen says. "I thought your meeting was yesterday."

A woman in heels pulls a rollerboard suitcase across the lobby, and its wheels clack along the marble floor.

Above them, trickling out from unseen speakers, there's the lobby's Muzak, a hybrid of acid jazz and bouzouki. "Ta Daxtilidia," set to a track of synthesized drums and a Casio keyboard.

Eleni says, "Things didn't exactly go as planned."

"Apparently not. You told me you were heading back to Aegina last night, and here you are, still in Athens."

"I couldn't sign the papers," she says.

"I'm confused."

"I didn't sell the Alectrona, Sue Ellen."

"Why not?"

Eleni takes a deep breath.

She says, "Because I think you should buy it instead."

She explains how the idea came to her last night, a few hours after she left Oskar in Lugn's conference room. Once she had fled the building, she had gone to Syntagma Square. The sun was setting; the sign on top of the Hotel Grand Bretagne glowed in the dusk, and outside the Old Royal Palace flags hung slack in the still air. She found an empty bench near the square's center and, not knowing what else to do, she sat, fixing her eyes forward on an old fountain. It was empty, but a group of people her age sat on its edge, their legs dangling into the basin as if there were water to cool them. To her east, periodic mobs emerged from the metro stop below the stairs leading to Amalias Avenue, and as she watched them flood the cafés that surrounded her, she realized that she was hungry—starving, actually; the only thing she'd consumed in the past eight hours was a single swallow of Oskar's parsnip drink, the taste of which still lingered, coating her tongue with a persistent film. Opening her purse, she found the sandwich that Stavros had made for her and, tearing away its foil wrapper, she ate it, first slowly and then with increasing urgency; the last half she took down with two monstrous bites. It was, she realized, a delicious sandwich—or, more delicious than any sandwich had the right to be, the ham and cheese and tomato perfectly proportioned, the mayonnaise spread with care. As she chewed, she began to cry, though this was something she didn't realize until a few moments later; when she had finished eating she brushed her cheeks and found that they were wet.

"I sat there for so long, I missed the last ferry," she says. "I had to sleep on my friend Sophie's couch."

This was true: she had texted Sophie from Syntagma Square. It was a short message (*does your sofa have any vacancies?*), which earned her a short reply (*as a matter of fact it does*), though from the simple exchange Eleni derived an extraordinary amount of comfort; while the rest of her life crumbled around her—while she cried over ham sandwiches and second-guessed decisions—she still had this: friends who were willing to put her up for the night, who could be asked favors without demanding to know their contexts.

"And that's where you had this idea?" Sue Ellen asks. "On your friend Sophie's couch?"

"They want to tear it down, Sue Ellen. They want to turn my parents' bedroom into a juice bar that makes these shit-colored drinks out of raw parsnips."

"From my experience, that sounds like most of Swedish cuisine." Eleni doesn't laugh, so Sue Ellen continues: "I'm not sure what you expected. They're developers. They develop."

"I understand that. What I don't understand, though, is why letting go of something also has to mean letting go of everything it used to be."

Sue Ellen leans forward and rests her elbows on her knees. On the glass table between them, the mohawked model on the cover of *Athens NOW!* stares up.

"I think you're grossly overestimating how much university professors get paid."

"As it turns out, I'm a very motivated seller."

Sue Ellen drums her fingers on the glass table, then reaches out to straighten the magazine.

"How would I care for it?" she asks. "I live in California."

"You could move to Aegina."

"I have a career—"

"You said you were bored with it."

"—not to mention a husband and a son."

Eleni rolls up the sleeves of Stavros's shirt. This morning, after Sophie had left for work, she had given it a thorough ironing, but still it bears the indelible creases of a second-day wear. She listens as, on the opposite side of the lobby, the elevators chime and their doors slide open. The truth is she had not considered this: the fact that Sue Ellen's life extends beyond the four weeks that she's spent on the island and the boundaries of their friendship; the fact that Sue Ellen was like her, like anyone: a person who existed in too many places at once; who was burdened with obligations and responsibilities from which it was impossible to extricate herself. To this end, Eleni's grand plan, which just this morning had the clarity of a solution, now takes on the opaqueness of a hypothesis. A theory formed in the hermetic universe of Sophie's apartment: a place where all she had to worry about was what she needed and what she suspected Sue Ellen wanted. Where the concerns weren't opposing forces and unpredictable variables, but rather whether Sophie had a second bottle of Syrah.

Still, Eleni keeps her focus. You don't balk when an investor points out an obvious glitch in your product. You offer an easy solution, and you move on.

"Your husband's a writer," she says. "He can live anywhere."

"He hates when people tell him that."

"And Will's graduated. He'll have a job of his own soon, anyway."

"That is . . . proving to be more difficult than expected."

Sue Ellen shakes her head. She reaches forward and adjusts the magazine, leaving it half an inch askew.

She says, "It's not going to work. Go back to Lugn, or whatever that company is called. Tell them that you've reconsidered."

Eleni hears her, but she refuses to listen.

"These Swedes, they want to run my family's hotel into the fucking ground," she says. "You, though . . . you understand why the Alectrona matters, why it's important—not just to me, but to you. A week ago, remember what you said? You were telling me that a part of you always thought that you'd end up here. You said that in another life you did."

She takes a breath.

She says: "Just *picture it,* Sue Ellen."

For a moment, Eleni thinks that she's managed to convince her. Sue Ellen's eyes drift away from the magazine, landing eventually on an undistinguishable point beyond the lobby's front door. And in her gaze, Eleni thinks she catches traces of what she's seen in the past, when Sue Ellen has talked about her first summer on Aegina: longing, wrapped in a quiet, defiant happiness. But then, as quickly as it's there, it's gone. Sue Ellen looks at Eleni and sets a hand on her knee.

"I have pictured it," she says. "In fact, I've been picturing it ever since your father made me a similar offer almost thirty years ago, and I think it's about time that I finally stopped."

Ginny Polonsky

"The problem," Ginny says, "is that Athens and its foreign lenders took way too long reviewing whether Greece had met its European bailout terms."

She's yelling, she realizes. But then, she's got a lot to compete with: two of the cab's windows are down, and the city's soundtrack—its honks, crashes, and strange, foreign sirens—assault her from all sides. There's also the driver's music, a medley of electro Europop that, at least to Ginny, sounds like variations of the same bad Cardigans song. Finally, there's his driving: the man can't seem to decide which part of the road he prefers, and each time he turns it's with such force, such ferocity, that her first inclination is to clutch her stomach. *I know there are a lot of options,* she wants to say. *But would it kill you to pick a lane?*

And yet, she presses on: "Yannis Stournaras said as much last year, when he spoke to Parliament's economic affairs committee!" she calls out as they barrel through a tunnel. "The delay hurt economic recovery— that's what he claimed. He said that because everyone dragged their feet,

Greek markets weren't able to bounce back. I'm inclined to agree with him."

In the rearview mirror, Ginny sees the driver nod and raise both eyebrows. She sits up a bit straighter and leans forward to catch his response; instead, he reaches down and turns up the volume—now she can feel the stereo's bass, vibrating against the back of her bare thighs. Leaning her head against the window, she lets the wind flip her curls across her eyes. She wants him to engage; she wants him to acknowledge, at least tacitly, how much she knows about his government's problems. Over the past three nights she's committed herself to studying the chaos unfolding in Greece. And while she may not entirely understand the wonky nuances of budget compliance, sectoral balances, and monetary union guidelines, she's nonetheless thrilled by the country's capacity for procedural drama. So much so, in fact, that she's obliged herself to form unshakable opinions about how the government should proceed. This, though, is routine for Ginny. Whenever she travels abroad, she accepts a moral responsibility to research and take stances on her destination's social, political, and economic challenges. Last March, before she went to Paris, she spent every morning for two weeks reading *Le Monde* on her phone. The same was true when she traveled to Chile, South Africa, and Iceland, and she pored—respectively—over translated editions of *El Mercurio* and the *Mail & Guardian* and *Fréttablaðið*. But then, that's just the sort of person she is: a global citizen. A member not of a single country, but of the whole of humanity.

Frustrated, she pulls a few stray strands of hair away from her lips and adjusts her sunglasses, which have started to slip down the bridge of her nose. She wishes that she still had Twitter. If she did, she would fire off commentary about what she's just observed. *Birthplace of Democracy?* she imagines punching into her phone. *More like birthplace of #APATHY.* She doesn't have Twitter, though; she deleted it a year and a half ago when, after spending an entire Saturday scrolling through Donald Trump's old tweets, she decided she couldn't occupy the same space as him, digital or otherwise. Reading his rants was like feeling his hot breath on the back of her neck—the precursor to a horrifically incompetent attack. It was also, she conceded, a drain on her productivity. She was so busy telling people what she was thinking that she couldn't reflect on what she actually thought. And so, she got rid of it. She fired off a straightforward *goodbye forever* to her 693 followers and nodded, satisfied, as the app vanished from her screen.

A space opens up in the traffic, and her driver lays on the gas. Ginny watches as, alongside the highway, regiments of billboards welcome her to Athens.

"How much longer to Piraeus?" she asks.

"One hour," the driver says, changing lanes.

"You said 'one hour' fifteen minutes ago, when we were at the airport." She takes off her glasses and squints. "I've got a ferry to catch at one o'clock."

The driver shrugs. He says, again, "One hour."

She slips her sunglasses back on to shield her rolling eyes—she knows how she can get when she's feeling pressed for time. Sinking deeper into the backseat, she thinks back to the beginning of June, when Claudia Min knocked on the door to the *Berkeley Review*'s office and asked if Ginny had a moment.

"For you, Claudia?" she had said. "Anything."

Two falls earlier, Ginny had taken one of Min's courses—an introduction to fiction that was a prerequisite for more advanced workshops. At first, she had been intimidated. She had seen Claudia's name on the cover of three novels, the last of which got her on the long list for the National Book Critics Circle Award. Two weeks into the semester, though, she happened upon a short story Min had published in *Granta*—a woeful character study about a woman deciding whether she should sell her apartment in Flushing. Ginny—gleefully—hated it. After that, her intimidation faded. Faded to the point where she had no qualms about saying things like *For you, Claudia, anything.*

Now, Min smiled and pulled up a chair. The *Review* was housed in an old utility closet on the sixth floor of the English Department: two desks, a Nabokov poster, and a ten-year-old iMac stuffed in a space the size of a California King mattress. When Claudia sat, her knees touched Ginny's and, for a moment, she tried to reposition herself, shifting her seat, adjusting her silk shawl. For her part, Ginny stayed put—this was her turf. Besides, she liked watching Claudia squirm.

She said, "So, what's up?"

"I was just wondering . . ." Claudia trailed off. She was always trailing off. Starting thoughts and not finishing them, letting half-bred sentences hang like flimsy clouds. Her prose was the same way, bloated with unbaked, doughy ideas. Ginny couldn't figure out if pregnancy had lessened her patience (she'd taken her test two weeks earlier) or if she was having a bad day. Either way, Claudia was driving her nuts.

"You were wondering *what*," she said.

"I was just wondering if you'd decided on what fiction you'll be publishing in the next issue of the *Review*."

Ginny leaned back; their shins touched, and Claudia flinched. The truth was she hadn't—to date, she had received only two submissions, a pair of stories by the same inept freshman. Drivel that she would have aesthetic qualms with publishing on a roll of toilet paper, let alone in the pages of her journal.

"We're doing final reads now," she said. "It's been a competitive pool, as I'm sure you can imagine. We're going to have to make some tough calls."

Claudia uncoiled her shawl and folded it across her lap.

"I figured that might be the case," she said.

"Why do you ask? Just, you know, out of curiosity."

"I've got this student. An advisee, really . . ."

Claudia's eyes drifted up to the ceiling. Behind her, the iMac's fan began to whir. As she counted the seconds, Ginny's blood pressure peaked.

"Claudia," she said, finally. *"Focus."*

"I'm sorry. My mind—it drifts."

"Yes. I know."

Claudia eyed her, the vacantness giving way to quiet indignation. For a moment, Ginny worried that she had gone too far.

But then Claudia looked down. She folded her shawl once more and said, "I've got an advisee who turned in a rather lovely thesis. Or, perhaps lovely's not the right word. Haunting, maybe? Yes. Haunting. Or, hauntingly lovely. I think that's probably best. In any event, I thought if there's room, or if you were in need of submissions, you might like to consider it for the *Review*."

Ginny dug a fleck of grime from beneath one of her fingernails—she didn't want to seem too eager.

She said, "Well, like I just told you, we've already got a *very* competitive pool. But if you want to send it over, I suppose I could give it a look over lunch."

Claudia stood. "You've always been so gracious."

Ginny ignored the tinge of condescension, the lifted eyebrow. She said, "Whose is it, by the way?" And then: "Don't forget your shawl."

Claudia reached down and snatched the silk from the seat.

"Will's."

"Wait, Will *Wright's*?"

"Is there another senior named Will in the department who I haven't had the pleasure of meeting?"

Ginny stood up.

She said: "Send it over immediately."

Five minutes later, she had the story up on the iMac's screen and her suspicions were confirmed: the son of a bitch had plagiarized it. This was not a surprise in itself. Will was a purple and clumsy writer—inarguably the worst in the department. Despite Claudia's simpering taste, her dangling prose, the fact that he had impressed even her was cause enough for alarm. So, obviously Will didn't write the story. The thing that did shock Ginny, though, was that the story he decided to plagiarize was his father's. She recognized it immediately. Dean had shared it with her in April, after she had suffered through an especially grueling workshop in which a story she had been particularly proud of had been eviscerated. Typically, harsh critiques didn't bother Ginny: she was an artist, and being an artist meant having thick skin. But this particular submission was personal. A month earlier, after having turned in two stories that were along the lines of her normal work (a cosmonaut named Nina wakes up one day and discovers that she and Vladimir Putin are the last two people on earth; a tenth-grade physics student stumbles on an equation that inverts gravity in men's restrooms), Dean urged her to submit something a little closer to home.

"Write about what's in front of your face," she remembers him saying to her. They were in a room at the Embassy Suites in Walnut Creek, and her nose was buried in the tangle of his chest hair. "Write about what you know."

So she did. She wrote about a junior at an unnamed California university who was wrestling with insecurities over issues like the width of her hips and her moral worth. Her classmates hated it. They called the protagonist grating and self-indulgent, and said that the only character with whom they had really connected was the girl's roommate—a bottle-blond twit who did nothing but preen and make fun of the narrator's cankles. Perhaps worse than all that had been Dean's reaction: as the onslaught progressed, he had done nothing to stop it. Instead, he sat back and watched. And at certain moments, Ginny thought she even saw him smile.

When the massacre was over and class was finally dismissed, she had gone to his office and cried.

"We all write things that don't work," he had said, stroking her hair as she sobbed.

She sniffled. "You don't."

"Not true. I do all the time." He sat across from her and booted up his computer. "In fact, I'll show you."

And now, sitting in front of the iMac in the *Review*'s office, she read the story a second time. When she finished the last page, she leaned back in her chair and closed her eyes. She didn't consider herself a religious person, but it didn't take her long before she decided that the day's events were a sign: an opportunity to use Will to reveal Dean's whereabouts. It had been a month since he had disappeared, and he had stopped returning her calls. Maybe, she figured, someone was looking out for her. Maybe she wasn't so alone.

In the back of the cab, she chews on a fingernail. Pulling a single knee up to her chest, she thinks of the email she sent Will—the one where she fawned over his *(Dean's)* story. In many ways, it had been fun to craft; she was, after all, a storyteller, and her enthusiasm for Will's work was nothing short of fiction. Still, that excitement paled in comparison to the ecstasy she felt when, five days later, she discovered twenty-seven missed calls from him on her cell phone. She really had been at a silent retreat in Ojai—she hadn't been lying when, upon finally calling Will back, she had told him that. Pregnancy, coupled with the burden of stalking Dean, had exhausted her, and so she had treated herself to a bit of R&R: some tofu *nao* for breakfast while overlooking a collection of shallow amber hills; a few *oms* in the afternoon while perfecting her downward dog. It rejuvenated her spirit and worked out the kinks from her bowels. It allowed her time to reclaim her center while Will, equipped with nothing but an iPhone and spotty internet, was left to panic.

"I'm in Greece, with my parents." Even now, as the cabbie pulls up to the curb next to the ferry terminal, Ginny can hear the unease in Will's voice, the clip of his strained vowels. On the one hand, she had been shocked that she had so easily wrangled the Wrights' location out of him; in a matter of two sentences, she not only uncovered the country to which Dean had fled, but also the exact locale—a rock called Aegina, moored in the Saronic Gulf. On the other hand, she had always suspected that Will only worked with half his brain, and the shoddy half, at that. The bigger surprise would have been if she hadn't succeeded in manipulating him— if, somehow, he'd wised up and saw through her guile.

"You walk from here?" the driver says, glancing in the rearview mirror.

"I walk? I'm *pregnant.*" The fact that she admits this surprises Ginny—it is, she realizes, the first time she's said it out loud.

"The police, they stop me," he says. "I'm sorry—you must walk."

She hands the driver forty euros and then digs through her purse, fetching the piece of paper where she had written down the name of the hotel where Dean is staying. Unfolding it, she says the word silently, then out loud: *Alectrona.* Finding it—the hotel's name—was a bit more difficult. While Will wasn't exactly bright, he would still surely become suspicious if, once he revealed his family was on Aegina, Ginny had suddenly asked for an address. So she had resorted to other means of investigation: calling the fifty or so hotels on the island one by one; impersonating a made-up classics professor, a certain Dr. Wendell, who needed to mail a rare manuscript to Sue Ellen Wright, posthaste; apologizing profusely, in an accent of vague European origin, for losing both the name and address of Dr. Wright's lodgings. It was tedious and frustrating work—half the time the phones rang unanswered—but then she figured sleuthing often was. Thankfully, she had the constitution for it. She was good at sleuthing. Sleuthing, Ginny liked to think, was her middle name.

"Oh, *hello,* Dean."

She brushes hair away from her eyes and winks at herself in the mirror. The ferry lurches to starboard, and she steadies herself, bracing one arm against the bathroom's wall and the other against the small steel sink. Once she's regained her footing, she inhales, her eyes watering as she teases out notes of coffee, gasoline, and piss.

Then, she tries again: "Oh, hello, *Dean.*"

But no—that's not right, either. Her voice sounds too languid, too bored, like she's just stumbled upon him at the cinema, coming out from some

tiresome Terrence Malick film. She should liven it up, let her words bounce
a bit, give them a little air.

"Dean," she says, widening her eyes, "why, hel*lo*."

Better, she thinks. Not perfect—she needs to work on not looking like
she's getting goosed—but better. Pressing her shirt against her midsec-
tion, she turns and looks at the profile of her stomach. She's not showing
yet—at this point, she figures the baby's just a coil of cells and veins and,
depending on what right-wing pregnancy websites she tortures herself
with, maybe a few fingernails. To some degree, though, she wishes she
was; she wishes she could surprise him with a belly, some visual proof of
why she's there. The sheer drama of it would be delicious. Glancing
down at her wrist, she unburies her watch from beneath a hairband and
wonders how much time she's got left before she reaches the island.

She doesn't like Greece. And while the country's politically apathetic
cabdrivers certainly don't help the situation, this isn't a new thing; she
just never got into the classics. Antigone was a whiner, and she stopped
reading *The Iliad* halfway through, when she discovered it was just a book
about a bunch of boys. She tried to change this—she felt, as a thinking
person, that the classics were something she should probably enjoy. She
had even gone so far as to take one of Sue Ellen Wright's classes during
her sophomore year at Berkeley—a seminar on antiquity and feminist
thought. The class had only mildly impressed her, and when it came time
to review it at the end of the semester, she gave it a tepid score of 3. To
begin with, in the middle of the term Sue Ellen slapped Ginny with her
first C. The grade was for a small assignment—a response paper on the
first sixteen lines of Euripides's *Medea*—but it was a C nonetheless, and
Ginny still counts it as one of life's greater slights. She wanted to know
who *had* managed to impress Sue Ellen; who *had* received an A. Or, maybe
she didn't—she suspected the answer might disappoint her. The fourteen
other women with whom she had shared the class were complete bores—
vapid little things with names like Lily and Kate, who considered themselves feminists because their favorite book was *Pride and Prejudice* and

they knew *Middlemarch* was written by a girl. Meanwhile, here was Ginny, quoting Adrienne Rich and Rebecca Solnit; here was Ginny, turning in five pages instead of the required two. And for *that* she was laden with a C? The mind boggles.

There was also the issue of Sue Ellen. Ginny often wondered whether she was too smart for her own good. Two years later, she can still remember Sue Ellen's tendency to bluster into class five minutes late; her tendency to stare out the window, as if lost in thought, whenever a student was reading aloud. These observations both enraged and fascinated Ginny. On the one hand, she felt she deserved better from her professor; at the very least, she felt she deserved her undivided attention. While Ginny didn't necessarily agree with the capitalistic direction of neoliberal education, the fact remained that the American university was a business, ergo she, as a student, was a paying customer who deserved certain courtesies. On the other hand, she was mesmerized by the ease with which Sue Ellen embodied the image of a thinker. She wore her ideas like a pair of old jeans, slipping in and out of them with comfortable lucidity. She didn't appear to be rankled by questions or uncertainty, and when she spoke, people listened—not just because she was the professor, but because her voice was buoyed by a sort of easy authority. Ginny, meanwhile, always feels like she's muscling her way to respect; for as long as she can remember, she's practically had to shout just to be heard.

She holds none of this against the woman. Nor does it factor into her motivation for coming to Greece to confront her husband. Ginny's not that kind of person. She's not in the business of napalming marriages—she's in the business of getting answers.

There is, of course, the concern that she'll encounter Sue Ellen before she finds Dean. This is a very real possibility that Ginny has considered, and that she considers again as she disembarks from the ferry and flags down a taxi. Luckily, she's prepared herself for this curveball, too. If she runs into Sue Ellen first when she arrives at the hotel, she'll fib. She'll say that she's just passing through. A quick jaunt in Greece before she moves on to somewhere more interesting, more exotic. Turkey, maybe. Turkey or *Iran*. Will mentioned that the family was on the island, she'll explain, and given just how much she adored the Wrights—all three of them!—she would be remiss if she didn't at least pop in and say hello. Then, at a moment that's appropriate, she'll pull Dean aside, tell him she's uh, *enceinte*, and ask him what the holy fuck is going on.

She takes a moment to collect herself once the cab drops her outside the hotel. After doing her best to flatten out the wrinkles from her shirt and the shorts she's been wearing for the past eighteen hours, she looks up and takes in the Alectrona. It's small—much smaller than she expected. Two stories of pale gray brick, topped with a red tile roof. A short iron gate leads to what she presumes to be the entrance, and as she passes through it she notes the rust coating its hinges, places where the white paint has flecked away. She doesn't bother knocking or waiting for someone to help her with her bags; passing a fruitless orange tree and tangle of bougainvillea, she pushes open the front door and lets herself in.

The lobby's clean, small, and, above all things, empty. She stands there for a moment, waiting to see if someone will come to fetch her, and when no one does she begins to poke around. An étagère to the left of the check-in desk holds a hodgepodge of relics: an old blue-and-white teapot, a wooden pipe, a gold horse the size of Ginny's foot. Examining them, she catches bits of her reflection in the case's glass and tries to improve on what she sees: collecting and repositioning loose strands of hair, wiping the grease away from her forehead with an inch of her shirtsleeve. When she's finished she returns to the desk, where she notices a small silver bell. The sort that you would ring at a deli counter, maybe, or an abandoned hotel in Greece.

Looking to each side of her, she chimes it once, then twice.

She clears her throat. She says, her voice cracking, "Hello?"

Still, there's nothing. No creaking footsteps from the second floor; no jolt of a door slamming. The only thing she can hear is the wind. Hiking her rucksack farther up on her back and tightening her grip on her suitcasc, Ginny ventures onward, making her way through an empty dining room and an adjoining kitchen, a galley with a stove, a sink, and a looming white fridge. There's an instant where she worries she's going to retch again—the scent of garlic and fried onions seeps from the kitchen's walls—but the feeling passes, and she goes back to wondering what she's been wondering since she arrived: namely, if she had somehow spelled the name of the hotel wrong; if, because of a minor error, Ginny will be playing Whac-A-Mole with Aegean inns late into the night.

But then she notices something: through the window on the kitchen's back door, she sees a patio, and the blue of a swimming pool. Pushing aside the window's yellowed lace curtains, she sees more: next to the pool, stretched out on a chaise longue, is a set of legs. Or, perhaps more specifically, *a set of very recognizable legs.* She feels her heart clutch in her throat and her palms begin to sweat. She breathes; she watches the legs twitch once and reposition themselves, and she recommits herself to her goal.

She swings the door open. As she walks over to him, her rucksack bounces along the base of her neck and her suitcase swings from her left arm. When she reaches the chaise, she stops and waits while the wind kisses her cheek. Though his eyes are hidden beneath a pair of dark Ray-Bans, she can tell he's sleeping: his hands are folded neatly across his chest, and his belly lifts and falls with a steady, smooth rhythm. She considers waking him with a kiss but thinks better of it—Dean detests being startled, and she would hate to kick things off on the wrong foot. Instead, she pulls out the tie that's been keeping her hair back, freeing an explosion of curls. She says, in a voice that's at once coy but assertive, sexy but controlled: "Hello, handsome."

Nothing happens, so she tries again. Repositioning her curls on either side of her face, she cranks the volume up a few notches and coos, "I said, *hello, handsome.*"

Nothing. Dean grunts once and sniffles. Then, after licking his lips, his tongue darting in and out like a snake's, he's still.

Overhead, a warbler dances on the branch of an orange tree and takes flight.

Closer to town, a dog barks, and a cat howls.

Her patience diminished, Ginny lets her rucksack drop from her shoulders before slamming her suitcase down on the pool deck. Dean wakes and leaps from the chair with a start.

She says, "Goddamn it, I'm *here*."

Dean

He thinks, Maybe if he closes his eyes for long enough, she'll disappear. She'll just—Christ, he doesn't know—evaporate. A sweating, red-haired mirage that gets sucked up by the unrelenting sun.

But he blinks once, then twice. He sees that Ginny Polonsky has not vanished. He sees that Ginny Polonsky is, indeed, very much still there.

"Oh, my God," he says.

"Are you surprised?"

"*Oh, my God.*"

"You're surprised."

Dean looks at the luggage gathered on the pool deck. Her ubiquitous rucksack, its threadbare canvas covered with iron-on patches from Planned Parenthood, the Human Rights Campaign, and the Marin County chapter of the Sierra Club. The same rucksack that he's seen balled up on the floor of his office, in the corner of her bedroom, and—on two occasions when Sue Ellen was out of town at a conference—at the foot of his bed. And then, next to it: a suitcase. A big suitcase. A suitcase bursting with multiple pairs of underwear, clean T-shirts, and whatever else it is that twenty-year-old women pack. A suitcase that, most important, portends a very long stay.

Staring down at the mess, he says, "Ginny—"

She smiles. "Yes, Dean?"

"—what the fuck are you doing here?"

She begins to answer him, saying something about Will, and a phone call, and a fateful if tedious visit from Claudia Min. But before she gets too deep (and Ginny, he knows, can get deep), he stops her. He shakes his head and waves his hands in front of his face until, finally, she shuts up.

"I didn't actually want to know why you're here."

"Then why did you ask?"

Her smile fades.

"I don't know. It was a rhetorical question."

She gathers her hair in a loose ponytail and drapes it over her left shoulder. Her neck's already pink, well on its way to burnt. Ginny was not made for the sun.

"You're wrong," she says. "It wasn't."

He picks up her rucksack. He'll throw her out if he has to, he figures. He'll haul her to the port and put her on a ferry himself.

"I'm not doing this," he says.

"Doing what? Properly defining a word?"

"Jesus Christ, Ginny."

"I'm sorry, Dean." She sits on one of the patio chairs and folds her hands in her lap. "I'm sorry that I'm a writer and I like language. I'm sorry that me wanting you to use the term 'rhetorical' correctly offends you so much."

"You know that's not what the issue is."

She stares up at him, and her scowl, her performative sternness, momentarily softens to a pliable confusion. Unfolding her hands, she rubs her palms against her bare knees and looks to either side of her, appraising the patio—its dead pine needles; its shallow pool—for the first time since she's arrived. For an instant, Dean sees her for who she really is: a girl a third his age with wild and unkempt hair; a girl who's suddenly found herself a long way from home.

Then she says: "This place is a dump."

"It has a certain charm."

"That's just a literary way of saying it's a dump."

Her rucksack is heavy. It tugs against his left shoulder and, slouching against its improbable weight, he wonders what she has in it. A barbell, it feels like. A barbell, a pair of shoes, and—he hopes; he always hopes—a copy of his book.

"You need to go, Ginny. I'll help you find a hotel in town, and I'll cover the ferry back to Athens, but . . . you need to go."

"Are you honestly insane?" She grips the side of her chair and stays put. "I've been traveling for over twenty-four hours, Dean. To get here I took two planes, a very unsafe taxi, and a *boat*. I spent eighteen hours in Frankfurt, where I ate a microwaved *hot dog* from a *cart* in the middle of terminal *D*. And I did it for you. Do you hear me? I did it all for you." She grips the side of her chair. "So, no, thank you. I won't be going any-where."

He grabs her beneath each shoulder, digging his fingers into her wet armpits, and, with a heave, he pulls her to her feet.

"You're leaving," he says.

"I'm not!" She pushes away from him. The chair teeters and tumbles over, clacking against the stone. "Jesus, Dean. I thought you'd be happy to see me."

Her lips quiver, and a series of small cracks along her cheeks threaten to deepen. He wants to see her cry, he realizes.

"Well, I'm not," he says. "I'm not happy to see you."

"Not even a little?"

"Not even a modicum. Not even a speck, an iota, a scrap, or a soupçon. In fact, I am, decidedly, *unhappy* to see you."

She starts sobbing, her tears moistening her cheeks not in elegant rivulets, but all at once, in a deluge. Her shoulders convulsing, she reaches downward and starts pulling at the hem of her shirt—a white tee bearing a cubist, Picasso-fied rendition of Nelson Mandela.

"I mean, what were you thinking?" he continues, feeling finally in control. "I came here to get away from you. You realize that, don't you? When I left without telling you, I was literally *running away from you.* What could have possibly made you think this was a good idea? No, don't cover your face with your hands—I want you to answer me. What could have possibly made you think this was a good idea?"

Ginny wipes her nose against her sleeve. Tendrils of hair have escaped her ponytail and now cling to her damp neck.

She says, in between a trio of guttural sobs: "Because I love you?"

He drops her rucksack and grabs both of her shoulders.

"You don't. Do you hear me? You don't."

Ginny shakes her head. "You're not allowed to tell me that."

"That's where you're wrong. I am, especially because you don't know what you're talking about." She pushes his hands away and sits down again, this time pulling her left foot under her rear. Christ, Dean thinks, repulsed: she's never looked so young.

"You're in love with my book, not me," he says. "Those are two different things."

"That's not true," she says. "And even so—they aren't that different. You *wrote* that book."

Dean shakes his head. "You're leaving—now," he says. "Will could be back any minute, and my wife's presentation is tomorrow. I want you off the island by then."

Ginny sniffles and mumbles something Dean doesn't quite make out.

"I can't understand you when you're blubbering."

"I said it's today!" Ginny yells. "Sue Ellen's presentation is today. I looked it up on Golden Age Adventures' website before I bought a one-way ticket and *crossed ten time zones* to see you. I swear to God, sometimes it's like I know more about your own family than you do."

Dean's pulse begins to quicken; there's a catch—shallow and brief—in his throat.

"No," he says. "No, she and I talked about it two days ago. It's on Saturday."

"Well, today *is* Saturday." Ginny releases her left foot from under her ass. The skin around her ankle is red and wrinkled, striped from the places where it's been pressing against the chair's slats.

"You know," she says, "you're really acting like an asshole."

Dean picks up the rucksack again and slings it over his left shoulder. Then he reaches for her suitcase and, finally, Ginny's wrist.

"Get up," he says. "Now."

"Don't touch me."

He doesn't listen to her.

He yanks her out from the chair and says, "We're going inside."

In the dining room, he searches for a spot where he might hide Ginny. Someplace far from the window, where he might reason with her—or, at the very least, coerce her into going home. A closet would be best, he thinks, were it not for the distinct possibility that she might suffocate or—worse—scream.

"Here," he says, shutting the door. "Sit there, at this table."

She does as she's told, plopping down in a chair. Its wooden legs wobble and creak.

"What are you going to do now?" she says. Her voice is still sad, but it carries something else with it: rancor and resentment. Ginny's impressive, youthful spite. "Fuck me?"

Dean looks at her legs, which she's presently sliding open. Her shorts ride up her thighs, uncovering freckles, and skin, and—finally—a few wisps of red hair. Reaching down, he shoves her knees back together.

"For Christ's sake, Ginny. No one's doing any fucking."

He is, he realizes, a little scared of her. Rubbing his bald spot, he looks down at the tiled floor.

Behind him, he hears her say: "I came here to tell you something."

"Yeah? Well, save it. I'm trying to think."

When does his wife's presentation start? He remembers her saying something about dusk—about all those geriatrics gathering with their walkers at the temple's steps, and Sue Ellen speaking as the sun dipped into the Aegean, and her stopping just in time for everyone to have a glass of cheap chardonnay before Zeus, or Poseidon, or Shiva, or whoever ripped a tear in the space-time continuum and carried them all away to that plush, easily navigable retirement home in the sky. No—he's making that last part up. Obviously he's making that last part up. But seriously, she did mention dusk, though, didn't she? Or maybe that's just the writer in him, adding dramatics where they needn't be. Maybe the presentation is actually in, say, an hour, smack-dab in the middle of the Greek afternoon— if that's the case, then he's even more screwed than he imagined. More important, though: *Why can't he remember?*

Because he's someone who forgets. He doesn't want to be—that's why he went along to Connie's, it's why he's trying to get Ginny to leave. He wants to be someone who not only remembers the hour of his wife's lecture, but who recalls—without blinking an eye—details like birthdays and anniversaries, promotions and deaths. Someone who writes thank-you notes within a week of receiving a gift, and visits sick friends in the hospital, and asks his guests about dietary restrictions before planning a dinner party. He wants to be someone who plans dinner parties. None of this comes naturally to him, though. Instead, he ignores. He buys himself Christmas presents, and always makes sure his wineglass is the fullest, and trolls negative Amazon reviews of his novels under the pseudonym Book Fan Beth. He'll try harder though, he thinks, as he listens to Ginny sigh behind him. And if he does, if whatever deific power brought him to Greece and Ginny to him decides to intervene on his behalf, then he promises he'll repent. He'll forgo his vices—his college coeds and Hollywood minxes—and become the sort of man he knows he's supposed to be.

He presses his palms together and closes his eyes. But then he opens them again. He's never prayed before, he realizes, and he doesn't know where to start.

Ginny says, "I think you'll be very interested in what it is I have to tell you."

"I doubt that," he replies. "I really, really doubt that."

On top of one of the room's other tables he sees his laptop; rushing to it, he flips it open. He'll follow Ginny's lead and look at Golden Age Adventures' website, he figures. Find a calendar for the cruise that lists the day's events. And while he's at it, he'll research ferry schedules, bus lines, and airfares. He won't shut the thing off until he's got a plan—an immediate one—to get the girl off the island and out of the country. He doesn't care what it costs him; he'll refinance his house if he has to.

But when he hits the power button, nothing happens: no illuminating screen, no whirring fan, no clicking of impossibly tiny gears. He hits it again, and then again, and then again, punching it harder with his thumb each time, until Ginny, who has now stood up and is hovering dangerously close to the window, says, "Jesus Christ, what did that computer ever do to you?" The problem is the battery: over the past two weeks, it's managed to die. If he'd actually been using the laptop to write—which is the ostensible reason that he brought it with him from San Francisco in the first place—then maybe he would have been periodically charging it. But he hasn't been writing. And so, this current quandary—a dead computer; an ungoogleable future—is no one's fault but his own. A spectacular display of lethargy, which has allowed the old PC's juice to bleed out at a slow, electric trickle.

"What's the Wi-Fi password here?"

He turns and sees Ginny standing next to one of the room's French doors.

"Get away from there," he says. "Someone might see you."

"It's the only place I get service." She pushes one of the doors open and sticks her arm outside. "Now tell me the password."

Dean says, "You won't be here long enough to need the password. Now goddamn it, Ginny, *get away from there.*"

"Well, I'm here *now,* aren't I? She leans out a little farther, trying to catch a signal with her mobile. "I want to post a picture I took on Facebook."

He lunges toward her and rips the phone away.

"Are you insane? What if Will sees it?"

"He blocked me three months ago."

"Frankly, I can't say I blame him."

Dean looks down at Ginny's mobile—a thin, rose-gold model encased in reclaimed wood. Its screen displays a photograph of Virginia Woolf looking thoughtful and forlorn, the tip of her equine nose reflecting light from some unseen source. Staring at her—those gaunt British cheekbones, those suicidal eyes—he suddenly has an idea. His fingers shaking, he connects to the hotel's spotty Wi-Fi and begins tapping on the screen.

"Hey," she says, taking a large step toward him. "What are you doing?"

"I'm buying you a flight." He doesn't look up. "I'm sending you home."

"God*damn* it, Dean! I don't want to go home!" Ginny reaches for him, but he holds the phone above his head. She's close enough now that he can smell her—the too-sweet notes of yesterday's deodorant and the yeasty ones of this morning's sweat. He pushes her aside and turns his back. There's a Lufthansa flight out of Eleftherios Venizelos at nine o'clock this evening. She'll have to spend the night in Zurich, but he doesn't care: he's four clicks away from freedom. He's almost there.

"Your son turned in an old story of yours for his senior thesis," she blurts out. "Will—he plagiarized you."

Dean gawks at her. "You're lying."

"I'm not." She's backlit—the sun floods in through the door behind her—and as he watches her chest heaving, her hair catching bits of light, he thinks she might burst into flames. "That shitty thing you wrote about the Laundromat. He turned it in to Claudia Min. She gave him an A minus. In fact"—she digs into her rucksack and pulls out a fistful of wrinkled pages—"I have it right here."

"An A *minus*!?"

"It's not a very good story, Dean. Anyway, aren't you furious?"

It's an interesting question: Is he? Maybe, he thinks—or, at least, conceptually he is. Both at his son's predictable ineptitude and Claudia's grading audacity *(an A minus)*. And if the immediate stakes weren't, well, *what they are,* he imagines that conceptual anger might transcend into something a little more palpable, a little more real. But alas, the present isn't exactly affording him opportunities for transcendence. Ginny, after all, is still standing there, very much in front of him. Her phone is still in his hand, the Lufthansa site open and begging for his credit card.

"I'll talk to Will."

"You'll *talk to him*."

"Yes, he's my son. I'll talk to him." He punches in the number of his American Express. "Now, where would you like to sit on your fourteen-hour flight from Zurich to SFO? The back of the plane sounds good, I think. Somewhere in the middle. I wouldn't want you to have to decide between window and aisle."

Lunging forward, she snatches the device from him and throws it out the open door. There's a moment where he thinks he can hear it falling—the whoosh of oxygen against its trim sides; the thick island air being split in two—but then that sound is replaced by something else: a splash.

"Ginny!"

"There's another thing, Dean."

"What the *fuck* were you thinking?"

He rushes over to the door and looks out, just in time to see the phone sinking to the bottom of the Alectrona's pool.

She says: "I'm pregnant."

Will

It's early—he's waiting for the nine o'clock ferry to Aegina—and from the bench where he's sitting he can see the mast of *Finja's Fantasy* rocking back and forth in its berth. Two small flags hang from the backstay, one German and one Greek, and he watches them flutter before he works his eyes downward, skimming past the boat's rigging and landing, finally, on a man's body. It's Dio, he knows, prepping the yacht for Klaus. Coiling thick braids of rope, scrubbing away cigarette ash from last night. Will wipes bits of sleep away from his eyes and stares for a moment longer. Then he spits out the stale gum he's been chewing and looks away.

What had happened before he read the book? He and Dio kissed, then undressed. Had paused their little Greek lesson long enough to slip out of their clothes and into each other.

It was difficult work. Getting belowdecks was hardly as easy as moving from a couch to a bed; on the boat, there were obstacles. Still, they did it, performing the acrobatics necessary to sleep together. They worked their bodies into strange new geometries, their breaths fogging the room's single porthole. Careful not to smash their heads on the cabin's low ceiling, they engaged in that familiar tug-of-war, stealing control from each other, only to relinquish it seconds later.

And it would have been fine, Will thinks now, if he'd left it at that, the simple victory of sex. He hadn't, though. Instead, he had convinced himself that a night spent with someone on a boat deserved meaning, a significance that lasted beyond sunrise. Reaching into his backpack, he fishes out the *tempelopita* he bought earlier that morning. The pie's still hot. Gingerly, he peels it away from its wax paper and breaks off a chunk, his fingers turning greasy from the phyllo dough and melted cheese. It's tart and rich—halfway between a Danish and a bowl of fettucine Alfredo. He looks into the pastry's steaming innards and decides that he hates feta. He decides he'd be happy to never see the stuff again.

He had returned to the bedroom belowdecks after discovering what his father had done. He had undressed, throwing his pants in with the sheets that he and Dio had kicked into a loose pile on the floor. He slept then, but fitfully; his mind kept racing back to what he had stolen from his father and what his father had stolen from him. While he wanted to believe that he and Dean were different, the evidence suggested they were more alike than Will was comfortable admitting. It was a thought that churned his stomach—twice he rolled over, thinking he was going to be sick.

Dawn had already started to creep upon him when he finally shut his eyes. When he woke up an hour or so later, Dio was still asleep on his stomach, his spine crosshatched with traces of oil and sweat. Will watched him breathe, the subtle rise and fall of his body. Then he slipped into his khakis. He draped his oxford over his shoulder and returned to the deck. Hydra dressed for morning was an entirely different island. The silence of 3 A.M. had given way to the crowing of roosters, the barks of distant dogs. Slowly, sunlight began creeping over the eastern edge of the harbor, washing everything, from boats to cobblestones to rough stone cliffs, in pale pink.

What was it that he had said to Dio when, persuaded by both certainty and anger, he had gone back downstairs to wake him? *I think I love you, and I want to stay with you.* Something awful like that, he thinks, throwing away the rest of the *tempelopita:* it's only been an hour, and already he wishes he could erase the memory. Unremember the way Dio had blinked and then shaken his head.

"Will . . ." he had started.

"I know it's a lot to wake up to, but just let me finish."

Dio sat up and rested a pillow across his bare thighs.

He said, "Go on."

His curls stood on end, and his lips were chapped. He looked fogged, annoyed. Waiting to go back to sleep.

Will hedged. He said, "I don't mean, like, forever or anything. Just until the end of August, maybe. Or September. I could help you at the school. Teach classes or something."

"You've sailed for a day."

"You said I'm a natural, though."

"You can't tie a bowline."

"Quoth Dionysus: *Fuck the bowline.*"

Outside, something rattled: a cart being dragged across the pier's uneven stones.

"It's a bad idea," Dio said. "You're supposed to leave in a day, anyway."

"Two," Will corrected. "I'm supposed to leave in two days. But that's what I'm saying—I don't *have* to go then—"

"No." Dio tossed the pillow to the floor and, standing, reached for his clothes. "You're not staying. You can't stay."

"Give me one good reason why."

Dio put on his pants and yanked up the zipper.

"Because you're on vacation."

"So what?"

"Because this isn't real." He ran both hands over his head, tangling his fingers in his hair. Will leaned against the cabin's wall and pulled his

knees to his chest. "Look"—Dio lowered his voice—"I know this all seems great right now. You come to Greece, meet some guy on Grindr, screw around on a boat. Get drunk with an old British woman. That's not real, though, okay? That's not actually life."

"Yeah? Then what is?"

"Here? You want to know what life is here?" Dio slipped his arms through his shirtsleeves. "It's the churn of tourists coming in and out. It's kissing the asses of fat fucks like Klaus so they'll toss you a few jobs when they're feeling generous. It's working at that shitty café on Aegina so you can make rent for you and your father."

He began fastening the buttons but stopped.

"What it's not," he said, "is this."

Will stared at his feet. He hadn't bothered to find his espadrilles, and now, in the half-light of the cabin, his toes looked dirty, caked in salt and grime.

He said, "So, what, you don't think I could stand it?"

"I think whatever delusions you have would disappear very fast."

"I think you're wrong."

Dio sighed, and his ribs, framed by each side of his shirt, pressed against his skin. Will watched him, waiting for him to speak, to punch another hole in his plan. When he didn't—when it became clear that Dio had done all his punching—Will looked away. He had a headache, he realized. A hangover that, after having been suppressed by the fantasy of a new life, was now gunning to wreak havoc on his morning.

He said, "This is humiliating. This is just really fucking humiliating."

"Hey, take it easy."

Will didn't respond. He crawled off the bed and pushed past Dio into the yacht's galley. He shouldered his backpack and searched through a small refrigerator for a bottle of water. There wasn't one; the only things he could find were one of the cans of Alfa left over from the day before and some orange juice. He thought for a moment, imagining the way the beer might calm his pounding head. Instead, he reached for the juice—one of those quaint European cartons with a tear-away foil top. What he wouldn't give, he thought, for something obtrusive, and fake, and American. One hundred and twenty-eight ounces of Sunny Delight, in a giant plastic jug.

"You don't get it," he said. "I have nothing to do back in California. My friends, they all graduated with these jobs at banks, or nonprofits, or Snapchat or something. Me, though? I've got nothing. Literally *nothing*."

"Maybe you should stop comparing yourself to everyone else."

"Oh, knock it off. The only people who ever say that are smug assholes and Buddhist monks."

"You think I'm a smug asshole?"

"Well, you're certainly not a Buddhist monk."

He finished the juice in two swigs, holding it in his mouth a second too long before swallowing. Finally buttoning his shirt, Dio explained that this had happened once before, two summers ago, with a kid named Jeff from Evanston, Illinois; that while they hadn't spent quite as long together as he and Will had, Jeff nonetheless succumbed to the same endless-summer fantasies.

"That's comforting," Will said. The acid from a hundred oranges raged against his gums. "It's wonderful knowing I'm a notch on a belt."

"That's not what I meant."

He didn't ask him to elaborate. He tossed the empty carton into the sink, and he left.

There was a moment when he considered telling him about his father's book. Dio was staring at him, waiting for an explanation, and Will nearly told him everything; he wanted him to know why going home wasn't an option, wanted him to know he wasn't just another kid with a crush. Now he's glad he didn't. He's glad he didn't buy into the belief that, in divulging a secret, he could somehow bind himself and Dio together; that by letting Dio have a part of him he would be creating an irrevocable bond. To do so would have been naïve, and he can see that now; instead of a bond, there would have been one more truth that was no longer Will's. A story that Dio could shape however he chose and tell to whomever he wanted.

Jeff from Evanston. Maybe he'll give him a call, he thinks, as a gull goes to town on the scraps of his *tempelopita*. Track him down and hit him up for a chat. See if he wants to talk about guys on Aegina named after lout-ish Greek gods. Local losers who, shackled by their own country's ortho-doxy, agree to suck only tourist dick.

But then, no—that's not it, either, is it? Resting his elbows on his knees, he remembers what Dio said to him: *the churn of tourists coming in and out.* The monotony of standing in one place while the world around you turns; the horror of having to stare at the same tired faces every time a cruise ship hauls out of port. No, Will realizes, Dio had not preyed on him, and to think otherwise was a fantasy in itself. A fairy tale in which Will was interesting and desirable, in which his greatest accomplishment was something more than almost getting a job naming potato chips. The truth, he realizes now, is that Dio was bored. Profoundly and stupidly bored. Will provided a solution, however temporary, not because of who he was, but because he was there.

To that end, if there's anyone who's capitulated to vulgar fetishes, it's Will. And not just with Dio, but with all of it: the islands sinking in the sea; the myth of some personal renaissance hiding in a bottle of Mythos. His parents, with their notions of language, literature, and history, have taught him to scorn tourism, the admit-one voyeurism of the Other—it was why, Sue Ellen said, they would never go to Santorini or Mykonos. The Wrights were travelers; they didn't use maps or take pictures—instead, they *lived.* How, though, was that any better? Weren't they all after the same thing? A desperate flash of transcendence, the possibility that see-ing an old church, a different sunset, might send them home somehow changed? Any differences that exist are cursory, a matter of aesthetics and staging: a girl with a selfie stick is content to have an epiphany among the hordes of Monastiraki. Will, meanwhile, requires Polly. Requires a voice, sweet and heavy with wine, telling him that he's *new.* Dio was right—this isn't his life. And yet, here he is, plundering from it anyway. Tearing it apart, looking for something to save him.

The cab stops outside the Alectrona in a cloud of red dust, and after handing the driver a ten-euro note, Will slips his backpack over one shoulder and slams the door. He needs to take a shower. Something to wash away the grime, and salt, and whatever traces of Dio still cling to him. When he enters the inn's foyer, though, he hears a rustling from the dining room, then his father's voice, calling his name. The sound causes Will to bristle, not just because it surprises him but also because of its timbre—a peculiar, idiosyncratic lilt that Will, like all sons of oversize fathers, uses to gauge if there's trouble ahead. He tries, in this case, to ignore it; instead, he focuses on what Dean has done. Dropping his backpack to the floor, he heads down the hall. As he walks, he whips together a diatribe to the beat of his gait—each step another word in how he'll dress down his dad: *You. Stole. My. Life,* and *You. Are. A. Creepy. Fuck.* As he gets closer and closer to the dining room, though, the rhetoric of prose gives way to poetry, and then to a genre not yet defined. A sort of free-verse accumulation of verbs and nouns and sputtered, melodramatic accusations. Stopping outside the dining room's threshold, he takes a breath and tries to rearrange his thoughts. He thinks of the times his father punished him whenever he screwed up as a teenager—how, after laying down Will's sentence, Dean would look at him coolly and express his *sincerest disappointment.* Those two words were, weirdly, the most painful punishment of all. And not because he actually thought Dean considered him a disappointment, but rather because they planted a seed, a germ of an idea that caused Will to worry that—maybe, actually—he was.

Now, taking a deep breath, he pushes open the door. Dean sits at one of the room's five tables, accompanied by an open bottle of white wine and a single glass. Before him are the unstapled pages of a story, spread out like shrapnel. While Will can't read everything from where he stands, there are a few key words that jump out at him: *Laundromat,* and the name *Mo.* His heart in his bowels and his stomach in his throat, he scans the sheets and finds the story's first page. There, finally, he sees it: his name—*Will Wright*—typed out in the upper left-hand corner, right alongside the thesis's due date and his professor's name. An admission of guilt, he thinks, in twelve-point, Times New Roman font, formatted courtesy of the MLA.

He says, "Shit."

"I'll say." Dean reaches for the bottle and pours himself a glass. "You want some of this? If I drink the whole thing on my own I'll get heartburn, and yesterday I ran out of Tums."

"What? Jesus, Dad, no, it's like three o'clock in the afternoon. How the— how the hell did you get my thesis?" Will pinches his eyes shut. "Fucking Ginny."

"First things first, Will: This is not your thesis. It is a story of *mine* that you *stole* and turned *in* as your thesis. And in terms of who gave it to me . . . I will neither confirm nor deny that it was Ginny Polonsky."

"Aside from Claudia Min, she was literally the only person who had it."

"I will . . . not deny that it was Ginny Polonsky."

"I swear to God, the next time I see her I'm going to kill her."

"No one's going to be killing anyone. What we are going to do, though, is sit down and talk about this . . . this plagiarism of yours." Dean takes a sip from his glass and shakes his head. "I mean, Jesus, Will, why'd you do it? I could have gotten you an extension! I could have helped you write something of your own!"

Will's jaw goes slack.

He says, "You have got to be kidding me."

Dean looks at him, quizzically.

"What's that supposed to mean?"

"It means I finally read your book."

His father's face brightens—"Oh!"—and then darkens—"*Oh.*"

"Christ, Dad! Did you think I wouldn't find out? Did you think I wouldn't read it?"

"In all fairness, kiddo, it's been four years and you still haven't finished *The Brothers Karamazov*." Dean rubs the back of his neck. "But did you . . ."

"Did I what?"

"Did you like it? I mean, did you think it was good?"

"I'm not answering that question."

"Your opinion is important to me!"

"You're disgusting." Will kicks a chair, and the sound of it toppling to the floor startles his father: Dean flinches in his seat. "What'd you do? Hire someone to follow me? Follow me yourself?"

"Don't be ridiculous. You know I think Dolores Park is for hippies."

"So you broke into my computer, then. Awesome."

"I did." Dean sighs. "Which I guess means we're even."

"We're not even, Dad. We're fucking *not*." Will is yelling. "Did it ever occur to you to help me? Did it ever occur to you that I was putting myself in danger, and I needed your help?"

Dean looks away from him.

He says, "I didn't want to be a helicopter parent."

"You're disgusting."

"You've mentioned that already."

"Well, let me mention it again: *you're disgusting*." He points at his father, then digs his hands into his hair. "I fucking worshipped you, Dad. I wanted to *be* you. And then, even when I knew I never could be, I was at least happy enough to be your son. I figured living in your shadow was better than not living with you at all. Jesus, even after everything you did to Mom, I told myself that you were still okay. That you were a person, and people make mistakes. But you're not a person, Dad. You're a leech. You're not just cynical, or well-read, or talented. You're not one of the enlightened few who *gets it*. You're just a fucking *leech*."

Dean drinks his wine and then, slowly, he looks up.

He says, "I mean, in my defense, you labeled that folder *Anatomy and Physiology*."

Will's exhausted. Sweat and spit coat his chin. He asks, "What's your point?"

"You never took that class. You were afraid of having to dissect a fetal cat. You took AP biology instead."

"You're kidding me."

"I got curious!"

"Well, what was *I* supposed to do? You named your folder *Unpublished Stories*!" Will presses the heels of his hands against his eyes. "And Jesus, Dad, you killed me off! You stole my life, and then you *killed me off*!"

"You're being way too hard on yourself. Some of the best characters in literature die. Think of that poor girl in *Little Women,* the one who ends up getting scarlet fever."

"You can't even remember her name."

"You get my point," Dean says. "Besides, can't you see this as an act of love? You're always saying that I never like what you write, but here it is—in a book!"

"It's not love, Dad. You're just fucking lazy. I mean, did it ever occur to you that I might want to *use* those stories myself? That I might want to turn them into something of my own? Christ, to that end, what else have you stolen from people? Is *any* of this book your own?"

Dean looks into his empty wineglass.

"All art is appropriation," he says.

"Oh, for God's sake."

"What *was* that girl's name?"

"I don't know what you're talking about."

"That girl from *Little Women*. It's killing me that I can't remember her name."

There's a cough that comes from the bathroom, then a woman's voice.

"It's Beth," it says.

Dean covers his face with his hands.

He says, "Shit."

"Who is that?" Will looks at his father, who is now shaking his head. "Dad, I recognize that voice. *Who is that?*"

Dean doesn't answer him, but only because he doesn't need to: Will knows who it is. On top of the voice's recognizable qualities—its knowing swing, its smug rhythm—he can only think of one person who wouldn't be able to resist the opportunity to call out the name of a Louisa May Alcott character from the bathroom. One person who, on the shittiest of shitty days, could manage to make things *just a little bit shittier.* Pushing the door open, he confirms his suspicions: Ginny Polonsky is there, sitting on the toilet with her knees pulled to her chest. Both her shoes are untied and in her right hand she holds a soda—a grape Fanta that, from the looks of the sickly purple syrup dripping from the ends of her hair, has recently exploded.

She says, "Wait, just so we're on the same page: You both plagiarized each other?"

"Ginny, please tell me you aren't really here."

"It's a pleasure to see you, too, Will."

She pushes off the toilet and marches past him. In a heap on the floor next to the sink lies her rucksack, its leather cracked and folded.

"What the hell is he talking about, Dean?" she says. "You *didn't actually write that book?*"

Dean rubs his bald spot. Once he's stopped, he doesn't remove his hand—he just keeps it there, poised on top of his head like a helmet.

"I thought I told you to stay in the bathroom until the coast was clear," he says.

"It was stuffy, and you know I suffer from claustrophobia." She sits at the table across from him. "Answer my question."

Now it's Will who steps in: "Someone needs to tell me what the fuck is going on. Someone needs to tell me what the *fuck* she's doing here."

"I have a name, you know," Ginny says. "And, besides, you're the one who told me where you were."

"That wasn't an invitation to fly halfway around the world."

She says, "Actually, Madagascar would have been halfway around the world."

"I can't believe this."

"Well, it's true. I looked it up on an app before I left." She looks down at her fingernails. "Greece is only about seven-eighths of the way there."

Will locks gazes with her for a moment, waiting for her to blink. She doesn't, though. She just keeps staring at him with this sort of wild, confused look, her head cocked slightly to the left like she's a parrot on a bender. *How,* her eyes beg, *could you not have known such a simple geographic fact?*

"I'm getting a drink," he says.

"Get me another bottle of wine," Dean says. "Nothing too sweet."

"How about you get your own damn wine?"

"How about you do what I say before I knock your head in?"

"You're a charming drunk. Has anyone ever told you that?" Dean doesn't answer, so he turns to Ginny. "And what about you, Miss Polonsky? Care for a drink? One of your performative Jim Beams, perhaps?"

She chews on one side of her lip.

"I can't drink," she says.

"We both know that's not true, Ginny," Will says. "Need I remind you of your spectacular performance at Ernie Castle's Halloween party last year?"

Now, she looks at him.

"You don't understand. *I. Can't. Drink.*"

Dean taps the base of his wineglass on the table. "For the love of God, Ginny, have a bourbon."

She whips her head around and clears the hair from her face.

"Are you kidding me?" she says. "You have *got* to be kidding me."

From where he's standing, Will watches them as they watch each other: the anger and betrayal lurking in Ginny's eyes; the detached resignation of Dean's slouch. He's confused for a moment, but then something clicks into place. A realization that's as repulsive as it is absurd—one that convinces him that he's not just standing on the brink of madness, but has rather spelunked into it, where he's currently dangling by a very thin rope. Below him, he imagines, is an endless assortment of Deans and Ginnys—a teeming mess of limbs, and ova, and inescapable red hair.

"Oh, my God. You knocked her up."

Ginny says, "I wish you wouldn't be so vulgar about it."

"So it's true?"

Dean moves his hand. He works it down from his bald spot, to his forehead, to his eyes, which he covers.

He says, in a tone that's as confessional as it is meek: "I made a mistake."

"You're kidding, right?" Will says. "A mistake is, like, wearing mismatched socks, or taking the Bay Bridge at rush hour. *Jasmine* was a mistake. You didn't make a mistake this time, Dad. You made a *baby*. Jesus, this is so fucked."

"I made a *zygote*." He shakes his head, his eyes still covered. "Please. We don't need to get sentimental about this. We don't need to start throwing around terms like *baby*."

Will says, "Maybe you should let Ginny talk."

She looks up at him, then back at Dean. Watching her eyes twitch, he finds himself hoping that she launches into one of her diatribes. Some impassioned speech about misogyny, and the sanctity of the female body, and the inherently patriarchal foundations of language, and—God, what else—Ophelia, maybe, yes, Ophelia, and how, like Ginny is now to Dean, she was a pawn in Hamlet's game, a casualty of his incessant and dizzying madness.

Instead, Ginny holds the can of Fanta to the side of her neck.

She says, "I feel like I'm going to be sick."

Dean reaches over and rubs her back. Ginny doesn't wince, nor does she turn away.

"Look, Will, I'm begging you," he says, his voice now soft and breathy. "Your mother can't know. Ginny's agreed to spend the rest of today and tonight at a hotel in town and fly back to San Francisco tomorrow after-noon. When we get back on Monday she and I will . . . well, we'll discuss the necessary next steps." At this, Ginny begins to quietly cry. "In the meantime, your mother—God, this would just kill her. This needs to be our secret. Okay, kiddo?"

"You want me to keep a secret from my own mother?"

"That's what I'm asking, yes."

"She's my *family*, Dad."

"Yes! Exactly! And what is family if not a bunch of secrets we keep from each other? Look, this will . . . this would be nuclear, okay? It would seriously destroy us, and just when we're starting to get back in a good place."

"I'm going to have to disagree with you, Dad: this place looks very, very bad."

Dean picks up his empty wineglass and, frowning at it, fills it with a little of Ginny's grape Fanta.

"And what if I do tell Mom?" Will asks. "What if I don't keep your secret?"

His father thinks.

"I'll call Claudia Min," he says. "And Chip Fieldworth. I'll tell them the story you turned in as your thesis was mine."

"So now you're blackmailing me. First you publish a bestseller with *my* work—"

"I don't mean to split hairs, but I did some substantial editing to that prose."

"—and then you *kill me off*—"

"Fictitiously!"

"—and now you're fucking blackmailing me."

Dean sips from the wineglass. Purple soda coats the stubble of his mustache.

He says, "I think I'd prefer to think of it as mutually assured destruc-tion."

"You know, he isn't wrong, Will," Ginny says. "I took History of the Cold War sophomore year—this is mutually assured destruction, but without the nukes."

"Shut up, Ginny."

"I'm just trying to be helpful."

"Well, you're not. You are not being helpful."

Ginny looks down and picks at a loose thread on her shirt.

She says, "I'd also like to point out that 'Anatomy and Physiology' and 'Unpublished Stories' are both really bad folder names. You are both so . . . so incredibly *bad* at this."

Will buries his face in his hands. He strains to hear something from the outside world: the distant honk of a horn, maybe, or the short, hard rattle of a warbler. He'll take anything that's not the hiss of his father's breath or the quiet gargle of Ginny's tears. How bizarre, how laughable it is to think that, not even an hour ago, he was moping about Dio and the death of a romance that, really, wasn't even a romance at all. He tries telling himself that there's comfort in this—that while you're staggering through one tragedy, it's important to keep things in perspective and remember that it's only a matter of time until a bigger one swoops in to take its place.

Uncovering his eyes, he says, "I'm telling Mom, Dad, because she deserves to know. And then, after that, I'll own up and tell Claudia Min about the story myself."

Dean begins to argue, but something stops him: a sound unlike anything that he or Will has ever heard. Something that's half siren's wail, half banshee's shriek—a pitch so high it rattles the windows in their frames.

Ginny, throwing her head back and screaming.

Ginny Polonsky

The first thing that made Ginny Polonsky feel stupid was a pink Easy-Bake Oven.

She had received it for her ninth birthday—it was the only thing she wanted. Even now, she remembers the thrill of opening it. The way she knew what the gift was as soon as she picked it up; the wonderful, fateful ease with which she removed the wrapping paper. For a week, she kept it in its box. Her family thought she was crazy, but Ginny didn't care. She liked the way it looked, sitting among her other toys—a pink treasure, protected by cardboard, framed by a harem of stuffed bears, unicorns, and lambs. Then, one day, her sister convinced her to take the next step. "The point of having an Easy-Bake Oven," Elsa said, "is to *actually bake something.*" And because Ginny was young and didn't yet know that some boxes are best left closed, she listened to her. She removed the oven and shed its packaging, and then she and Elsa went about making brownies, stirring together one of the grainy mixes her parents had bought her. When they were done they tasted awful, nothing like anything her mother had ever made. Upset, Ginny began to worry: For the rest of the oven's working life, would she be expected to *make* things with it? Cookies with burnt, brittle edges; cupcakes whose insides were doughy and undercooked? When she wasn't using it, would her parents ask what was wrong with her? Would they question buying her future toys she coveted? She imagined them whispering that she was lazy or ungrateful; that in wanting to *admire* the oven as opposed to *bake cute things* with it, she was shirking some crucial duty she had as a daughter.

And so, two nights after the brownie disaster, once she had dutifully cleaned the oven, she went about dissecting it. She wanted to see what made it so different, so entirely inadequate, compared to the oven her mother used. Opening the pink door and removing the device's feeble little tray, she was confronted with a curiosity: a lightbulb, small and round and splattered with a single glob of brownie batter. Her mother's oven had no bulbs—rather, upon inspection, Ginny found an elaborate series of tubes, a heating element powered by such adult forces as fire and gas. Kneeling on the kitchen's tile, she felt duped and dumb: she had thought she was so old baking with Elsa, so impossibly mature. Really, though, the world had tricked her. It turned out, she was nothing but a kid, turning on the same kind of light that topped the princess lamps in her room.

There were more disappointments after that, more opportunities to feel stupid and naïve. They ranged from the small (saying *nauseous* when she meant *nauseated*; having to pretend to understand the latest Pynchon) to the momentous (not getting into Smith; thinking November 8, 2016, would turn out differently). Each of them she recalls vividly, perfectly, as if they're specimens she's preserved in jars. Here's when she just missed getting into the National Honor Society; and here's when her aunt Sharon died. Here's when she overheard her mother tell her sister that *she'd always be the smarter one*, and here's when Ginny started to believe it. Little balls of anguish and despair, neatly contained and turning yellow in jars of formaldehyde. A history, she likes to think, presented like a display in a house of oddities—a whole life tracked by its enduring regrets.

Which means that none of this should be new to her. She should be able to compartmentalize the sinking feeling in her chest, the way her knees suddenly feel light. She can't, though; every time she tries to screw the top onto this new jar, it pops off again. The reason, she suspects, is Dean's book—or perhaps, to be more specific, the realization that Dean's book is not actually Dean's book at all, but a forgery, a lie. What does that say about Ginny? She loved that book—it was, in so many ways, the map that steered her through the last ten months. And now she finds out that the thing that saved her is basically a cheap act of theft—the literary equivalent of a Katy Perry song. This realization leads her to other, more troublesome territory. She thinks, for example, of the things she did to him in that diner bathroom and, in turn, the things she let him do to her— the ways in which she inserted herself into the Wright family. At the time, she had found it thrilling; she was, in many ways, living the plot of so many bawdy novels: the aloof literature professor falling for the promising (she is, she still holds, *promising*) nubile writer. The fact that this particular aloof literature professor was married didn't register to her—or, if it did, it appeared as a blip, a dot that flashed across her radar when she felt her life needed a little narrative tension. She told herself that any obligation she felt to Sue Ellen as another woman was contrived, a reinforcement of the patriarchal standards she so vocally abhorred. After all, how many times had she read about the ease with which men commit adultery, only to escape the consequences? By forcing herself to adhere to some cosmic feminine allegiance, Ginny was giving men another pass—a chance to fudge the rules while she was bound to some unattainable sisterhood. Real freedom, she decided, was allowing herself to do whatever the fuck she wanted. How stupid that had been, though—how terribly and unfathomably stupid. She had invested her faith in a mutable philosophy instead of a basic sense of compassion. She had preferred the easy protection of an *ism* to the complications of other people.

What else? She thinks of Scarlett and her foam cups. She thinks of melting ice caps and overfished oceans and how, no matter how many trees she plants and protests she attends, she will never be able to save them. She thinks of how uncomfortable the flight was across the Atlantic, and what it felt like to have morning sickness in the Frankfurt International Airport. And then she thinks of Dean: the horror and dread that befell him when she told him she was pregnant; the entreaties he'd made to her as, over a bottle and a half of wine, he tried to persuade her to get rid of their child. Or, no—not their child, but her child. Can she regret how naïve she had been about that? Can she regret her child? She looks down at her belly button, poking out from the bottom hem of her shirt. Maybe she could, she thinks; in fact, she probably should. She probably should, but, somehow, she refuses to. She can't.

Will and Dean continue to argue, and Ginny looks down at her rucksack. Reaching for it, she runs her finger along one of the patches on the outside flap—an iron-on shield from Greenpeace, which shows an orca jumping over a rainbow. She picked it up at a rally, somewhere near the Embarcadero. It was hardly a year ago, but still she can't remember what it was about—all she knows is that she wore a black crop-top that said FUCK YOUR DIRTY OIL. There had been chants—there are always chants—but as Ginny joined along with them, she remembers not completely understanding what she was saying. But then, was this so different from the other rallies she'd attended, or the other town halls where she had stood in line behind a microphone to speak? How often in her life had she raised her voice, only to parrot back a thread she had read on Twitter? How many times had she violently committed herself to a cause without ever stopping to consider if she actually agreed with it? The truth, she realizes, is that she doesn't know what she believes. Rather, all she knows is what she doesn't know—which, weirdly, feels like more than she's ever known before.

The problem, though, is that she can't put this feeling in a jar, like all her other regrets. Rather, this time around, it's Ginny who feels like the jar—a vessel that's been emptied of what is essential. The naïve notion that love lasts in perpetuity, or something. Her youth. Disappointment, meanwhile, is all the stuff that storms around her, throwing her against things like the Aegean, and Greek islands, and the Wrights. Threatening, as it were, to shatter her. Listening to Will and Dean argue about who will tell what to whom (as it turns out, neither of them is very good at blackmailing), she thinks about all this, *feels* all this: the way the world seems to be pressing against her, wrapping its fingers around her neck, filling her cheeks with a new and impossible heat. And then, because all other options have been scrapped from the table—because, really, this is the only way out, and *out* is a place Ginny Polonsky would very much like to be—she screams.

It's unlike anything she's ever heard. A guttural, primal roar that starts somewhere near her hip flexors and then travels, gaining volume and collecting little bits of rage, to her throat. At first it terrifies her—her own scream terrifies her—but then she comes to sort of love it. Or, if not love it, then embrace it, clench her fists together and shut her eyes and let her sound fill the room until she's out of air and the two of them have, totally and utterly stupefied, gone quiet.

"Shut up," she says, once she's taken a breath.

"Ginny—"

"I said to shut up, Dean. You are talking. Talking, as you know, is not shutting up."

He opens his mouth, preparing to argue, but Ginny lifts an eyebrow. "One more word, and I swear I'll do it again," she says. "I swear I'll make that sound again."

From where he's standing, Will stares at her. His nose, she sees now, is red and beginning to peel: the scorched aftermath of a sunburn. For the first time since he arrived, there's silence. Ginny takes a moment to center herself, to breathe. Outside, a breeze rattles through the pines, and as she listens, she tries to imagine what wind might look like, if anyone were ever lucky enough to see it. After a minute or so, though, she notices that

Will and Dean are still watching her, waiting for her next move. The problem, of course, is that she doesn't have one; her immediate plan had been to get them both to *just stop talking,* and now that she's accomplished that, she's planless. She looks down at the table, where a faint sigma has been carved into the wood. Tracing it with her thumb, she thinks.

She says, "Okay, here's what's going to happen. Dean, I'm going to publish that story with Will's byline, and you—you're going to let me. *And* you're going to keep your mouth shut about it, because, honestly, that's the least you can do for both of us."

Will shakes his head. He says, "Ginny, I already said that I don't *want* the story published. I want to tell Claudia what I did. I want to do the right thing."

"Will, please," Ginny says. "The only thing that's more obnoxious than a liar is someone who's self-righteous about the truth. Besides, without that story the only thing the *Review*'s got is an anecdote about a pair of crickets. *Literal crickets.*"

"And what if I don't let you do that?" Dean says. "What if I call Claudia myself?"

Ginny doesn't miss a beat.

"Have at it," she says. "I'll call *The New York Times, The Washington Post,* and *The New Yorker.* I'll get on Twitter and tell the world what a fucking fraud you really are. Which, really, would be a tragedy. That book means something to a lot of people, and just because it's been ruined for me, that doesn't mean it should be ruined for them."

He thinks she's bluffing: "Go ahead. No one cares about books anymore, anyway."

She's not: "Nice try, Dean. The internet cares about everything."

She's sweating, which she's just now noticed. A trickle works its way down her spine to the waistband of her pants.

"And what about—"

"About *our baby?*" Ginny looks down at her belly. "Tell your wife whatever you want. Or don't tell her, for all I care. I'm not here to ruin lives—you seem totally capable of doing that on your own."

She walks to the bathroom to collect her rucksack, and as she does so, she glances at herself in the mirror. Her eyes are ringed with dark crescents, and her skin is pale and clammy. Sighing once, she slaps a bit of color into her cheeks and tries to smooth a few of the wrinkles from her shirt.

"We should think this over," Dean says, once she's returned.

"It's not open to workshopping." Ginny slips her sack over her shoulder. "Now, if there aren't any more questions, I'll be leaving. There's a four thirty ferry, and I plan to be on it. I've been here for less than two hours, and already I need to get the fuck off this island."

She's feeling good. That's what she thinks as she storms out of the dining room and into the foyer: she's feeling good. Or, if not *good,* exactly, then better, more in control. Less the girl who cries in Walnut Creek diners, more the woman who knows when it's time to leave. She knows that there are issues she'll need to tackle, ranging from the logistical (booking a room in Athens; finding a flight home; *pregnancy*) to the more emotionally complex *(what is she supposed to do now?),* but she figures she'll be in a better state of mind to think about all that once she's left Aegina and extricated herself from a situation that she—Ginny—has helped to make largely inextricable. She tightens her rucksack on her shoulders and lifts her suitcase with both arms. From somewhere within the inn, she can hear Will trailing after her, begging her to *wait* and *talk* and *slow down.* Ginny doesn't, though; she just keeps going. She hasn't called a cab, but she figures she'll walk to town if she has to. She's feeling strong. Hopped up on the sort of hard-won clarity that she suspects writers are referring to when they talk about epiphanies.

Except, she isn't able to. Walk to town, that is. Because just as she's starting the trek along the drive that leads from the hotel to the main road, she encounters a taxi, dodging divots as it drives toward her. She pauses and sets down her suitcase as the cab rolls to a stop five yards away. In the backseat, Sue Ellen Wright hands the driver a few euros and opens the door as she waits for her change. She looks younger than Ginny remembers—or maybe *remembers* is inaccurate, given that for the past year she's done less to remember Sue Ellen than she has to construct an entirely new and dismal version of her, an awful shrew, which allows Ginny to believe that she's saving Dean instead of wrecking a home. Now, she watches as Sue Ellen straightens her shirt and scratches the back of her neck. Watches, in other words, as she turns from a convenient trope into someone entirely and undeniably human. Somewhere deep in her gut, Ginny feels a rumbling. At first, she wonders if it's the baby doing tiny somersaults atop her bladder. Soon, though, she realizes it's something else: hunger—she hasn't eaten since Frankfurt—coated with the sticky stuff of guilt.

Sue Ellen closes the door and the cab leaves.

"Hi, Dr. Wright," Ginny says.

She removes her sunglasses.

"I know you," she says.

Next to her Ginny hears heavy breathing. Glancing over, she sees Will, who whispers, "Shit."

"I . . ." Ginny struggles. Her stomach rumbles again. "I took your seminar on antiquity and feminist thought? It was something like two years ago, though, so if you don't remember me, I totally—"

"Ginny Polonsky." Sue Ellen's smile widens and becomes genuine. "You wrote your final paper on the *Thesmophoria*."

"Yes." Ginny nods and draws circles in the dirt with her foot. "Ginny Polonsky. That's me."

"I'm confused—are you here to see Will?" Above them, a warbler cackles. Sue Ellen looks beyond Ginny to her son. "Will, what's going on?"

"Actually—"

Will presses his hand against Ginny's back, and she feels her shirt stick to the base of her spine.

"Hi, Mom," he says. "Uh, yeah, she's here to see me. She's on her way back to Athens from, uh, Patmos, right?" Ginny stares at him and doesn't nod. "Anyway, her flight's early tomorrow morning, and she was just on her way out."

Sue Ellen's quiet. She nods, and the space between the three of them seems to stretch and pull.

"I see," she says eventually.

Will reaches down and picks up the suitcase.

"Here, Ginny. Let me get you a cab."

With his free hand he grabs her arm and starts to tug her, burrowing his fingers into her flesh. At first, she allows herself to be led, tripping over her own feet as Will drags her past Sue Ellen and down the drive. Then she digs in her heels. She pries his hand away and yanks herself free.

"We aren't really friends," she says. "Will and me, I mean. We sort of used to be, but we aren't anymore."

"Ginny," Will says. *"Please."*

She ignores him.

She says, "I guess what I'm trying to say is that I'm not here to see him."

For a moment, the sun ducks behind an errant cloud and the world darkens, the afternoon's long shadows bleeding and disappearing into the earth. There's a breeze, and the air swirls with familiar and foreign scents: pine and brittle scrub. The chalky dryness of an evaporating summer.

Sue Ellen crosses her arms. She says, in that unmistakable tone of a mother who has sensed something awry, "One of you needs to tell me what the hell is happening here."

When does a person grow up? Ginny wonders. Is it when she realizes the adults in her life—the parents, the teachers, the politicians making laws—are just as screwed up as she is? That their mistakes aren't noble or mature, but rather mundane and selfish? Or is it something beyond that?

A coming to terms with the world as a brutally indifferent place? A forum of pain, joy, energy, and struggle that's ambivalent to the desires of any single person? Perhaps more to the point: When, and how, does this change happen? Do we undergo a singular experience—a trauma or a quest—from which we emerge fully formed, like a butterfly springing from its cocoon? Or is the process gradual: Do the millions of tiny scars we earn each day eventually blunt us, rubbing off the sheen of childhood?

Ginny doesn't know about any of that. The truth, she suspects, hides somewhere in a gray area. What she does know, though—what she's absolutely certain of—is that part of growing up is admitting when you're wrong. Coming clean and ripping off the Band-Aid. Being able to say *Look, I really screwed up,* and then taking those steps, small as they initially may be, to set things right.

And so, Ginny Polonsky takes a deep breath.

She closes her eyes, and she says: "I slept with your husband, Dr. Wright, and now I'm pregnant. It was stupid, and mean, and selfish, and I don't think I've ever been so sorry in my entire life. And while I don't really know much about you, except that sometimes you stare out the window too much during class, what I can tell you is that you're better than he is, and you're better than I am. You're better than both of us, and you deserve more."

Dean

A list, if not comprehensive then very close to it, of all the metaphors he's used to illustrate regret: wineglasses, pillowcases, and a half-finished sheet cake. Empty picture frames, scuba gear, and fading star-shaped tattoos. Unused bicycles, chipped front teeth, and—once—the entire country of Czechoslovakia. A boat that never touched the water; a plane without any wings. Missed sunsets, broken vases, coffee that grows cold as the morning stretches into the afternoon. In other words: life failing to come together. Opportunities forgotten in dark corners, left to gather a thickening layer of dust.

He knows that all of these are absurd; they smack with the precise sort of self-conscious, literary hand-wringing he professes to loathe. Regret is not a Joni Mitchell song or a broken umbrella. Rather, it's literal, it's visceral, it's a feeling. It's weight, composed of air, hindsight, and consequence. It's the sensation of choking; the quick clenching of his bowels. An unbearable burden that crushes him as he watches, from the relative safety of one of the Alectrona's bedrooms, as Sue Ellen listens to Ginny, her face settling into a familiar, devastating pallor.

What else is regret? How does it manifest itself beyond those brutal physical sensations? In memories, he suspects. A deep and unfathomable flood of them. Here he is with his wife, taking turns holding their infant son as he cries through his first ear infection; here they are a year earlier, giggling over the earnestness of parenting books. And there is, of course, more: birthdays and holidays and the blessed mundanity that fills the space between them. A chain of Friday nights and Saturday mornings; of soccer games and first dates and bleary-eyed breakfasts. And then, somewhere buried within all that, is the moment they met. It had been at a social mixer for doctoral candidates organized by the Graduate Assembly. Dean wasn't a graduate student—he had just started teaching creative writing as an adjunct—but he didn't know anyone in Berkeley, and the department's administrative assistant had taken pity on him and had forwarded the invitation, so he decided to attend. They had rented out a bar on Durant Avenue—the aim, as far as Dean could tell, was to break free from the tropes that typically characterized the academy's attempts at forced socialization, and yet still, upon entering, he was confronted with the same platter of wrinkled celery and gray-skinned carrots; the same landscape of stilted conversations. He hovered at the periphery of the room for an hour, he remembers. Occasionally, someone would approach him. They would see him nursing his IPA and they would come over to where he was standing, scooting slowly, with the practiced timidity of scholars. The interaction would then follow a familiar pattern: after a brief rally of small talk, he would ask them about their dissertation, a topic that—regardless of his interest—he would try to keep in the air for as long as possible, delaying the inevitable moment when the conversation turned toward him and he was forced to admit that he wasn't a scholar at all, but a part-time teacher of stories; that, in fact, his academic pursuits stopped after he received his Masters of Fine Arts—a degree that, in the face of medieval history, ethnosociology, and nanophysics struck him as little more than finger painting.

They were nice to him. Or, if not nice then gracious. They listened to him as he talked about his writing, which at that point consisted of a handful of published stories and a single novel—a quiet, slim thing with the sort of sales that his agent and publisher described as modest. They asked the right questions, and nodded at the right moments. When he mentioned that the book at been reviewed in *The New Yorker*, they smiled and said that was *really something*. Still, as he spoke he found himself turning embarrassed, then ashamed; more and more he began to apologize for being there, and his became speech riddled with self-deprecating tics. The book wasn't a big deal and anyone could write—really it was just a matter of being bored enough. Here, after all, were people who had committed themselves to a life of knowledge, of uncovering worldly truths. Meanwhile, he had settled for playing make-believe.

He met her as he was leaving. After his second IPA he decided that he had taken enough of these peoples' free beer, and that it was time to go home. Besides, he led a workshop at eight o'clock the next morning, and while the last hour and a half had filled him with more self-doubt than his most recent royalties report, the act of teaching—of planning a class, of engaging with students—still felt fresh and relevant; it made him feel part of something larger than himself. She was standing, he remembers, just to the right of the bar's exit. When he tried to slide past her she jutted out an arm, as if it were a turnstile, and clocked him in the nose.

"Ow," he said, rubbing the spot where she had bumped him.

"And where exactly do you think you're going?"

She was wearing a plain white T-shirt and a pair of dark Levi's. Her hair was pulled back off her face, and beneath each eye was an asymmetrical spattering of freckles. To her left were two other graduate students—a pair of men who greeted Dean with brief, unfriendly nods.

"I—I was just going."

She kept her arm where it was, her hand planted against the opposite side of the door frame.

"Not without paying, you aren't."

"I didn't realize there was a toll for leaving."

"You've either got to pay or suffer here with the rest of us." She sipped her beer. "No one escapes hell for free."

"Uh, okay." He rubbed his nose again. He worried that it might bruise. "What's it cost?"

"Ten bucks."

"That seems pretty expensive."

She shrugged. "Happiness ain't cheap."

Both of the men snickered—not with her, but at him.

Dean dug through his pockets but came up short: a crumpled five, three ones, and half a toothpick. Even if he had the cash he wasn't going to pay—he wanted to leave, but he wasn't a pushover. Still, he decided to play along. He liked how jealous it was making the men beside her.

He said, "I've only got eight."

Sue Ellen sucked her teeth and shook her head. "Guess you're not leaving, then."

"This is ridiculous."

"Let me make it up to you."

He brushed his hair out of his eyes. He was tired, he decided. He wanted to go home.

"How?"

She took the eight dollars and slipped her arm in his.

"I'll let you buy me a drink."

Was that their first date? Or, had it been week later when, exhilarated and nervous, he'd called her at the number she had given him when she finally let him leave. He doesn't know, and he supposes it doesn't matter. The fact is they saw each other again; they kept seeing each other until suddenly they were married. In the beginning, she terrified him. Whereas he had never had a passport, hers was overflowing with stamps, evidence of travel to places like Greece, and Turkey, and Egypt—countries that, for Dean, constituted a mythological worldliness that made his own life feel as expansive as a snow globe. She was calm and unbearably collected; while Dean wanted to be near her all the time, Sue Ellen seemed at ease in love—her heart she doled out in pieces, while he offered his up all at once. His blunders—and there were many of them—seemed tragic, and world-ending: a spilled glass of wine would have him apologizing for weeks. Hers, on the other hand, just added to her charm. The first time they slept together, she tripped and toppled over as she was shimmying out of her jeans. Springing up, she brushed her hair from her eyes and smiled at him.

"That was my *grand jeté*," she said. "What would you like to see next?"

These are histories he hasn't thought of in years, and now, still standing at the window, he wonders where he's kept them buried away. When, and how, did Sue Ellen turn from someone he worshiped to very simply his wife? When had they allowed themselves to become such different people? Had it happened quickly, or rather inch by inch—two continents separating until a vast and impassable ocean lay between them? Or, had one of them actually stood firm, while the other drifted? He suspects that this latter theory is closer to the truth: Sue Ellen hasn't changed, so much as he has.

He waits ten minutes—long enough for Ginny to run away and for Will to follow her—before he ventures downstairs. He finds his wife sitting by the side of the pool. She's taken off her shoes and her legs hang over the edge, the water swirling around her knees. Next to her is a glass filled with a clear liquid—ouzo, he guesses, poured over two cloudy ice cubes.

Approaching her, he says, "You know, they say that if you drink that stuff on the rocks it gives you a worse hangover."

"Get away from me." She doesn't look up.

"Sue Ellen, let's please just talk."

"I'm serious, Dean. Get away from me."

He shoves his hands in his pockets and stares down at his shadow, which in the afternoon sun elongates, stretching until it dissolves into the pool.

He says, "I don't know what to say."

"You can't say anything."

"I'm sorry."

"That's not good enough."

With one hand he reaches around and rubs the back of his neck, now dampened with a cold, nervous sweat. Looking up, he takes stock of the Alectrona—its gray stone walls, its baked-tile roof, the way the orange tree, set against that washed-out façade, seems to have been robbed of its green by the sun.

"I'll fix it," he says.

"Oh, save it, Dean. You got someone pregnant. You got a *student pregnant*." She shakes her head. "I don't know whether to strangle that girl or offer to pay for her child care."

He feels a rush of indignation. "What, so this is all my fault?"

"Yes," she says. "It is unequivocally your fault."

"*She* came on to *me,* you know. She weaseled her way into my workshop, and then *she* came on to *me*."

"And then what? You just happened to trip and fall inside her during office hours? Jesus, Dean, listen to yourself."

"Don't be vulgar, Sue Ellen."

She stands up, and water drips from her calves. The glass she leaves where it is, sitting on the pool deck. The ice has started to melt, turning the ouzo cloudy, the color of watered-down milk.

"Don't tell me how to act—you slept with a child." She wipes her hands against her shorts. "Did you think about that? Someone who's two years younger than our son. At least with Jasmine you were screwing around with someone who was old enough to rent a car. Who was there to vote for Barack *fucking* Obama. But Ginny, Dean?" Sue Ellen covers her eyes with her hands. "Jesus Christ."

He lets her cry for a moment, then cautiously takes a step toward her. She immediately steps back.

"Hey," he says. "I told you I would fix this, and I will. I promise you."

"Yeah? And how exactly do you plan on doing that?"

"I'll talk to Ginny," he says. "We'll go back to Connie."

"Connie," she spits, and finally reaches down for her drink. "Connie isn't penance, Dean. She's not there to absolve you whenever you screw up." Sue Ellen swallows some ouzo, and her eyes pinch shut. "We never should have gone to her in the first place."

"Sue Ellen—"

"No, I'm serious. We never should have gone to her. That—that was my mistake."

"I'm not going to let you do this," he says. "I'm not going to let you rewrite the entire history of our marriage just because I fucked up."

"I'm not rewriting history, Dean. I'm just finally recognizing it."

She looks down and swirls the ice.

She says, "Do you remember how, after our first session with Connie, we went to that dinner Charlene Jackson was having to celebrate getting tenure? We weren't going to go, but then Connie mentioned that we should do something together—something that didn't involve fighting or yelling at each other."

"Of course I remember," Dean says, though really, he doesn't. Watching her stare into her glass, he wonders what else she's holding on to that he's already forgotten, what sort of memories she's used to construct the record of their marriage, and how wildly they might differ from his own.

"Anyway," Sue Ellen continues, "I can't remember the name of the restaurant where they had it. Can you?"

"I can't." He ventures a guess: "It was in the city, though, wasn't it?"

"No, Oakland," she says. "There weren't enough seats, so we spent most of the time standing up, balancing plates. You were drinking Sancerre, and

I had beer and kept eating these bruschetta they were passing around. I was emotionally wound up, and starving, and wanted something that would make me feel tired and full." She looks into the glass again. "Jesus, isn't it insane that I can remember that—what I ate and why I ate it, I mean—but I can't remember the name of the goddamned restaurant?"

Dean nods. He begins to tell her that he agrees, but she shakes her head.

"We tried our best to follow Connie's advice and not to talk about the session, and we did an okay job. There were a few times when we would drift, or where it was clear that one of us was thinking about something the other had said, but mainly, I think, we managed to avoid it. Your book had just gone into its third printing. Mostly, we talked about that."

"Sue Ellen, your lecture's in an hour. Can we just—"

"I'm not done." The ice has finally melted. She finishes her drink and holds the glass at her side. "Charlene hired these students to act as servers at the dinner. There was a group of them—three boys and two girls. They'd all been in her Ovid seminar the semester earlier, I think, and she wanted to help them earn a little extra cash. You know how she can be like that. Anyway, at one point I was standing by the bar, and I looked over and saw you on the other side of the room, watching one of the girls. Someone was talking to you—Rick Jenkins, maybe?—but you weren't really listening; it was like you were in your own world, where it was just you and this—this girl. You watched her wherever she went. I thought you were going to break your neck."

Dean says, "It's not a crime to look."

"Of course it isn't. Lord knows I look all the time. But the thing is, Dean, it's *how* you looked. Like you didn't care who saw you. Like she belonged to you, and you were ready to eat her alive."

She clicks her wedding ring against the empty glass and continues. "You know, once I heard someone say that success doesn't change a person so much as it teases out the person they were all along."

"Oh, for God's sake, Sue Ellen. The people who say that sort of shit are business moguls and politicians, and the only reason they say it is so they can be quoted on some tear-away calendar."

"Maybe," she says. "But that doesn't mean they're wrong. I mean, look at you, Dean. You're hungry now. You're hungry in a way where I actually don't know how to make you feel whole. And I remember realizing it—that's what I'm trying to tell you. I remember realizing on that night that, if you'd had the chance, if you were given another Jasmine, you'd do it again. And there'd be another Jasmine, of course. Because, really, there always is. The history of the world is one of men not keeping their zippers up in front of Jasmine. I mean, for Christ's sake, *that is why Troy fell*." She runs her hands over her hair. "Here we were, torturing ourselves with Connie, and the whole time I knew that, at the end of the day, you'd just end up doing it all again."

"Please don't blame yourself for this, Sue Ellen."

"Oh, don't worry, I'm not." She looks at him. "I'm saying I was stupid, but I'm not blaming myself. Those are two separate things."

"Then why did you stay?" Dean asks. He's feeling cornered, exposed. "Why are you still here?"

"Will," she says. "And inertia. I thought if we could just keep going, keep riding the wave, then things would work out. You'd stop looking—or, at the very least, I'd learn to live with it again. It's why I agreed when you suggested we all come here. Somehow, I figured the sheer inertia of *us* would help us find our footing. But that's not how it works, is it? Inertia doesn't solve problems so much as it keeps broken things together."

There is, for a moment, a pure and perfect silence, a void in which he can't hear the call of the warblers or the crunch of tires on gravel. But then, as quickly as he notices the quiet, it's gone. A ferry blows its horn. Somewhere closer to town, a rooster crows.

He says, "Sue Ellen, let's get through today. Then we can work this out. We can go home."

She shakes her head.

"I don't think you understand," she says. "I'm not going home."

Will

August 3
Aegina

The harbor is a madhouse. One of the larger ferries—the *Poseidon Hellas*—
has just delivered a thousand passengers to the island's port, and it's within
this chaos that Will searches for Ginny. It is, predictably, impossible. On
all sides of him, queues materialize haphazardly, hard-baked travelers
arranging themselves into rows without knowing what those rows are
actually for. Their luggage, inevitably, scatters: rollerboards are felled
facedown on the stone sidewalk; duffel bags are trampled by sets of sandaled feet.

He finds her, finally, not within the chaos but adjacent to it, lingering
just on the outskirts of bedlam. She's sitting on the curb along Leoforos
Dimokratis, a hundred yards south from the dock itself. A little farther
down, the red dome of Ekklisia Isodia Theotokou casts half-moon shadows
over a rocky beach. Her knapsack rests on her knees, and in her right
hand she holds a half-eaten nectarine, its skin broken and ragged, its flesh
the color of marigolds. From a safe distance, he watches her, considering

his next move as she stares down at the fruit, turning it slowly to let the juice drip down her fingers. Then someone knocks him—a woman carrying a purse on one arm and a leather weekend bag on the other. Whipping her head around, she glares at Will and shouts something at him in Greek.

Ginny looks up, sees him, and sighs.

She says, "You found me."

"I didn't peg you as such a fast runner. Especially with luggage."

"I did track in high school." Behind them, the woman who yelled at Will climbs in the passenger side of an idling Peugeot and slams the door. "Actually, that's a lie. Once I got to the main road, I hailed a cab."

Ginny takes another bite from the nectarine, this time working her way around its pit. Readjusting her knapsack, she pulls her knees closer to her chest. Sweat forms rings beneath her armpits and flecks of sand mix with the freckles on her wrists. Will lowers himself to the curb and sits next to her. At the other edge of the harbor, the last of the departing passengers boards the *Hellas*.

"You're going to miss your ferry," he says.

"I got a ticket for the *Flying Dolphin*. I don't like the idea of a boat, which carries cars, which carry people. That's too much carrying in one place."

"Jesus Christ, you're weird."

She says, "Yeah, well."

Will rests his elbows on his knees and listens to the noises in the port: horns honking and the waves breaking against the quay. The squabble of gulls fighting over a plate of cold french fries. He wonders if he'll miss these sounds when he leaves tomorrow, or if he'll even be able to distinguish them from the waterfronts of Oakland, of San Francisco. He wonders if places have their own individual soundtracks or if it's just his wishing that makes it so.

"Why'd you do that, Ginny?" he says, finally.

"Why'd I *do* what?"

"I don't know, sleep with my dad? Follow us here? Tell my mom that Dean fucking *knocked you up*?"

He expects an apology, but she doesn't give him one. Instead, she turns to him and wipes nectarine juice from her face.

"What else was I supposed to do?" she says. "I fucked up, okay? Is that what you wanted to hear? Well, there. I said it. *I. Fucked. Up.* But that doesn't mean I'm going to pretend like none of it happened, because I can't. I can't just *pretend* I'm not pregnant."

"You could have for five minutes in front of my mom. She didn't have to know."

"Yeah, Will, she did—you said it yourself. She needed to know the truth, which, in case you haven't noticed, your family doesn't seem exactly adept at telling."

"You realize she'll leave him, don't you?" Will asks. "Like, you do realize my family's totally fucked."

She says, "Two things: One, a family is more than a broken marriage. And two: I sort of get the feeling that happened long before I came along. No offense."

Will doesn't respond. He knows she's right, he just hates that she has to be the one to say it.

Ginny sucks on the nectarine's pit, then spits it into her hand.

She says, "You're not an asshole like your dad is, Will. I actually think you're a sort of okay guy. I know you don't like me—you've never liked me, and you probably really don't like me now, but you're not an asshole."

He closes his eyes. His lips are dry, cracked. He can't remember the last time he had a sip of water.

"I don't not like you," he says.

"You hate me."

"Knock it off, Ginny."

"You do," she says, her voice rounding at its edges. "You and Cassie both hate me."

"Maybe because you slept with my dad."

"You hated me before that."

He tears a bit of dead skin away from his lips with his teeth.

He says, "The truth is I don't hate anybody."

"By saying that you don't hate anybody, you're at the very least admitting you don't like me."

She turns the pit over in the palm of her hand, letting it dry in the sun.

"Ginny, I think you have more pressing things to worry about right now."

"Probably, but this feels weirdly important."

"Well, that's too bad, because I'm not doing this."

She drops the pit and presses it against the pavement with her foot.

"Why'd you unfriend me on Facebook?" she asks.

"You have got to be kidding me."

"Will, I'm twenty years old, single, pregnant, and sitting on a curb in Bumfuck, Greece. Humor me. Tell me why you unfriended me on Facebook."

He leans back on his elbows. Bits of gravel and sand press into his forearms.

"Christ, I don't know. Because I didn't need to read every knee-jerk epiphany you had every time you skimmed an article on the *Huffington Post*."

"I don't *skim* them."

He doesn't acknowledge the correction. He decides that she's asked, so he'll tell her.

"And you started doing that thing."

"What thing?"

"That thing where you were posting the entirety of *Moby-Dick*, one sentence at a time."

"It was the one hundred sixty-eighth anniversary of its publication." She presses her sunglasses, a pair of pink-tinted aviators, farther up her nose. "Besides, that book is one of the greatest contributions to American literature."

"It was annoying."

"It was art."

"No, Ginny. It wasn't art. It was objectively annoying." He looks at her and sets his hand against her shoulder. "*You*, actually, can be kind of annoying."

She doesn't brush him off. Instead, she leans into him a little, letting first his fingers and then his palm press against her.

"I think that's probably true." Then: "I'm sorry your father stole your life."

"Yeah, well."

"I can't believe I thought he was so incredible. I can't believe so many people think he's so incredible."

"Let them think it," Will says. "Being incredible seems like a pretty shitty gig, anyway."

He watches a skiff bob in the water, its dock lines going loose then taut as it rises and sinks. He tries to imagine what he would say if, a month ago, someone had told him that right now he would be here, sitting on a curb in Greece, having this conversation with Ginny Polonsky. He would call them crazy, sadistic. And yet, here he is, settling into a fate that he regards now as inevitable. There are no surprises, he decides. Just futures he's been too lazy to imagine.

"Will?" she says.

"Talk to me, Ginny."

"What am I going to do?"

"I don't think I'm the person to ask. I can't even write my own thesis, let alone tell you how to live your life."

She turns to look at him, and he catches his reflection in her sunglasses: his hair is shaggy and disheveled, and his cheeks are patched with the uneven beginnings of a beard. He blinks, and it stings: salt crusts the edges of his eyes.

"I was serious about what I said to Dean," she says. "I'm going to publish it. No one's ever going to know."

"It hardly seems like it matters now."

Ginny sighs and stares back at the water. The crowd from the ferry has thinned, and as he looks at the port Will wonders if Dio is among the stragglers still hanging around the docks. He hadn't told Will what ferry he was taking back from Hydra, and as he was fleeing Will hadn't bothered to ask. The fact that he had woken up next to him this morning now seems inconceivable, the memory already so faded, so blurred by other stimuli, that he would swear that years separated him from it, rather than a handful of hours.

"Jesus, Will, what am I going to *do*?" Ginny says again.

"Ginny, you and I both know that I'm not the person that can, or should, make that decision for you."

Her knapsack falls off her knees, and she makes no move to pick it up. The flap falls open, and a tube of mint lip balm rolls out onto the street.

"You know, an hour ago, after I said all that stuff to your dad, I was feeling good. Really good, actually. Like that moment *after* you rip out a hangnail, and the sting's already going away. I got in a cab to come down here, and I kept saying to myself that I had this. That I'd, like, Hannah Horvath or *Gilmore Girls* this shit, and I'd come out on the other side with a daughter, and a cute new haircut, and some grand understanding of what life actually means."

"No one actually wants to be Hannah Horvath," Will says. "Or Lorelai Gilmore, for that matter."

"That's not the point." Ginny shakes her head. "The point is that no one *can* be Hannah Horvath or Lorelai Gilmore. No one can be them because life doesn't have neat series finales where you get a resolution but also a digestible cliffhanger, you know? Life has mistakes and implications and consequences that aren't fair and—I don't know. When I was in the cab I somehow forgot that. Either that, or I'd never really realized it to begin with." She reaches up, loses both her hands in her curls. "Jesus, Will. I can't have a kid."

And then, for a third time, she says: "What am I going to *do*?"

Will leans forward again, this time resting his hands on his thighs. Behind them, he hears the whir of a scooter, slowing as it prepares to round a corner.

"Ginny, I've told you: I. Don't. *Know*."

"Well, try." She tugs at his shirtsleeve. She's trying to smile, but it's tight, labored. Her cheeks quiver.

What, he wonders, is he meant to tell her? That things will be okay? That, through a few adjustments of chance, their courses will miraculously correct themselves and their lives—lives that suddenly feel somehow stuck between young and old—will settle back into the patterns that, for the past twenty-two years, they've been imagining for themselves? He'd be lying if he said that; he'd be hiding behind sentimentality.

He says, "You're going to go home."

"What?"

"You asked me what you're going to do, and I'm telling you. The first thing you're going to do is go home. You'll get on that *Flying Dolphin*, and then your Lufthansa flight. You'll cross the sea like fucking Odysseus, and you'll go home. Then, once you're there, you'll make a decision. Because I'll tell you one thing: you aren't going to make one here. Not when you haven't showered or eaten in, like, thirty-six hours, and you're sitting—to quote you—on a curb in Bumfuck, Greece."

He reaches out and gently tugs on her ear. "This is not a place to make a decision about the rest of your life."

Ginny leans forward. She pulls her knees to her chest and rests her chin upon them. Ten yards away, the tide churns in shallow loops, an endless feedback of salt and sand and ruin. She breathes, and the air rattles as she exhales.

"What if I make the wrong decision?"

"You won't," Will says.

"How do you know that?"

"Because you're smart. Because you're Ginny Fucking Polonsky. Because even though you've made some massive mistakes, you're still the bravest person I know, and whatever you decide will be the right thing for you."

"You're just saying that."

He nods.

"You're right, I am," he says. "I think what's probably more likely is that, whatever you do, you'll end up regretting it, or questioning it, at least once or twice. But then that will go away. It'll go away because it has to, and because I think that's how these things just work. Pretty soon, the thing you've done will become the only thing you can imagine doing."

Will glances over at Ginny and sees that she's started to cry.

"Besides," he says. "I'll be there to help you. Build a crib, go to a doctor's appointment. Whatever."

"Why would you do that for me?"

"Because I don't have a job, and I'm bad at being bored." She leans into him and buries her head against his neck. "Jesus, Ginny, because I'm not a monster, and it's the right thing to do."

She's quiet, and he feels the warmth of her breath against his skin, the dampness of her cheek on his shoulder. Around them, the island's minor tumult continues, oblivious: mothers slathering sunscreen on antsy children, old men twirling their worry beads beneath the shade of pin-striped awnings. Ships, their masts scraping the lower boughs of the sky, unfurling their sails and drifting out to sea.

Sue Ellen

August 3
Temple of Aphaía, Aegina

They arrive an hour late, at six forty-five in the evening, when the sun has begun to sink behind the Peloponnese and the temple is washed in the Hesperides' golden light. A pair of buses brings them. Giant vehicles whose doors open with hydraulic hisses and upon whose sides are painted three triremes, the ancient warships the Achaeans sailed to the beaches of Ilium. Beneath these vessels is a name, stenciled on in a violent, muscular font: MYRMIDON COACHES, it reads. THE FINEST IN LUXURY TRANSPORT. The passengers unload slowly—they move deliberately as they descend the buses' steps; they pause and gather themselves before huddling in groups. An hour earlier a few Golden Age Adventures staff members unfolded eighty-five chairs into a regiment of tight rows, and it's into these rows that Gianna now tries to usher the cruisers, leading them to their seats with stiff pats to their backs. Her efforts are futile; they resist her. There's too much to see, too many views of the Aegean. And so they scatter, fanning out among the temple's grounds, tilting back their sun hats to get a better look at its pediment. Flustered, Gianna chases them. She barks out instructions like she's commanding soldiers, their swords traded for flimsy gossamer scarves. As she passes by Sue Ellen, she apologizes, breathlessly, and promises she'll be able to start her presentation shortly.

From behind the lectern that's been erected for her, Sue Ellen smiles and nods. She's not listening. She's not watching, either. She's looking down at the notes she's prepared, wondering what happens next. It's an uncertainty that exists both in the short term and in the long term, the existential: *What happens next?* Dean had not reacted well when she said she was not returning to Berkeley; when she'd told him that, rather than repeat their cyclical mistakes, the same, prophesized sins, she would instead grasp at the single lifeline she had, the one Eleni had thrown her. At first, he cried. He begged her to come home, to stay. There were dramatics—the sort that, now, she's uncomfortable recalling. He dropped to his knees; he held her waist and buried his head against her stomach. His nose nestled into her belly button, and she froze. She felt like she was watching a bad movie or reading a scene from one of his books. The sentimentality, the empty performance of his love, angered her.

"Get up." She softly pushed his head away. "This is embarrassing."

"Don't you care how I feel?" he asked, standing.

"No," she said. "And neither do you."

He asked her again to reconsider, and again she told him no, she wouldn't. If anything, his hysterical pleading reaffirmed her decision. For the past year, Dean had made her feel like she and Will were burdens to his success. Chains, more or less, that held him back from the pleasures fame provided. Staring down at the top of his head and feeling his body convulse against her thighs, she realized that she had this equation in reverse. Without her, without Will, Dean was lost. He was a name on a bright red cover. A stack of books among a hundred others, waiting on a discount table to be bought.

He turned cruel, then. Before storming upstairs to pack his bag, he told her she was living in a fantasy that would end in disaster. He mocked her with the same high-pitched laugh she had often heard him use to patronize his students and their son. What the hell did she know about taking over a business? he asked. What the hell did she know about running a hotel? Nothing, she told him. Nor did she know anything about moving abroad, or escaping a marriage, or abandoning the only career she had ever had. But then, twenty-two years ago, she had also known nothing about being a mother. She had known nothing about cutting food small enough for a toddler to eat or worrying late into the night until a teenager came home. She had known nothing of the daily and colossal frustrations, the unending terror and joy. But she did it. She learned on the fly. And while she wasn't perfect—she couldn't have been—she raised a son who was thoughtful, compassionate, and good.

She sees him—Will—now. He's standing behind the last row of chairs, just to the left of center. He's changed clothes since she last saw him. Now he wears a freshly ironed shirt and a pair of slacks she bought him last summer. He grins and gives a clandestine wave. She winks back, then smiles. Tonight, over their last glass of scotch, she'll have to explain her decision: that she's leaving one home to return to another. She wonders what those words might sound like. She wonders if she's even capable of saying them.

A placard with the Golden Age Adventures logo hangs from the front of the lectern. With two fingers she smooths down the tape that holds it in place, pressing air bubbles out from under the adhesive.

She looks down at her notes again.

What happens next?

Gianna finally wrangles the cruisers, herding them into the rows of chairs. Once they're seated, she passes out small blue notebooks emblazoned with the company's logo, along with matching ballpoint pens. She encourages them to take notes and to jot down any questions they might have during Sue Ellen's lecture. There won't be a test, she promises, to a response of polite laughter, but still, she encourages active engagement. This isn't just any cruise—this is a Golden Age Adventure, and they came here to learn. Watching this, Sue Ellen wonders how much they're paying for this, how much they're paying for her. If what she has to offer is a pop commodity, in the words of Charles Winkler, she wonders just how expensive it's become. Whatever it is, it doesn't matter. This is the first time she's doing it, but it will also be the last. She's done resurrecting worlds for everyone but herself.

But then—is she? Gripping the lectern, she feels her throat tighten; she worries that Dean was right. She worries that she's giving up everything she has for a fantasy, a life that wasn't meant for her. She doesn't know what she's doing—that's definitely true. She admitted as much to Eleni, who she called once she left Dean. The last time she had seen her was that morning, at the Hilton. She'd told her she could stay the night in her hotel room after she declined her offer to buy the Alectrona—it was late, and she doubted she would be able to get in to see anyone at Lugn Escapes that evening. She had left just after dawn, while Eleni was still sleeping on the rollaway cot she had ordered from the front desk—there was a breakfast Gianna had asked her to attend, and Sue Ellen hadn't wanted to wake her. Before she slipped out, though, Sue Ellen ironed one of the shirts she had brought and laid it out on the bed. Next to it, she placed a note: *For your meeting,* it read. *Don't take no for an answer.*

"I got late checkout and ordered room service," Eleni said, when she picked up the phone. "I'm sorry."

"Where are you now?"

"I'm about to get on the metro. I'm supposed to meet Oskar in an hour—he said he couldn't see me until six o'clock. I spent the whole day practicing my groveling."

"Cancel it," Sue Ellen said.

"What?"

"Cancel it. The meeting."

She listened as, upstairs, Dean stomped and threw suitcases.

"Look," she continued. "You should know I don't know the first thing about running a hotel."

On the other end of the line, there was a siren, then a trio of car horns.

Eleni waited for the sound to clear, then said, "I'll help you. I'll come back from Athens on the weekends for a while. I'll do whatever you need."

"The only C I ever got in college was in microeconomics, and for the past twenty years I've paid someone to do my taxes."

"Stavros does all the accounting. I taught him how to use Excel, and it turns out it's the only thing he's good at."

"My cooking sucks, and I don't know how to make a bed with hospital corners."

"No one actually likes hospital corners, anyway. They make it impossible to get comfortable."

A door slammed, and Sue Ellen swallowed. "What if I'm beyond help? What if this is a mistake?"

"It's not."

"How do you know? You hardly know me."

"Because I know," Eleni says. "Because my father loved you, and I know."

Now someone in the audience coughs. She looks out at the bodies assembled in the chairs in front of her. On the terrace of the Hilton in Athens, she had obsessed over the physicality of getting old, the way the human form succumbed to years. How silly that had been. Aging—real, honest-to-God aging—has so much less to do with the physical burden of years than it does with the cumulative weight of experience. If anyone knows that it's her. Never has Sue Ellen felt so old as when she sat in Connie's office, watching Dean cry. Finding a gray hair, watching her skin sag—those were comedies compared to dealing with the wreckage of her husband's affair. Now she tries to imagine the individual histories these people shoulder—the triumphs and the inexorable defeats. This woman in the front row has mourned one lover and deserted another. The man next to her—the one doodling—he's still hoping the pieces of his life will hold together; he's still grasping the anemic threads of fate.

She worries that the weight of experience is crushing—that, no matter how far you run, you're stuck with the mess you make. She worries it's impossible to escape a buried life.

There is a final memory, one that's escaped her until just now: Sue Ellen is lying on a blanket in the *eleonas* with Christos, her hands folded behind her head. She's just told him how, earlier that day, she had received a letter from a friend in her doctoral program, a woman named Gayle who was spending the summer in Rome, assisting with the excavation of the Crypta Balbi. It was fascinating, Gayle had written—in a neglected site on the Campus Martius, they'd managed to uncover imperial porticos, along with renovations that were made centuries later, in the medieval period, when it became the Chiesa di Santa Maria Domine Rose. On top of that, there was evidence of a Renaissance-era convent and artifacts from an eighteenth-century church. A time line, Gayle wrote, rooting itself deep into the dirt; the whole of Rome's history, preserved in a single city block.

Her eyes fixed on the olive leaves above them, Sue Ellen explained to Christos how she read the letter once, then a second time, and then began to cry. How many times did Rome, the Eternal City, need to be destroyed and rebuilt? How many times did Athens? Despite her training, it was a thought she had often, whenever she was in a place with any history, and occasionally it saddened her. Civilization was not poetry, heroism, or myth; it was, instead, a sort of layer cake. City foisted upon city, life foisted upon life. The newer iterations replacing the old ones, burying them with their collective mistakes and regrets.

"You're looking at it wrong," Christos said to her once she had finished. "It's not destruction—it's rebirth."

She rolled her eyes and folded her hands behind her head.

She said, "*Rebirth.* How romantic."

"Maybe." He propped himself up on his elbow. "But that doesn't make it wrong."

A bowl of olives sat between them, and she reached for one.

"You're telling me that all the head shops next to the Agora are a rebirth, not a destruction."

"No," he said. "Or, yes."

She threw the olive at him. He brushed it from the front of his shirt.

He said, "Knock it off, I'm serious."

"All right, then," Sue Ellen said. "Explain yourself."

Above them and to the north, two thunderheads merged.

Christos repositioned himself, brushing his arm against Sue Ellen's.

"Take Aphaía," he said.

"I thought we were talking about cities."

"Just—bear with me here." He repeated himself: "Take Aphaía."

"Fine." Sue Ellen closed her eyes. "Taking Aphaía."

"Well, first, according to you, and at least in some myths, she was living on Crete, as Bretomartis—"

"*Brit*omartis."

"—when she fled from King Minos, threw herself into a fishing net, and disappeared."

Sue Ellen sat up.

"That sounds more like a death than a rebirth," she said.

"Yes, fine, but *then,* in addition to being called Britomartis on Crete, she emerged here, on Aegina, where they called her Aphaía and worshiped her as a mother goddess. A temple is built to her."

"Which, later on, gets mislabeled as the Temple of Jupiter Panellenius. Another death."

"*Which* then gets *relabeled* years later as, indeed, a sanctuary to Aphaía." He picked the olive from the blanket and threw it back at her. "And now you're studying it as the subject of your dissertation."

Sue Ellen was quiet. She stared up and watched the clouds darken.

"To disappear and reappear," Christos said. "To be born, to die, to be reborn. *Re, re, re*: an implication that something existed before, in another form, and now has the opportunity to live again. You can tell me that cities, and history, and life are about destruction, and maybe that's true. But they're also about something else. They're about re-creation. *Re, re, re*."

She pulled her knees to her chest. There was wind, and when it picked up she could see the velvet undersides of olive leaves.

"But how do we know what phase we're in?" she asked him. "How do we know if Rome's rising or falling? How do we know if the flames we see are flames of civilization's failure or the beginnings of something else?"

Christos shrugged and ate an olive. "We don't, I guess. Or maybe we do, and it's a matter of perspective. Maybe it's a matter of picking where you are, in the rise or in the fall, and saying that—regardless of what the historians and philosophers decide to call it—for you, this is a beginning." He spat out the pit in the palm of his hand. "What is it that Homer tells the muse at the beginning of *The Odyssey*? '*Start from where you will.*'"

Sue Ellen looked at him and reached for his hand.

She said, "I think it's going to rain."

Start from where you will. Pick a point in the epic of the hero's wanderings, and call that the opening of your story. It's a deceptively simple instruction, she thinks, looking at the expectant faces before her. For any beginning she chooses won't really be a beginning at all. It will carry with it the baggage and histories of the many lives that came before it, and when it's gone, the lives that come after it will be built upon its back.

Sue Ellen turns and looks up at the temple behind her. She knows these columns better than she knows herself. And yet tonight she feels like she's seeing them anew—not for the first time, but through another lens. She feels like she could spend the next twelve hours learning them all over again, running her fingers along the rough stone until the moon has been charioted clear across the sky. Beyond the sanctuary—beyond the hill-crest, and the mastic trees, and the pointed tips of pines—lies the Aegean, the wine-dark sea, now turned brassy as another day dies. Rising from it, even farther off, are the shadows of the Peloponnese, dark reliefs of mountains emerging from the twilight. *Sing in me, Muse, and through me tell the story.*

She hears the creaking of chairs and a chorus of intermittent coughs. They're waiting for her, she realizes, turning back. They're trading per-plexed looks and whispering in one another's ears. Their pens are readied in their ancient hands, and their notebooks sit open on their laps, empty.

Will, her son, catches her eye and nods.

A few feet to his right, Gianna taps her watch.

Sue Ellen smiles. She thinks, Ruins are not endings—they are the foun-dations for lives that have yet to come.

She says, "Let's begin."

Acknowledgments
and Author's Note

There are a number of people who helped in the creation of this book, and who thus deserve my deepest gratitude. Before I thank them, though, I'd like to offer a quick note: while most of this novel operates in the real world, I have taken a handful of small liberties. To begin with, ferry schedules between Aegina, Athens, and Hydra have been altered for the purposes of the story. Likewise, while Berkeley certainly offers creative writing courses, the only undergraduate degree it grants in the subject is a minor, which is under the auspices of the Interdisciplinary Studies Department.

I'd be remiss if I also didn't point out that while Eleni may be bored with life on Aegina, it's actually a very beautiful island and an extraordinary place to visit, as is the rest of Greece.

Finally, Ginny Polonsky dismisses *The Iliad* as a book about a bunch of boys. This isn't an opinion that I share.

Now, on to the main event . . .

Thank you to Richard Pine, Eliza Rothstein, and the rest of the team at Inkwell Management for more than a decade of support and advocacy on my behalf. Jason Richman and Sam Reynolds at UTA have also been tireless advocates, and deserve buckets of gratitude and appreciation.

At Flatiron Books, I'm indebted to James Melia. Every author should be so lucky to have an editor who works with such dedication and, more important, humor. Thanks also to Amy Einhorn, Bob Miller, Patricia Cave, Marlena Bittner, Nancy Trypuc, and Greg Villepique.

I was fortunate enough to have a wonderful group of early readers whose guidance helped shape this book into what it's become. Ali Bujnowski, Chris Rovzar, Gerold Schroeder, Peter Schottenfels, Yona Silverman, Clare O'Connor, and Elizabeth Dunn—thank you, thank you, thank you.

My parents, Deborah and Steven Ginder, taught me that reading was something necessary and vital from the time I was old enough to crack open a book. I wouldn't be writing if it weren't for them.

Edith Hamilton's classic *Mythology: Timeless Tales of Gods and Heroes* and Emily Wilson's wonderful new translation of *The Odyssey* were both essential reading as I tried to create my own world of wandering and regret. I recommend them both.

Finally, to my husband, Mac McCarty: thank you for keeping me sane, even when it seems like insanity is imminent. I love you.

Recommend

Honestly, We Meant Well

for your next book club!

Reading Group Guide available at

WWW.READINGGROUPGOLD.COM